TERROR FOR NOW

Bob Howard

ISBN-13: 978-1-945754-49-4

Cover designed by Getcovers

This book is a work of fiction. Names, characters, places, and incidents either are a product of the author's imagination or are used fictitiously. Any resemblance to actual persons, living or dead, events, or locations is entirely coincidental.

This book is dedicated to my wife, Dawn, and our two children, Drew and Julie. Because of them, I'm a lucky man.

ACKNOWLEDGMENTS

Contributions to fiction are most often derived from fact, and I'm constantly surprised by the facts I discover when I do research for a book. In this book, I couldn't help feeling a debt of gratitude for the soldiers who fought to defend the Aleutian Islands. I don't think enough people know what sacrifices they made for a few miserable pieces of rock.

The modern resources available for research are opening doors to information that we didn't have at our fingertips before, and I appreciate the people who have put the information out there for me to pick through. Because of their contributions, I didn't have to invent the entire story.

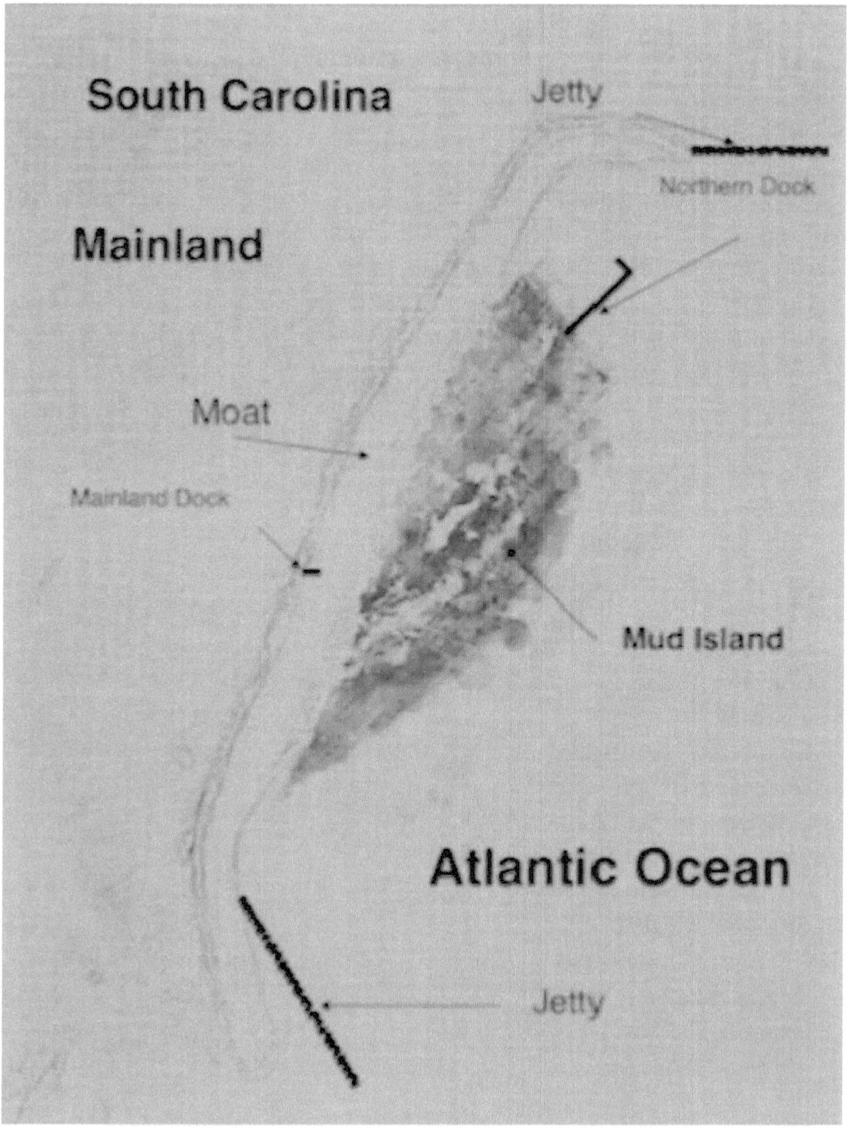
South Carolina
Jetty
Northern Dock
Mainland
Moat
Mainland Dock
Mud Island
Atlantic Ocean
Jetty

Table of Contents

1

Minnesota

International Falls Airport - The Beginning of the Infection

The news of a worldwide panic reached International Falls, Minnesota, shortly before the strange disease that would kill its small population. Local television programming was interrupted by two nervous anchors who constantly spoke directly to each other rather than to the camera. It was as if they needed verification before they continued. The journalists were a well-known couple because it was the only TV station in the area.

The small airport restaurant where passengers preferred to wait for their flights was almost full despite the fact there was only one scheduled departure, and it was still over two hours away. The patrons were silently glued to the broadcast, not wanting to miss a single word. The handful of waitresses were doing their best to serve the larger-than-normal crowd while keeping their eyes on the news, and they took orders from their tables in lowered voices.

Everyone was curious about the unscheduled arrival of a Frontier Airlines flight no one recognized, and the female anchor read a headline about the plane as if a UFO had descended onto the runway. It was currently the only passenger plane parked near the building. The other occupants on the tarmac were six single-engine Cessnas lined up in a neat row.

The male anchor reminded the viewers if they didn't know already, that the town only received flights from Skywest, a company that partnered with Delta. The plane could be seen from the restaurant, and some of the silence in the restaurant was caused by a feeling that the passengers on the plane were watching them. It would have surprised them to know the anxious passengers sitting inside the plane felt the same way.

A banner moved across the bottom of the TV screen, and the viewers were torn by a desire not to miss something that was spoken while reading the headlines. According to the banner, North Korea had launched a missile from its only submarine, but unlike its previous missile tests, the missile had flown inland and landed in the North Korean city of Chongjin. Unsurprisingly, no updates were coming out of North Korea about the tragedy, but over six hundred thousand people were living in Chongjin, and satellite information indicated the possibility that the missile had been a nuclear weapon.

The headline on the banner changed from North Korea to France, and the news only bore a small similarity to the first headline, but as small as it was, it was still enough to startle the viewers. The military had been brought in to help the police control protests that had grown violent, and they had reportedly used lethal force. The banner said hundreds of protesters had been shot in the streets of several cities, including Paris.

The reporters were reading the headlines as fast as they came in, and sometimes the stories overlapped with the banner at the bottom of the screen, but every headline ended with the same phrase. They were developing stories that would be updated as soon as more was known. The female anchor told their audience they wouldn't take any commercial breaks, and she promised they would stay with them as the stories unfolded. She had barely finished her promise when the lights flickered in the studio, and the broadcast ended with static.

The whispers in the restaurant rose in pitch and then escalated into shouts when the lights in the restaurant went out. The TV screen became black, and silence descended on the room as everyone listened for something to fill the void. If not for the light streaming through the windows from the outside, the restaurant would have been dark, but the normally welcome view was occupied by the Frontier Airlines plane that was still stranded on the tarmac. It represented the unknown and was eyed with suspicion as if it had brought bad news with it.

There was a collective sigh of relief when the lights blinked on, and the sounds of appliance motors hummed from the hidden corners of the restaurant. A few people cheered as if there was someone who deserved a reward for restoring the electricity, and they were joined by clapping when the news reappeared on the TV screen. Waitresses who had stood where they were when the lights went out walked among the tables again, giving the appearance that they were linked to the loss of power. Offers of coffee refills were collectively declined in favor of alcoholic beverages.

The news continued to broadcast the unbelievable stories on the banner and directly from the anchor team. They informed the viewers that the unwanted Frontier plane was being turned away without allowing passengers to disembark, and the report was supported by the appearance of a police car and a fuel truck next to the plane. Some of the customers rushed to the windows the same way people were drawn to the sight of an automobile accident.

They could see the pilot leaning from his small window, and his finger-pointing gave them a sense that his discussion with the police officer was less than cordial. The exchange ended with the pilot and deputy both making finger gestures that were easily interpreted.

The ground crew from the fuel truck finished their task and withdrew from the side of the plane, but the deputy stayed where he was and asserted his authority that the pilot should take his passengers elsewhere. It wasn't a surprise when the pilot turned the plane away in a tight circle that sent his jetwash across the deputy's car. There were equal amounts of laughter and jeers as the deputy chased his hat across the luggage loading area.

During the local drama, the anchors talked about concerns that there was some kind of infection that was being spread from people who had left major cities, and as word spread through the restaurant, the cheers for the deputy reflected the fear the customers felt toward the passengers on the plane. No one wanted them to bring the infection to them, even though there was no proof the newcomers were infected. The male anchor confirmed information from the air traffic controllers at the airport that there were six flights requesting permission to land as they circled above the airport, and the customers spontaneously chanted not to let them land.

The sense of unity displayed by the patrons of the restaurant was shattered when an announcement came over the airport's public address system.

Attention all passengers of scheduled flights. Due to circumstances beyond our control, all flights out of International Falls Airport are canceled. Normal service will resume when further information is received. Please check our website for updates. Thank you again for choosing Skywest Airlines.

The immediate silence that followed the announcement was similar to when the lights went out, but it was more sharply broken by shouts from angry customers. It hadn't occurred to them that the scenario that had played out on the runway would have a direct impact on them. If planes couldn't land, they couldn't leave. The scheduled flight they were supposed to be on was one of the planes that circled overhead.

There was a general stampede toward the ticket counters. Everyone wanted to be the first to get compensation for their inconvenience. The restaurant manager was shoved out of the way several times as unpaid checks were left on tables. His efforts to slow the exodus ended when a customer punched him across his face, and he fell in a heap to the shiny linoleum floor.

The ticketing agents had anticipated the reaction from the disappointed passengers, and by the time the first of them arrived at the counter, the agents and TSA staff were gone. Signs on the counters said they were closed, and the passengers would be allowed to return the next day to reclaim checked luggage. Steel curtains were pulled down over the gates leading to the concourse. With no one available toward whom they could vent their frustrations, the angry ticket holders gradually left, but not without vandalizing the lobby.

The staff sat with their injured manager in the restaurant and watched the news. His ego was more bruised than his face, but at the moment, the ice bag he held against his right eye was a useful way to avoid looking at anyone. Employees from other parts of the airport joined them, and the waitresses passed out snacks. They all knew each other, and each of them felt the same as the manager. They were part of a small city of less than six thousand people, so many of them had grown up together. All they could do now was give each other moral support, but they didn't know what was happening.

The news from around the world was still as frightening as the first reports. Mobs had stormed the Vatican, and even though it was thousands of miles away, the enormity of the violence wasn't lost on the people who had lived their lives in the city known to some as the *Nation's Icebox*. They all saw when a military aircraft appeared as a fast-moving dot in one corner of the screen, and the unmistakable trail of the missile that dropped from its wing caused the watchers to scream. The explosion ripped through the mob of people in front of the Vatican.

The audience in the restaurant was paralyzed by the reports that came in from around the world, but the full impact didn't sink in until the banner said the names of cities in the United States. Washington DC, New York, Chicago, Atlanta, and Los Angeles were all asking the federal government to send help, and the President had left the White House for his own safety. The female anchor apparently took that as a bad sign, and she chose that moment to unclip her microphone and leave. She ignored her coanchor when he asked where she was going.

A waitress named Beth was sitting with the restaurant manager, and she decided she should follow the reporter's example. It was time to go home. When she stood up, she stopped and stared at the place where the Frontier Airlines flight and the deputy had their confrontation.

"Is that the same plane?" she asked no one in particular.

Several people answered at the same time that it wasn't, and the TV was abandoned again. Everyone watched through the windows as planes landed at the far end of the runway. In their limited experience, it was virtually an airshow as six passenger planes landed in the space of five minutes. The first plane was already approaching the terminal, and someone had opened a door despite ground crews not rolling stairs out to greet them.

One of the male spectators said, "That's not something you see every day."

He was obviously referring to the behavior of a member of the flight crew who had jumped out of the open door as if falling to the asphalt wouldn't hurt. The flight attendant hit the ground hard, and despite the way her legs bent at unnatural angles, she pushed herself up and ran toward the terminal. It was more like hopping on one leg while dragging the other, and she fell on her face after going only a few feet. The watchers at the windows backed up a step as if she was one of the infected people the anchors had talked about.

A tall, heavyset man appeared in the doorway next, and he walked out of the exit without jumping. He stepped through the opening no differently than someone would have done if the door had been level to the ground. His body followed the direction of his foot, and he did a spectacular head-first dive. After his head hit the tarmac, he didn't move.

The flight attendant must have heard the impact because she took only two seconds to see what was happening behind her before resuming her efforts to reach the terminal. This time, though, she didn't try to run. She crawled faster.

After the big man exited the plane, a steady stream of passengers and crew followed. One by one, they poured from the door without regard for the height of the plane, and a pile of people grew where the man had landed. Newcomers to the pile landed and then rolled, and the watchers inside the restaurant screamed when they saw some of the crippled passengers get to their feet. As they stood, some fell onto the pile a second time because they had injuries to their legs, but all of them were drawn to the sound of bodies landing…at first.

Inside the restaurant, some of the watchers cried, and there were occasional reactions to the scene that resembled the manner in which baseball fans yelled in pain when a batter got hit by a pitch. No one could actually feel the pain, but they understood what it must've felt like. They also couldn't hear the flight attendant screaming for someone to help her, but the airplane passengers who managed to stay erect once they got their feet under them heard her clearly. It was a much more enticing sound than the noise made when new bodies arrived on the pile. One by one, they turned in her direction and took unsteady steps toward her.

A cockpit window slid open, and the pilot squeezed his head and shoulders out as far as he could. He cupped his hands around his mouth and yelled at the passengers. Even though the people in the restaurant couldn't hear him, there were whispers that the pilot must be trying to help the flight attendant. When someone in their place of safety asked if they should help her, the reaction was so loud that the injured passengers momentarily turned their attention to the row of windows on the terminal.

There was a chorus of "Be quiet" and "shushing sounds" from the crowd inside as they took another collective step away from the windows.

Someone said in a really low voice, "The pilot must've locked the cockpit door."

"What's that got to do with anything?" answered an angry spectator.

The restaurant manager had long forgotten about the ice bag he had been holding against his head, and he was beyond caring about good customer service.

"Where have you been for the last few hours, moron. Those people are infected, and the pilot isn't," said the manager. "That's why he was able to land the plane."

The insulted customer would have protested the rudeness of the manager, but the majority of the crowd appreciated his authoritative explanation of the circumstances that led up to the scene they were watching, and they told the man to shut up. They resembled a crowded theater that had experienced a temporary interruption of the movie as they returned their attention to the screen. An uncomfortable silence descended on the room.

Outside, the pilot had managed to yell loud enough to get the passengers moving in his direction. The plane had been full when it landed, but nearly all of the one hundred and twenty-two passengers and crew had taken their turn at the exit. The people inside the restaurant couldn't have known that the injured passengers were making a strange groaning sound, and the sound agitated them. The more the pilot yelled, the more they groaned, and the more they groaned, the more agitated they became. The pilot looked like a performer on the stage of a rock concert as the passengers reached upward toward him, and the injured flight attendant disappeared somewhere below the windows as she crawled away.

The excitement below the cockpit window continued for a few minutes until a second airplane coasted slowly to a stop behind the first one. The reaction from the crowd of 'fans' outside was immediate, and they left the pilot in favor of the new arrival.

Inside the restaurant, a few of the patrons did the same thing. They left the windows and returned to the news broadcast, hoping to learn more about what was happening. They suspected they were witnessing people who were infected, but so far, they hadn't seen the worst that could happen. Aside from the injuries and the erratic behavior, they hadn't witnessed what would happen when the infected people encountered an uninfected person.

The man still at the anchor desk was reporting that several planes had landed without permission at the International Falls Airport and that it was unsafe to have contact with any of the passengers. He said he had a source on the scene. Considering the number of people who had cell phones aimed at airplanes so they could record videos, it was a surprise to find some people were making calls. The banner on the bottom of the screen had been updated to say the infection was transferred when uninfected people were bitten by the infected.

"Wait a minute," said the anchorman. "We have more information, but I can't confirm it at this time. It appears that the infected are actually dead when they try to infect someone else. I'll give you a confirmation when we get that from an official source."

"I don't see anyone out there trying to bite anyone else," said one of the men watching the news. He was the one the manager had called a moron earlier, and a few people guessed by his latest comment that the manager had hit close to the mark with the insult.

A waitress asked him, "Do you see many people by the planes who look like they could be alive?"

The man took her question as an invitation to assess the crowd outside. It made the waitress roll her eyes so hard that it hurt.

"How can you tell them apart?" he asked.

She spoke slowly, as if he wouldn't understand if she said it too fast.

"How is the pilot different from the rest of them?"

Before he could answer, she said, "I'll give you a clue. The pilot is smart enough not to body surf over the mosh pit."

A few customers who were watching the exchange between the waitress and the man burst into nervous laughter. More than one agreed with the manager's opinion of the moron.

Someone at the window yelled, "The deputy's back."

The TV was abandoned in favor of the live event again. The deputy was closer to the windows, and he had retrieved the flight attendant from her hiding place next to the terminal. He helped her into the passenger seat of his police-issue Chevy Tahoe and then quickly got behind the wheel. He didn't know for sure what was happening, but he knew there was a difference between the flight attendant and the rest of the passengers. He drove out of view around the corner of the building, unaware of the ovation he received from the people inside the restaurant.

The ovation was well deserved, but Deputy Harold Stone had only done what he believed was his duty. He always considered himself the kind of law enforcement officer who would run toward the problem instead of away from it. He was also trained in first aid, and he figured as soon as he had put some distance between himself and the runway, he could stop and tend to the injuries of the woman who rode beside him. As he drove, he gave her sideways glances to assess the damage.

"Where are you hurt besides your legs?"

He could see that she had shattered the bones of both legs, and she had to be in tremendous pain. He could also see a pool of blood on her seat, but he couldn't tell where it was coming from.

She tried to speak, but her sobbing came in bursts every time she opened her mouth. When the woman turned a bit in her seat, he saw her name tag.

"Dorothy, can you answer me? Where are you hurt?"

Dorothy pointed toward her legs with her left arm, and he caught a glimpse of a jagged tear in her upper arm. Whatever it was that had cut her missed the brachial artery, but the flesh on her arm had been ripped away from her like a peeled banana.

"We need to get the bleeding stopped on your arm."

Deputy Stone pulled the Tahoe to the side of the road and reached into the back seat for his first aid kit. He only took a moment to open the kit and tear the wrapper from a roll of sterile gauze, but Dorothy was already unconscious. She slumped against the passenger door of the Tahoe.

He reached for her exposed neck and felt for a pulse. He found it, but it was getting weaker with each passing second.

"At least she's alive," he thought, and her position against the door gave him easy access to the injury on her arm.

He pressed a large gauze pad against it and held it in place as he made quick loops around her arm with the roll. He saw her stir a little, and she attempted to lift her head from the window. There was a faint sound, and Deputy Stone thought she was trying to speak. He watched a trail of blood-tinted saliva trail from her mouth down to her lap, and he was sure she would only barely survive the trip to the hospital even though it was only a short drive.

"There," he said. "That should at least hold you until I can get you to the Emergency Room. You're going to need a lot of stitches, but I've seen worse."

In truth, he had never seen anything like it. Even when he had helped a hiker attacked by a mother bear protecting her cub, the claws hadn't flayed the man's skin open like the woman's arm. Something had dug into her fleshy arm and pulled away as if they were trying to pull off a piece of her.

The Deputy sat back in his seat and put the Tahoe in gear. It was good that he didn't pull away from the shoulder of the road without checking his side mirror because a caravan of vehicles passed him at high speed. He even had his blue lights turned on, and the other drivers didn't seem to care or even notice.

When the last car went by, he got in line and accelerated. Until today, if someone saw his blue lights in their mirror, they moved over to let him by, but today didn't seem to be like any other day. The procession of vehicles ahead of him ignored his lights, and the deputy was surprised when a car came up behind him and then moved to the other lane to pass.

"What the hell?" he mouthed at the driver, but the man didn't even glance in his direction.

It seemed like every car in front of him was headed for the Canadian border, and within a few minutes, Deputy Stone realized the number of cars in front of him had increased. Their group had caught up with the traffic jam at the border, so he turned on his siren.

The driver of the car that had passed him seemed to realize the logjam of vehicles would benefit from the presence of a police officer, so he edged closer to the shoulder of the road. Deputy Stone took advantage of the opening and quickly moved up to the rear end of the next car. That driver ignored him until Stone nudged him with the front bumper of his car. The driver gave up his spot, but a solid wall of stopped vehicles was in front of him. No one else had room to move out of the way, even if they wanted to.

His injured passenger regained consciousness, and Deputy Stone saw she had lifted her head from where it had rested against the window. Beyond her, he could see the driver of the last car that had moved over for him, and the man was frantically pointing at the former flight attendant. Stone didn't know what the man was trying to tell him, but it seemed urgent, so he lowered the passenger side window.

The man yelled at the top of his lungs, "She's got that infection. Get out of there."

It sank in when Dorothy turned in the direction of the shouting driver. The growl that escaped from her mouth was feral and ugly. She reached out the open window with one arm and clawed at the air, trying desperately to reach him. The vehicles were close together, but the man had just enough time to raise his own window. Her fingertips brushed against the glass and made a tapping noise. The driver didn't hesitate. He crawled across the inside of his car and climbed out of his own passenger door. Deputy Stone watched the man abandon his vehicle rather than be next to the woman.

In hindsight, Stone knew that the man in the other car had saved his life by yelling at him. It gave him the precious seconds to open his door and get out. As he escaped, Dorothy reached for him, but her bandaged arm didn't move with the coordination it needed to grab his jacket. Stone stood outside the open door for a moment and stared inside at the creature Dorothy had become. She was already climbing over the center console, making that feral growling sound, and reaching for him.

Deputy Stone swung the door shut and turned toward the scene that had developed outside the car. People were leaving their cars and running toward the border all around him. Some were leaving cars with people still inside them, and when he moved closer to those cars, he saw the occupants were much like Dorothy. They didn't appear to be human anymore.

In the traffic jam ahead was a car with all four doors open. A woman fell from the rear door on the driver's side and was attempting to get to her feet. Her legs were shaking, and her head hung heavily to one side. People running past her dodged her outstretched arm until one man deliberately slammed the door into her. Stone thought it should have injured her, but it only knocked her down. As soon as she pushed the door away, she got up for a second time.

Screaming behind him drew his attention away from the woman, and he saw that more injured people were wandering through the narrow gaps between the cars. One man was avoiding them by jumping from the rooftops and hoods of the closely packed cars. He was making fast progress until someone grabbed his leg and pulled him to the pavement. Deputy Stone couldn't see what had happened when the man had fallen behind the cars, but the screaming reached notes higher than most people could have.

He couldn't remember the last time he had pulled his service weapon, but it slid from his holster as if he had done it every day. Deputy Stone could hear the screaming and panicked voices around him, but his ears only registered the eerie sound of music playing in a nearby car. He recognized the song by the Carpenters because his mother had collected their vinyl albums when she was young. The lyrics were so out of place in the mayhem around him.

Dorothy pressed her face against the glass and slapped a wet hand against the window. *We've only just begun to live. White lace and promises…*The song and Dorothy's face were both unreal to him. They didn't match, and he was momentarily undecided between holstering his weapon and shooting someone. Another growl came from behind him, and the decision was made for him.

The man was so close that the gun was pointed into his stomach as soon as Deputy Stone turned around. He pulled the trigger and watched the man get punched by the blast. It had sounded muffled because the barrel had been pressed against him, and Stone knew the bullet most likely exited from the man's back. The man sat heavily on his rear end but didn't put his hands to his stomach or lower his eyes to the bullet wound. Instead, he rolled over and used his hands to push himself from the pavement. The man was now on his knees facing away from the Deputy, and Stone could see he had been right about the bullet. There was a large wound above the man's waistline where it had passed through the man.

Still on his knees, the stranger rotated the upper half of his body until he could see Deputy Stone. He growled again and laboriously got up.

The music faded, but the sounds flooded over Stone as he raised the gun and shot the man in the forehead. This time, he was a little further away, and Stone didn't see any evidence that the bullet had gone out the other side. It had rattled around inside the man's skull at high speed and scrambled his brain. The stranger collapsed to the pavement and didn't move.

Deputy Stone had never shot anyone, and even though he was sure he had been forced to do it, he didn't like how it felt. His legs were numb, and he could hardly command them to move, but something made him turn and run from the scene where he had just committed his first murder.

Running blindly, he knocked over dozens of people who reached for him as he went by, and he wasn't always sure if they really needed help or if they were like Dorothy and the stranger he had shot. He pushed and shoved until he was away from the traffic jam and ran with every bit of strength he could muster. He ran on the road until he saw the airport, then he climbed a fence and took a shortcut across the runways.

The crowd had thinned inside the restaurant that faced the planes. Most of the people decided it was time to get into their cars and leave. Some of them had been behind Deputy Stone in the traffic jam. A few patrons had taken advantage of the untended bar and were solving the world's problems by self-medicating and providing commentary about the crisis.

"I think it's the zombie virus that infected the deer," said one man. "I heard on the news that you couldn't eat venison, but I wasn't going to stop eating venison because someone wearing a necktie said to."

"Are you infected?" asked one of his bar mates.

"What? Why would you ask a dumb question like that?"

"Because you're saying all of those people out there must've gotten infected by eating bad venison. Say, isn't that the deputy out there? What's he doin' running around out there?"

Deputy Stone had run past the airplanes and was followed by a much slower-moving crowd. He disappeared through a door by the luggage entrance. Less than five minutes later, he reappeared in the doorway of the restaurant.

"Get the man a beer," said the man who had shared the zombie deer theory.

2

Canada

Last Island - March 2023

Winter on the frozen lakes above the border had always been brutal. Still, even the hearty residents who lived in International Falls, Minnesota, before the infected dead arrived would have told everyone it was colder than they could recall.

Warmer weather was just around the corner, but June couldn't come soon enough for Garrett Carson. Although he had wanted to live out his life in a cold environment that was hostile to the infected dead, even he had a limit to what he could endure. He thought he had experienced what it was like to be cold while he and his fellow survivors were stranded in the airport in Columbus, Ohio, but he had learned since then that it had been merely practice for what life would be like north of the Canadian border.

Garrett had just turned fifty when the apocalypse began, and he often wondered if his wife and children would recognize him seven years later with his long hair and gray beard. He was also more muscular from doing manual chores to survive. He hardly resembled the man who had piloted the President of the United States out of the nation's capital on the first day. He hoped his family was alive somewhere, but if he really believed they had made it out of the crowded cities around Washington, DC, he would have tried to find them.

It seemed more uncomfortable than usual as he huddled inside the makeshift hunting blind he had erected about a mile from the island. It was only a hut made of lightweight branches he had dragged across the snow-covered ice. He selected a spot facing northwest, piled the slender stems into the shape of an igloo, and then stretched a yellow tarp over it. A few short bungee cords held the tarp in place, but the snow fell fast enough to weigh it down.

Garrett wasn't hunting for wild game. There wasn't likely to be anything worth hunting out on the frozen lake at this early hour. He figured the temperature wasn't higher than twenty degrees, and any game worth shooting would be foraging for food on one of the larger islands or across the border of the US to the south. Today wasn't for hunting…it was just for watching.

Something had made the tracks in the snow the day before, and he hadn't seen anything similar in a long time. People lifted their feet when they walked through deep snow or left smooth ruts with their skis. He had heard snowmobiles once a couple of years ago, and their tracks were deep but easily recognized. Game prints were rare out on the lake, but just like skis, they were always shaped like the feet of the animals that made the tracks.

The swath of disturbed snow Garrett discovered was over a dozen feet wide, and it could only have been made by a group of the infected dead. They didn't lift their feet when they walked, and their sideways gait brushed the snow to the left and right as they shuffled forward. Garrett didn't like seeing evidence that a horde had passed so close to their home, but even worse, they should have been frozen long before they reached this part of Rainy Lake.

Anne had begged Garrett to find another way to locate the horde. She didn't like the idea of him sitting in a hunting blind out in the open. There wasn't any evidence that the infected dead had reached the island they had called home for the last few years, and she thought it would be a better idea to reinforce the traps and barriers they had built around the lodge. Jon and Susan agreed with Anne. Jon suggested that they could spend a few days surveying the coast that surrounded the island. If there were infected dead nearby, they would find their trail.

Garrett didn't want to wait for the trail to lead to the island, and besides, he was worried about why the path of disturbed snow had ended on the lake. The heavy snowfall during the previous week had covered any clues he might have found that would explain where the horde had gone.

In the last hour before dawn, Garrett was ready to build a fire to fight off the cold, but it was still too risky. Besides, he had already suffered through the worst part of the night and didn't want it to be for nothing. He told himself he could make it a few more hours, and if nothing happened, he would listen to the others and do it their way.

Binoculars weren't very effective against the driving snow. Besides making the lenses wet, the swirling white flakes made everything appear to be moving. The best he could hope for was to see something in the distance change, so he focused his eyes on the horizon. The sun rising behind him might reflect off of anything that moved, and it would be far enough away if he needed to abandon his hiding spot.

Garrett wasn't sure if his eyes were playing tricks on him. The line that marked the horizon appeared to be thicker than before. It wasn't moving, or at least he wasn't sure if it was, but the pencil-thin line that had been there had changed. For the next ten minutes, it grew in size in the middle until it wasn't thin anymore. To the left and right of the place where the line swelled, the horizon remained as he expected, but Garrett knew something was coming closer. Thirty minutes later, he could see the swaying heads well enough to know it was what he feared most. A horde of the infected dead was crossing the lake, and they weren't affected by the freezing temperature.

He got a break when the snowfall dwindled to a few random flakes falling through the morning light. The sun rose high enough for Garrett to tell that the horde was about thirty or forty individuals heavily clad in winter gear. He wondered if they were possibly alive for a moment, but he realized that a large group of living people wouldn't waste energy walking through deep snow side-by-side. They would follow in the tracks of the leaders. Then there was the tell-tale swaying motion as they slowly advanced.

Garrett was still puzzled about where the other horde had gone and why their tracks had abruptly ended, but his questions were answered when he saw the different dark shapes that materialized with lightning speed on both sides of the horde. The horde stopped moving forward and broke apart into disorganized smaller groups that were harassed by the fast-moving dark shapes. He knew they were wolves, but Garrett couldn't recall seeing wolves get that big.

He was already cold, but the spectacle unfolding in the distance gave Garrett a different chill. If the horde had gotten closer to where he was hiding, the wolf attack might have happened near enough for him to have been detected. The snowflakes that still fell were drifting toward him, so Garrett knew the wolves wouldn't catch his scent, but even at this distance, he knew they would see him if he moved. The sun behind him wouldn't reflect from his binoculars, so he could watch the scenario run its course.

The wolves worked together to spread the groups of infected dead apart, and once there was enough distance between them, the swarming attackers took their prey to the ground. The horde was gone in a matter of minutes, and Garrett could only see the furry shapes moving between the bodies. He discovered why there was no evidence left behind from the previous horde when he heard the excited yapping from the north. Once again, he was grateful that the wind came from the northwest as the rest of the wolf clan arrived. Young pups and older, less agile wolves joined the hunting party for the feast.

Clouds rolled in, and the snow fell heavily again. Large, wet flakes blanketed the lake's surface, and Garrett knew they would cover whatever remained of the horde within an hour. The red stains would be gone, and the only evidence of the attack would be the uneven path that the horde had traveled. He didn't know which was worse: hordes of the infected dead that survived the extreme cold or wolves that could decimate a horde so completely. How the crew of Executive One had survived on Last Island without being discovered by the wolves was his biggest worry.

******

Garrett waited for an hour before trusting that it was safe to leave. He saw how the enormous wolves spread out in a loose circle around the clan and faced outward. They surveyed their territory while the others fed, and Garrett wondered if he would survive if the beast facing in his direction somehow discovered him. He could raise his rifle and aim before it reached him, but it wouldn't be long before the rest of the pack had him surrounded.

When he was sure they were gone, he quickly released the bungee cords and folded the tarp. The wolves had gone north, but if the wind shifted, they would probably pick up his scent and find him before he reached Last Island.

Jon King saw him practically running through the deep snow a quarter of a mile from the island. The lodge had a tower next to it that served as a fire watch, but it also gave them a place where they could safely search for the infected dead. During the few summer days when it got warm on Rainy Lake, they spotted bodies in the water and washed up on the beach, and the tower made it possible to survey more of the coastline of Last Island near the lodge.

Jon had been in the tower waiting for Garrett to reappear, and he was really cold. Despite the wool cap and hood of his jacket, his bald head never felt warm enough. He had continued to shave it even in the cold climate, but it gave the group something to tease him about and had been good for morale.

When he saw his old friend, his first instinct was to focus his binoculars behind the running man to see what was chasing him. The snow blocked his view, so he was forced to climb from the tower to warn Anne and Susan that Garrett might be in trouble. They had all prepared their gear for an immediate departure, so it was simply a matter of pulling on their heavy coats and grabbing their rifles.

The snow they had cleared from the compound surrounding their lodge left only a concave path to follow to the gate. It was filling in with new snow so fast that it wouldn't be visible within an hour. The wind blew drifts against the barriers they had erected around the perimeter, creating dunes that hid the ugly, sharpened spikes that faced outward. They had only found the infected dead impaled on the spikes during warm weather, but the first snowfall had arrived so suddenly this year that they had found bodies frozen only a few feet from their protective barrier. For that reason, they had to approach the gate from the outside as if there were deadly traps to the left or right. The infected might be frozen, but it would be a sad irony to step on one and be cut by sharp teeth.

After pulling the tall gate inward against the snow, Anne and Susan went to each fencepost that supported the entrance and lit oil lanterns they could use to identify the safe path. Jon poked the drifts in the middle of the trail with a long pole just to be sure no infected had wandered into the place they always kept clear. They closed the gate and ran single file toward the frozen lake where they knew Garrett would appear.

The dock was over forty feet long and stood eight feet above the ice. Anne and Susan ran the length of the wooden structure and took up positions behind a barricade of sandbags. From there, they knew they could visually locate Garrett but would also have a clear sightline to shoot anything behind him. The driving snowstorm significantly diminished their range.

Jon ran from the island's beach in the direction where he had last seen Garrett, and he shouted his name as he closed the distance. He knew he could easily pass his old friend and become lost on the frozen lake. He was gratified when he heard the response, but there was no way he would do what Garrett yelled.

"Go back…run."

Garrett was close enough already for Jon to zero in on his position, and Jon saw the dark silhouette of his old friend running out of the gray and white background. There was something else behind him, and Jon could see that it could run faster and take longer, leaping strides. If he had run away as soon as he had heard the order, Garrett would have died. Jon lifted his Browning X-Bolt Max rifle and sighted in on the shape behind Garrett.

Garrett heard the single bullet pass by, and even though he also heard the impact, the animal made no sound. It tumbled to a stop only a few feet away, and he saw Jon had hit the massive beast in the head. Jon came up beside him.

"Good shot."

"A lucky shot," said Jon. "It was moving so fast that I was only trying to slow it down. I couldn't even tell where its head was."

"We need to get out of here," said Garrett. "There were at least twenty in the pack."

Anne and Susan could barely see the two men until they were almost back to the shoreline, but they could see how hard they were running. That could only mean there was still something after them even though they had heard the single shot from Jon's Browning. They ran ahead of the two men to get the gate open. The men trudged through the deep snow and helped push it shut as soon as they were inside. They were breathing hard and yelling that they needed to hurry.

The concave path to the lodge was barely visible, but they made it to the front porch steps before the first wolves arrived. A pair of them hit the gate hard, but it held. Jon laid the barrel of his rifle across a porch rail to steady his aim, but Garrett stopped him.

"Don't waste your ammo. There are too many of them, and we have a new problem. Let's get inside so we can talk about it."

The lodge was sturdy and built to withstand the harsh climate. The walls and doors were thick enough, and they had closed the heavy shutters for the winter. The wolves were big, but even if they could get into the compound, they couldn't get into the lodge.

Susan had become the doctor for the former flight crew, and she was practically turning Garrett in a circle to see if he was wounded. He kept protesting that he was fine, but she knew he would say that even if he was bleeding out. Satisfied that he wasn't hurt, she turned her attention to Jon.

It was only natural that Susan Morris and Jon King had become a couple, just like Garrett Carson and Anne Hill. The latter were both about fifteen years older, and they occasionally acted like they were their parents, but when things got rough, they all had to defer to the other's skills. Jon let Susan check him over, but then he joined Garrett and Anne as they made sure the doors and windows were secure.

They gathered around the fireplace and nursed cups of steaming coffee while they got warm. Garrett didn't seem overly anxious, but there was clearly something he wanted to tell them.

"Was it the size of that wolf that has you jumpy?" asked Jon.

"No, I didn't even know it was there until you shot it. I thought I had left the pack behind, and they hadn't detected me. The wind must've shifted, and they got my scent."

He took a big gulp of his coffee, and his eyes focused on a spot inside the fireplace. The others waited for him to tell them what had his eyebrows so raised.

"I saw a horde of the infected walking across the lake."

Susan said, "You mean a frozen horde that had been walking across the lake, right?"

"Nope. They were still walking."

They sat silently for several minutes, each weighing what it would mean if the infected dead wouldn't freeze.

Anne said, "Over the years, how many would you guess we've put an end to while they were frozen?"

Jon snorted, "Who's counting? Hundreds would be my guess if you count the first ones at the Columbus airport."

They had gone from one frozen infected dead to the next and scooped fuel onto their heads. Then they set fire to them until the snow-covered airport tarmac blazed with light. When the fires burned out, their former navigator had compared the blackened heads sticking out of the snow to his aunt's Thanksgiving ham because she had always seasoned them by piercing the outside of the ham with cloves. Remembering Terrance Simmons always made them a little sad. As far as they knew, he was still alive, but they didn't think they would ever know for sure.

Susan picked up the conversation by adding to her last question.

"How can that be? It can't be over twenty degrees outside."

"That's what I was thinking," said Garrett. "I set up a shelter before dawn and waited at a spot where I found evidence that a horde had passed through, but there weren't any bodies. I found out I was right about the horde, but I also solved the mystery of the horde's disappearance. Packs of wolves are ranging farther south."

"It must be because there's an abundant food supply," said Jon.

"There were plenty of frozen bodies to eat before," answered Susan. "We've seen wolves dig up the infected dead when they couldn't find anything else to eat."

Jon shook his head.

"That wasn't what I meant. A moving horde would throw off a scent that could attract a wolf pack from miles away."

"I agree," said Garrett. "The noise a horde makes is almost as bad as the smell. Wolves from other packs are probably still converging on this area."

Anne had been the Senior Flight Attendant on the crew of Executive One, and over time, she had become the voice of reason for the survivors. When the other three let the hardships wear them down, Anne would remind them that they were still alive for good reasons. One of those reasons was the isolation they enjoyed. Her maturity and sense of responsibility for the group made her take on the role of a psychologist at times, and it didn't hurt that she was as remarkably healthy as Garrett.

"We're still far enough from the nearest towns," said Anne. "Whatever is causing the infected to make it so far north before they freeze, I doubt they would have made it to Last Island."

Garrett nodded and moved a little closer to her. He put one arm around her shoulders and drew her into a hug. Although they had left the formality of marriage customs behind, the gesture was as familiar to the group as if family members had done it, and they all felt the security of their home.

"Anne's right," said Garrett. "There's probably a simple explanation. If I had to guess, I would bet there have been other groups of survivors who had the same idea as us. They made it to a place where they could survive for a short time, but their luck ran out. They were still in a warm enough place when they started walking, and they just hadn't frozen yet."

"We were lucky," added Jon. "We came here at the right time of the year and got this place ready to last through the winter. I don't think we could've done it without help, but that's all just history now. Other groups haven't been as lucky as us."

A silence descended over them as they each were lost in their thoughts. Garrett was always the father figure because he had been the captain of the flight crew. He would never stop worrying about the rest of his crew, and his thoughts turned to the cache of supplies they had collected at the lodge when they settled on Last Island. He knew they still had plenty of everything they needed, but it wasn't an endless inventory. No matter how much they replaced, the quantities grew smaller in every category. There was less food, ammunition, medicine, and maintenance material. He had even reused nails when he repaired a hole made by a tree that fell onto the roof.

Anne was thinking the same thing. Survival meant replacing everything she cooked, and as she prepared meals, she itemized the ingredients on a shopping list so she could balance what had been used against what was left. As the list grew longer than what was still in the inventory, she knew they would be forced to make a supply run across the border. It wasn't something any of them wanted to do.

Jon knew his friends well enough to guess what they were thinking. He was slightly amused by how easy it was to read the meaning behind the furrowed lines on their foreheads, but it also made him sad to see them so worried.

"You two should see yourselves right now. It's not that bad, is it?"

Garrett heard Jon's question and lifted his eyes from a spot on the wall in the distance. There wasn't anything particularly interesting on the wall. It was just what Garrett did when he thought about something too hard. The question sank in as his eyes regained their focus, and he was a little embarrassed that he had been so obvious.

Anne had the same reaction as Garrett but turned her head away from Jon and Susan. She didn't want them to see that she was so afraid of having to make another supply run. Jon felt bad for calling them out because he knew they would always feel responsible for him and Susan. He apologized before they could even answer.

"Hey, I'm sorry. I didn't mean to make a joke out of it. I know you guys are just thinking ahead."

"It's okay," said Garrett, "but I feel like we have three new problems. There should be fewer infected dead out there, not more, and they shouldn't be walking. I thought we would be able to make at least one more supply run while they are frozen."

"What's the third new problem?" asked Susan.

"The wolves are most likely responding to their new food supply like the rats did back at the Columbus airport."

Jon said, "The food chain has been disrupted again, but why did it take so long to happen?"

"I've been giving that a lot of thought," said Garrett. "What if there were a few successful evacuations of larger groups? If they settled north of our island and began hunting game for food, the wolves had to leave their territory to find food. As they found a more abundant food supply, they moved closer and closer to the source. Without going there, we can't know for sure, but we couldn't have been the only survivors who headed for a cold climate to get away from the infected."

"So, you're saying you think the abundant food source is somewhere south of here near International Falls, and the infection caught up with them?" asked Jon.

"Exactly," said Garrett. "I thought they would have frozen faster, but the point is, whether the infected are frozen or not, we'll have to deal with the wolves."

"We need to know," said Anne. "We can't wait until next winter for the next supply run, and we can't do it in warm weather for a lot of reasons."

They all knew what Anne was talking about. The only way to get enough supplies was to cross the border into Minnesota, and they couldn't carry as much as they needed in their small boat. The best way was to tow sleds across the ice using snowmobiles.

One time, they had done it during warm weather using trucks to carry the freight across a long, narrow bridge to a dock closer to the north side of their island. The sound from their engines had attracted so many infected dead to the bridge that they had been forced to abandon their cargo to escape with their lives.

They had used the boat to cross Rainy Lake to a place closer to the US border. Anne returned to Last Island and remained at the lodge while Garrett, Susan, and Jon made the supply run. She waited until a designated time and then took the boat around the island to dock on the north side to wait for them. If all went well, they would return with truckloads of supplies and make several short trips from the bridge to the island using the boat. Things only went well at first.

They found three cargo trucks that miraculously started after little effort, and a local food distribution warehouse had everything they needed. They loaded the supplies quickly and sped away from the town, excited about their success. The excitement faded at the bridge's midpoint when they saw a large horde of infected dead blocked the road ahead. When they attempted to back away from the approaching death, they saw that the road behind them was no longer an option either.

With hordes approaching the trucks from the front and back, Anne had appeared below the bridge with the boat. She had taken it upon herself to leave their rendezvous and follow their progress across the bridge. When she saw that they couldn't go forward or backward, she coasted quietly to the bridge with a spotlight aimed at the cab of the truck in front. Her three friends knew their only chance was to escape while they could, and they used a rope to lower themselves into the boat.

Years later, the trucks were still parked out there on the bridge. They had retrieved most of the supplies in small amounts per trip, but they had learned their lesson about making supply runs during warm weather. They weren't convinced yet about the threat of infected dead during freezing weather, but the wolfpacks were something they hadn't anticipated. Humans couldn't outrun the wolves.

Anne left the others by the fire and went to the kitchen. When she returned, she had a tray of sandwiches. They shared the chores, but since Susan had become the doctor for the group, Anne tried to do a little more of the cooking. She also kept a close eye on the remaining food supplies.

"We might as well eat even if the pantry isn't as full as we would like it."

Everyone helped themselves to the food, and Garrett marveled at how his wife had adapted to a world where there were more hardships than they had known before that day when their plane had been drafted into service to fly the President to safety. One of the first things she taught herself was the art of making bread, and even her sandwiches were wonderful.

"Anne, I don't think I could ever say it enough," said Garrett, "and the same goes for Susan and Jon. I don't know how we could have survived without you. We all bring something special to the group, but some of the little things mean the most."

"There's nothing little about this sandwich," said Jon. "I don't know how you do it."

Anne would have normally accepted the praise with feigned humility just for fun, but her grim expression gave away her true feelings.

"I can only reiterate what I said before," said Anne. "We're backed into a corner. We have to cross the border again, and we have to do it soon."

"That's why I was out on the ice in the first place," said Garrett. "I was making sure we could do it without problems."

Jon added, "I think you got a couple of questions answered. We have to watch for the predators. The wolves may not be the only hunters out there. We may run into bears and mountain lions."

"I thought it would be too early for bears to be hunting," said Susan.

Garrett shook his head and pointed at Jon.

"You might be right. That many wolves could be a sign that they're also getting bolder. They could find where a bear is hibernating and attack it. At the very least, even if the bear survives the attack, it will be awake."

"And hungry," said Jon. "The big cats in the area will be stalking the big game that's being diminished in the usual hunting grounds. That could be why we haven't found any deer or moose tracks."

Anne poured more coffee while Garrett stoked the fire. They all knew they had been living a good life compared with the rest of the world, but their mistake had been thinking they could survive indefinitely as a small group. Now, they were faced with taking risks they knew could end their survival, and losing even one group member would be more than the others could bear.

"It's settled," said Garrett. "We can't put it off, and this time is going to be the hardest supply run we've ever made. Let's get our gear ready so we can leave tomorrow morning."

"All of us?" asked Anne.

Garrett gave her a solemn nod.

"The snowmobiles will make enough noise to make the predators keep their distance, but now that they've tasted human flesh, we can't count on them being too afraid of us. If we have to stop for any reason, we should expect to be attacked. We're going to need an extra gun on this trip."

"How many days should we plan to be gone?" asked Susan.

Garrett gave it some thought and said, "That depends on whether or not the old places have been picked clean. Judging by the hordes of infected dead, I expect that other survivors found the warehouses at the food distribution center. Let's plan to be on the road for at least a week. We usually last that long, even if we only plan for three or four days. It's still early, so we have plenty of time to prepare and get some rest before doing this."

3

Mud Island

The Coast of South Carolina - March 2023

Chief Joshua Barnes was thinking about whether or not he could refer to sitting on top of the houseboat as a vacation. He considered the definition of the word and made a mental list of the things people used to do when they took time off from work. He held up his index finger first as he added boating to the list.

"That wasn't fun," he said to himself. "Not unless you think it's fun to get shot at."

Traveling from Charleston to Mud Island was easy when they had helicopters, but the trip was much easier by boat than by car. He could have used the MRAP, but the roads had become impassable to the point where it wasn't worth the work to clear them. Not to mention the bridges by Georgetown that didn't exist anymore. Still, the MRAP was less likely to draw gunfire than an open boat.

The Chief and his friends had spent seven years locating survivors and bringing them into the fold, but there were still renegades who resisted attempts to convince them that the survival of civilization depended upon keeping the number of living people higher than the number of infected dead. How people could resist joining with others was beyond his comprehension, but it was even more confusing why they would shoot at someone in a boat.

When he had passed between several small islands less than ten miles from the shelter on Mud Island, a sniper had taken out the windshield on his Boston Whaler. He was glad Iris had been sitting on the deck toward the back and hadn't been hit, but the anger that flared inside the Chief burned hot as he lifted the microphone on his radio and called out the location of the sniper to the AC-130 that was at an altitude that made it undetectable.

If the sniper had fired a shot into the air just to draw his attention, the Chief would have been glad to make a new friend. He would have followed the precautions they had used since the beginning of the infection, and he thought it was a shame that the sniper didn't give him a chance to extend an olive branch. Instead, the Chief turned the wheel hard to starboard and increased his speed toward open water. He heard a second shot pass too close for comfort, and the sound of it erased any sympathy he may have felt for someone else who had survived the infection for seven years.

The drone of the AC-130 became audible as it descended, and the Chief could imagine the sniper searching the sky for the source of the once-familiar sound. He took a moment to be sure Iris was still safe where she crouched in the stern, and then he watched along with her as the silver aircraft dipped into a spiraling dive. He knew that spiral meant the crew had acquired the target. There was a barely visible flash on the plane's left side, and the Chief dropped his eyes toward the tiny island where he knew the sniper had to be hiding.

The Chief still held his index finger in the air, and his eyes refocused on it as if he had forgotten why he held it in the air. In his mind's eyes, he could still see the puff of smoke that meant the sniper had joined the ranks of the dead. He remembered hoping that there had only been one idiot on the island.

The Chief held up a second finger and added the weather-related activities to his mental list. Cold mornings accompanied by rain weren't things anyone would enjoy on vacation. A broad smile stretched across his face when he raised a third finger. There was one thing that he liked about vacations even before the apocalypse.

"Peace and quiet," said the Chief.

The roof of the houseboat was one of the few places outside where he could sit without constantly looking over his shoulder. The ocean stretched out in front of him, and he didn't have to worry about the infected dead because they wouldn't be able to see him even if they somehow managed to cross the moat to Mud Island.

"Who're you talking to?" asked Iris, "and what's with the fingers?"

Her smile matched his own as she climbed into full view on the ladder attached to the side of the houseboat. The Chief felt a little bit self-conscious with his fingers raised into the air, but his smile spread even further.

"I was listing the reasons why this trip could be called a vacation."

"I hope one of the three things you came up with was spending some quality time alone with your wife," said Iris as she sat in the folding chair beside his.

"That was number one," he lied, but a small laugh charmed Iris into not really wanting to know what he had listed.

"Okay, I'll rephrase my question. What're you thinking about?"

"It seems like forever ago when Tom showed up on top of this houseboat, and then you somehow survived the trip to the coast. Before then, I never really thought about things like vacations. You know, things that ordinary people did. We worked on cruise ships, so it was like we were always on vacation."

Iris put a hand on her husband's and said, "I don't want to sound pessimistic, but it doesn't matter anymore. All roads lead to this point in time, and what matters is that we're here together."

"But where does the road go from here?"

Iris knew the Chief better than anyone, and she knew his question was based on something more significant than vacations. They could exchange idle comments about whether or not they were on vacation, but the Chief must be thinking about their next mission. She knew his mind was restless as long as there was a challenge for him to overcome, and ever since he had returned from Wyoming, he had been different. When she had asked him what was wrong, he had brushed off the question with the excuse that he had a lot on his mind.

Kathy filled in some blanks when Iris asked her about their mission. Most of it was exactly as the Chief had told her, but Kathy had suspected it had something to do with the military. Kathy said the Chief was fixated on the idea that the US military must have survived somewhere. Just as they all suspected there were nuclear submarines other than their friends in the British Royal Navy, the Chief was convinced that a base must have survived.

Captain Miller told Kathy and the Chief he believed the military would have survived in remote pockets like Guantanamo Bay or Diego Garcia. The Chief agreed, but he had trained as a Navy SEAL in the

Northwest, and he was sure that elements of the Air Force and Navy could have made a stand in Alaska. The climate would have given them an advantage over bases on the mainland, and the wilderness would have been an inhospitable environment for the infected dead. Besides the harsh weather and terrain, there were predators that would have found the infected dead to be another food source. Their scent alone would have attracted every wolf, mountain lion, and bear within hundreds of miles.

Iris squeezed her husband's hand.

"You know I'm going with you this time, right?"

"It's a long trip."

"England was a long trip. I haven't measured the distance, but I could use a change of scenery."

Iris smiled at the Chief but tilted her head to one side when she spoke. That was her way of asking him if he understood her. She knew he was listening and hearing every word, but there was a big difference between hearing and understanding.

The Chief knew her question about going along was rhetorical. When they returned from Wyoming, he saw how Kathy and Tom had been. If Tom had been with them to witness the number of times Kathy had come close to dying, the Chief doubted he would ever let her out of his sight again. He had wondered several times if he would have had the courage to face Tom with bad news. It had been bad enough to answer Tom when he asked if there had been any close calls. The bandages around Kathy's hamstring and where Captain Miller had bitten her were all the answers he needed.

They both turned their heads toward the beach when they heard the sound of water splashing. The woods at the end of the dock blocked their view of most of the beach, but they could see well enough to tell the blue crabs were pulling a human body away from shore. They could tell it was one of the few infected dead that still managed to find its way to their island. There was a time when they washed ashore so often that the Mud Island family was forced to patrol the beaches to eliminate them. Now, the blue crabs did the job for them.

"Did you remember to shut the door when you came up here?" asked the Chief.

"No, I thought we might have crab cakes for supper tonight," answered Iris.

The last time one of them left the door open on the houseboat, they had discovered the blue crabs were no longer content to wait in the water for unsuspecting prey. Three of them had foraged through the houseboat in search of food. Not only had they gotten as large as cats, they had become much more aggressive.

"Just once, I'd like to get a straight answer to a reasonable question."

"Coming from you, that's a tall order," laughed Iris.

The Chief had the decency to grin at her rather than to disagree. Everyone in their group of survivors knew the Chief was the master of sarcasm. He was deadly serious when necessary, but given the opportunity to twist someone's words, he couldn't help himself. It was as if he felt obligated to make people regret their choice of words.

The Chief stood up from his deck chair and stretched.

"It's time to go back. I could sit up here for hours, but I don't want to navigate the woods back to the shelter after sunset. Those stupid crabs can smell us, and I don't plan to help them become better hunters by teaching them they can wait in the bushes for us to pass by."

The Chief climbed down the ladder and then gave Iris a hand, even though she was quite capable of doing it without help. He had to admire her tall figure and how slim she was in jeans. Her long, silver hair was in a ponytail that hung to the middle of her back, and despite the color of her hair, she moved with the grace of a woman half her age.

Iris noticed him checking her out and asked, "What are you thinking, old man?"

"Is it 'pick on the Chief day'?" he answered. "Can't a man appreciate the way his wife looks?"

Her grin was enough to answer his questions. Even though they had loved each other before the apocalypse, it was the end of civilization that had brought them together. They regretted not admitting their feelings before the infection but were glad they had survived and gotten a second chance. Not everyone could say the same thing.

They pulled machetes and thick gloves from their belts and walked the length of the dock toward the nearly hidden path that led to the shelter's entrance. They tugged on the gloves and kept their eyes aimed at the underbrush, watching for the slightest movement.

In the days before the infection, the Chief and Iris could have enjoyed the hike across the island, but a moment of sightseeing was all it would take for the aggressive crabs to attack. There was always the possibility of running into the infected dead, but the blue crabs had upended the food chain. Millions of infected dead had walked into the ocean a few years ago, and the blue crabs had greedily welcomed the extra food. They had so much to eat that they didn't have to compete with each other for meals, and they not only multiplied in numbers. They had grown in size.

As the new food source dwindled, the crabs were forced to evolve again. They were no longer content to wait in the shallow water for people to stumble over them. They came out of the water and hunted for their next meal. Eventually, they would turn on each other, but for the time being, there were still enough people and infected dead to satisfy their hunger.

New growth of trees and vines hung down over the shelter's entrance and hid the big door that resembled a bank vault. The Chief still remembered the first time he had seen the door, and it always amazed him that good fortune had given all his friends a chance to survive the infection. He knew it had only been sheer luck that he, Kathy, and Jean had spotted Ed in a boat near the island. If he hadn't gone outside when he did, they would never have known the shelter was there, and they might not be alive to think about it.

When they crawled through the hatch inside the shelter and made their way to the kitchen, they were greeted by Kathy and Tom. They were setting out plates for supper, and the smell of the food made the Chief's stomach growl.

"I'm not even going to ask you what it is," said the Chief as he pulled out a chair at the table.

Iris said, "I promised him crab cakes, but I've got my heart set on bacon."

"No thanks," said Cassandra as she emerged from the room beyond the kitchen. She was followed closely by Sim. "Crab cakes would be a hard pass for me, but I wouldn't mind shooting a few of the sneaky little devils."

"They're not so little anymore," said the Chief.

The comment earned him a withering glare from Cassandra.

"You think I need to be reminded of how big and mean they can be?" she asked.

The Chief couldn't help himself, and Kathy laughed before he even finished his answer.

"Sorry…I thought you would be over that little incident by now."

Cassandra opened her mouth to give him a piece of her mind, but Kathy held up her hand to stop her.

"You should know by now not to feed the trolls. Now, sit down and eat before it gets cold, or he'll take your share."

The lighthearted banter continued for another minute, but they gradually settled into eating and discussing a variety of topics between bites of food.

"I think we should go to Alaska," said the Chief.

There was a brief silence around the table as everyone stopped talking and eating. The eating part was resumed, but no one spoke.

The Chief added, "We can make a detour along the way and check on our friends near International Falls."

Sim choked on a mouthful of food and coughed long enough for Cassandra to slap him on the back.

"Stop coughing. You know he does that on purpose, and the longer you choke, the better it makes him feel."

The Chief acted innocent and kept talking as if nothing had interrupted him.

"If things haven't worked out for them, they might reconsider our offer to return with us."

"I'd like that," said Sim. "I don't care much for how you delivered the news, but I liked the headline. I miss them. We went through a lot together, and I can't help wishing they had come with us. At least I would know for sure they're safe."

"Not to change the subject," said Tom, "but what's in Alaska?"

Between bites of food, the Chief answered, "Remember the last survivors we picked up near the border of Mississippi and Alabama?"

"The people who came from Texas?"

"Yeah, they said there were rumors about the Air Force setting up a safe zone in Alaska."

"That's a long way for a rumor to travel," said Cassandra. "Did they say how they heard about it?"

Kathy added, "That's also a long way for people to travel, which is pretty much the only way rumors travel these days."

The Chief took a moment to think back to what the group of survivors said because he knew why the others were questioning the information. It wasn't the first time they had heard about a military enclave making a stand against the infected dead, and it wouldn't be the last time.

"I spent a few hours with them to see if it was just something they heard other people talking about, and it sounded like solid intelligence to me. What really caught my attention was something about a secret base. The inside is off-limits to civilians, but the military fortified the area for survivors. Does that sound familiar to anyone?"

Iris said, "It seems like most of the shelters are underground because everyone expected the apocalypse to come in the form of a nuclear war. It's no secret that Russia would have tried for a foothold in North America by attacking Alaska. They never got over the fact that they used to own it. I would have wanted my own survival shelter in my backyard if I lived in Alaska."

Tom was stirring his food with his fork, and the Chief noticed he wasn't joining the conversation. The Chief was good at reading expressions, but he was having a hard time reading Tom's mood. He couldn't tell if Tom was upset or angry, but he could tell something was bothering him. He caught Kathy's attention and gave her a subtle gesture with one index finger. She saw the motion and where it was pointed, and her expression changed.

Kathy shrugged her shoulders at the Chief. If she was aware of something bothering Tom, she would have given him a nod or waved him off so he would let it go for now. Instead, she leaned forward on her elbows and put her face lower than Tom's so he couldn't miss the fact that she was trying to get his attention.

"Something wrong?" she asked.

"Huh? Oh, don't mind me. I was just thinking about what the Chief said."

"Which part?"

At first, Tom seemed stumped by the question but answered, "All of it."

This was one of those times when the Chief felt like he had been dropped into the middle of a problem and didn't have all the facts. He was always glad to have Iris next to him when that happened. If it was something about Tom and Kathy's relationship, he would hand it off to Iris as fast as possible.

"I'm all ears," said the Chief. "Would you care to be a bit more specific?" His tone was more serious than he had intended.

Tom realized that everyone at the table had stopped eating and had their eyes on him, waiting for him to continue. He had been so preoccupied with something that it hadn't occurred to him that Kathy's question was from everyone. He had a guilty look on his face.

"Sorry, Chief. That was more abrupt than I meant it."

The Chief still sounded less than forgiving.

"Apparently, you have a problem with my suggestion about going to Alaska. Is it because you weren't invited along when we went to

Wyoming?"

The conversation had started between the Chief and Kathy while they were on the trip and continued when they got back. Tom had expressed his displeasure in strong terms, and the Chief was still unable to put some of it behind him. Kathy had told the Chief that Tom wanted her to take a less risky role in the group, and he was worried that something might happen to her. The Chief doubted Kathy had told Tom about how close she had come to making his worries come true.

"No, it wasn't about that," said Tom, "but this would probably be a good time to bring the question up. Would this be another adventure with my wife while I wait at home?"

Tom had been a professional baseball player before the apocalypse, and he was a big man. He appeared to grow visibly bigger when he sat up straight to deliver his question. His reaction caused the Chief to stiffen, and he would most likely have stood up if not for the firm grip of Iris' hand on his leg under the table. Its pressure also made him take time to think about what he should say next. They had about seven years of friendship behind them that had to count for something, so the Chief took the high road.

"You're right, Tom. If I had that all to do over again, it would've been both of you making the trip, or it would've been neither of you. I won't put you in that position again."

It was meant to be a conciliatory statement to help the two men get past some hard feelings, and it had the desired effect, but it also opened the door for Sim to ask his own question.

"Does that include me?"

Sim was of average height and weight, and although he wasn't a liability in a fight, he would never be as capable as his wife, Cassandra. She wasn't a physically imposing woman, but she was very skilled at combat. The Chief had said repeatedly that he would defer to her skills in urban warfare.

The tension in the room had gone up as soon as everyone realized there were unresolved issues between Tom and the Chief. They had respect for each other, but as long as the Chief was in charge, he would decide who was suited to go on a mission and who wasn't. It had never occurred to him that Tom would disagree with that, so he didn't ask for Tom's opinion when he arranged the trip to Wyoming. Now, the Chief was offering Tom an olive branch. With a little coaxing from Iris, he understood he should have at least discussed it with Tom before making a unilateral decision. Sim's question was well-timed and was asked so innocently that even Tom laughed.

"What did I say that was so funny?" asked Sim.

Cassandra put her arm around her husband and gave him a strong hug.

"Darling, there isn't one of us who could navigate the way you do, but don't throw your hat in the ring when it comes time to decide who should go into a firefight."

It earned him some credit with the rest of the group when he didn't get offended by their laughter or by what his wife said. Instead, he took the opportunity to get everyone to laugh again.

"It was always the same way when we would pick volleyball teams in high school."

"That's my man," said Cassandra.

When everyone settled down again, Tom surprised the Chief with a tactical question he hadn't thought of.

"I'm actually over what happened before, Chief, but I have a genuine concern about seeking out the military. I mean, put yourself in their shoes. How do you think they're going to react when they see a pre-infection AC-130 gunship coming in for a landing? Their first reaction will be defensive, and their second will be gratitude that you returned it to them."

It might have occurred to the Chief before making that mistake, but he had to admit, it wasn't the way he had imagined it. He expected the United States military to be happy to see others had survived, and their information about other storage facilities and shelters would be a welcome surprise.

Kathy said, "You haven't forgotten about Huntsville, have you?"

"No, I haven't forgotten," said the Chief. "I just think the honorable behavior of the US military branches is what sets them apart from other countries. What happened in Huntsville was a subversion of the Army because of bad leadership. I believe we're going to find that most units will still remember what their duty is."

The Chief saw Cassandra and Kathy share something with eye contact, and they saw that he had noticed. Kathy didn't wait for the Chief to ask if there was something he should know about.

"The Air Force silo in Wyoming was a history lesson we should all study. They started as a strong military unit caring for the people they were sworn to protect. They fed them, clothed them, mended their wounds, and put a roof over their heads to keep them safe from the elements. Despite all of the good things they did, they would tell you they had failed in the long run because it wasn't sustainable. They gradually evolved into a blended unit that resembles us, but the reason we were sustainable is that we didn't evolve into what we are…we started out like this."

The Chief thought back to their beginning and remembered how they started small. They were just a handful of survivors, but one of the first decisions they made as a group had been to seek out other survivors who needed their help. It wasn't enough to survive. They realized survival wasn't living unless they had a purpose, and that purpose grew as they opened more shelters. When they reunited Tom with his wife, it was more than a gesture. It defined them as humans.

Iris said, "This is a conversation that would benefit from Jim Miller's input. As I recall, he deserted because he felt like the military was already moving away from their prime directive, so to speak."

"He deserted because the doctors and scientists wanted to bring the infected dead back to the ships to experiment on them," said the Chief.

"We remember," said Tom, "but that was a bad idea, and the ranking officers behind that decision were ignoring the risk it posed to their own people. I wonder how long it took before the infection broke free from containment. Like Hampton always says, if you let the infection get behind your lines of defense, sooner or later, it will break free."

"I wonder why they didn't understand that," said Sim. "There's one simple argument I would have made if I had been in Captain Miller's shoes. If it was a good idea to experiment with pathogens in laboratories on ships, why wouldn't they have been doing it that way instead of in labs like Fort Dietrich, Maryland, or Wuhan, China? There were labs scattered all over the world, but I'll bet there weren't any at sea."

That was an argument everyone at the table could get behind. If the pathogen escaped from a lab on a ship, it could only spread through a limited population. Still, there was something unnatural about the idea of making a ship's crew seem expendable. It was like condemning them to die just because they worked on the ship.

Cassandra added, "I guess the same could be said for putting those labs in remote locations. When did it ever make sense to put them in densely populated cities?"

The discussion ended with the last question, and they ate in uneasy silence. There was a lot to consider. On the one hand, they felt like it was natural to hope there were more survivors, and the military was likely to have withstood the infection somewhere. On the other hand, Tom was right about the AC-130, and the military would feel entitled to take it from them. They would also believe they were entitled to the supplies recovered by the Mud Island survivors, and the Chief couldn't deny that he would feel the same way if he were in their shoes.

"I think I know what we should do," said the Chief, "but I'd like us to agree before we do anything. If anyone has any objections, feel free to express them."

Kathy stopped him and said, "I'll bet we're all thinking the same things you are. I'll be surprised if you hear any objections."

The Chief saw the nods of approval around the table. Their goal had always been to expand to new locations. It was the only way they would be able to keep the human race from extinction.

"Okay," said the Chief. "I can't remember the last time a plan was approved without anyone hearing the details first, but I appreciate it. I think you just told me you trust me to make the right decisions, but if there are any concerns about Captain Miller, I think our best bet would be to hide his identity. I propose that we should follow the rumors to locate survivors in Alaska. We can visit Sim's old friends along the way, but when we reach Alaska, we're going to land the plane far enough from the military bases to avoid detection. We can hike the rest of the way."

"How many of us are going?" asked Iris. She knew she wasn't the only one who was thinking the same thing.

"Anyone from our core group who wants to," he answered. "If Captain Miller wants to go, I suggest we get used to calling him Jim. I noticed he's already growing a beard. Shannon said she liked it when he quit shaving and let his hair grow longer, so he already looks more like a civilian than he used to."

Everyone at the table liked the idea that Jim Miller had met Shannon. Despite years of seclusion, she had adjusted quickly to her new life. She had followed him around like a puppy at first, but as she became used to her new surroundings and so many friends, she sought new ways to fit in with them. Shannon impressed everyone with the amount of work she put into combat training. She was determined to be accepted by them in every way, and that included going with them when they went on a mission.

"Hearing no objections," said the Chief, "vacation is officially over.

I'll make arrangements to rendezvous with the rest of the gang tomorrow."

4

Rainy Lake

Last Island - March 2023

Sunrise came earlier than they wanted because sleep came later for all of them. They had always left someone behind at the lodge to guard against the infected dead, predators, and the occasional poachers who discovered their island. This expedition to International Falls was the first time they would all make the trip, and it gave them a feeling like they were saying goodbye to their home.

Since they had made preparations before turning in for a couple of hours, they only had to make breakfast. The morning meal was usually an opportunity for lighthearted discussions about plans for the day. Someone always had a project they wanted to finish, and they discussed the details to enlist help or suggestions. They worked well as a team or independently, but breakfast was a time for ideas. This morning was different.

They went about the business of cooking and then ate in silence. They seemed lost in their private thoughts but were aware of the glances across the table. It was as if they all sensed the dread that they shared. They remembered living in constant fear at the airport. From the day they first landed in Columbus to when they were finally free to leave, they had lived with the fear of the infected dead. They feared for the safety of each other more than they did for themselves, and this time was no different. They knew this breakfast might be their last meal as a family, and they tried to eat without wondering if they would all be alive at the end of the day.

The foursome almost finished the meal without speaking, but Garrett decided it created a dangerous atmosphere. They were already being too defensive if they let themselves worry so much before leaving the lodge. They were acting like a sports team that was playing not to lose instead of playing to win. He understood that was a sure way to lose as a leader, and he had to say something to motivate the others.

"Now I understand what it must've felt like for you, Anne. When we made supply runs before and left you behind. We always talked about our plans while eating breakfast, and everything was said in a way intended to make you less worried. Now that we're all making this trip together, it feels like we can't even reassure each other."

"It was a lonely feeling watching you three as you ate breakfast. I never knew if it would be our last meal together," said Anne. "Now we all feel like that."

Jon added, "We all wondered the same thing, but we put on a good face for you. We didn't want you to worry."

"It's not too late to fix things," said Susan. "I think you just said what we were all thinking, so let's put on our big boy pants and talk about it."

Susan's choice of words was just what they needed. They didn't laugh, but it lifted their spirits, and as they finished their meal and cleaned up the kitchen, they did it with a conviction that they would return safely from the supply run.

The temperature was still hovering around twenty degrees, but the snow had stopped falling. There were moments when the sky was so clear and refreshing that they appreciated the wilderness and its harsh climate. The cold air stung their cheeks as soon as they left the warmth of their cabin, and they pulled scarves from around their necks upward to cover their faces.

"With good visibility, we should be across the lake in less than an hour," said Garrett, "but I want to take our time because we don't know where that horde came from. If there are more, we don't want them to see us first."

"If we had done this yesterday," said Jon, "we might've run right into them. We should be able to see anything on the ice all the way to

International Falls. By the way, have you thought about how far we're going?"

"We never made it to Walmart," said Susan.

Susan was only partly serious about it, but it was a standing joke they all laughed about every time they made a supply run. In the early days of the infection, they had become isolated in the Columbus airport while millions of people died. When they talked about what they would do after they were free to leave, Anne had said they should probably go to the nearest Walmart for supplies.

Jon had said at the time, "If you think Walmart was crowded before, can you imagine what it was like on the first day of the infection? There were probably people wheeling out big flat-screen TVs by the dozen."

The image of people looting flat-screen TV sets during an apocalypse had given them laughing fits, but they didn't miss the real point of his comment. There were plenty of things in Walmart that would aid their survival, but it was all gone on the first day. Whatever was left after the first day had most likely been picked clean in the seven years since.

The same had been true for most of the stores, but Garrett and Jon were both pilots and had good heads for engineering. Garrett had told Susan more than once that pilots had to be natural engineers to believe airplanes were capable of flying. When they broke into buildings that other survivors had looted, they came back with odds and ends that had been left behind because people didn't recognize the value of raw materials. To prove their point, they had good indoor plumbing and a still that made some of the smoothest moonshine in Canada.

Their early efforts to make the snowmobiles run on the product from their still had resulted in an explosion, and they had abandoned the idea, but they learned from their mistakes and figured out how to make an alternative fuel from the corn storage bins at a farm near the airport.

"Walmart it is," said Garrett as they uncovered their snowmobiles. "It's about time we satisfied our curiosity even though we aren't likely to find anything worth keeping."

"That's too far inland," said Jon. "It's far enough from the center of town, but we have to go through some areas that were too populated."

Garrett didn't answer immediately because they were all busy with the tarps and the gear they needed to take along on the trip. They had attached converted cargo containers used on automobile rooftops to carry more supplies if they got lucky. Jon said they looked like coffins on the backs of the snowmobiles, but they did the job well. Plus, they kept the supplies dry and made the snowmobiles more aerodynamic.

"We've talked about this before, and I understand the risks. If we run into any of the infected dead, they'll most likely be buried under the snow. We need to take it nice and easy so none of us ram into a mess of them and wreck. I also figure that we can avoid some of the congested areas by using the Rainy River until we get to the Fort Frances Toll Bridge. The banks are low enough for us to get off the ice before the bridge and back on the river after the water treatment plant."

"Someone's been studying the maps again," said Susan.

She was already straddling her snowmobile and ready to go. Hers was painted bright yellow. Garrett's was red, Jon's was blue, and Anne covered hers in red, white, and blue stripes. The different colors allowed them to identify each other from a distance if they got separated.

Garrett smiled at her and said, "How else would I know we can get off the Rainy River the second time at the sewage plant? There's a boat ramp there, and we'll only have to use one street for a few blocks to get to the Trans-Canada Highway. We'll practically be in the Walmart parking lot."

One by one, they started their engines and moved toward the gate. Jon got there first and pulled off to one side to open it for the others. It was a routine they had used dozens of times. Garrett revved his engine and went through first, followed by Anne and then Susan. They didn't stop to wait for Jon, but they only coasted away from the entrance. He made sure the gate was secured behind them and then caught up. He noticed that all three of them had looked over their shoulders as they coasted away, but he didn't think they were checking on him. It was more likely that they felt like getting one more view of their home on Last Island.

Garrett followed a trail from their compound to the shore of Last Island. It was deep with snow, but they had used the same route over the years and kept it clear of debris. They removed branches when the snow melted, and of course, they wanted to be sure no infected dead had made it their last resting place. Even as the first winter snowfalls began, they inspected the trail daily to ensure they wouldn't wreck a snowmobile before they even reached the lake.

There was a slight bump as each vehicle crossed the line between the shore and the frozen lake, and as each of them felt the jolt, they increased their speed. The steady hum of the engines sounded like a small airplane on the ice, and even though the cold bit at the exposed skin around their goggles, it was an exhilarating feeling to be moving with so much freedom. They let the distance between them increase by a few yards, and even though they were in line with each other, the line was crooked. If someone had trouble, they didn't want to compound the problem by rear-ending them.

On the lead snowmobile, Garrett watched for anything unusual as the distance decreased between them and their first significant landmark. The railroad bridge that crossed the border between Canada and the United States was dark against the bright sky behind it, and Garrett could see something was wrong. He knew he should be able to see under the bridge, and it appeared to be lower than it had been.

Garrett held up a fist to indicate he was decreasing his speed because of a problem, and the rest of the group slowed with him. When he stopped, they coasted into position on his left and right. He pointed at the bridge.

Jon was the first to ask, "Why can't we see under the bridge? Could snow accumulation have possibly been that much?"

They all carried binoculars, so they pulled them from their backpacks and studied the bridge silently. It didn't take long for them to realize the bridge had collapsed. It had gone unused for years with the weight of a freight train sitting on its tracks, and the weather finally took its toll. They had passed under the train several times but had never inspected the cars to see what they had been carrying. They suspected it was raw materials, such as ore and lumber. Some of the cars were cylindrical, so they were most likely filled with chemicals. They doubted there would be anything of use to them on the train, so they had simply passed under it, watching for signs of danger.

"Something is moving in one of the cars that's hanging over the edge," said Susan. "It's the boxcar on the right side."

Garrett, Jon, and Anne focused their binoculars on the railroad car Susan had indicated.

"Did you mean something's moving or something's falling from the car?" asked Anne.

They all saw the human shape fall from the boxcar's open door. The huge vehicle hung down at a steep angle above the section of the bridge that had collapsed. They wondered how anyone could still be alive inside the train, but mostly, they wanted to know how the falling body could suddenly reach the open door.

Jon said, "The boxcar is hanging at such a steep angle. How could someone fall out the door? I mean, they would need to climb up the inside wall and pull themselves out, right?"

"Whoever or whatever that was," answered Garrett, "they didn't fall like someone who was alive. They weren't waving their arms or anything. They fell like a sack of potatoes."

As they watched, a second person fell from the open door, and each of them watched for signs that the falling person was even aware of what was happening. They saw that Garrett was right, and that could only mean it was an infected dead.

"Oh, no," said Susan. "That has to mean one thing. The boxcar had been completely full of infected dead when the bridge fell. The door must've slid open when the boxcar dangled over the edge. The infected dead are piled so deep in one end of the car that they're crawling out."

"I wonder how many of the boxcars are full of people," said Jon.

"Even worse," said Garrett. "If the cars are full of the infected, they'll thaw out as soon as the weather gets warm. On the bright side, this explains where those hordes came from."

Anne said, "From here, I count forty-seven boxcars capable of carrying people, but I can't see both ends of the train. Why were they on the train in the first place?"

Jon answered, "Escaping, but it doesn't really matter, does it? My only concern is making sure they stay inside the train. Is it worth our time to check the locks on all the doors?"

"No, I don't think so," said Garrett. "They've been sitting on those tracks for years and wouldn't have gotten out if the bridge hadn't collapsed. Let's take care of what we came for, then check it out on our way home. If nothing's changed by then, I think it's safe to assume they'll be there a few more years."

Garrett stashed his binoculars in his backpack and pulled his goggles down from his forehead to cover his eyes. He gave everyone a moment to follow suit, then he surged forward in the direction of the bridge. They wouldn't know if there was a gap they could pass through until they got closer. If the only opening was below the falling bodies, they would have to find the infected that were below the bridge and be careful not to be in the wrong place if more fell from the car.

As the distance between the snowmobiles and the bridge grew

shorter, they could see there were two gaps. Besides the larger gap below the dangling boxcar, there was a narrow spot further to the left. It was closer to the beginning of the bridge, and the span that had collapsed was still attached at that end. The train tracks were angled downward to the frozen river, and a dozen railroad cars sat on the slope.

Garrett came to a stop for a second time, but they were close enough to see everything without binoculars. Jon, Susan, and Anne coasted to a stop. The problems posed by the collapsed bridge were worse than they had thought.

The end of the collapsed span had fallen heavily onto the river, and the combined weight of the bridge and the train cars had punched a large hole in the ice. It had refrozen, but the first car in line was partially submerged. There was no way to know if the collapse had been long enough ago for the ice to become as solid as it needed to be for them to cross it.

The part of the bridge that was still connected to the collapsed span was under pressure from the weight of the train, and if it broke free while they were on the river, it would crack the ice over a hundred yards in both directions. They would be sucked into the water under the ice if they were near enough to it.

"The banks are too steep for us to climb on snowmobiles," said Garrett. "I know we can backtrack and go onto land further from the bridge, but we would lose a lot of daylight."

"Want to go home and try again tomorrow?" asked Anne.

Garrett shook his head and answered, "There aren't any guarantees that the weather will be this clear tomorrow. At least we can see far enough ahead of us to know if there's a problem. Besides, we don't see any wolves tailing us, but they could be on land. I'm for making a run through the big gap. Let's string ourselves out about fifty yards apart. I'll go through it slowly and make sure I can get to the other side first."

"I don't really like the idea of you taking on the role of crash dummy," said Anne.

Garrett had to grin despite himself, and the situation made him think of Chief Barnes. They were both leaders, and they had been forced by their sense of responsibility to take risks for their people. They hadn't been around each other long, but they had recognized their similarities instantly. Sometimes, he asked himself what the Chief would do, and he always knew the answer.

"I wouldn't ask any of you to do something I wouldn't do myself, so

I'll go first. I'll signal for you to come through, but watch me closely. If I swerve or point at anything, it means to avoid that spot."

Anne knew there wasn't any sense in arguing with him, so she gave him an understanding nod. She pulled her goggles back down over her eyes so he wouldn't see the tears welling up.

Garrett stood up on his snowmobile to see further ahead and then drove quickly toward the bridge. He concentrated on the spot where they had seen the last body fall and went slightly to the right. If he was correct, the infected had fallen in larger numbers to the left when the boxcars had separated. It didn't take long for his suspicions to be confirmed.

He could only guess how many of the infected had fallen onto the ice, but there were hundreds. A blanket of snow had covered them, but the protruding limbs that still sluggishly waved in the air were enough for him to wonder if their cold sanctuary was really as safe as they had thought. Other survivors must have been trying to flee to a cold climate just like they had, but to go further north would mean hardships they might not be able to endure.

Garrett shifted his weight and pointed with his left arm extended. He made a smooth turn to the right but kept his eyes on the ice directly below the hanging boxcar. The end of the pile of infected dead was a twisted mass of bodies that had fallen since the snow had stopped. None of them were capable of walking because the fall had been the final insult to their mangled bones, but they heard his snowmobile approaching and reached for him with anticipation. He saw the pile shift as one slipped down to the ice in an attempt to crawl toward him.

He didn't need to get closer than he was in order to tell that the gap was wide enough. The distance between the last of the infected dead and the shoreline on the Canadian side was at least twenty yards wide, and he had learned from experience that the ice would be more solid near land. As he went through the gap, he watched with fascination as a body landed on the pile.

Garrett's red snowmobile was easy to see against the stark whiteness of the background, but since the others were at an angle to his course, the falling body appeared to be dropping straight toward him. They held their breath until it landed well to his left. Then, they saw him signal for them to follow his path.

It took several minutes for them to catch up with Garrett on the other side of the bridge, but they eventually gathered along the shoreline to talk about the next move. They turned off their engines and pulled back the hoods of their heavy coats. It was safe to say that they were all getting a bad feeling about this supply run.

Anne said, "I've got that same nagging urge to come and rescue you guys again, but this time I'm with you. Maybe we should go back and try to make our supplies last until warm weather melts that mess."

Jon pointed at the mound under the bridge and said, "After the ice melts, everything you see over there is going to be in the lake. There's no way to know what that's going to do to the water supply."

"It's already in the water," said Susan. "The cars that landed on the ice and punched a hole probably dumped hundreds of infected dead into the lake. They're probably drifting away under the ice as we speak. Depending on when the bridge collapsed, they could already be bumping against the shoreline of Last Island. Who knows what's going to crawl out of the lake after the ice melts?"

"So, exactly why are we making a supply run?" asked Jon. "We should be leaving instead."

"And going where?" snapped Anne.

She made it sound more angry than she was, but if she was really angry, Jon would know it wasn't anger toward him. They were all frustrated by the way things were developing.

Garrett said, "We wanted our lodge to be permanent, but maybe our friends who brought us here had been right when they offered to take us in."

"We don't know if they're even alive anymore," said Anne.

It wasn't like her to be so pessimistic, and her quick answers silenced the group for a minute. It was natural for Garrett to take charge and lift up the woman who had been thrust into the role of his wife and mother to Jon and Susan, so he searched his mind desperately for the right thing to say. He barely opened his mouth to speak when they all heard the sharp crack that sounded like a gunshot, but it wasn't followed by the whistle of a bullet passing by.

Their eyes widened as a second snapping sound drew their attention to the massive mound under the bridge. It was like watching a mountain being blown out of existence by dynamite. It appeared to expand before it shrank, and they all knew at the same moment that the ice had collapsed under it. The sound of gunshots was coming from the cracks that snaked away from the center like spider veins. None of them needed to be told what to do.

Going back the way they had come was no longer a question as they raced along the river into the middle of International Falls. Behind them, the ice let out shrieking protests louder than their engines, and all they could do was try to outrun a fate worse than death. They glanced backward, but all they could see behind them were great sheets of ice pointing upward as the weight of bodies and railroad cars stood them on end.

When they passed below the next bridge where traffic had been allowed to cross between the two countries, they knew they had to get off the river soon. Garrett saw a hard-packed slope along the shoreline on his left and hoped it would support their snowmobiles if they kept up their speed. He didn't know what had happened to create the slope, but he could only pray it was solid. If they stayed on the river, they would die when the ice broke around them, so he took his only option.

All four vehicles went up the slope, and as soon as Garrett reached dry land, he swerved around to see if the others were still with him. He was relieved to see the blue, yellow, and striped vehicles come over the crest of the bank one at a time. He coasted back to the edge and watched as the ice split down the middle of the river.

"So much for going to Walmart," said Anne. "It's on the other side of the river."

The pitch of her voice was much higher than normal, and it gave away how frightened she was. The rest of them wouldn't have hidden it any better than she did.

Susan added, "They're probably picked clean anyway. That's where the most people died on the first day because everyone needed batteries and camping gear."

"The food section would've been stripped of canned goods," said Jon, "and don't forget the toilet paper."

They had said the same things many times before, but it was nervous chatter this time. This time, it wasn't really about Walmart at all.

Garrett dug around in his backpack and pulled out a map. He spread it out across the front of his snowmobile. The others all cut off their engines and gathered around him to see what he was trying to find. They all knew the area well enough to know he wasn't lost, but the days were still too short for them to spend a lot of time making new plans. It would be good to know exactly where they were and where they could find shelter for the night if they had no other choice.

"We're here," said Garrett, "and I know the last place any of us would want to spend the night is an airport, but we know we can get the snowmobiles under protective cover and maybe even find some useful gear."

After escaping death on the ice, the four friends would be happy with anything that made them feel safe for the night, but they had survived inside the Columbus airport for years and often said they never wanted even to see another airport again. After they had settled in at their lodge, they had never found a reason to visit the local airport, even though it was only a short drive from the lake.

Garrett gestured toward the road and said, "That's the fastest way to get there, and unless we run into more problems, it shouldn't take more than fifteen or twenty minutes."

"I really had my heart set on rummaging through Walmart," said Anne as they returned to their vehicles. They knew she was still trying to ease her nerves after watching the ice collapse in the river when she added, "Do you think they had any air fryers left?"

They were forced to detour several times, and it took almost two hours to reach the airport. They had learned that snow drifts were traps, and there were no longer straight paths between one location and another. Some of the drifts towered above the streets and threatened to collapse on them if they were disturbed. Garrett was careful to let the three riders behind him know when they should stay on either side of the road.

The small drifts usually covered rusted cars and trucks that had been abandoned during the early days of the apocalypse. Sometimes, there were frozen bodies inside the tangled metal, but the prospect of being cut by metal covered with rust was almost as frightening. Susan had discovered medical supplies in the trunk of a car a few years earlier, and the kit contained tetanus shots. They had inoculated themselves against the deadly infection, but they didn't see the need to test their luck, and they carefully avoided the low snowdrifts.

The airport finally came into view, but Garrett almost preferred the streets with their snowdrifts. The wide open area directly in front of the airport terminal was undoubtedly the runway, and the flatness was deceiving. It was dotted with small hills that were likely to be airplanes, but the lack of trees around the runways had allowed the wind to sweep the snow across the hills and fill in the paths between them. He surveyed the hills with his binoculars, hoping to identify a safe route to the terminal.

Jon, Susan, and Anne got off their snowmobiles and walked over to stand beside Garrett. The airport was like a toy replica compared to the Columbus airport, but the miniature facility still made them feel like they had gone full circle.

"The facilities in the concessions section of the Columbus airport were bigger than this whole airport," said Jon. "We had it made compared to the people who were trapped here."

Susan leaned against him and said in a shaky voice, "You know, I don't even remember where we were scheduled to go on that first day, but I remember every detail of Columbus. Every day was a struggle to survive, but the worst one was the first day. Remember all the people on the runway and the faces against the windows of the planes?"

"We have to go around," said Anne. "You know the gaps between those hills were full of people."

Garrett shook his head from side to side.

"The operative word is 'were.' When this place thawed during the first summer, they got up and walked away. If anyone survived inside the airport until then, that's where all of the dead people from the runway went. Follow me, and stay in my tracks."

Garrett's snowmobile glided forward at a slow speed. The other three fell in behind him at a closer distance. He changed directions several times, his keen eyes spotting hidden dangers before most people would. One area had filled in with snow so well that it appeared to be flat, but he didn't like how deeply the skis under his vehicle cut into the surface. Once he managed to navigate around the hazard, he saw that it had been a luggage vehicle that had been abandoned. He would never know whether it was luggage from an incoming or outgoing plane, but it was still fully loaded, which could mean useful supplies. He held up a hand to indicate they were stopping.

"Let's take a break, folks. Just think of it as a rolling Walmart."

"Now, I know why you suggested the airport," said Jon, "and I guess we're going to be spending some time in the luggage area inside. You expect to find anything good?"

Garrett was already clearing away the snow that covered the luggage, and he pulled at the strap of a large piece of baggage that appeared to be made of waterproof material.

"If this was outgoing luggage and it was stuff that belonged to people trying to escape the infection, they wouldn't have left their guns at home, and this is gun country. I'll bet the TSA people who were checking bags finally gave up and relaxed the rules. I mean, people were frantic."

It wasn't the first time Garrett had been right about a hunch, but he wasn't just looking for guns to resupply their arsenal. He was searching for anything survivors might have packed. While some of the suitcases would be stuffed with family photo albums, some would hold items that allowed the people to stay alive long enough to take more pictures.

The waterproof bag had either been packed by a video gamer or a survivalist because it was stuffed with packages of beef jerky. It wasn't as fresh as one of Anne's sandwiches, but none of the bags had expanded like something inside had gone bad, so he decided to ignore the expiration dates.

"Hopefully," he thought, "I'll find something more worthwhile in another piece of luggage, and there's plenty more of it to go through."

5

South Carolina

Myrtle Beach Airport - March 2023

Returning to Myrtle Beach wasn't a trip down Memory Lane that Tom wanted to take, but it made more sense to meet with the AC-130 at that airport than the one in Charleston. The airport was within walking distance of the beach, and the runway was so close to the pier where they planned to come ashore that they would be able to see the plane waiting for them.

When the Chief gave everyone the plan details, he explained that the AC-130 would already have the rest of the group aboard. The Chief, Iris, Kathy, Tom, Cassandra, and Sim would travel by boat to a pier near South Ocean Boulevard and then walk to the airport. One of the soldiers permanently stationed at Mud Island would accompany them and then return their boat to the shelter.

The pier was right where the maps said it would be, but it had been hit by a large yacht. It and the yacht were still locked together, and both had burned into a charred mess.

"We can beach the boat, but watch out for crabs in the shallow water," said the Chief.

"You're kidding me, right?" said Cassandra.

The Chief thought she meant they would have to beach and said,

"We don't have a lot of choices, but the boat can take it."

"What makes you think I was talking about the boat? I can't believe you think you need to tell us to watch out for crabs."

The Chief hid his amusement because it was funny but not so funny at the same time. Even before the infection, blue crabs were common along the East Coast. Now, they were the dominant species and weren't picky eaters.

He let the boat coast straight toward the beach and listened for the sound of the hull scraping along the sand.

"Single file over the bow, everyone. Hit the sand running, and don't stop. When the crabs hear us, they'll move our way fast."

The front end of the boat rose upward as the sound of scraping increased. Cassandra pushed Sim hard enough from the bow that he didn't even get his feet wet when he landed. She landed so close behind him that she practically knocked him over, but she hooked one arm around him and helped him keep his balance. He would have objected, but he knew why she did it, and he didn't want to experience what she had when she fell off the trawler's bow near Beaufort. The crabs had attacked mercilessly, and she still had the scars to prove it.

They didn't turn around to see what was happening behind them, but they could tell everyone was doing the same thing they had. If they stopped, they would keep the others from reaching the safety of the sand dunes.

The Chief was the last one to leave the boat, and he was becoming worried about the crabs. He wasn't as worried for himself as he was for the soldier who had taken the steering wheel from him. If he didn't get the boat back into deep water and power up the engine soon, the crabs would overwhelm him.

There were small 'v' shaped wakes in the water where the crabs were already moving their way, and the only way to keep them from climbing into a small boat was to keep moving.

After landing on the sand, the Chief turned and put both hands on the bow. He charged forward and gave the boat the strongest push that he could before letting go. He had become shin-deep in the water, and he knew he wasn't going to outrun the crabs that had gotten between him and the beach.

The soldier in the boat pressed the ignition switch, and the engine roared to life. There was only a brief pause before the bow lifted upward, and he cut the wheel hard to port. The boat picked up speed and turned at the same time. He didn't know it, but the Mud Island survivors saw that his maneuver scraped several large crabs from the left side of the boat. Crabs were tenacious about not letting go of their prey, and some of them sacrificed their pincers as the boat made another sharp turn to starboard.

The Chief was too busy to watch what was happening on the boat, but he was grateful for his combat boots. He managed to dodge the grasping pincers of at least a dozen of the hungry predators, but there were two of them clinging to his right foot. He had to ignore them, or the others would catch him before he got away.

"Hold still," yelled Cassandra.

The Chief didn't realize he had gotten far enough away from the spider-like creatures, and he was still moving his feet too much for anyone to help him. For a wild moment, he thought Cassandra was going to shoot at the crabs hanging onto his leg because she had her rifle pointed in his direction.

"No...wait."

Cassandra pulled the trigger, and a large crab ten yards behind the Chief exploded. At the same moment, Kathy swung her machete in a downward arc and neatly severed the legs from the crabs on his boot.

The Chief gave Cassandra a withering stare.

"Sorry," she said. "You kept blocking my shot."

"One of these days," said the Chief, "I'm taking you to the beach to let you take out your frustrations on those things. You can shoot them to your heart's content."

"I've already done that. It didn't help," said Cassandra.

The Chief moved to the front of the column without a word to the others. They hid their grins but knew it wouldn't be the best time to make a comment. With the sun at their backs, they needed to focus on the ground in front of them.

There had been a time when the beach would have been crowded with people, even in March. People would be beachcombing for interesting shells and for the occasional trinket lost by someone else. There would be people sitting on blankets and old men with metal detectors and headphones making sweeping gestures over the sand.

There had also been a time when the beaches were crowded with the infected dead. Escaping people were backed up to the ocean's edge with nowhere to go, and when they had to swim for their lives, they were dragged away by the strong currents that often ran parallel to the shore. Some of them survived, but the vast majority didn't and were deposited on beaches further south.

When the hordes of infected that died on shore reached the water, those in front were pushed into the surf by the weight of the bodies behind them. They floated or sank, but all of them were at the mercy of the food chain.

Now, the beach was empty except for the crabs that patrolled the entire area between the water and streets that ran parallel to the coast. The streets were mostly covered by drifting sand, and the column of survivors scanned smooth surfaces for footprints or signs that the crabs were foraging further inland. The footprints were almost always made by the shuffling feet of the infected dead, so they resembled furrows dug in a cornfield.

The Chief stepped sideways several times to deliver blows to attacking crabs with a machete. Kathy had moved to the second position, and when the Chief was forced to step aside, she automatically watched the path directly in front of him. She warned him several times of the quiet creatures moving to intercept him.

At the rear of the column, Tom reminded everyone that it was important to keep moving. Crabs didn't care what they ate, so they were swarming on the ones that were injured by the Chief's machete, but some were close enough to make him walk backward.

They eventually crossed a wide area between two hotels, and their defensive posture changed. They walked in three pairs with their eyes moving over the debris left over from years of decay. Overgrowth that covered abandoned vehicles also provided hiding places for the infected dead, but even worse, there were still people like the one that had shot at the Chief and Iris. Fortunately, the bright sunlight made it easy to see what was behind the obstacles ahead.

"There's the airport," said the Chief, "and our friends are right on time."

The AC-130 didn't need as much runway as most planes its size, but even airports as small as the one at Myrtle Beach had become junkyards at the beginning of the apocalypse. Most of the junk had been small planes and airport service vehicles, but desperate people had driven their cars onto the runways, where they either collided with each other or were abandoned. Landing the plane was difficult, but Chris Hampton was in the pilot seat and had the experience to find enough room to get the plane on the ground. From a distance, they could see the cloud of dust behind the plane as it touched down.

The Chief said, "Hampton must have used the runway and some flat ground next to it. That dust cloud means he landed on dirt. Let's move."

The group broke into a trot but never ignored the next pile of debris or blind spot. Several times, they changed directions because there appeared to be remains of bodies, but none of the corpses were moving. Decayed bodies were always a sign that the battle for survival had continued in the area, but there was no way to tell if it had been won or lost.

Fifteen minutes later, they were close enough to the AC-130 to tell that Hampton had opened the side door for them. He would wait for them to be closer before dropping the steps, and he was watching for signs that other survivors had seen him land. For the same reason, the Chief had told everyone to sheath their machetes and have their automatic weapons ready. They still carried their M4 rifles because they had such a large supply of ammunition.

They crossed the last stretch of grass as Hampton lowered the steps, and as usual, the Chief stepped to one side to provide cover for the others. Once they were inside, he followed. He stowed the steps and closed the door, and Hampton began the take off as the Chief climbed into the cockpit. He gave Hampton and Jim Miller a thumbs-up to let them know everyone was aboard and no time was wasted getting into the air.

Over the roar of the engines, the Chief shouted, "You must've seen something coming when you landed."

Jim Miller pointed out the window on the right, and the Chief leaned in for a better view. Hampton tilted the wing slightly, and the Chief saw that a horde had formed on the main highway from the town of Conway toward Myrtle Beach. Even after seven years, they still drew the attention of other infected dead with their incessant groaning and growling. It bonded them together into mindless groups that didn't stop moving until an obstacle blocked their path.

The Chief put on a headset so he could talk without needing to shout.

"Thanks for the smooth pick-up, fellas. It looks like twenty-four hours from now could have been too late."

Tom squeezed through the door of the flight deck and gave the Chief a nudge.

"Did you see that horde? I was watching through a side window, and it's the same down there as it was the night that Molly and I escaped from Myrtle Beach. How can there be so many of them seven years later?"

"We're flying northwest," said Hampton, "and a steady stream of the infected is coming from that direction. They must be people who tried to survive in the Appalachian Mountains."

"Lots of people had the same idea," said the Chief. "They thought higher ground would be safer, but they didn't consider the long-term goals like food and shelter. They probably built modest shelters, but a safe building wasn't much good without food to last the winter...one winter, maybe, but not six or seven."

Colleen was the next person to work her way through the door of the flight deck. She good-naturedly elbowed Tom and the Chief for more space, and they did their best to move for her. They were big men, and they could only give her so much.

"Everyone in the back wants to know our ETA," she said.

Hampton keyed his microphone to broadcast throughout the plane.

"This is your captain speaking. We'll be heading roughly northwest for most of the flight. Our cruising speed will be an average of three hundred miles per hour, and our altitude will be just under ten thousand feet to avoid the possibility that someone still has anti-aircraft weapons. We expect to arrive in International Falls, Minnesota, around 1:00 PM Central Time, so you have plenty of time to relax and watch the in-flight movie. Once again, thank you for choosing Mud Island Airlines."

It was Shannon's first mission since she had left the Wyoming shelter to be with Jim Miller, and she was excited. She was also enjoying the light-hearted attitude of her fellow survivors. It was likely to be a dangerous trip, but she wouldn't have known it judging by the joking the rest of the group did. She was seated against the right side wall of the plane to get a good view through one of the port side gun portals, and she felt free after spending so many years in isolation.

Sim took over the front seat from Captain Miller because he was a former flight navigator and also because the Chief wanted to spend some time discussing their trip with the rest of the group. He told everyone that it would be best to keep Jim Miller's military background a secret and that everyone should call him Jim.

He also told them the airport at International Falls was smaller than Myrtle Beach, and because of the harsh climate, he expected to find less of a threat from the infected dead. He had instructed Hampton to make a pass over Last Island and then fly to the airport. If Sim's old friends saw the plane, they wouldn't know they were friendly unless they had managed to locate a radio and get it operational. The Chief felt like a former flight crew would have done that, but on the off-chance they didn't have a way to communicate with them, Kathy had prepared a package they could drop with a message from Sim.

After everyone had been briefed, they settled in for the trip. It would only take about four more hours, so they really did have time to relax. There wasn't an in-flight movie, but there was a deck of cards, books, and gun portals. The view from the portals was spectacular and enjoyable, but they would also take turns using binoculars to locate signs of survivors. If they saw someone alive, they would mark the location on the map and drop a backpack stuffed with survival gear. A note was included in the backpack that gave the location of the nearest shelter and how to make contact with them.

For obvious reasons, the instructions for contacting the shelters were vague. There had been rogue elements like the one at Fort Knox that would take advantage of their generosity, so new arrivals would be screened when they showed up on the doorstep of any of the shelters. Now that Fort Sumter was fully operational again, there was room for anyone with good intentions.

Iris was stretched out on several blankets toward the back of the plane, and the Chief decided it was a good chance to get some quality time with his wife.

"Mrs. Barnes, I remember finding you in a similar place on the flight to Nova Scotia, but you had a serious expression painted on your pretty face. What's with the big smile this time?"

"I'm smiling because we've come a long way. Remember why I was frowning the last time?"

"I do. It was something about doing more to help other people survive. Can I take it from your smile that you feel like things have gotten better?"

"You can. We still have a lot of work to do, but we've located so many shelters and supplies. Now, we only need to keep finding people."

"That's why we're going to Alaska. I'm not sure about the decision made by Sim's old friends, but I think the inhospitable climate of Alaska makes it a logical choice for the US military to set up shop."

"Do you really think they'll let us go about our own business after we find them?"

The Chief saw his wife's upbeat smile fade a bit, and he knew that would be one of their biggest risks on this mission. He had tried to imagine what he would do if he were the man in charge of the military, and a group of survivors showed up with all of the gear they carried. He had to admit, there was a very real chance that they would become conscripts in someone's militia.

"I wish I could answer that," he said. "I was tempted to tell everyone we should try to act like we aren't as functional as we really are, but anyone would see through that. No one left surviving the apocalypse survived on luck alone. I think our best bet is to find them first, and then we can tell them as much or as little as they need to know."

"One thing hasn't changed about you," said Iris, "and I really like it."

The Chief liked the smile on her face as she spoke, so he gave her his best grin back. That grin had charmed everyone he had ever met if they had a good heart.

"What hasn't changed about me?"

Iris laid the palm of her hand on the side of his face and studied that grin. She also saw in his eyes that he was enjoying her mood.

"Well, despite the times when you had to take matters into your own hands and dish out justice, you haven't become jaded. You still have faith in the possibility that we'll meet good people. You trusted Sparks, and he abandoned us. Somehow, you've managed to keep your trust available to strangers. How do you do it?"

He didn't have to think about it very long because it was something he never let himself forget.

"Yes, we've met our fair share of bad actors, and we'll meet more of them, but we've also met so many people with good intentions and good plans. Where would we be if not for Andi coming to our rescue with her ocean-going tugboat? Where would we be without the help of the British Royal Navy? I can't stop believing that our military did something big like England did. All we need to do is find them."

Iris saw in her husband's face all she needed to see to know that she would follow him to the end of the Earth for what he believed in. If he thought there was something big out there that was worth finding, then she had to believe it too.

"What are you two whispering about back here?" asked Kathy. "Do you want me to string some curtains across this area?"

"Do you have any?" asked the Chief as he gave Iris a sideways glance and winked.

Iris gave him a playful slap on his arm, and he feigned surprise.

"Pull up a seat," said Iris. "We were just talking about things. You know, where we've been and where we're going to."

"Sounds like that John Denver song, *Poems, Prayers, and Promises.*"

"That's about right," said Iris. She tilted her head to one side and tried to remember the lyrics. "That song was really about the best in all of us, and it makes me miss those days when we had the leisure to search for it in everyone."

Kathy chuckled and said, "You're in a mellow mood. What did he do to you?"

Before Iris could answer, Jim Miller joined their little group with some news. At the same time, they felt the aircraft tilt to the left.

"Someone shot a signal flare from the side of a mountain. We're getting ready for a drop."

"We're still over the Blue Ridge Mountains?" asked the Chief.

Jim nodded and said, "We've been over this area before, so it must not be a permanent settlement. Could be that they're survivors working their way south toward one of our settlements."

Just as rumors of a military base in Alaska had reached the Mud Island survivors through people from Texas, rumors had spread about them to the places they had yet to establish footholds. Survivors were constantly drifting out of hiding in search of a safe place to live. Whoever the people were who shot the signal flare, they didn't know how close they were to so many shelters. If they could stay alive for a few more days of travel, they would be close to permanent survival.

Even though their mission was to locate survivors and attempt to balance life against death, one of their first rules was to maintain vigilance. The flare was likely a signal from someone who spotted their plane and had desperately welcomed the opportunity to make contact with people who could save them. Whoever was on the ground, the plane represented their last best hope of survival, but that wouldn't be an assumption taken for granted in the plane.

The protocol for new contact was to circle the area once or twice to visually assess the risk of dropping to a lower altitude. If they saw nothing that threatened their safety, they would descend until they found the survivors, and then they changed their assessment to include the likelihood that the survivors were in imminent danger. On several contacts, they saw that the people were surrounded by hordes of infected dead, and they had used the lethal power of the AC-130 to eliminate the threats. They had little doubt that the rumors spread the farthest were about the silver plane that came out of nowhere to save people.

The first pass around the area gave them very little information because the mountains were under a white blanket of snow, but if there had been a horde moving anywhere nearby, that white blanket would have been disturbed. They descended lower and saw deer moving through an open area, and that was a good sign. Hampton put the plane into an attack spiral to give the Chief and everyone else a good view of the target area, and he knew if anyone took a shot at the plane, it would be the last shot they fired.

The Chief told Hampton over his headset that they had a visual on about a dozen people who were waving frantically at them from a ridge on the side of a mountain. He said they were out in the open, and it was safe to make a drop. He instructed Hampton to change his flight path and fly directly at the ridge. If they dropped too soon, the package would fall to the base of the mountain below the people.

Iris was watching with Kathy through one of the gun portals as they dropped the package. She had helped to prepare the backpacks, and she knew that one of the most important items included was the map that showed the locations of shelters. She knew that this group of survivors would be excited to see how many choices they had. Along with the maps were matches, water purification straws, antibiotics, a semiautomatic handgun with a box of ammunition, a suture kit, and a portable fishing kit. There was a package of foil rescue blankets that held in heat better than most cloth blankets, a box of chem-light sticks, and several flares that released huge clouds of colored smoke. Last but not least, there was a handheld radio with instructions describing when to use it and what to say. If the instructions weren't followed, the shelters wouldn't respond.

"This is the part I enjoy the most," she shouted to Kathy over the sound of the engines. "Some of the people we find haven't had a way to make a fire in months. This will be like Christmas to them."

After the drop, Hampton circled back around to see how well they had delivered the package, and they saw the survivors celebrating around it. With a little luck, they would be warm and celebrating inside one of the shelters within the next day.

The supply drop only took a few minutes from start to finish, but it left all of the people on the plane with a good feeling about the mission. They were off to a good start whenever they had the chance to spread goodwill, but when it included saving lives, it made them feel like it was already a success.

Kathy left the back of the plane to visit Hampton on the flight deck.

She wanted to compare notes with Sim and Hampton.

"Gentlemen," she said. "Would you guys mind giving me some information for the record?"

They had expected her visit, and Sim handed her a sheet of paper that detailed the exact position where the survivors were located at the time of the drop. She also wanted to compare observations with them about the number of people they had seen. Everyone who had a clear view of the party on the mountain reported seeing at least a dozen adults, and there appeared to be surprisingly more children than usual. Colleen had spotted as many as ten children using her binoculars. That made them a higher priority to rescue.

At the beginning of the apocalypse, the loss of children had been due to direct attacks by the infected dead. As the years passed and survivors found new ways to protect their children, the losses were caused by a lack of medical care. Simple injuries led to infections without antibiotics to help their immune systems fight off the worst symptoms. Common childhood illnesses prevented by vaccines took the world back to a darker time when diseases that had been eradicated made their comeback.

It was important to know the number of children in the group because they would get medical care as soon as they got to a shelter, but the number of children in this particular group meant the shelters would send out search parties to intercept them.

Kathy spent the next half hour making radio contact with the shelters in Huntsville, Guntersville, and Charlotte. The goal was to find the survivors they had just seen and to get them to safety before they encountered the infected dead. They would be relieved when they got confirmation that the people had been brought in.

The Chief took over in the pilot seat to give Hampton a break. He verified their position with Sim and learned he had estimated their progress correctly.

"We're a little less than halfway to International Falls," said Sim.

"Are you excited about seeing your old friends again?"

Sim shrugged his shoulders, and the Chief was surprised by the gesture. He had expected Sim to be anticipating the reunion more than the rest of them.

"What's up?" asked the Chief.

Sim acted like there was something interesting outside the window, but the Chief saw him make a quick backhand swipe across one cheek. It wasn't that Sim was afraid to show his emotions in front of the

Chief. It was his fear that they would get bad news. A million things could have happened to his friends by now, but they all boiled down to one of two outcomes. They were either dead or alive, and Sim had seen enough death to know his friends should have gone with him when they had the chance.

"I didn't have much time to get to know your friends," said the Chief, "but Garrett Carson seems like someone who doesn't have to ask himself at the end of the day if he had done everything he could to keep everyone alive."

For a second time, Sim didn't react the way the Chief expected. Instead of accepting the reassurance that his friends were fine, Sim locked his eyes on the Chief.

"There were more of us before you arrived. Remember? Garrett did everything he could, but sometimes people die. Even you have to admit, luck has kept this group alive plenty of times."

There was one thing about the Chief that all of his friends knew. He had a positive outlook that left no room for self-pity or looking backward to things that might have been. He could empathize with Sim about the losses his group had shared, but he could rejoice in the fact that five of them had survived. He also wasn't going to count the rest of the group as dead until he knew they were.

"This is more about you than them, isn't it."

Sim was a bit surprised by the question, and it seemed to him that the Chief was calling him out for something. He wasn't sure if he was supposed to be angry or at least insulted.

"What's that mean?" he asked with a sharp edge to his tone of voice.

"You left them twice," said the Chief. "You never got over the guilt you felt for leaving them the first time, then you left them again. You feel like you're responsible if they didn't make it. Are you saying they would have survived better with you along for the ride?"

Sim felt like someone had just let the air out of the personal balloon that carried around his guilt. He could see it mentally, and it was crashing to the ground.

When Sim had left the airport in Columbus, Ohio, he had every intention of making his way south to a warmer climate. He had left more for himself than anyone else, and he returned mostly for the same reason, but he had also gone back to them because he was afraid. He had seen for himself what was still out there in the world, and he didn't feel like he could survive alone. When he left them again, he left with his new friends because they were a more formidable force, and he knew he would have a better chance of surviving. He told himself he had left for Cassandra, but he also felt that he had left his friends behind to die.

The Chief didn't wait for him to answer. Instead, he reached over and rested his big hand on the smaller man's shoulder. There was plenty of reassurance under that grip.

"We'll find them," said the Chief. "We'll find them, and this time they'll be leaving with us."

6

Yelizovo

Kamchatka Peninsula - The Beginning of the Infection

Oleg Volkov had planned for this day. He and his wife, Galina, had talked about it only between themselves and one other person. They brought her younger brother into the conversation because he had a boat that could make the trip. It was a rusty piece of junk that Oleg didn't completely trust, but Pavel Ivanov swore his *Svetlana* would last longer than the relationship with the woman he had named the boat after. That might not be the best endorsement, but he also swore that his boat could make the crossing from the Kamchatka Peninsula to Alaska. It had been a fishing boat and sometimes a trawler with a crew of eight, but it wouldn't need a crew to cross the ocean near the Aleutian Islands.

According to Pavel, sailors in the Russian Navy stationed in Petropavlovsk joked about how easy it would be to disappear to Alaska. They said it was only a matter of reaching Attu Station, where the Americans still had an Air Force monitoring base. Getting captured was as simple as holding their hands in the air and asking for asylum. The rumor was the Americans would treat them very well, and they would live out their lives in their own homes on their own land.

At thirty-two, Oleg was only a year older than Galina and seven years older than Pavel. His tall, muscular frame made Galina look even smaller than her diminutive five feet made her seem. He had served in the Army for a few years, and although he never talked about what it had been like, Galina knew it had changed him, and she didn't want to see it do the same thing to Pavel. Their parents had passed away only a year ago, and she was all he had. Oleg was strong and a good provider even though he still limped from a wound he wouldn't talk about. When he came to her with the idea of escaping to Alaska, she didn't hesitate for a moment to agree.

Oleg and Galina delivered fresh produce and other goods from Yelizovo to Petropavlovsk for the Navy, but on each trip to the coast, they always made a detour with extra canned foods and survival gear. The hold of the *Svetlana* was nearly full, and the plan was to make one last trip tomorrow morning. Then they would pretend their truck broke down as they were leaving Petropavlovsk to return home. They would appear to be forced to remain in the port until the next morning, but they hoped to escape in the *Svetlana* under the cover of darkness. The bribe for the harbor master had already been paid, and the patrols would recognize the *Svetlana* by the green lantern on the bow.

That had been the plan, but they had no way of knowing the world was about to turn upside down. They were in their modest apartment in Yelizovo when the news reports turned grim. The city of forty-thousand people was too small to keep the news from reaching every citizen within the first hour, but it was also too big to deal with the panic that paralyzed the helpless population.

Pavel arrived within thirty minutes of the first reports. Oleg and Galina Volkov were glued to the small screen of their TV as if they were in shock and were incapable of breaking free.

According to the broadcasts, big cities fell first because there were too many people who needed help, and there was no way to tell who could be saved. Perfectly normal in appearance, other than their bandages, the infected worked side by side with the uninfected, totally unaware that they had lost the war before a single battle had been fought.

Hospitals were places to be avoided, but the need for medical care drove the injured to go to them anyway. People who survived long enough to reach hospitals never left them alive. A steady stream of off-duty doctors and nurses flocked toward the chaos with the common thought that they could help, only to find that they were the ones who needed to be saved. Salvation would never arrive.

Police departments sent their officers to help the medical personnel, first responders, firefighters, and Emergency Medical Technicians who were either at the hospitals or attempting to reach them. It was almost as if hospitals were the vacuums of death, and there was a constant suction that pulled the rescuers toward them.

After the hospitals became breeding grounds for the infected dead, the direction of the chaotic flow was reversed, and death spread outward. Those who were trying to reach hospitals were forced to run from them, but the more populated the city, the harder it was to reverse the tide that pushed the living forward. The crowds of infected dead collided with the living, and the living were folded into the hordes of the dead.

It was only different in small towns because word spread quickly that it was safer to stay home, but as the infection spread outward from the cities, towns were swamped by the tidal waves of people escaping urban areas. Rural communities rallied to confront 'city folks' and to turn them away, but eventually, they were overrun.

Some parts of the world lasted a bit longer than others. The remote Russian peninsula of Kamchatka was enduring a driving rain that swept in from the west over the Sea of Okhotsk. It was bitterly cold, but the exodus from the Russian mainland, Sapporo, Japan, and the Russian border with North Korea had already begun. Despite the frigid elements, thousands of refugees boarded boats of all sizes in hopes of reaching Yelizovo on the east coast of the peninsula. It was rumored that the Russian military was organizing a relief effort to stop the spread of the infection, and as refugees converged, the rumor took on a life of its own. It grew into a promise of safety, but in reality, it was dying as fast as any other city that had an airport.

The rumor began as Russian military units evacuated bases on the mainland, and the population of Yelizovo exploded from thirty-six thousand to fifty thousand on the first day of the infection. The tidal wave of infection that swamped every major city in the world was racing ahead of the mass exodus of refugees and was waiting for them as they arrived at their safe haven.

The infected dead arrived in Yelizovo, Kamchatka, Russia, on the passenger planes that carried hundreds of living victims who had sustained injuries inflicted by fellow passengers. They flooded out of the planes, and Yelizovo became another center of death.

The Russian military units didn't try to stop the hordes of infected dead that fed on the steady stream of refugees. Instead, they abandoned their posts and spread out on the Kamchatka Peninsula. With its wild terrain and active volcanoes, it was an inhospitable corner of the world where the infection wouldn't find them.

Pavel Ivanov was breathless as he burst into his sister's small apartment. It was totally dark, with the exception of the small area where the little TV set cast its light. Oleg and Galina sat close to each other in that spot, and Pavel was just a dark shape as he emerged through the door. Their eyes were so accustomed to the brightness of the broadcast that he could have been one of those infected people, and if Oleg had been holding his old army rifle, he would have shot Pavel before he could speak.

"We must go," shouted Pavel. "Tonight...we must go now, not tomorrow morning. The Navy ships in Petropavlovsk are calling for all crews to return for duty, and they are going out to sea to get away from this thing...this infection. They are even making men leave their families as conscripted crew members, so we must get to the *Svetlana* before the sun is up to avoid being seen."

Oleg had been frightened by the sudden arrival of his brother-in-law, and he was on his feet shouting back at him even as Pavel was delivering the news.

"I could have shot you. What were you thinking coming in here like that?"

He stopped when Pavel got to the part about the Russian Navy forcing men to join. Despite his limp, he knew they would value him more over civilians who had never served. If someone recognized him at Petropavlovsk, they would make him a noncommissioned officer, and he would be shot if he refused.

"Are you packed?" interrupted Pavel.

"Everything is in the truck," said Galina. "We just need to say goodbye to our neighbor, Sofiya. Her daughter is away, and she will be afraid."

Oleg and Pavel both reacted at the same time. Oleg grabbed his wife's arm as she got up to go to the door, and Pavel stepped in front of her.

"We tell no one we are leaving," said Pavel. "You said so yourself. No one can know, especially now. If you tell her, she will want to come along, but first, she will call her daughter and want to pack. We must leave immediately."

Galina turned to her husband for support, but in the glow of the TV set, she could see him nodding. He gently applied pressure to her arm and guided her toward Pavel and the open door. Pavel handed her coat to her as Oleg pulled his on over his broad shoulders. He almost followed them out the door before he remembered the rifle leaning against the wall behind the sofa. As he retrieved it, he turned the volume up on the TV. It was best that people thought they were home.

The street outside their apartment building was usually quiet after nightfall, but there were more people down the street. There was yelling and cursing, and in the short time it took for the three of them to climb into the truck, there were screams unlike any they had ever heard. Even to Oleg's ears, the screams were more anguished than those he had heard on the battlefield. For some reason, they sounded like the screams that came from prisoners who were tortured.

"It cannot be," he thought as he started the engine and pulled away from the curb. "Not here."

It took thirty minutes to reach the outskirts of Yelizovo. They were ahead of the exodus that would follow at dawn, but they found themselves in a line of vehicles that were being funneled through a checkpoint. Armed guards stopped each vehicle ahead of them, questioned the drivers, and either let them pass or directed them to a side road. The vehicles on the side road were met by a large crowd that was kept behind a barrier by more guards.

"What are they doing?" asked Galina.

Pavel figured it out and said, "If they have room in their cars, they are being made to take passengers. How much room do we have in the back?"

"If we take passengers, they may find out about the boat," said Oleg.

Pavel nodded, "But if we refuse to take passengers, the guards will take the truck and give it to someone else. How much room do we have?" he insisted.

Just as a guard arrived at the window and pointed at the side road where they knew they would be told to go, Oleg grumbled that he thought there was room for ten people with the supplies.

Pavel leaned over him and said, "We have room for twenty if they do not mind standing, Comrade."

The guard enthusiastically directed Oleg to follow him as he walked past the waiting cars on the side road. They were led to the front of the line, and twenty people were hustled gratefully to the back of the truck and loaded inside.

"Why did you do that?" demanded Oleg. "I should put you out here and let them have room for one more in the front with me and your sister."

Pavel was unfazed and said, "Did you want the guards to decide how much room we have and take a closer look at the supplies? Those people may be sitting on your boxes, but if the guards had seen what you have back there, they would have taken everything for themselves."

"Go," said Galina. "The guards are saying go."

Oleg put the truck in gear and crept forward through the checkpoint, leaving behind a crowd that had grown since their arrival. When they were rolling on the open highway, he decided to tell Pavel that he had been right, but when they got to Petropavlovsk, he should make them unload just as quickly. He didn't want any of them to even see the *Svetlana.*

It was still dark when they reached the port at Petropavlovsk, and they thought they had escaped the terror that descended on Yelizovo only hours later, but as Oleg pulled to the side of the road and shut off the engine, they heard the commotion in the back of the truck. They only had a brief moment when they felt like they would make it to their boat when the tailgate of the truck fell open with a loud bang.

Oleg thought it was a gunshot, so he took his rifle with him to investigate. It was a good thing he did. If he had gone to the back of the truck without it, he wouldn't have been able to defend himself. He didn't know why there were people coming toward him with outstretched arms. He had time to wonder about the growling sound they made, but there was no mistaking the bloodstains on their clothing. Oleg had seen wounded soldiers and had been one himself, but in his assessment, the people coming from the back of his truck seemed more dead than alive. He took aim and fired.

The first time he pulled the trigger of his AK-47, the bullets tore through the chests of the nearest people in the crowd. Those people were thrown backward into the second row, and everyone fell over in a pile. Pavel and Galina stood behind him and watched in stunned silence as the people got up again…all of them.

Oleg caught on faster than some people would have because he had been in combat. He took aim again, but this time it was at their foreheads. One by one, he eliminated them all. When it was over, the trio stood without speaking and stared at what he had done.

"Tell me I had to do that," said Oleg. "There was something wrong with them, and if I had let them, they would have killed us."

Galina had been on the verge of losing her grip back in their apartment in Yelizovo. Some of the scenes where the infection had spread beyond control showed people doing unspeakable things to each other. They were like rabid dogs as they tore away the flesh of their victims using their teeth. Reporters and cameramen stood by doing their jobs in the name of getting the story out. Now, Galina had watched her husband execute close to two dozen people who had appeared normal when they boarded the truck. Now, she cried silently and was unable to answer his plea for absolution.

In the quiet darkness next to the truck, Pavel spoke up and told Oleg what he needed to hear. After the sound of the gun, it seemed like it was even quieter than normal, but they each had ringing in their ears. As the ringing subsided, they felt a million miles away from the tiny apartment and the infection that had caused them to leave ahead of schedule.

"They were infected. If you had not stopped them, your wife would be dead now."

Oleg saw it clearly in Pavel's choice of words. He saw his wife being held down and torn apart by the mob. It had been on TV, and he had seen it with his own eyes. In Moscow and St. Petersburg, there had been chaos and violence beyond what he had seen in combat, and they had been afraid that Yelizovo would be the same until Pavel had dragged them away. The bodies in front of him were all the proof he needed that the infection was everywhere.

"We have to go," said Pavel. It seemed to him that he was always pushing Oleg forward.

"What if this thing…this infection is happening in America too?" said Oleg. "The news said it was everywhere."

"The Americans would have a way of stopping it," said Pavel. He spoke directly to Oleg, but he gripped his sister's arm and pulled her back toward the cab of the truck. "Come, Galina. We should go to the boat while we can."

Galina moved as if she were in a trance, but she allowed herself to be taken back to the front seat. Pavel went around and climbed in next to her on the passenger side while Oleg closed the tailgate. They heard two more shots when he found two more of the infected still inside the truck. They had been too severely injured by their fellow passengers and were unable to walk.

When Oleg climbed behind the wheel, he kept his eyes straight ahead as he started the engine and drove away. He kept the headlights turned off so no one would see them on the stretch of deserted road. They only had to go another mile before they would reach the place where Pavel had left the boat.

The *Svetlana* was untouched and unnoticed in the cove where she was anchored, and Oleg was careful to let the truck roll to a stop without using his brakes. The red glare from the tail lights might have caused the end of their journey. Pavel had picked the spot well because the boat was practically docked against the bank, and trees hung low over it for cover. Even if there had been a full moon, the shadows from the trees would have hidden its shape.

In a low voice, Pavel whispered, "Talk as little as possible. Sound carries over the water, and we don't want to be discovered."

"What about the green light on the bow?" asked Oleg.

"That was for the harbor patrol not to shoot at us tomorrow night. Now they will shoot us and take our boat," said Pavel.

As if to confirm his answer, there was a burst of machine gun fire only a hundred or so yards south of their position. The hot bullets must have hit fuel lines or tanks on a boat because it burst into flames.

"That is what I am talking about," whispered Pavel. "We did not know the boat was there until it exploded. A guard will likely be shot for destroying it."

In the light cast across the harbor by the explosion, they saw what Pavel meant. Dozens of shadows from boats that were attempting to escape from shore appeared from the darkness, and more shots were fired at them. There were screams for help and orders barked through bullhorns by the harbor guards. They could hear them ordering all boats to come to the docks to receive refugees.

"It would be no different than our truck," said Oleg. "They will load the boats with the infected, and everyone will die."

"We are far enough from the fire. I do not think we will be seen," said Pavel. "We should move the last of the supplies from the truck, then when we leave, I will stay close to shore until we are farther away before crossing the harbor."

Pavel showed them that he was as good as he had bragged. Once they had unloaded the truck, he had taken his place at the helm of the boat while Oleg and Galina huddled together in the corner of the cabin behind him. He steered away from the dock and skillfully maneuvered the *Svetlana* along the shoreline. Sometimes it seemed he was too close, and they expected to hear the grinding of the hull against solid rock.

Pavel assured them that the water was deep enough, and the curve of the shoreline would prevent anyone from hearing the low rumble of their engines. Even if someone heard them, they wouldn't be able to locate the source of the sound.

"Now, we go to America," announced Pavel.

They traveled north of the fire in the harbor, and once it was no longer even a pinpoint of light, he turned the wheel hard to starboard, and the boat glided toward the open sea. The moonless night was ink black, and a slight chop met them as they left the relatively calm waters of the harbor. They at least had good luck not facing a storm coming down from the icy waters in the north.

"Should we put the green light on the bow?" asked Galina. She already had it in her hand and was reaching for the on switch with her other hand.

Pavel practically knocked it from her hands, stopping her from giving away their position by turning on the light.

"No," he shouted. "That was our signal before things changed. If we light it now, they will kill us all for the boat."

Pavel would have said more, but each of them heard the sound of another engine that was a much higher pitch than the low rumble of the *Svetlana.* It was a higher pitch because it was traveling at a faster speed. Pavel cut the engine off, and they slowed until they were only coasting. The fishing boat rocked from side to side in the gentle chop that hit their bow on the port side.

"Why did you stop the engines?" said Oleg.

"Stay quiet," snapped Pavel. He was becoming frustrated with his sister and his brother-in-law.

In a low voice, he said, "Do I have to explain everything to you? Sound carries out here, but if they have not heard us yet, they might not see us because they are moving so fast."

A white spotlight blazed across the water on their starboard side. It was only about fifty yards away, and they could see the way it was being played over the water in an arc, and that arc was being slowly expanded toward them. In the next five or six sweeps it would illuminate their boat, and there was nothing they could do. They braced themselves for the inevitable, and no one had to be told to stay quiet because they weren't even breathing.

Three sweeps later, the light stopped moving as it landed on another boat that was unluckier than the *Svetlana.* It was also sitting motionless in the harbor until the light hit it. Its engines roared to life as it tried to outrun the owner of the spotlight. They heard Russian commands barked over a bullhorn, and the high-pitched engine moved closer.

Pavel started their engines again, hoping that the noise coming from the other boats would drown out the churning propeller of the *Svetlana* as they made their escape. Instead of resuming the original course to the west, Pavel turned the steering wheel and once again went north. He had enough fuel for them to hug the coast for at least another hour, and it was possible that the Russian navy had expanded their grip even outside the harbor.

A series of bright flashes erupted along their starboard side as an invisible vessel on their right launched missiles at a target behind them. It was too late to warn each other not to watch, and they were all momentarily blinded by the explosions.

"Someone else is trying to leave the harbor," said Galina. Her fear was made more obvious by the shaking of her voice. It was easy for her to believe the next missile launch would be aimed at them.

A secondary explosion caused a burst of light that showed how accurate Galina was. There were hundreds of boats in the harbor, but it wasn't clear if they were coming or going because they were pointing in all directions. The ship that was burning was too damaged for them to tell where it was going, but a second volley of missiles hit a boat that was definitely entering the harbor. It was a ferry that appeared to be carrying hundreds of people.

"Where are they coming from?" asked Galina. "Why are they trying to go to Petropavlovsk?"

Oleg answered, "Refugees who will be surprised when they learn that they are going to a place that is far worse than the place they left."

Galina heard something in her husband's voice that frightened her, and she wondered if he was talking about the people on the ferry or if he was talking about them.

"We are refugees now. What if this thing…this sickness is in America too?"

Oleg put his arm around his wife and drew her closer.

"It most likely is, *moya milaya,* but the Americans will not be shooting at each other. They will be protecting their people."

Oleg always called her his sweetheart when he was feeling affectionate, but lately, it had seemed he was saying it more often when she was worried.

There were more explosions behind them, and some of the missiles were being fired from land. They watched as graceful, white-hot streaks arched across the black sky. An explosion at the end of the streaks confirmed they had found their target.

Oleg understood the questioning look from his wife and answered it.

"Tracer bullets. They help the gunner adjust their aim toward the target. They must have detected an aircraft. Those were air defense batteries in Petropavlovsk."

The explosions faded as the *Svetlana* increased the distance between the refugees and the harbor, and Pavel adjusted their course toward a heavily forested expanse of the Kamchatka Peninsula. It provided relative isolation for them as they gradually turned northeast toward the Commander Isles.

It was the beginning of their high-speed run past the Russian monitoring station on Medny Isle. If they made it to the Near Islands, which were the property of the United States, Pavel planned to hide behind the first island for a least a day. The water would be shallower on the northern side of the island, and there would be less chance of detection by Russian submarines.

"Get some sleep," he said over his shoulder. "It will be a long night, and I will need you to stand watch while we are anchored tomorrow."

Neither Oleg nor Galina felt like sleeping at first, but the monotony of the rocking boat and the thrumming engines began to take their toll. They curled up inside sleeping bags and drifted into a fitful sleep.

It felt like they had just closed their eyes when Pavel yelled to wake up. Both Oleg and Galina dragged themselves awake and pulled themselves up using the back of the captain's chair. They weren't prepared for what they saw happening only a mile away.

Two Russian warships sat parallel to each other and traded heavy gunfire as if they were eighteenth-century tall ships doing battle. They were so close to each other that they were using small arms, and some of the cannon blasts went harmlessly high over their targets. If the *Svetlana* had been behind either of the ships, they would have been in the path of those blasts, but from their vantage point, they could see down the middle between them. Both ships were crippled and listing, ready to slip below the surface together.

Beyond the two ships was Medny Isle, and they could see that the military station was also under attack. A third Russian vessel was firing every weapon at the station. The *Svetlana* was merely an innocent bystander, witness to a scene that was being played out in a thousand ways across the planet, and just like other bystanders, they fled as fast as their boat could carry them to the first island considered to be American territory.

Pavel watched the darkness ahead while Oleg and Galina were glued to the battle behind them. They still couldn't believe they were seeing Russian ships turn on each other and the small listening station on the island.

"Why would they do that?" asked Galina in a low voice as if they could still be detected.

"The sickness must be on the ships already," answered her husband. "We were smart to leave when we did."

"You can go back to sleep, or you can take over for me," said Pavel. "I was going to stay awake until we crossed north of the Near Islands, but we have about eighteen hours to go."

Oleg slid into the captain's chair as Pavel held the wheel in place. Pavel pointed at the compass and told him to just stay on course and not to worry about running into anything because they were in open water.

There was room for Galina on the chair with Oleg when he moved over a bit. It wasn't really comfortable when the fishing trawler bounced on the waves that were crossing the bow, but she didn't feel like sleeping, and he felt like he could use the company. Besides, Oleg wasn't convinced that Pavel could say with certainty that they wouldn't run into anything. They had already seen their share of unexplainable things in one day.

Galina put the strap from a pair of binoculars around her neck and lifted them to her eyes. Oleg was relieved to have her watching for him because all he could see was the compass in front of him.

"Can you see anything?" he asked.

"No, I can tell why Pavel got sleepy. If we have to do this for the next eighteen hours, I will go mad."

Oleg felt his wife's weight rest against him, and as much as he wanted to lay his head down, he didn't have the heart to wake her up when her breathing became rhythmic. He just had to focus on the compass and not let himself listen to her for too long. He almost welcomed the irregular bouncing of the boat.

7

Airport

International Falls Airport - March 2023

Although the Crew of Executive One had been isolated in their retreat on Last Island, they had a good idea of how things must have happened at the airport. They had seen enough at the airport in Columbus, Ohio, to know there had been chaos.

They had all assumed the large, snow-covered wall at one end of the terminal was either a building or a protective barrier, and even though it blocked the passenger drop-off exit, they assumed it was supposed to be there. The truth only became apparent as they pulled luggage free from the snow. It didn't matter anymore about how a plane had come to a stop in the front parking lot of the airport or how luggage had become strewn, unopened, under the plane. It was simply something that piqued the curiosity of the four friends.

"I know I'm asking the obvious, but aren't the runways on the other side of the airport?" said Jon. "There isn't even a taxiway around to the front."

Garret was wondering the same thing until he realized the left side wing had been sheared off.

"The pilot knew he wasn't taking off again, so he drove the plane around to the front entrance. I think they tried to get away from the infected that were on the runways."

Anne added, "They must've done okay at first if they had time to unload luggage, and the main cabin door is still open."

Susan filled in the possible final piece of the puzzle.

"The pilot drove the plane around the terminal because he was trying to get the plane as close as he could. I think they were planning to go straight from the plane to the roof of the building."

"I thought we had seen everything," said Garrett.

Susan continued, "The wing broke off as they turned the corner, and look at the way it fell."

She pointed at a place where the plane was wedged against the building. The wing was buried under deep snow drifts, but just enough of it was visible for them to see that the wing had acted as a temporary barrier under the plane. The passengers and crew of the plane bought themselves a few precious seconds to make their escape.

"But the pilot couldn't get the passenger door close enough to the building," said Garrett, "so they had to jump. Someone inside must have tried to help them by driving the luggage carts out to meet them. See how that one cart is directly below the cabin door? It gave them something softer to land on."

Even though the train of luggage carts was mostly buried under the snow, it all made sense because the four friends had seen the desperation of so many people stranded inside airplanes at the beginning of the infection. They had been luckier than any of the victims they saw on the runways of the Columbus airport, mostly because they weren't carrying a full load of passengers. Seeing the broken plane parked in front of the building brought back a flood of memories they wanted to forget, but it was important that they were remembered. To forget what happened that day was an invitation to become careless.

"This luggage has been here a long time," said Susan. "Anything worthwhile has probably been damaged by the weather if it wasn't well sealed. If people followed the rules and kept their prescription medications in their carry-on bags, we might have to climb up there onto the plane to check the overhead storage compartments."

Anne said, "It's been a long time, but I think you've forgotten what scared passengers were like. The pilot undoubtedly announced over the PA system that it would be faster if everyone left their bags behind, but by the time he suggested it, everyone was already in the aisles with their bags in their hands."

Susan remembered how people didn't listen on a good day and knew Anne was right. On a bad day, they were like an undisciplined high school class during the last period of the day on Friday. If the pilot told them to leave their bags, they would have given him a hundred reasons why they couldn't.

"Let's see what we can find around the plane," said Garrett. "Watch for expensive carry-on bags that have good seals."

Clearing away the heavy snow with small camping shovels was hard work, but they eventually found where carry-on bags had been abandoned. Garrett and Jon kept digging while Susan and Ann broke the locks and searched through the long-forgotten personal items.

"Bingo," said Susan and held up a value-sized bottle of acetaminophen. "The seal isn't even broken, so we just scored five hundred of these babies. Now, all we need is a few antibiotics and something a little stronger for when I have to stitch up this accident-prone group."

Over the years, their luck had also continued when they considered how seldom Susan's medical skills were needed, but there was always the fear that one of them would be severely injured and need something more than a splint or some stitches.

Garrett said, "I'm not letting you do any more oral surgery on me unless you find something stronger than that acetaminophen. I want something that has a warning label on it that says the effects may be increased by the use of alcohol. In which case, I plan to consume a large amount of alcohol."

They all laughed, but it hadn't been funny at the time. Garrett had suffered quietly with an abscessed molar until Anne noticed the way he winced while chewing his food. She mentioned it to Susan, and Garrett finally let her take a look. It was badly infected, and Susan had to open it, drain it, clean it, and then do something she had only the faintest idea of how to do. She had stitched fingers, feet, shoulders, and scalps, but gums were by far the hardest. From the pained expression on Garrett's face, she guessed he would rather have been shot.

The pile of empty bags grew, and the assortment of marginally useful items they found were tucked away in their own supplies, but most of the contents of the carry-on luggage were junk to them. Still, there was a fascinating but morbid curiosity that drove them to inspect everything closely. It felt as though they were getting a glimpse through the eyes of the people who had packed those bags, and it made them ask questions about that final day. Did the people know what was happening as they packed their bags? Did they realize it would be the last bag they ever packed?

As they rummaged through the clothing, personal effects, and technology that was useless to them now, the seasoned survivors of Executive One were forced to remember their own private thoughts on the morning that became the end of life as they knew it. Garrett remembered breakfast with his wife and children the most. It seemed like it had been a century ago, but the details were still vivid. The fog of time and distance hadn't clouded his memory of wiping maple syrup from the chin of his youngest child.

The silence of his three friends told him that they were deep inside their own memories. That morning, over six years ago, they had all begun the day as if it would be like any other day, and they had packed accordingly. If they found anything really useful, it would most likely have been the belongings of someone who planned to be away from home for an extended trip, but there was one other possibility. It occurred to him that they should be focused on a carry-on bag that was different in some way. If the person had taken the flight at the last minute, they might have packed something they were less likely to stow in the overhead storage compartments.

"Hey, everyone. If we have time to find everything, that would be great, but has anyone seen backpacks or small bags that were likely to have been kept close by? You know, things that could've been put under seats?"

They all took a moment to survey their surroundings. Anne found a red backpack that was more suitable for use on a college campus than for camping. She held it up in the air.

"Something like this?"

"Exactly. Whoever had that with them wanted quick access to it."

Anne opened the straps and shook the contents out. A plastic bag full of brown bottles with white caps fell at her feet.

"You're a genius," she said to Garrett as she read the pharmacy labels. "The owner of this bag had some serious health issues. We've got antibiotics, antifungals, and some serious pain meds. If Susan has to put stitches in your mouth again, you'll get the good stuff first."

She tossed the bottle to him, but even though it was right at him, he was distracted and missed the catch. It took Anne a moment to realize why. His eyes were fixed on a spot behind her, and the first thing to cross her mind was that the infected dead had found them. She turned to defend herself from the coming attack that wasn't there.

Susan and Jon were also staring at something, but they were both holding a hand over their eyes to shade them from the sun. Anne realized none of them were frightened, but they were all mesmerized. She lifted her eyes to an area above the horizon, roughly in the direction of Last Island, and she caught a glimpse of something in the sky when it reflected light back at her.

"Is that a…?"

She stopped her question at the last word, and Garrett finished for her.

"Plane."

"It's circling our lodge," said Jon.

Garrett said, "I can see that, but why?"

The answer became obvious when the plane stopped circling their home and lined up a flight path that matched their trip across Rainy Lake.

"They spotted our tracks," said Garrett, "and it won't take them long to follow them right to us."

"What should we do?" asked Susan. "Should we hide?"

"That's an AC-130, and if it's stocked with its original armament, they'll be able to find us no matter where we hide. The only thing we can do is hope they're friendly."

The sound of the plane grew quickly as it flew across the lake toward the bridge. It tilted its wings as it passed over the collapsed bridge. Their tracks ended there because they disappeared when the ice broke behind them.

Jon said, "If they're following our tracks, they're probably thinking we went into the water where our tracks end."

Garrett nodded and said, "Unless there's someone really good at tracking behind the controls. We'll know in a minute if they fly low over the river banks looking for exit tracks."

The plane did another circular pass over the bridge and then flew down the middle of the river. They got the answer to the question about the tracking skills of the pilot when the plane made a smooth turn to the right until it did a circle. It crossed its previous path at a right angle and flew directly at them.

"Everybody wave," said Garrett. "We have company."

******

Everyone on the plane tried to find a window or viewport that would allow them to see Last Island. The bright snow reflected so much light that they had all dug out their sunglasses. The tracks from snowmobiles were the only scars on the white landscape below them, and because they hadn't followed in each other's tracks, the Chief knew all four people had ridden away from the lodge.

It was a subtle confirmation to Sim that there was a chance all four of his friends had survived since he had seen them the last time. There was always a chance that the tracks belonged to someone else, but he took them as a good sign.

As quickly as the tracks gave him hope, the collapsed bridge at the end of the tracks took it from him. It was almost as if they had ridden straight over the edge of the ice into the frigid water, and on the first pass over the bridge, they were appalled by the number of bodies that floated motionless in the gaps between large chunks of ice.

The Chief didn't need to be told to circle the devastation again. He tilted the plane into a pylon turn and spiraled as close to the bridge as he could. After completing the turn, he told Sim to watch the Canadian side of the river. He used the PA system to tell the rest of the group to watch the left side of the river for tracks that matched the snowmobiles, and he flew down the middle.

He heard several voices say, "I see tracks on the port side."

After he straightened out from the high-speed turn, the Chief lined up the plane with the new set of tracks. He saw the airport ahead, and his first thought was how ironic it was to find the crew of Executive One at another airport. He wagged the wings of the AC-130 in response to their waves.

******

The first time the Mud Island family had visited the northern border of the United States to help the crew of Executive One, they had used helicopters. It would have been their preference to do it the same way instead of landing a plane on the snow-covered runway, but the durability of the AC-130 made it the logical choice for the long trip to Alaska.

"Let's hope there's enough usable aviation fuel down there," said the Chief, "because I need to make at least two or three passes over the runway before I can tell where it's safe to land."

Over the intercom, the Chief made an announcement that had everyone scrambling for a better view of the runway.

"I need all eyes on the ground to assess the runway for obstacles. I'll make passes until we know for sure where to land. If we hit a buried car, we'll only snap off our landing gear if we're lucky."

The first pass over the runway was less than encouraging. Several of the crew reported hills that were likely to be buried vehicles, so the Chief widened the possible landing area. His theory was that there might be fewer buried vehicles in the buffer zone next to the runway.

"Chief, wait to make the next pass," said Sim. "It appears that our friends on the ground understand the problem."

Garrett had hardly hesitated. He didn't know who was in the plane, but he knew they couldn't land without help.

"Everyone back on the snowmobiles," he ordered. "We need to show them where to land."

It wasn't perfect, but from the air, the Chief could see where they were going when the four snowmobiles spread out in a straight line near the end of the runway. Two were about thirty yards apart, and two were closer to each other in the middle. They drove as straight as they could across a field that angled away from the runway and left a visible trail in the snow.

High above, Sim said, "The two in the middle are showing us where we should put our landing gear."

"Let's do this," said the Chief. "Everyone put your seatbacks and tray tables in the upright positions. Brace yourselves and hope they didn't miss anything buried in the middle."

In the back of the AC-130, everyone found a way to secure themselves. The general opinion was that takeoffs and landings were the most dangerous parts of flying, but this particular landing would be harder than most.

The plane bounced and slid from side to side, but the Chief kept his big hands on the controls and tried not to overcorrect. He knew that any mistake he made would mean a long layover at the International Falls airport while they tried to fix the plane, and that was all on the assumption that it could be fixed…and that they lived through it.

Twice he was tempted to abort the landing and increase the power to the engines. The Chief felt the plane under him hold the line as the wheels got solid traction, and he focused his attention on the centerline. He kept the front landing gear in the middle of the path created by the snowmobiles, and after what seemed like an eternity, he watched his speed drop enough for them to stop in time.

He announced over the intercom, "Welcome to International Falls. You are now free to move about the cabin."

In the back of the plane, there was some good-natured grumbling about the skill of the pilot and the bouncy landing, but Shannon's comment was the one that showed she had caught on to their sense of humor.

"The in-flight service on this airline is the worst. I never even got my peanuts."

The Chief released the brakes and let the AC-130 roll forward until they reached the end of the makeshift runway. Then he rotated until the plane faced the opposite direction. He didn't want to run the risk of getting stuck if bad weather came in again, and he figured that the snow would have been packed harder where they had landed. That would work to their advantage unless it had a chance to freeze.

"Let's get our friends and some fuel and get back in the air as soon as possible," he said.

******

Garrett, Anne, John, and Susan had spent years working in the airline business, and then they had spent years living in an airport. In all of those years, they didn't think they had ever seen anything as beautiful as the gunship. The icing on the cake was who stood in the open door of the plane. They never expected to see Terrance Simmons again after he left with their rescuers. They always hoped he was still alive, but from what they had seen in Columbus, Ohio, and in their cold corner of the Canadian and Minnesota border, they didn't think it was possible. They knew that he had gone to the deep South, and where it was warmer, there were more of the infected dead.

Sim was smiling from ear to ear, and he couldn't believe that all four of them were still together. He jumped down from the plane and ran to greet them. The laughing and tears were nonstop, but in the middle of it, they all talked at the same time. There were good-natured jokes about Sim finding his Southern version of sweet tea, and Sim told them he had made a ham just for them that had been seasoned with cloves.

They groaned at the memory of the night when they set fire to the frozen heads of the infected dead.

Behind Sim loomed the big man who had led their rescue before, and they broke away from Sim to give him a proper welcome. They also marveled at the way they had arrived. Garrett said he had always wanted an opportunity to fly an AC-130 gunship, and the Chief told him he would be glad to give him his chance.

They all took turns shaking hands and exchanging hugs, and Jim Miller introduced Shannon to them. When Sim broke the news to them that he and Cassandra were married, the celebration went on for several more minutes before they got down to business.

Standing beside the airport terminal with the silver AC-130 behind him, the Chief made the offer short and sweet.

"We'd like to enlist your help with a mission. We could use your piloting skills, but we want to extend the same offer we did before. We think we're stronger together, and we would be even stronger with you guys on our team."

The Chief knew from the past that asking them to come along for their own sake wasn't the way to convince them, so he appealed to their egos. What he didn't expect was how ready they were to say yes this time.

Garrett said, "You guys chose the right time to show up. As a matter of fact, I don't think we could've lasted another year up here."

"Seriously?" said Kathy. "You look healthy. Did something go wrong?"

"We're out of supplies," said Garrett. "This is the first time all four of us have gone out together on a supply run, and it's a good thing we're all here. There are more predators coming down from the north and less supplies to be found, not to mention the trainload of infected dead that are contaminating the lake."

"It was the Chief's idea to check on you," said Sim. "We're on our way to Alaska from South Carolina and planned to just visit you, but we hoped you would also consider going with us."

"There's nothing for us here anymore but trouble," said Garrett. "If we stay, someone will die. Don't get me wrong, we've had a few good moments in our private corner of the world, but I didn't know it would be this hard."

Even as Garrett said it, he could see in his mind's eye the times they had all sat around the fireplace and embraced the warmth of the fire and friendship. They wanted more times like that, but they knew the price could be high. There would be a night sooner or later when there would only be three of them sitting in front of the fire, and then the warmth would also feel empty.

"You gave it your best shot," said the Chief.

It only took a few minutes for them to unload their gear from the snowmobiles. They didn't need everything they had with them, so they were repacking quickly. Garrett happened to glance toward Anne as she packed something from one bag into another. It was a crude wood carving he had made. It was supposed to be a deer, but he broke the antlers and wound up with something more like a bear. It had been on the mantle over the fireplace.

Anne noticed she was caught and said, "I didn't know if we would ever go back again, and you tried so hard to make it."

"It was our first winter when I was feeling like a frontier woodsman."

He had to laugh. He had gone from mowing the grass on weekends to stalking game and carving wooden animals. He had been better at cutting grass, but life didn't give him a choice.

While they got ready, Hampton and Tom stretched fuel lines from a tanker truck over to the plane. It was an added bonus that no one had ever bothered to use up the readily available supply, and they knew that they could stop there to refuel on the way home.

They finished sorting out their gear and carried it to the plane, and Garrett told the Chief he had one request.

"Would you mind making a pass over the island so we can see it one last time? We weren't there long, but it was home."

"You're going to be in the pilot seat, so feel free."

Garrett was too excited about flying the AC-130 to even think about the fact that it had been close to seven years since he had piloted a plane. It didn't occur to him until he felt the power of the engines as he opened the throttle. The plane was lined up perfectly with the tracks they had left in the snow, and he surveyed the unfamiliar instruments.

The Chief was in the copilot seat watching Garrett enjoy the moment.

"It's just like riding a bike, Garrett. Let it come back to you."

It was a familiar feeling for Anne, Jon, and Susan in the back of the plane too. Jon had been across from Garrett in the copilot seat over a hundred times, but he was fascinated by the inside of the AC-130. The weapon systems were well cared for, and they appeared to be nothing short of lethal. He had to strap in for takeoff, but he wanted to take a closer look at everything as soon as he could.

Moments later, Garrett circled Last Island doing a pylon pass so everyone could see their lodge. Through the open ports, they waved at their former home, but it was a bittersweet farewell when they saw wolves inside the fence. They knew they had left at the right time.

Food was the next order of business on the flight to Alaska. Colleen and Shannon had talked about how much they were looking forward to meeting the crew that had flown the President out of Washington at the beginning of the infection, and somehow they had strayed to the topic of how they had survived in an airport and then to how they had survived living on the edge of the wilderness. They came to the conclusion that the crew of Executive One would enjoy a meal prepared from their fresh food supplies.

Instead of dipping into their MRE boxes for 'simulated' lasagna or meatloaf, they announced with some fanfare that there would be an in-flight meal service preceded by appetizers and followed by dessert. Although they hadn't starved on Last Island, the four friends had become a bit lean from living on their limited supplies, and they appreciated the food that the ladies prepared.

Salads with real tomatoes and cucumbers on a bed of lettuce were a novelty, and they realized those were things they had given up when they chose to live in the middle of nowhere. They had found substitutes, but they didn't compare with the real things.

The salads were followed by beef stew and rice that had been cooked and sealed before they left Myrtle Beach, and for dessert, they served hot peach cobbler.

The Chief took the plate that had steam rising from the food and gave Colleen a sideways glance.

"Do I need to ask how you heated up the food in an airplane full of munitions?"

"No, you don't need to know."

When everyone was full and the plates were gathered, everyone settled in and talked about what they had been doing to survive. The four newcomers were amazed to hear that Sim and his friends had actually traveled across the Atlantic to England to reunite an astronaut with his family. Just the idea of getting there was incredible, but they had also made it back with the help of a Royal Navy submarine.

They were also fascinated to learn there were so many shelters already occupied by the Mud Island family and that there were resupply shelters scattered throughout the country. Above all, they were relieved to hear that the survivors were constantly finding other people who were welcomed into their shelters.

In the cockpit, the conversations between Garrett and the Chief were about the same things, but there were darker sides to their adventures. The Chief told Garrett about how Sparks had stranded them on an island near Nova Scotia, and then he had returned the favor by forcing Sparks off the plane on the dark airstrip with no way to leave. Garrett listened without comment and had a sense that the Chief hadn't shared the details with many people before him. It was one leader to another, and he was explaining why he did what he had to do.

When the Chief finished, Garrett said, "You gave him more of a chance than I would have. I would've shot him in the leg."

The Chief doubted Garrett would have shot him, but he appreciated the gesture. They talked about the missile silo to move past the dark episode with the Brotherhood, and the Chief told him about the Air Force shelter that would have succeeded if they had begun with more resources. He explained to Garrett why he believed Alaska was the logical place for the US military to make a stand, and he laid out their plans once they got there.

"I agree with your reasoning, Chief. If they are in Alaska and we show up with this plane, the military is just going to thank us for returning it to them. Have you decided how to approach that little problem?"

The Chief grinned as he said, "I've got a few ideas."

8

A Safe Place

Fairbanks, Alaska - The Beginning of the Infection

Governor Brandon Burgess and United States Senator Linda Worth had been pressured relentlessly by the oil industry to get the White House to open more land for oil exploration. A trip to Dutch Harbor on Amaknak Island wasn't what either of them had on their schedules, but the oil companies had insinuated their donations might be better spent on rival party candidates during the next election. They had complied with the 'request to tour the oil production facilities as if it had been in the best interests of their constituents. The Governor also had to live up to the legacy left by his father, the long-time Congressman from Alaska, Roy Burgess.

One good thing about flying out to the Aleutian Islands was the food. There was no shortage of good seafood restaurants in Alaska, and they knew their hosts would want to impress them by putting on an exceptional luncheon. At least that would make the trip worth their time.

The helicopter that picked them up in Juneau had an oil company logo on the side, and the passenger compartment lavishly included all of the amenities afforded to people of their importance. They settled in for a comfortable trip even though there wouldn't be much to see on the flight because the weather report promised another day of heavy fog and rain. The Governor inspected the label on a bottle of expensive whiskey and then poured them each a generous glass of the brown liquid.

A second helicopter trailed behind them that belonged to the US Army. The crew was dispatched from Joint Base Elmendorf-Richardson to escort the two officials on their trip, and to them, it was just another mission despite the odd reports that had been coming in from cities across the country. On board the Sikorsky UH-60 Black Hawk were four soldiers, the pilot, and the copilot. One of the soldiers was perched in the open door behind an M240 machine gun. If any of the stories on the news were true, they felt well-prepared to deal with them.

The pilot of the Blackhawk, Captain Roy Conrad, opened radio contact with Adam Ramos, the pilot of the private craft, and they exchanged basic flight information as well as introductions. Captain Conrad was surprised when his counterpart broke typical military protocol with an unusual question.

"UH-60, do you have any information other than weather conditions on Amaknak Island?"

"Standard Flight 260, say again."

Ramos repeated his question to the pilot of the Black Hawk, and there was a long pause while the two Army officers talked about how much they could say. Their orders had been to provide armed protection for elected officials, but there was nothing in their mission briefing that indicated what the threat would be. Off the record, they were convinced the threat was related to the events anyone could have heard about on the local news.

"Standard Flight 260, additional information would be nothing but speculation. Our orders are to provide an armed presence and retrieve your passengers in the event of hostile action."

The civilian pilot paused this time. He and his copilot were undoubtedly doing the same thing the military pilots had done, except in their case they were attempting to figure out how to get the officers to bend the rules a little.

"UH-60 Black Hawk, are we on a secure channel?"

"That's affirmative."

The military pilot's short answer carried a hint of skepticism. He couldn't recall ever being ordered to provide an armed escort for elected officials on a routine trip to the islands, but he hadn't questioned the unusual assignment. He had flown training flights to the Aleutian Island chain several times, and he was always glad to log more hours of stick time.

Adam Ramos dropped all formal protocol and said, "If it's just us up here, what can you tell us about the reason we have an armed escort? I've hopped these islands hundreds of times, and I've never had a babysitter."

The friendly, informal transmission didn't cause the Army officer to break from protocol, but there was something in his tone that made the pilot and copilot in the oil company helicopter nervous.

"Standard Flight 260, communications are restricted to mission-critical information. Be advised that you should use lethal resistance to prevent taking on additional passengers at any locations including Amaknak Island."

Ramos and his copilot, Michael Bailey, aboard Standard Flight 260 were confused by the advice, especially since there might be senior company executives at the landing area to greet them. If one of them wanted to ride with the Governor or the Senator, it wouldn't be something they could prevent, and they weren't even sure what the man had meant when he said to use lethal resistance. They decided they weren't going to get the military crew to tell them anything worthwhile, and between the two of them, they agreed they didn't need permission from their escort before taking on additional passengers.

Typically, helicopter pilots are very hesitant to fly under any conditions other than Visual Flight Rules, but those rules were meant for places where fog would eventually dissipate. If pilots waited for that to happen in the Aleutian Islands, they might have to wait days or even weeks. For that reason, most of the traffic between the islands was by boat. Since the Governor and Senator didn't have much advance notice of the meeting, they were forced to take the more risky way to travel.

"UH-60 escort, be advised that we are beginning a slow descent to Amaknak Island. Cloud and fog density require rules for instrument meteorological conditions. The fog ceiling is described as extremely low. We recommend you maintain your position until we have landed and can advise you of the level of risk."

The military crew didn't like waiting above the fog, but landing two helicopters in close proximity to each other when the visual ceiling was only a few feet from the ground was unacceptable. Before they could make an objection, they saw the private helicopter disappear into the thick fog. They knew the civilian pilots were probably former military pilots, and they were giving their undivided attention to their instruments, so they were left with no choice other than to comply.

Inside the fog, the choices were even more limited. Ramos kept the aircraft level by using the artificial horizon indicator, and Bailey called out their decreasing altitude. Ground personnel were tracking the landing and continually echoed the altitude called out by the copilot. When Ramos finally saw the ground below the helicopter, he was only six feet above the tarmac. If he had been less experienced, he might have overreacted and caused the aircraft to stop its descent too quickly. He might have increased his altitude and become confused when he reentered the fog and then found himself descending the last few feet too fast.

In the passenger compartment, Governor Burgess put on a show of steel nerves for the Senator, but inside he was panicking and ready to scream. The Senator had closed her eyes and gripped the narrow table between their seats. All they could see through the windows was the fog, and after descending a few hundred feet with no horizon to watch, neither of them could tell if they were going up or down. It was disorienting, and the sudden appearance of the ground below them made Senator Worth collapse even lower into her seat than she had been.

The wheels touched the ground at the same time, and everyone on board exhaled in relief, except the Senator. She was sobbing between gasps for air. Governor Burgess was already pouring them another round of drinks. This time there was twice as much in each glass. She snatched hers from him when he held it across the table. After a big gulp, she began sputtering as if she was having a stroke, and without warning, she passed out.

The side door opened, and Adam Ramos climbed in with an oxygen mask fastened to a portable tank. He saw the Governor reaching across the table toward the Senator with a glass of bourbon.

"That won't help her, Governor. She needs oxygen more. Let me get this on her face."

Governor Burgess retrieved her glass and downed the rest of the drink. He felt better after the bourbon, but he felt like something else was wrong. Every helicopter trip he had ever been on ended with the pilot shutting down the engine before opening the passenger door.

"Captain, why are the rotors still turning?"

"I thought you knew, Sir."

"Knew what?"

"I thought the orders must've come from your office," he said as he got the face straps around the Senator's head. "The air traffic controller on the ground said not to land just as our wheels touched the pavement. There was something about the state of Alaska activating its emergency preparedness program. Isn't that something you would be in charge of?"

"I don't know anything about it. If they said not to land, then why did you land?"

"Because a helicopter doesn't work that way, Sir. We were already decreasing our rotor speed for touchdown. We didn't have time to throttle up again. They're turning at ground idle speed now."

The Governor pointed at the cockpit and then straight up.

"Well, do it now."

"We need to refuel, Sir. Give me fifteen minutes."

Captain Ramos backed out of the open door and slid it shut as he went. He left the Governor with his bourbon and the Senator with her oxygen tank. He wasn't sure which one was more pale, but he was worried about why the Senator hadn't woken up.

He ducked low as he ran away from the spinning rotors and hoped the runway fuel truck was near enough for a hose to reach his helicopter. He hated the idea of refueling with his engines on and a fog ceiling so low, but he also hated the idea of turning them off. At least Michael Bailey was a good copilot who would make sure no one got near the controls while he was away from his seat.

A ground operations technician came toward him through the dense fog with the end of the fuel hose. Ramos saw he wore a name tag that said *Sewell*, and he gratefully let the man do his job. Within a few minutes, the Sikorsky was refueled. Before Sewell could disappear back to his truck, Ramos caught his arm and shouted his questions.

"What's going on? Why the state of emergency?"

"I don't have any verified information," yelled Sewell over the sound of the helicopter, "but if you caught any national news before you took off today, then you know there's some crazy stuff happening."

At first, Captain Ramos wondered why the man was yelling louder as he went on, but then they both looked up at the rotors. They had the same thought and expected to see the rotors had picked up speed. It was definitely louder than before.

The Army UH-60 descended through the thick ceiling of the fog far too close and too fast for comfort, and the Blackhawk touched down so hard it was a surprise that the landing gear didn't collapse. Ramos and the ground technician both dropped flat to the tarmac and covered their heads expecting the rotors of both helicopters to overlap. It would be a miracle if they didn't because helicopters didn't land that close to each other on a clear day, let alone in heavy fog.

When the Army pilot ran to them in a stooped-over position, Captain Conrad was greeted by two angry men, but he didn't care.

"You guys can yell at me later. Right now, we have people coming our way, and I don't know their intentions, but they shot at us already."

From the other side of the UH-60, there were long bursts from the M240 followed by an explosion at the end of the airstrip.

"What's happening?" yelled Ramos.

"People are killing each other in Dutch Harbor," answered Conrad. "You need to have the Governor and the Senator in the air sixty seconds ago."

"Why? Why are they shooting at us?"

"They want our helicopters or at least to fly out in one. We could use some fuel, but you need to get in the air first. We'll stay on the ground to provide cover for you, but you need to keep your passengers safe while we do it."

As if to emphasize what Captain Conrad said, there was another burst of machine gun fire. The M240 was firing tracer rounds, but the fog was so thick that their streaks disappeared before they reached their targets. The only reason they could tell they were hitting their targets was because the return fire stopped, and the explosions were where the shots had come from.

The civilian pilot didn't need to be told again. His copilot had heard the shooting, and he could have sworn he heard stray bullets go by his window. He had wanted to go and see for himself what was happening, but he couldn't leave his seat with the rotors turning. When Captain Ramos climbed into his seat, Bailey saw how his hands were shaking as he buckled his seatbelt.

"We need to get out of here fast," he said. "Someone's shooting at our escort."

Even as he said it, he heard bullets hitting their own helicopter. Neither of the men was hit, and the controls still responded for the time being, so Ramos increased the rotor speed. They lifted from the tarmac without any consideration for what might be above them. The fog ceiling was still so low that the ground and everything else disappeared immediately.

On the tarmac, Sewell, the ground operations technician, managed to get fuel into the UH-60 faster than he had ever done. He clapped a hand on the side of the helicopter and gave them a thumbs-up signal. On the other side of the helicopter, there was the steady sound of the M240 pouring rounds into a target that was lost in the fog. It lifted upward, but Sewell didn't bother to watch because the fog was so thick that the helicopter seemed to disappear.

There was always a chance that the two helicopters would collide with each other, but as the UH-60 emerged into clear air above the clouds, the private Sikorsky carrying the Governor and Senator was nowhere in sight.

"Standard Flight 260, what's your location? We don't have you confirmed on instruments or visual contact, over."

Captain Conrad repeated the message, and there was a burst of static through the speakers and headsets, but they couldn't tell if it was a response. He tried several more times without success. As he made his broadcasts, Conrad circled above the impenetrable clouds below them. He also tried to raise the airport they had just left behind, but he got the same results. His copilot, Captain Hank Rowlands, watched the instruments for any contacts, in part because he was worried that they might be too close to each other but also because no contact meant they had most likely gone down somewhere.

After almost ten minutes, the Army pilot radioed their base to report that they had lost contact with Standard Flight 260. Strangely, the report was received without emotion, and Captain Conrad received orders to return to the base. The crew had the feeling that the report didn't come as a surprise to the base. They turned the craft to the northeast and increased their forward speed to maximum.

Behind the Army UH-60 and flying in the opposite direction, Adam Ramos was suddenly unable to adjust his altitude according to his instruments. Ramos and Bailey both realized they were in trouble at the same time and as the copilot repeatedly shouted Mayday into his microphone, Ramos tried to make sense of the instrument display.

The altimeter wasn't increasing or decreasing, the artificial horizon indicated their yaw was fluctuating, but the pitch was almost level. The airspeed indicator was frozen at twenty knots. Even worse, the compass said they were flying away from the mainland toward the west. Captain Ramos didn't know if the helicopter was going up or down, but if the compass was correct, they were going the wrong way, and they didn't know how to report their position. All Bailey could include in his Mayday was their last known location and where he thought they might be.

They instinctively wanted to trust their controls and the pull of gravity on their bodies, but they knew that part of being disoriented was a natural instinct to pull back on their controls. If the artificial horizon was wrong, they might pitch too high and either stall or roll over on their back.

There was a loud knock on the door to the private cabin, and Ramos opened it to find the Governor was frantic. The rapid take-off combined with zero visibility through the windows had caused the Governor to become disoriented. He had thrown up on the table and had a cut on his forehead which meant he had taken off his seatbelt and had been thrown about the cabin.

The Governor thrust a folder into the pilot's hands and yelled, "Take us here…you have to take us here. We'll all be safe."

Ramos took the folder, but he kept his eyes on Senator Worth across the table from Governor Burgess. It appeared that she was regaining consciousness, but it was hard to tell behind the oxygen mask. He saw her eyelids flutter, and her head lolled from one side to the other, but she seemed oblivious to what was happening around her. She certainly hadn't noticed that the Governor had vomited and that there were undigested chunks of food in her hair.

Ramos shut the door and decided the Senator didn't need to hear it from him, nor did the Governor need to hear that the only thing they thought they knew for sure was their course. There was always the possibility that the compass was also malfunctioning, and they just thought they were going west.

Michael Bailey continued to call out the Mayday over the radio, but he saw the folder the Governor had forced into Adam's hands.

"What's that?"

Ramos had forgotten he was holding it at first, and he wondered where it came from.

"Oh, the Governor says to go here, and we'll be safe."

"Go where?"

"I don't know…I didn't open it. I don't think the Governor understood what I was trying to tell him. How can we go somewhere when we don't know where we are?"

"We have to get above these clouds," said Bailey.

Captain Adam Ramos was normally calm under pressure, but this time he snapped.

"What do you think I've been trying to do? We could be flying straight at the ground for all we know. Can you tell which direction is up?"

Bailey had stayed in his seat longer than Ramos, and he knew his friend was trying hard to read the pull on their bodies as the aircraft flew forward. He didn't take the outburst personally.

Captain Bailey said in a calm voice, "I think we're flying level. We should pull back and go up. If either of us feels too many G's, then we're pitching too high and going to stall, but we need to at least try."

Ramos felt a measure of calm return and nodded at his copilot. If he was wrong, they would feel it in time. He pulled backward on his controls. The artificial horizon stayed where it was, and neither of them felt the pull of gravity in their seats. The altimeter indicated no change.

The sunlight burst through the clouds unexpectedly, and he almost overcompensated, but they were relieved to be out where they could at least see the sky in front of them. That was when they knew for sure that they had lost the ability to increase their altitude. Even though they couldn't see the ground through the thick clouds, they could tell they weren't going higher.

"We must've been hit by some of those bullets in the wrong places. If we can manage to decrease our altitude, we have to sit down somewhere," said Ramos. "We can't just keep going west, or we'll run out of places to land."

Bailey didn't disagree, but without an altimeter or artificial horizon, they could fly straight into the ocean. He was at a loss for any safe suggestion they hadn't tried, so he said the only thing they could do.

"I agree. If we can't go up, maybe we can still go down. The only choice we have is to try to decrease our altitude and hope this fog doesn't go all the way to the ground. Let's agree on how much stick should be used for one degree of pitch, then do everything we can not to use more."

While they were in clear skies, they were able to gauge how fast they approached the top of the clouds, and when they were sure they had a one-degree downward pitch, they could see they were descending gradually. Adam Ramos drew on every bit of his experience and concentrated on keeping his stick position steady. The clouds rolled over their windows, and once again, they were flying blind. All they could hope for was enough space under the fog to allow them to react, and they had to force themselves not to look down too intently. If they did, they knew their instincts might cause them to react too quickly and change the down angle. They were going to land hard, even at a one-degree pitch, but they had to land.

At the wrong moment in their descent, there was pounding on the door to the passenger compartment for a second time, but over the sound of the rotors, there was also a high-pitched scream.

******

Despite having lost his lunch, the Governor kept drinking. It was the only thing he could do to settle his nerves. He felt better when sunlight appeared through the windows, but the thick blanket of clouds below them was unrelenting, and he felt lost.

Long before Brandon Burgess became the Governor of Alaska, he had been a private citizen who loved his guns. He was an avid hunter who had shot his fair share of big game. He had also watched the lights go out in the eyes of the animals he had shot. The familiar blank stare in the eyes of Senator Worth didn't match with her body. The eyes had gone as cloudy as the view outside the helicopter window, but he had never seen the lights go out in an elk's eyes while the rest of it tried to stand up.

Senator Worth was still securely fastened in place by her seatbelt, but she was pushing against it with her arms and legs as if she could get the belt to break or the clasp to release. Behind the oxygen mask that had slipped toward the right side of her face, her lips were curled back in a feral grin, and the Governor watched as she ate the soft plastic of the mask. She chewed at it like bubblegum, but her mouth opened wide in his direction.

He had also never heard an animal growl at him after it was dead. Senator Worth leaned forward as far as her lap belt would allow her and chewed through the face mask until it fell away. With it gone, the Governor had a front-row seat that allowed him to see that the woman had already eaten her tongue along with the mask, and the wet gurgling of blood and plastic made him push back harder into his own seat.

The narrow table between the two passengers was just wide enough to keep Senator Worth from getting a grip on the Governor as he sucked in his stomach and pushed at her grasping hands. He slapped at her arms, knocking her away repeatedly, but she persisted until her bony fingers slipped under the leather band of his wristwatch. When he attempted to pull free, he only succeeded in pulling her closer to himself. He cursed at his own decision not to wear a stretch band on his watch and used his right hand to undo the buckle of the band.

Governor Burgess had always heard there were more nerve endings in the back of the hands than any other part of the body. When Senator Worth lowered her face to the back of his right hand and wrapped her teeth around it, he became an instant believer in what he had heard. The bite was a searing, white-hot pain that made him scream on such a high note that even he didn't think it had come from himself. He pulled his hand free, and Senator Worth sat back heavily in her chair. He watched in disbelief as she chewed.

The door slid open behind the Governor, and whatever it was that Adam Ramos was going to say, it fell short of a complete sentence.

"Is that...?"

Senator Worth was still chewing on a sizable portion of the Governor's hand, but she was already leaning forward and reaching across the table. When the door opened, she adjusted her attention toward the pilot. He was behind the Governor, but his voice seemed to attract her interest.

With her next open-mouthed growl, a piece of the Governor's hand fell on the table in front of her, and she ignored it. She wanted some of the pilot as he leaned from his seat into the passenger compartment.

Governor Burgess was cradling his right arm against his body, but he had turned to face Captain Ramos.

"She bit me. She did this."

Judging by the unhealthy pale appearance of his face, Ramos knew the Governor was probably seconds away from a heart attack. It would be hard enough to give him CPR inside a helicopter, but doing anything to save his life while dodging the grasping hands of Senator Worth...or whatever she had become, would be impossible.

The Sikorsky had been designed for the maximum comfort of its passengers. There was no extra space available in the cockpit, or Captain Ramos would have dragged the Governor out of the passenger compartment to get him away from something he couldn't understand. He knew there was a first aid kit in a wall compartment, and there was even a portable defibrillator if he could get to it, but Ramos knew it would put him within reach of the Senator. For a moment, he considered the possibility of using the defibrillator as a taser on the Senator, but he had been trained to use it and knew they didn't work that way.

"Bailey, you have the stick. I have to help the Governor."

Ramos climbed out of his pilot's seat and into the passenger compartment. The Governor was still clutching his right hand against his chest and appeared to be crying, but he was mumbling between sobs that he needed help. The Senator was attracted to his whimpering and was reaching for him again, but as soon as Ramos was inside the compartment, she redirected all of her energy toward him. He dodged her hands and timed his movements better than the Governor. He caught the Senator by the back of the left arm and pulled her forward over the table instead of pushing her back. She was still strapped into her seat, but he had her upper body on the table and was able to grab her by the back of the head and hold her face down.

"Governor Burgess," he yelled. "I need you to open that cabinet. There's a first aid kit inside."

The Governor assumed the kit was to patch him up, so he didn't hesitate to retrieve it, but once he had it out and open, Ramos told him to unwrap the package that contained the silver thermal blanket. He was confused but did as he was told. When he handed it to Ramos, he understood better and was opening the container of medical tape even before Ramos asked for it.

With one hand holding the back of the Senator's head, Ramos used his free hand to shake out the blanket that was like a big sheet of foil, and he wrapped it around her head. He bunched up the excess and managed to put a long strip of tape around her neck to hold it in place. Once her head was completely covered in the foil hood, Ramos pulled her arms behind her back and used more tape to tie her wrists together. When he let her go, she thrashed from side to side, but she wasn't going to break free.

"Let's take a look at that hand," said Ramos.

The Governor didn't look any better than he had before, but at least he was calm. He quit crying and watched Ramos as he worked on the bite wound.

"I'm sorry, but this is going to hurt. I've got to disinfect the wound."

Ramos didn't give the Governor a chance to react. He poured alcohol from a plastic bottle in the first kit over the bite, and the

Governor screamed in pain. He resumed his crying, but Ramos didn't blame him. The scream really got the Senator fired up, though.

After adding antiseptic and covering the bite with gauze, Ramos used more of the tape to keep it covered.

"I'm sorry, Governor, but that's the best I can do for now."

Ramos was really worried about the shade of blue around the Governor's lips compared with how pale he was. Something told him there was more to the injury on his hand than just being bitten. Yes, it was traumatic, but Governor Burgess was taking on a resemblance to his traveling companion. Oxygen hadn't helped her, so Ramos found one of the glasses that had rolled away while he wrestled with the Senator. The Governor gratefully accepted it. For some reason, Ramos also felt like it was important for the Governor to be wearing his seatbelt.

"Here, let me get that for you."

He leaned across and helped the Governor put the seatbelt into the clasp and pulled it tight.

"Stay put, Sir. Captain Bailey and I have some work to do, but we'll have you on the ground in no time."

"Are we going to the place I showed you?"

For a moment, Ramos didn't understand what the Governor was asking him, but then he remembered the folder he had forced into his hands.

"Yes, Sir. I left it with Captain Bailey. We're heading there now."

Once he returned to his seat and closed the door to the passenger compartment, Ramos retrieved the folder from the gap between the seats where he had left it. Bailey was maintaining the one-degree down angle, but he had his eyes glued to Ramos, waiting for him to tell him what had happened in the passenger compartment. Ramos didn't want to look at him because he wasn't sure what to say.

Captain Ramos opened the folder and scanned the documents inside. They were all marked *TOP SECRET,* and there was a map with coordinates marked in bold, red print near Joint Base Elmendorf-Richardson. The heading on the top of the map said *Project SOUL.*

"I don't know what's going on, but I just tied up Senator Worth because she bit Governor Burgess."

Captain Bailey turned in his seat as if to open the passenger compartment door, but Ramos put a hand on his arm to stop him.

"I also had to bag her head with a thermal blanket and tape, but something tells me if we don't get the Governor some medical attention soon, we'll need to do the same thing to him, too."

9

Attu Island

The Aleutian Islands - The Beginning of the Infection

"I don't know who I offended to draw this duty, but I really must've stepped on someone's toes hard. Does it have to rain every day?"

Complaining was considered to be the national sport on Attu Island among the handful of soldiers assigned to the 'unofficial' outpost. Even though the island was designated as a national monument and considered to be uninhabited, there were people in the US Army who considered it to be the first line of defense if the Russians decided they wanted to take Alaska back. They were on their way to the mess hall and looking forward to getting inside where it was dry.

"No, Private Ritter, it doesn't have to rain every day. You've obviously forgotten it didn't rain last Tuesday," said Sergeant O'Reilly.

"That was two weeks ago, Sarge."

Although Corporal Mincey didn't usually correct her boss, she knew it was just good-natured fun.

"I stand corrected, Mincey. Ritter, it doesn't rain every day. It's clear every other Tuesday. As for who you offended to get assigned to this merry band of misfits, I think it's obvious that the rest of us must have offended someone, and they sent your sorry rear end here to punish us."

Despite the insult, Ritter laughed along with the rest of them. He had been the last one assigned to the unit, and when he received his orders, he had thought someone was pulling a prank on him. His official job description was infantry, but he had been hoping to be sent to one of the Army technical schools to be trained to operate a sophisticated weapon system. He didn't even know where Attu Island was.

Six weeks later, Ritter was still trying to figure out who he had offended, but at least the orders said it was temporary duty. In the Army, the word 'temporary' wasn't always the way it sounded, but he was sure new orders to a school would arrive at any time.

Ritter had gone to a computer and searched the internet for anything useful about Attu Island and found that the Army didn't even have an official base there. It was basically just the closest island to Russia which was still United States territory, and the last military presence had been decades ago. Actually, the last human presence was decades ago.

It was raining when a helicopter landed and deposited his squad of seven men and women on a plateau overlooking the beach. If the weather had been clear, they would have seen that it was seven hundred square miles of barren land that wasn't worth writing home about…not that they could write home. There was a mountain dominating the island and surprisingly, very few trees. Their encampment was on a ridge that would give them a view of the southern approach to the island, but they were invisible unless someone knew to look for them.

When they unloaded their gear from the helicopter, they expected to find an established compound. What they found was a circle of camouflaged Quonset huts with a large generator in the middle. Two of the huts were quarters for the enlisted personnel, one was the mess hall, one was the latrine, and one did double duty as the officer quarters and operations.

Complaining began within minutes after stowing their gear in their quarters because the windows didn't open. That was when they learned about the rats. They were large, mean, and constantly trying to find a way to get inside the Quonset huts, and for some reason, they had been able to figure out windows. As soon as a window was opened for fresh air, they would scramble across the rocks and leap toward the gaps. The soldiers found out the hard way that rats could make their bodies incredibly flat to squeeze through the smallest of gaps. After too many close calls, the windows were welded shut.

After six weeks of living on Attu Island, the squad had adapted to the dampness and even the presence of the rats. They went everywhere in pairs or groups, and they carried repurposed mop poles to keep the rats from getting too close. At first, they would shoot the rats, but that had an unexpected side effect. Rats were cannibals, and wounded rats were food to other rats, so everyone carried their mop poles like spears.

As they filed inside the mess hall, they watched their feet to make sure none of the rodents took the opportunity to slip by them. Mop poles were leaned into the corner by the door, and they grabbed meal kits from a stack.

"Don't touch the food if you haven't washed your hands."

The voice that bellowed at them from the kitchen at the far end of the hut was Mullins, a grizzled veteran who had been up and down between Sergeant and Corporal three times.

Mullins was presently a Corporal, but the Lieutenant had recommended him for promotion again. He was a good cook, but he was also the man you wanted with you in a firefight. He had volunteered for the miserable outpost on Attu Island because he said it would do him some good to get away from people. What he really meant was that he needed to be away from easy access to bars, and after six weeks on Attu Island, everyone had run out of the little bit of liquor they smuggled with them in their duffle bags. They suspected the Lieutenant still had some stashed away, but there was no way to get at it.

Corporal Mullins stood at the head of the serving line and waited. One by one, they raised their hands for him to see as if that was proof they had washed them. It was mostly a ritual, but it was their way of showing him the mess hall was his domain. He nodded his approval, and they all lowered their hands to ladle out the meal.

"Yo, Mullins," said Corporal Mincy. "I don't know how you do it, but man, you can cook. Where do you get all this food from? I know you can't go hunting. There's no game out here."

"It's not hard to make rat taste good," said Ritter. "A little salt, a little pepper, and some onions is all you need, right, Chef?"

"You're eating the rat meat, Private. The Corporal's eating chicken because she outranks you, and she's nicer."

"But we're eating the same thing," Ritter protested.

"You just keep thinkin' that, and you'll be fine," answered Mullins through a grin, "and don't call me Chef."

The whole squad was at the table, but the Lieutenant usually ate his meals in his quarters. On Army bases, the officers had their own mess halls, but in the field, they often ate with their men if they were a small unit. If there were several platoons, there were enough officers to set up a separate mess hall, and it was normal for them to eat separately but not alone in their quarters. No one said anything about it, but on Attu Island, it felt like Lieutenant Gleaton should be spending more time with his men because they were all so isolated already. They saw him as standoffish and a bit of a 'stuffed shirt.'

"Has anyone figured out why we're camping out here in the middle of nowhere?"

The question came from Shirley Talbot. She was also a Private who had joined the squad straight from basic training.

"Not that I'm saying it's a bad idea to have a base out here, but it seems to me that it would be worth putting more into it."

"What…you want a PX or something? Maybe a McDonalds?" asked O'Reilly. "Those golden arches would look mighty fine outside."

Private Talbot was new to the squad, but she had caught on early in basic training. You weren't allowed to dish out grief if you couldn't take it from someone else. She laughed along with them.

"I can smell those fries from here," she said.

"Those aren't the fries," said Mincy. "Ritter doesn't shower."

Despite the rain pattering on the curved metal roof and the rats that were drawn to the smell of food and were most likely inspecting the door for a small crack, the squad enjoyed the meal and carried on as they ate. If they had to spend a few months on a miserable island, it was good that they liked each other. Mullins was glad to watch them enjoy themselves as they ate his food. He took pride in his work, even if he would never openly admit it.

Private Thomas Hupp was one of the few people allowed to go inside the operations center, and the rest of the squad couldn't resist taking the opportunity at meals to ask him questions. O'Reilly was allowed to know what went on inside, but the others considered him to be off-limits because he was the squad leader.

Mincy decided it was her turn to give it a shot, and she leaned toward him. She gave him her best smile and waited.

Hupp was uncomfortable with her so close to him. As a squad, they knew the limits that were part of sharing quarters and tight spaces with members of the opposite sex. There was harmless flirting from time to time, but if Mincy had touched Hupp, O'Reilly would have stepped in fast. He knew that morale would take a detour if he allowed it to go too far.

"You look real nice tonight, Mincy, but that ain't gonna work," said Hupp. "The Lieutenant would have a chopper pick me up and take me off this island in leg irons if I say anything that's classified."

They all liked Hupp, and it was all for fun, so they didn't push too hard. Corporal Mincy sat up straight in her chair and feigned rejection. She let out a heavy sigh.

"I must be losing my touch."

What Private Hupp didn't tell them was that they had been sent to the miserable island to monitor activity around the Kamchatka Peninsula, and it didn't take a full-sized military installation to do the job anymore. A few decades ago, the Coast Guard had a LORAN station on Attu Island. The acronym stood for Long Range Navigation, and it relied on a series of similar locations that relayed information to each other. Those stations became obsolete when satellites began doing the job more efficiently. Now, their tiny operations center was using satellites to track the movement of Russian ships as they left Petropavlovsk.

When they finished their meal, they did something that made them feel more like a family than just a squad of soldiers. Even though Mullins griped at them for doing his job, they formed a line at the sink and washed their own dishes. He stood by and grumbled the whole time, but just like the handwashing ritual, it was something they needed to do.

Everyone else returned to their quarters except Ritter. It was his turn to wait for Mullins to finish storing the leftovers and cleaning the rest of the kitchen. He offered to help, but as usual, Mullins said it would get done faster without anyone under his feet, so he waited dutifully at one of the tables. An hour later, the amount of time Ritter expected, Mullins was ready to leave. He came out from behind a locker carrying his own repurposed mop pole, but he had a six-inch knife fastened to the end.

"Care to go hunting for tomorrow morning's breakfast?" he asked.

Ritter studied the man's face and gave him the same answer he gave every time.

"Only if I don't have to skin it."

They both clicked on flashlights and aimed them toward the ground before opening the door. A surprised rat darted away as soon as the light reflected from its red eyes, and Ritter kept his beam on it as long as he could before it disappeared.

On Attu Island, clear weather was the exception rather than the rule. Besides the neverending rain, there was always fog. Sometimes, the fog would be above them like a low-hanging cloud, and sometimes, it was below them, blocking their view of the beach, but most of the time, it surrounded them. As Ritter and Mullins left the mess hall, it was so thick that they couldn't see the other Quonset huts.

"Man, I'm glad the Sarge decided we don't need to post guards at night," said Ritter. His voice seemed to be dampened by the fog like he couldn't make it echo even if they were inside a big room.

"Even better," said Mullins, "remember when the Lieutenant wanted to send out night patrols? O'Reilly had locked eyes with the Lieutenant until Gleaton blinked. Then he ran off to his quarters."

"I think Lieutenant Gleaton's afraid of O'Reilly."

"Don't let O'Reilly hear you say that. He still believes in the chain of command. He just had to let the Lieutenant know what's what, if you know what I mean."

"Yeah," said Ritter, "and I'm glad we don't have to go out at night. If we didn't get a rat bite, we would most likely have someone break a leg stumbling around in this fog. Man, is it ever thick tonight."

In the first week of their stay on Attu Island, they learned quickly how easy it was to get lost in the fog. The main group had left the mess hall and gotten off course on their way back to their quarters. The next day, they were alarmed to find how close they had come to the cliff above the beach. To keep it from happening again, they had staked a rope along the ground that ran from each hut to the others.

The rats ate the ropes in one day.

Private Talbot said she had lived on a ranch, and they marked trails with stones. Everyone agreed that the rats wouldn't eat rocks, and it would be even better if they painted them. Everyone thought the suggestion was hilarious because the Army was well known for painting anything that wasn't meant to be moved, and as if to prove the point, someone had included white paint in their supplies.

Having the white stones to follow as they made their way back to their quarters was an instant relief, and they had made it an even bigger project by marking both sides of the path. They panned their flashlight beams to the left and right and were almost to the door of the Quonset hut when they heard the Lieutenant outside the operations center. They couldn't see him, but they could hear him cursing.

"Lieutenant, is that you?" asked Mullins.

"Who the hell do you think it is? Of course, it's me. Get over here."

Mullins mumbled in a low voice to Ritter that he should have ignored the jerk when he heard him making noise. He didn't have to worry about his voice carrying too far in the fog, but the Lieutenant was used to the men saying things behind his back, so he repeated the order. Ritter aimed his flashlight at the path that led to the operations center.

"Thanks," said Mullins. "Might as well find out why he's outside by himself."

It didn't take long to cover the distance between the Quonset huts, and Ritter aimed his flashlight where he knew the Lieutenant was standing.

"Would you mind getting that light out of my eyes, Sergeant?"

"It's not Sergeant O'Reilly, Sir. It's Private Ritter and Corporal Mullins."

"Where's Sergeant O'Reilly, and why hasn't anyone done anything about these rats?"

The enlisted men had all felt like the Lieutenant was out of touch with the big picture, but they had kept quiet out of respect for O'Reilly. Mullins had gone back and forth between Corporal and Sergeant because he couldn't always hold back the smart comments, and this seemed like a good time to let one out.

"Would you like for me to do something about the fog while I'm taking care of the rats…Sir?"

He deliberately paused before adding the title of respect at the end of his question.

Even in the swirling fog and without a flashlight aimed at the Lieutenant's face, Private Ritter could tell the officer was fuming, and if he had been able to see Mullins' face, he would have bet money that the Corporal was grinning.

The Lieutenant wasn't entirely sure he could court-martial the man for what he said, so he went back to giving orders that could be followed.

"Go get Sergeant O'Reilly. Tell him we've been ordered to investigate an incursion."

"An incursion, Sir? What kind of incursion?" asked Mullins.

"Do you see these bars on my shoulders, Corporal? They mean I don't have to explain everything to you. Go tell the others to fall out in full gear in ten minutes."

Mullins was silent on the way to their quarters, and Ritter knew the man was highly irritated by the idea of going anywhere on the island at night, especially in the thick fog. Whatever it was the Lieutenant had in mind, he knew it wasn't something O'Reilly would try to talk him out of because he doubted the Lieutenant wanted to go on a patrol anymore than he did.

When Mullins found his way back to the quarters and relayed the message to the rest of the squad, there was enough disbelief to go around, but ten minutes later, they were in full gear and standing quietly outside the operations center.

"Listen up, people."

The Lieutenant didn't need to command their attention because they were already waiting for him to speak.

"SATCOM has detected an incursion on the east side of the island, and they want us to find out what it is."

O'Reilly didn't want to question the Lieutenant in front of the others, but he knew that whatever it was that had been detected, it wasn't likely to be a threat at night in the dense fog. He had to be really sure it was something SATCOM wanted and not just the Lieutenant going off half-cocked.

"Sir, did SATCOM have more intel? Is the incursion land-based and moving?"

Lieutenant Gleaton was clearly anxious, and if he wasn't more afraid than he wanted his soldiers to know, he might have lost his composure. The pause before he spoke said as much as they needed to know because they caught the shaking in his voice when he answered.

"There's…there's something happening stateside that they can't explain. Everyone…all branches of the military are on alert, and SATCOM says there's a chance that it's everywhere."

"What's everywhere, Sir?"

O'Reilly was careful to use a tone that the Lieutenant wouldn't interpret as insubordinate. It was almost conversational between the two of them and not in front of the whole squad.

"Mass casualties in urban areas. Emergency services are overwhelmed."

"I'm sorry, Sir. You're not making any sense. Something's happening back home, but we're not being recalled? We're being ordered to investigate something on this worthless piece of rock in the middle of nowhere?"

The Lieutenant would normally have cut O'Reilly off in the middle of his question, but everyone watched in stunned silence as Gleaton's military training failed to kick in. Even in the dark and shrouded by the heavy fog, they could see the man's face pale, and he clutched at his stomach and doubled over to vomit.

Corporal Mincy whispered, "What's happening, Sarge?"

"I don't have a clue, Christine."

The Sarge only used a first name when he was worried. It was his way of trying to calm people down, but at this particular moment in time, it had the opposite effect. Private Hupp took a chance he normally would have passed on. Since he was the only one with access to the operations center with the Lieutenant, it was his responsibility to ask the question for the rest of them.

"Sir, would you like for me to verify the message from SATCOM for you?"

Most of them were expecting another outburst, but Gleaton didn't even seem to hear what he had asked.

"Sergeant O'Reilly, put someone on point, and let's move out. Our objective is about six miles up the coast. If we follow the beach, we won't get lost in the fog, and the rats prefer higher ground."

Someone said something about the rats preferring anywhere they could find something to eat, but the others ignored the comment. All they could do was follow orders, and if that meant going for a walk on the beach, it was marginally better than going inland and breaking an ankle by stepping on the wrong spot. Besides, even when they walked along the inland trails during the daytime, there were places where they used their hands to pull themselves over steep hills. Grabbing a rat in the dark wasn't fun.

They had to follow a narrow trail that dropped steadily downward toward the beach to the east. It felt like they were in a sewer tunnel because the sides of the trail were so close to their shoulders, and they had to turn sideways at the tightest places. Ritter was on point with O'Reilly close behind. The Sergeant helped Ritter by keeping his flashlight beam aimed ahead of him instead of at his own feet. Ritter was grateful for the extra visibility in the dense fog.

Even though the mop handles weren't standard military weapons, everyone had theirs held out in front or to the side except Private Talbot at the rear of the column. She managed to keep one hand on Hupp's shoulder while swinging her pole and flashlight from side to side with her other hand behind them. It was disturbing the way the rats followed them.

The narrow trail ended abruptly, and the fog wasn't clinging to the beach the way it had on the rocky slopes. They felt like they had walked out of the sewer tunnel onto the barren beach with a low ceiling above them. They could literally reach upward and part the fog with their hands. It was a relief, but the downside was that they couldn't see the sky above them, and no light could reach them from the moon. They could hear the gentle lapping of water on the beach, but no light reflected back from its surface until their flashlights reached it. To make matters worse, it began to rain again.

"This is plain spooky," said Corporal Mincy. The low-hanging fog and steady drizzle made her sound like she was talking from somewhere far away. She was behind Lieutenant Gleaton and Sergeant O'Reilly, but Corporal Mullins was behind her, and that made her feel safer.

Ritter didn't realize they were at the shoreline until he saw the water swirl around his feet. He took a couple of steps away from the next little wave and led the column away from the water at an angle. They were at least on flat ground and could increase their pace without worrying about stepping into a crevasse or slipping on a rock.

"Guys, there's something happening back here," said Talbot.

The column came to an abrupt halt, and Talbot walked into Hupp hard enough to push him into Mullins. She managed to keep her flashlight aimed at the rats so everyone ahead of her knew what she talking about. The rats weren't following them at slow speed anymore. Instead, they had begun to scamper away from the column as if the humans weren't going fast enough. Everyone kept their flashlights on the rats as they passed the column as quickly as their short legs could carry them.

O'Reilly was talking to the entire squad, but he made a point of facing Lieutenant Gleaton when he said, "There are only two things that make rats run that fast. They're either about to be roasted with a flamethrower, or there's food up ahead. I don't see anything burning behind us."

He turned his attention to the flat beach ahead and said, "Ritter, keep your eyes open for something that washed ashore."

"Yes, Sergeant."

Before starting forward again, Ritter stood where he had stopped and searched as far as he could see in the beam of his flashlight. He was glad that the pea soup fog was above his head. When he finally saw something different, it looked like something had been dragged out of the water onto the beach. He could see the trail, the drag marks that plowed up the wet sand. He followed the trail with his flashlight, and the rest of the column stepped up beside him to do the same.

The area where the trail stopped was a swarming mass of rats, each of them competing for a share of the food. Whatever it was they were eating, it had managed to crawl about twenty feet before falling a few notches on the food chain, and that meant it had been alive.

"What should we do, Sarge?" asked Ritter.

O'Reilly kept his eyes on the feeding frenzy but relayed the question to the Lieutenant.

"What's the plan, Lieutenant? That can't be the incursion SATCOM wanted us to check out, could it?"

"No, we're still a couple of miles from the objective. I don't even know what that is. I mean, what are they eating?"

"Looks like a beached seal," said Mincy. "Poor thing."

Ritter moved as close as he could without distracting the rats and studied the drag marks. They were deeper toward the edges.

"Do seals wear shoes?" he asked.

Six more flashlights were aimed at the spot where Ritter was shining his light on the soles of a pair of street shoes. The toes were pointed downward.

"Street shoes," said O'Reilly. "Not boots, not sneakers, and not deck shoes. I wonder how he got here."

Mincy said, "I wonder how he got from the water to where the rats got him."

"We're not going to get any answers standing around talking about it," said Mullins. "I feel like we're sitting ducks out here waiting to end up face down under a pile of rats just like him."

"I agree," said Gleaton. "Let's go while the rats are busy."

Ritter led the column across the drag marks, but everyone kept their flashlights on the squirming pile. Talbot kept hers aimed backward until they were far enough down the beach to no longer be able to see any part of it. No one spoke because they were using all of their senses to probe the darkness that surrounded them. Their feet made a small squishing sound as their combat boots pressed into the damp sand. Other than that, there was nothing but the soft lapping of the water onto the beach and the light patter of the rain.

A mile later, Ritter's first thought was that they had somehow gone in a circle, but as they got closer to more drag marks in the sand, he saw there wasn't a body under a pile of rats. The trail in the sand was a confusing mess at the start, and it gradually became more distinctive.

O'Reilly saw why Ritter had stopped and told everyone to wait where they were. He walked ahead and then followed the trail toward the rocky terrain. He came back feeling like something was seriously wrong on Attu Island, even more than usual.

Mincy said, "You're scaring us, Sarge. You look like you've seen a ghost."

"I thought I saw someone walking up the trail, but if I remember this stretch of beach from the last time we came over here, that trail gets too steep about a hundred yards inland. If someone went up there, they'll be back soon enough. You want to wait on them, Lieutenant?"

Gleaton shook his head. "Our objective is still a couple of miles from here. Whatever it is, we need to stay on mission. We can check it out on the way back."

"It's starting to rain harder," said Corporal Mincy. She held out a hand and watched the water make a puddle in her palm.

"Hang on a second, Lieutenant. With all due respect, Sir, I feel like I'm leading my people into something without proper intel. I know you've got your secrets, and we've got a job to do, but it seems like a collision of our job and yours right now. Can you at least tell us what SATCOM sent us out here for? Is it something we can be ready for?"

They could see the Lieutenant was weighing the request, and he finally gave in.

"SATCOM doesn't know enough to tell me anything. That's why they said they want us to investigate. I can tell you that a helicopter took off from Alaska. It was carrying the Governor and a US Senator. It made a stop for fuel near Dutch Harbor on Unalaska Island."

O'Reilly said, "You mean it was island hopping the way we were six weeks ago. Let me guess, they landed at the Adak Island airport, too?"

"They aren't sure, but it wasn't long after Unalaska when SATCOM was asked to track them. They reported that they sustained some damage when they left Amaknak Island but didn't say how or the extent. All SATCOM knew was they flew in this direction."

"Why?"

The question came from more than one of the soldiers, and Lieutenant Gleaton was momentarily caught off guard. He hadn't even realized that the soldiers had formed up around Sergeant O'Reilly. It was just the sort of gesture that made him feel like O'Reilly was more in charge than him.

Gleaton almost put the thought into words, but he remembered some advice he had gotten from a fellow officer. Never take the time to remind enlisted men that they were subordinates. They already knew they were not officers, and reminding them was a sign of insecurity. Privately, he knew that he was insecure, but at that moment, standing on the dark, miserable beach, he felt like he needed them more than they needed him.

"The Governor and the Senator didn't think they needed to explain themselves. Their offices said they were touring the oil facilities on Unalaska, but they couldn't explain the detour all the way over to Adak Island."

"Forget the detour to Adak," said Corporal Mullins. "What in hell made them detour in this direction? I mean, it's not like we're all that close to Amaknak and Dutch Harbor. I think we might actually be closer to Russia."

There was a bit of nervous laughter from the squad, and to everyone's surprise, even the Lieutenant joined in. It felt strange to him, but it also felt like he had bonded with the others. It might be a bit premature on his part, but something told him that SATCOM would be satisfied when they reported that their mission had been a success after finding the missing helicopter.

10

Svetlana

Near Attu Island - The Beginning of the Infection

Pavel Ivanov was grateful for the compass because the fog was the thickest he had ever seen in his life. During the morning hours after sunrise, Oleg had gone out to the bow, where he sat and listened for even the faintest sound other than the water lapping against the boat. It was unnerving to be inside a fog bank so thick that Pavel could barely see Oleg. Galina made them breakfast of oatmeal and fried bread. She carried some to the pilothouse and the bow. No one spoke above a whisper, and they felt as though the silence would be broken at any moment by another boat or, even worse, a tanker ship that was crossing between the Aleutian Islands.

The fog covered the deck with enough moisture to make everything reflect the light, and it seemed to blind them even more. Galina squinted her eyes against the glare as she made her way back from the bow to the pilothouse.

"Oleg wants to know if you have an update on our position. He said to tell you that he has been listening for the sound of water against land so he can tell when we are close to the American islands. He is beginning to worry that we might pass by them if we are off course."

Pavel was a bit irritated by the comment.

"Tell Oleg we are not off course unless he took his eyes off the compass last night while he was at the wheel. Tell him if we miss the first islands, we will still reach the next ones, and if we miss them, we will not miss Alaska."

Galina considered what she should do, but there was no way she would stoke the tension they all felt by delivering that message. She gave her brother a hard stare that he pretended not to see, then left him to his work.

At the bow, she said to Oleg, "Pavel says we are on course, and we should be near the American islands soon."

"How soon?"

Galina had considered the possibility that Oleg would ask the question, so her answer sounded more natural.

"We have been traveling much slower than we would have with better visibility, so we might not reach them until tonight."

"Tonight," he said with exasperation. "It would be dangerous to approach an unknown beach at night, especially if this fog is still so dense."

Galina playfully poked her husband on the top of his arm. It was something she did when she really wanted his attention, and he knew when he gave it to her, she would be smiling.

"What?" he asked.

"Are you forgetting that we got away? We were leaving anyway, but the things on the news…the killings and all those people trying to escape. We got away. We could be in a worse place right now."

Oleg knew she was right. It was just in his nature to worry about what was going to happen next.

"Yes, *moya milaya.* We are in a better place now than we were. I worry that it will be the same in America, but we will know that when we get there. I will try to worry less and remember that we are at least safe."

The dull thud near the port side of the boat wasn't loud, but it was different than the sound of water lapping against the hull.

"Did we bump into something?" asked Galina.

Oleg was already leaning as far over the rail as possible without falling and staring intently at the gentle swells. There was something floating on the surface of the water, and their forward speed was causing it to bounce along the boat as it moved toward the stern.

"Whatever it is, it must have a rope attached to it because it is staying close to the boat."

One look toward the bow was enough for him to know he was right, and he switched to the starboard side to see if there was something there. His suspicion was confirmed when he saw a bright orange life jacket had been caught by their bow and held against the boat by their momentum. A long cord stretched around to the port side, and when Oleg returned to that side, the object that was attached to the cord had stopped traveling along their hull.

"What is it?" asked Galina.

"I do not know. Get your brother…hurry."

Galina ran up to the pilothouse where Pavel had been watching his brother-in-law reacting to something, so he had her take the wheel as soon as she arrived. He made his way forward but stopped long enough to grab a long pole with a hook and a javelin-type point on the end.

"Is there something in the water? What do you see?"

Oleg pointed to the object on the port side.

"Whatever it is, it seems to be tethered to a life jacket that got caught on the bow."

Pavel saw the long cord and instinctively reached over the side with the long pole. He easily caught the cord with the hook and pulled upward, but between the drag created by their forward speed and the weight of the thing in the water, he couldn't bring it closer. Oleg put his hands on the pole near Pavel's, and they pulled together.

As soon as they had the heavy object partially above the water, they knew what it was. It lifted water-swollen arms toward them, and its head lolled backward, exposing the wrinkled skin of its face. There were deep cuts along the cheeks that were washed clean by the salt water, and they could see the jawbones and teeth on the left side.

Pavel didn't need to tell Oleg to let go before he let the long cord slip over the edge of the hook. He ran to the starboard side of the bow and used the javelin to poke at the life jacket until he managed to push it to the port side. It and the body tied to it both slid out of sight in seconds.

Neither of them spoke for several moments as they weighed the implications of their catch. They knew what they had left behind, but they also knew what was ahead. Galina could also tell by the way they both turned their eyes toward the pilothouse.

"This does not have to change our plans," said Oleg. "The Americans might have the same problems, but we cannot go back."

"Did I say we have to go back?" snapped Pavel. He saw

immediately that Oleg was getting thin-skinned by his short temper because his brother-in-law had turned red.

Pavel raised a palm toward Oleg and said, "Wait. I have been a jerk toward you since yesterday. You have been strong about all of this. You took care of things back at the truck in a way that I am not so sure I could have done by myself. I treat you like dirt because the *Svetlana* is my boat, but I could not have escaped alone."

The apology was overdue, but it was sincere, and for all they knew, it might have been what would help them survive whatever it was that they were going to face in the days ahead. Galina was gratified as she watched from the pilothouse and saw the men exchange hugs.

They went together to the bow, where they discussed the meaning of the man…or thing that they had encountered. They were in agreement that the life jacket meant it was from another boat, and they were likely to encounter more. Whether it was debris from a wreck or people, they had to decide what they were going to do.

"Are we going to rescue survivors?" asked Pavel. He felt like he already knew the answer, but he needed to hear Oleg say it.

"It would be like the truck," answered Oleg. "How would we know if it was safe? The news reports were saying that the infection spreads when someone gets bitten. If we pull someone aboard and they are bitten, are we going to throw them back in the water? What if they bite one of us?"

Pavel nodded and said, "If we want to survive, we should not take the chance."

Both of them heard the sound at the same moment that Pavel finished speaking. It was the unmistakable crash of water against rocks, and it was too close. Even though they couldn't see ten feet from the bow, they knew if they continued straight ahead, the *Svetlana* was likely to crash into land.

"Which side do you think the sound came from?" yelled Pavel.

"I think the port side."

Pavel ran to the pilothouse while Oleg leaned as far over the bow as he could, hoping to hear where the sound was coming from but wanting desperately to see land.

Pavel took the wheel from Galina and saw Oleg frantically pointing to his left…to the port side of the bow, and despite what Oleg expected, Pavel turned the wheel hard to the left and increased the forward speed as far as it would go. He saw Oleg trying not to fall over the bow while flailing his arms to signal that they were turning the wrong way. There wasn't time to explain it to Oleg, but if he could, he would have told him they needed to stay near the sound, but they also needed to stop in time. His best guess was that they were passing the island on its southern side, and if he could turn fast enough, he could do both.

Oleg was afraid that Pavel had misunderstood and thought he was indicating which direction he should turn. At another time, it would have been amusing because he appeared to be trying to erase something in the air. Then he pointed again, but this time it was straight ahead. Then, it was a little to the starboard side, and Pavel knew he had done it. As Oleg pointed more and more to the starboard side, Pavel eased the wheel back to a zero bearing. He had guessed correctly, and on their right was the western tip of an island.

An hour later, Pavel had navigated around the northern side of the island and was about to reach the eastern tip. All he had to go by was Oleg's ability to tell where the waves hit the beach, but as they were about to make their final turn to the starboard side, there was a break in the fog, and he could see a small cove where they could drop anchor. It would be a nice place for them all to get some sleep. He steered the boat past a natural outcropping of stone that curved outward from the beach. The water in the cove was calm, and he stopped the engines before dropping anchor.

Galina had stayed inside the pilothouse mostly because the turn Pavel had made was so sharp, but she was also afraid. The silence that descended on them when the engines stopped was a blessing.

"Where are we?" she asked her brother.

"If I am correct, this is an American island called Attu."

Attu Island - The Beginning

Sergeant O'Reilly moved back in the column to be even with Lieutenant Gleaton and leaned sideways toward him. He kept his voice conversational and remembered how the man had seemed to be gratified by a feeling of acceptance by the squad.

"So, there wasn't really an incursion, was there? You just said that to keep from talking about whatever it is that's happening stateside."

It seemed for a moment that the officer wanted just to answer the question, but O'Reilly saw him avoid letting him get a good look at his face. He dipped his head down and away, and O'Reilly remembered that the man had gotten sick back at the base.

"You're worried about your family, Sir. I get it. You're stuck out here and can't do anything to help them. What can you tell me about whatever it is that's going down?"

O'Reilly didn't think Gleaton was going to answer him because he waited so long. He was ready to take the man's silence as his answer and was about to move back to the front of the column when he finally spoke.

"SATCOM said there's some kind of disease that spreads like wildfire. It's causing the dead to come back to life, and people are eating each other. It's happening everywhere in the world."

O'Reilly had been a sergeant long enough to hear some tall tales, and he had long ago developed the ability to tell when someone was feeding him a line or telling the truth. Lieutenant Gleaton was sarcastic at times, but he hadn't been inclined to get really creative. O'Reilly didn't think the man was making up what he said.

"Where's your family, Sir?"

There was another long pause before he answered, but Gleaton finally said, "The Base has an emergency plan for dependents. We have a place in the dependent's quarters. If this thing is real, there's supposed to be a plan to get families into some kind of shelter."

"I never heard about that, Sir, but if they have a plan, then I'm sure your family is safe."

"It was part of the orientation for dependents. My wife brought home a big manila envelope of stuff. I guess since we're so close to Russia, they figured they needed to be ready for a nuclear war."

O'Reilly remembered an Army class about nuclear decontamination, fallout, radiation, and the whole deal. One of the details that stood out in his mind was that the whole thing, from start to finish, was likely to be about thirty minutes. They would detect multiple launches from Russia, and the clock would start ticking. You had to be somewhere safe in thirty minutes, or you could forget about it. He recalled one guy in the class said that was just enough time to get his lawn chair and a cooler of beer. He said he would be outside well into his third beer when the nuclear warheads arrived. If he was lucky, he would be drinking number four.

This wasn't a nuclear war, though. They would've had more than thirty minutes. As soon as that thought crossed his mind, he knew why Gleaton had thrown up. Given the facts, they had been told just enough to cause a hundred more questions. If it had been a nuclear war, maybe someone would want to know who had done it to America, or maybe someone would want to know why, but when it came to a disease that made the dead come back to life, no one would know where to begin with the questions.

Apparently, Gleaton was having the same thoughts because he asked Sergeant O'Reilly his questions as if the NCO knew more about it than he did.

"If this is happening everywhere, how did it spread so fast? I mean, how can the dead even come back to life? Is there a cure? No one here is sick, so it has to spread to a population, right?"

O'Reilly knew that Gleaton didn't really expect him to be able to answer his questions. He was only asking them because he was afraid for his family.

"Sir, whatever this is, I'm sure the command took care of your family. I mean, they had people assigned to do that, right?"

Gleaton canted his head to one side the way he usually did when he remembered something. O'Reilly had considered getting the man into a poker game so he could watch for all of the 'tells' the man had.

"There was a whole division assigned to the welfare of families. According to the orientation documents, someone would pick them up in a bus within thirty minutes of the announcement that there was an emergency."

"Thirty minutes," thought O'Reilly.

The squad came to a sudden halt as Private Ritter held up a fist. O'Reilly moved up next to him, and he saw something large was beached up ahead. It was big enough that the top of it wasn't visible in the fog.

"What's that look like to you, Private?"

"A boat, Sarge…a nice one. Judging by the furrow it dug in the sand when it beached, I would say it drove straight into the beach with a lot of speed. Must not have seen the island until it was too late."

"Who would be driving around out in this fog without using instruments? Let's take a closer look. Lieutenant Geaton, could this be what SATCOM wanted us to check out?"

"Only if the Governor and the Senator are on board, Sergeant. I don't expect they got out of their helicopter and took a boat."

As they got closer to the dark hull, they aimed their flashlights toward it and saw it was a luxury yacht. It was about one hundred feet long and had probably belonged to a millionaire. There wasn't any movement they could see, but they could hear something that became clearer as they got closer.

"Is that music, Sarge?" asked Corporal Mincy.

All he said back was, "Everyone be on your toes and be ready for anything. Something ain't right. Ditch your rat-stickers and switch to sidearms. Mullins, you, Hupp, and Talbot scout the other side, and I'm not just talking about the boat. Keep your heads on a swivel."

The trio gave the boat a wide berth as they circled around to the other side. They were hardly out of sight when the rest of them heard Shirley Talbot scream.

The rest of the squad reacted the way any close-knit group of soldiers would, and they ran to the rescue of one of their own. If their nerves hadn't already been frayed by the fog, the darkness, the rats, and from just plain not knowing what was going on, they would have set a perimeter and then gone to see why she had screamed. After all, she was in good company since Mullins was leading the group.

All of their flashlights combined were more than enough to illuminate the area, but Private Ritter had the presence of mind to launch a red flare. It disappeared into the fog above, but when it burst above them, the light filtered down and cast an eerie glow over the beach. Mullins had a man by the back of the neck and was in the process of throwing him at a group of people who were standing ankle-deep in the water. When he threw the man, he knocked over three more who didn't even try to dodge the flying body.

"Is everyone okay? Talbot, what happened?" yelled O'Reilly.

Before she could answer, Mullins said, "Jerk tried to bite her. He was standing by the bow where we didn't see him right away, and he just grabbed her."

"Talbot?"

"I'm fine, Sarge…just startled. I'm sorry I screamed."

O'Reilly wondered what would have happened if he had been the first person to go around the bow. He might have screamed, too.

"Forget it, Private. I think everyone here would've done the same thing."

"Everyone except Mullins," she answered. "He grabbed that guy quick. I mean, that guy had my arm almost in his mouth when Mullins grabbed him."

When he saw that Talbot was okay, O'Reilly turned his attention to the people in the water. There were six of them and not one of them was in good shape. They kept falling down and getting back up while the squad of soldiers watched them closely.

"Everyone move away from the boat. If there are more on board, I don't want them falling over the side on top of us."

They all moved in a semicircle so that the strange people were between them and the boat as they came out of the water. As they walked up onto the wet sand, they took heavy steps toward the row of soldiers. They walked as if their legs could hardly support them.

"Weapons ready," said Sergeant O'Reilly. Then he said to the group of people, "That's close enough. Stay where you are. Why did you try to bite one of my soldiers?"

The reaction he got to his question was far from what he expected. He didn't really know what he expected, but it wasn't a groan. It came from the one that Corporal Mullins had thrown, but as soon as that one groaned, the others chimed in.

Lieutenant Gleaton moved up beside O'Reilly's right shoulder and said, "I think this is what SATCOM was talking about. They look sick."

"So, what are we supposed to do about it?" he answered. "Was there something from SATCOM you forgot to mention?"

O'Reilly had his sidearm aimed at the man who groaned first, but he couldn't resist putting his eyes on the officer's face, so his head was going back and forth between the two. He saw that the man was getting too close, but the Lieutenant hadn't answered him.

"I said that's close enough," he shouted at the man.

His shout seemed to have an effect on all of the people coming behind the man because their chorus of groans became a nonstop racket.

"Sarge?" said Corporal Mincy.

All of them were nervous, and they didn't know if they should withdraw a few steps, hold their ground, or shoot.

"SATCOM said the only way to stop the dead after they come back to life is head trauma."

O'Reilly didn't lose his cool with officers very often, but he was rapidly reaching that point with Lieutenant Gleaton. His earlier sympathy for the man was forgotten for the time being.

"You're just now getting around to telling me that?"

Sergeant O'Reilly said to the squad, "Hold your fire unless you have to. I need to test a theory first."

To the slowly approaching man, he said, "Sir, I'm giving you one last warning to stay where you are, or I'll shoot."

The groans intensified, and Sergeant O'Reilly shot the man in the chest from less than six feet away. The bullet must have hit the man squarely in the sternum because the impact tossed him backward into the rest of the group. They all fell over this time because they had bunched up behind the man in front.

The squad of soldiers stood in a line with their sidearms raised. They waited and watched as the people struggled to their feet. The first two that got up were facing in the wrong direction at first but gradually turned back to the beach. Then the third, fourth, and fifth ones got up. The soldiers were all watching the one O'Reilly had shot, and they had a hard time not saying something out loud…all except Mullins.

"That's messed up."

O'Reilly had just shot a man at nearly point-blank range, and even though he had done a tour in the Middle East, it wasn't something he could say came easy for him. He had purposefully shot the man in the chest to test his theory, and part of him felt like he had just killed someone. What Mullins said was something he would never forget as he took aim at the man's head and pulled the trigger.

This time, the man simply collapsed to the sand in a heap, but the other five people all seemed energized by the sound of the gun. Even as Sergeant O'Reilly gave the order to open fire, there was already a series of pops from the rest of the squad. They didn't need to be excellent marksmen, but they all were, and it was over in a matter of two seconds.

"I've never shot a real person before," said Ritter.

Mullins let out a sound that was half laugh and half cough.

"I don't think you've shot a real person yet, Ritter. I can't say for sure what they were, but they weren't real people."

O'Reilly glared at Lieutenant Gleaton and told everyone to form up around him.

"The CO has something he wants to tell everyone. Tell them, Lieutenant, or I will."

It didn't take long because the CO didn't have as much more information than what he had already told O'Reilly. The main thing he had left out was that the Joint Base in Alaska had told him they couldn't spare the resources to recall them.

"So, no one is coming to get us?" asked Corporal Mincy. "What about our families? Is someone at least going to let them know we're still alive?"

O'Reilly put a hand on her shoulder to let her know they were all there with her and that they all had family somewhere. Her voice became shaky when she asked if there was a possibility of them contacting their families by satellite phones, and they all saw the way Gleaton avoided answering.

"Let's secure the area around this boat," said O'Reilly. "We have our own survival to consider at the moment."

Throughout the duration of the encounter, everyone was aware of the music playing somewhere inside the boat, but it had been ignored. There was something incongruous about listening to a song that was at the top of the charts while they shot people in the head, and each of them had tuned out the sound.

"Is that a radio station or an album?" asked Ritter. "If that's a working radio, maybe we can get some news."

The top of the boat wasn't visible even while the red flare had drifted downward, but they all knew a boat like this one would have sophisticated instruments for navigating. Why it would hit an island at high speed was a good question, but when they considered the condition of the people in the water, the answer was obvious…the infection had been on board.

O'Reilly asked, "Does anyone know anything about yachts this size? How many people will it take to crew one of these things? How many passengers do they carry? We just shot people who were probably on this thing."

Private Hupp added, "There was one on the beach getting eaten by the rats, and then there was the trail in the sand that might have been one more."

"Let's assume there are more still in the water that will wash ashore sooner or later," said O'Reilly. "What about my question? No one here ever got curious about how the other half lives? What's the guess on the number of staterooms?"

"I went to a party on one after high school graduation," said Mincy.

"Okay," said the Sergeant, "assuming you at least took a tour, let's check this thing out with you on point with Ritter. Where do we start?"

"There's a swimmers platform at the stern, Sarge. We might have to wade out to it, but it would be the easiest place to board."

They formed up on Ritter and Mincy and walked to the stern of the yacht. They didn't need to be told to keep a close eye on the water as they waded about twenty feet to the platform.

"This thing must've been really moving to go so far up the beach," said Hupp.

"No chatter," O'Reilly said over his shoulder.

Ritter stepped up onto the platform and listened. There was a new song playing somewhere inside, and small lamps along the stairs lit up their path to the main salon.

He whispered back over his shoulder, "The good news is that there's still power."

Mincy added, "There's probably an outside entertainment area and then a main area inside. The one I was on had a dining room, a lounge, and a game room. There were bars everywhere."

O'Reilly had to remind everyone except Gleaton that they weren't there for a party.

"If I see anyone touch the booze, I'll send them back to the base by themselves."

They knew he would never do that, but they got the message. They also knew O'Reilly well enough to know that the stock of liquor on the boat wouldn't go to waste. There would be a better time to deal with the booze.

Ritter raised a fist when his head was high enough to see above the top of the stairs. Then he extended two fingers. After a few seconds, he added a third. He backed downward one step and whispered.

"They don't appear to be different than the ones in the water."

O'Reilly answered, "Shoot to kill unless one speaks and uses real words."

Ritter and Mincy went up the steps onto the outside entertainment area. The door to the main salon was open, and they stood shoulder to shoulder to take aim at the three people. In the dim light from somewhere inside, they could tell that the people were the same as the ones in the water, and they didn't hesitate to eliminate the threat.

It took almost a half hour to go through every room of the yacht, and they eliminated two dozen more of the groaning people. The beautiful floors, walls, and furnishings were all stained by blood or damaged when the yacht hit the beach, but the soldiers were still amazed by the luxury they saw.

After clearing every room, they gathered in the main salon to discuss the next move. They still had to investigate the 'so-called' incursion further up the beach that involved the Governor and Senator, but there was still power in the batteries of the yacht, and O'Reilly wanted to make use of it. He told Ritter to stand watch on the bow and had Talbot go to the stern. They both had orders to stay dark, but they should shoot anything that walked like the people they had already encountered.

"Lieutenant, we need to use this yacht's satellite system to find out what we can about the rest of the world. SATCOM isn't going to tell us anything. Maybe someone else will. Hupp already checked out the system and thinks he can get some broadcasts. There's also a lot of supplies, and we should consider the probability that we're going to be stuck on Attu Island a little longer than we expected. We should haul as much as we can back to our base and start rationing."

Gleaton nodded without comment, and O'Reilly judged by the glazed-over eyes that the man was back to thinking about his family.

"Okay, people. You've all done good so far, and I believe you deserve something for it. Everyone pour yourself one drink. No more than three fingers in a glass. If I see anyone take more, they're cut off. Someone get a glass to Ritter and Talbot. You can sip it, savor it, or shoot it. I don't care which but show some self-control. In the meantime, Hupp is going to see what he can do about getting us in touch with the outside world."

O'Reilly knew that Mullins would probably find a way to talk someone out of their free drink, but he wasn't going to make an issue out of it. After everyone was situated around the big screen TV that magically dropped down from a hidden panel in the ceiling, or overhead, as Mincy called it, Hupp announced he had a satellite connection. The sixty-inch screen lit up with an image that silenced the room.

11

New Alaska

Campbell Airstrip - March 2023

The flight from Minnesota to Alaska was almost enjoyable. The Mud Island family was always aware of the dangers on the ground, but it felt like there were two families flying together in the AC-130, and for a short time, the infected dead world below them didn't exist. Sim had nicknamed his former crew mates the Executive One family, and Kathy had pointed out that the Mud Island family had started with four people. Regardless of where they started out, they all felt like they were in the right place, and they had a good feeling about Alaska.

"How much longer before we see our airstrip?" asked the Chief.

Sim checked the charts he had spread out across his lap and said, "Ten minutes seems about right."

Garrett Carson had taken the copilot's seat to help the Chief as he landed the plane on the old runway. Part of his job would be to assess the condition of the runway while the Chief made a low pass. Over the years, the runway might have developed cracks in the pavement or been littered with debris that would prevent them from landing the plane. If they wanted to remain undetected, the old World War II airstrip was their best bet. It would have been better if it had been at least ten miles further away from the big joint military base, but it would have to do.

The backup plan was not much of a plan at all. If Campbell Airstrip turned out to be too dangerous, they would have to decide quickly if they wanted to fly past it and be totally exposed to detection by landing at Anchorage International Airport. There weren't any other options unless they wanted to take a chance that the military would let them land at the airbase and be allowed to keep their plane.

Garrett said, "The last place I want to be is at another major airport."

"I'll second that," said Sim.

"How much fuel would we need to reach that short runway across the bay from the base?" asked the Chief.

"More than we would want to use," said Sim. "We would have to circle the bay to avoid detection, and then there's the problem with the length of the runway. It's only three thousand feet long, and we need two hundred more feet."

"I guess Campbell Airstrip had better work out. I can see it up ahead. I'll approach from the south, make a pass, and bank hard to starboard to keep as much distance as possible between us and the Army base. Let the gang in back know that we need all eyes on the ground to assess conditions."

As the Chief lowered the altitude of the AC-130 to get ready for the pass, everyone found a position that would allow them to see the ground. The treetops seemed close enough for them to touch, but they slid by underneath the plane so fast that they were a blur. The trees ended with a wide-open field on all sides of the runway, and the Chief let the plane drop even lower. He stayed in a straight line along the right side of the runway so more people could have a view through the gun ports.

Visual reports came through the Chief's headset even as they were banking to the right at the end of the runway. There were no major obstacles that would prevent landing, and there were only a few infected dead in the area near a building. The assessment should have made him happy, but the Chief was back in his element when he had something to worry about, and he was worried about why the runway was so clear.

"All hands, report," he announced. "Did anyone see evidence of recent activity?"

Kathy had always demonstrated keen powers of observation, and she had seen something that felt wrong.

"Chief, there were tire tracks leading to a parked vehicle. It's a green utility truck with a roll-up back door."

"That's what I'm talking about, everyone. Someone cleared the runway, and it might have been recently. As soon as we're on the ground, I want one group to check out that vehicle and see if there are any more signs of recent activity."

It only took a few minutes for the Chief to turn in a tight circle that brought them back around to the beginning of the runway, but before the wheels were on the ground, Cassandra and Kathy had everyone assigned to squads. Garrett and Sim would guard the plane while the Chief and Cassandra would lead two squads in a reconnaissance of the airport. In the Chief's squad were Kathy, Jim Miller, Shannon, Hampton, and Colleen. Following Cassandra were Iris, Tom, Anne, Jon, and Susan. Everyone was heavily armed with M4 rifles and 9mm handguns, but they had their machetes in their hands. If they hadn't been detected when they landed, they didn't want to draw attention with gunfire.

The Chief turned the controls over to Garrett and went back to get ready with the others. Garrett rotated the plane and taxied it to a spot near the service building where the truck was parked, but he kept the engines running. As soon as the two squads were out the door, he took his foot off the brakes and let the plane roll to the end of the runway. He rotated for a second time before shutting down the propellors.

A silence descended over the airstrip, and the Chief's squad moved as quietly as they could toward the truck with the tracks behind it while Cassandra's squad went toward the service building. It wasn't a large building, but it had a rusty garage door with broken windows on it. They would be able to hear if there was anything inside.

The squads both knew the arrival of the plane would have been loud enough for anyone to hear, but no one on the ground would expect them to send armed people out to secure the airstrip as fast as they did. If they were lucky, there would be no one inside the building, but if anyone were home, their attention would be on the plane at the end of the runway. Even at a distance, the array of weapons that bristled from the left side would be enough to paralyze any resistance.

The Chief crossed the tracks behind the truck and saw that it was mud that had probably frozen while still wet. That meant they were older than they thought. From the back of the truck, he could see the reflection of someone moving inside the cab. He signaled the rest of his squad to let them know. Kathy and Jim moved toward the driver's side while he continued along the passenger's side, followed by

Shannon. Hampton and Colleen covered the closed door on the back.

Chief Barnes was a big man, and if the occupant of the cab even glanced toward the rearview mirror, they would see him easing along the side of the truck, but there was no indication that they saw him. He was also a combat veteran, and he had seen a soldier pull open a door that was rigged with an explosive device, so he wasn't about to repeat that mistake. He bent down and scooped up a handful of gravel, then tossed it at the mirror.

Inside the cab of the truck, two faces competed with each other for space at the window. They were both badly decayed and had been inside the truck for a long time. The Chief backed up toward Shannon, and together, they retreated to the back of the truck. Kathy and Jim joined them so the Chief could tell them what he thought they should do.

He pulled everyone into a huddle and said in a low voice, "There's no need to open the truck. Whoever cleared the runway might have left surprises attached to the doors. Remember, there were a lot of military people in this area when the infection went down, and we have to think like the best of them. A random truck sitting at an old airstrip might seem like a prize to some people, but out here, if it looks too good to be true, then it probably is. Let's hold our position while Cassandra's squad clears the building."

It didn't take long for Cassandra to signal that they were all clear, and the two squads regrouped next to the side of the service building where there were no windows. They had the cover of the building on one side and some trees close behind it.

"Well, that was boring," said Cassandra. "I don't think anyone has been here in a long time."

"Nothing but a couple of infected dead in the truck," said the Chief. "Anything inside the building?"

Cassandra shook her head and said, "Nothing but a sign above the door that says *Welcome to New Alaska.*"

"Okay, everyone. Let's get the rest of our people and start walking. No need to leave a guard on the plane. Garrett and Sim have been disabling key systems that we can fix in a hurry when the time comes. We have enough daylight left to reach the Joint Base if we don't run into trouble."

******

"Remind me never to say that again," said the Chief in a voice barely above a whisper.

"Say what?" asked Kathy.

"If we don't run into trouble."

They hadn't made it a single mile when they came to a ragged fence that was a patchwork of chainlink and boards. The materials were placed over the gaps between trees and nailed in place. It didn't run in a straight line, but it went in a general direction to the southwest, and it was solid enough to keep the infected dead on the other side. From the place where they were hiding, they could see another fence about fifty yards away, and it was roughly parallel to the first one. In between the two fences were close to one hundred of the infected dead.

Jim Miller said, "That can't be an accident. Someone created a channel to run them through. Since it goes southwest, I think that's the way the fence builders wanted the infected to go once they got between the two fences."

The Chief said, "I almost always agree with you, Jim, but Anchorage is southwest of here, and the base is almost due north. I'm betting it's a kill zone. A mobile force of people on either side can draw them to the fence and eliminate them."

"You think the ends are open?" asked Jim.

Sim was able to answer the question with a map of the area. He spread it out and pointed to a spot.

"We're about here. This is the trail we crossed a few minutes ago. It's called Old Rondy Trail, and you said at the time it would be easier to follow it than go through the trees, but it was too open."

The Chief nodded and said, "It looks like it goes straight to the Army Base, but I don't want to walk right up to the front door, and if Jim is right that the fences create a kill zone, the Army would be using that trail to travel along the fence on the other side."

Sim moved his hand along the center of the kill zone all the way to the open end at the northeast side and said, "And here's your garden variety natural barrier on the other end. That's not a deep lake. From what I can tell, it's just an area that floods when South Fork Campbell Creek overflows its banks. Any infected dead that get in there will get so bogged down that they won't be able to get out."

Jim said, "That mobile force you mentioned could pick them off like ducks on a pond, but they don't have to. They can just let them rot after they get stuck in there."

Hampton had been listening and pointed out an even more likely scenario.

"After enough of them cross the creek and get stuck in that bog, they'll make a racket. If we keep following the fence to the northeast, we should hear them soon. The sound will draw more of them toward the kill zone, but it will also draw predators that will feed on them."

Kathy asked, "What kind of predators can we expect?"

"Bears and wolves," said Garrett. "I don't think there are any big cats in Alaska…British Columbia, yes, but not here."

"That's good to know," said the Chief, "and bears are hungry this time of year. They're just coming out of hibernation, and the smell of rotting flesh will drive them wild. They'll come from miles away."

"That's why the kill zone is so smart," said Sim. "It looks to me like the infected get funneled toward the wildlife."

"Whoever came up with this idea has time and resources," said Iris. She usually took a back seat to the strategy sessions, but if she ever felt like there was something wrong, she added her two cents to the conversation.

Iris had been a leader in the times before the apocalypse. She had passed up on a permanent relationship with the Chief because she recognized that they were two people who were cut from the same cloth. The Chief was always going to be out front, and so was she. It wasn't until after the infected dead had destroyed so much of their world that they realized they had passed on an opportunity to lead together. She kept her shelter society safe on Governors Island for years, but as soon as it was safe to leave again, she had gone in search of him. Now, they had an equal say in whatever they did.

Iris continued, "The military would have come up with this idea. Creating kill zones is a strategy as old as civilization, and it was taught to everyone in uniform. They would've studied a map just like ours and picked this spot to build their fences. One reason is that living people would stay on Old Rondy Trail while the infected would follow the noise to the swamps."

The rest of the group saw exactly what Iris was saying. It was a way for the military to sort out who was or wasn't supposed to reach safety. If she was correct, someone had created a brilliant way to eliminate the infected dead and provided an 'underground railroad' for survivors. It wasn't hidden the way the term would imply. As a matter of fact, it was out in the open for everyone to see because the infected didn't know what it was. At the same time, it was in the open, so it would draw in the living who followed the trail.

She finished her observation with, "Living people who walk up the Old Rondy Trail will be scrutinized long before they reach the front door, and they will be judged by how they act as they travel."

Chief Barnes felt particularly proud of his wife at that moment, partly because she had presented a strong case for the existence of the two fences but also because she saw something that they had all missed. Whether they had followed Old Rondy Trail or chosen to stay in the woods as they had done, they were most likely already under observation. The question was, how would their observers judge their decision not to follow the trail?

The Chief gestured for the whole group to come closer into a tight circle. With all fourteen of them in a huddle, he was able to tell them all at the same time not to react to the possibility that they were being watched.

Keeping his voice low, he said, "I can't stress enough that anyone watching us will think we're dangerous. The size of our group, the way we move, our weapons. They're going to treat us as a threat until they know otherwise. We have to figure out a way to make them curious about us but not afraid of us. Any suggestions?"

"A white flag?" asked Cassandra. "We would be sending a message that we know they're out there, but we mean them no harm."

Colleen said, "I'm not ex-military like some of you, but I always felt like a white flag was a way of surrendering. I've never really understood how it can be used for a truce."

"It's simple." said Cassandra, "If you wave the flag, you're surrendering. If you send someone forward with it held high, it's offering a truce."

"Offering a truce comes from a position of power," said Tom. "I think they have the upper hand no matter how good we think we are."

"Anyone have a better idea?" asked the Chief.

Next to Shannon, the member of the group who was presumed to be the least likely to provide an inspirational solution was Anne. She was considered to be rock solid as a team player, and she had earned her stripes and survived just like the rest of them, but they had to admit, she surprised them with her idea.

"I kept a souvenir from the shelter in Columbus," said Anne. "I don't know if I ever thought it would be useful, but when our crew got commandeered to fly the President out of Andrews Air Force Base, I don't think he or any of his staff knew what a big deal it was to us. It was history in the making, and to our knowledge, it was the first and last time it would happen under emergency circumstances. Afterward, they treated us like we didn't do anything that made us important enough to save. Anyway, I took something, and I've kept it as a reward I felt like we deserved."

Anne dug into the bottom of her backpack and pulled out a sealed package. She peeled away some tape and pulled out a piece of thin silk cloth. They all saw that it was much bigger than it looked when it was folded, but they all recognized the flag with the Presidential Seal.

Garrett was the most surprised member of the group.

"You kept that to yourself for a long time," he said.

"I wasn't trying to keep it a secret. I just never got around to telling you about it. I thought maybe someday we would build a memorial to Mike and Addison and put this on it. They shouldn't have died in that shelter after surviving so long at the airport."

Tears welled up in her eyes when Anne mentioned their lost friends who had died together, and they all saw how intensely personal the flag had been to her. She handed it across the circle to the Chief, and he took it as reverently as he would pass a folded flag at a funeral for a fallen soldier.

"I'll take good care of this for you, Anne."

"You can only promise to try," she said. "I'm just glad I could help."

Walking under the flag of the Presidential Seal would be enough for the military to be intrigued and, hopefully, not threatened. It would come from a position of power, but the people in charge at the base would want to know their right to claim that position. Introducing themselves as the crew of Executive One should give them that right. After all, they had rescued the President of the United States.

They only needed a few minutes to find a suitably straight tree branch and attach the flag, and it also didn't take long for them to decide that Anne should carry it, and she gratefully accepted the honor.

They formed up in one column and moved south to put some distance between themselves and the fence that marked the kill zone. It didn't take long for them to reach the Old Rondy Trail, where they turned to the northwest. Their next obstacle was in front of them. They would have to cross the open end of the kill zone, and even years after the beginning of the infection, there was no shortage of the dead walking out of Anchorage.

There was still a very thick tree line on both sides of Old Rondy Trail, which made it the perfect cover for whoever was watching them, but despite the forest, they felt exposed. Their best guess was that the military would want to see how they handled themselves if they ran into the infected dead. It didn't take long for them to be put to the test.

The Chief was on point, with Kathy and Cassandra next in line behind him. Anne was next in line, holding their banner high. Garrett wanted to protect his wife, so he was behind her. The rest of them followed behind him. Everyone had machetes drawn because anyone who was keeping score would give them negative points if they used their guns.

From his point position, the Chief told Kathy to pass along instructions that they should only go after infected dead that came onto the trail. The sides were too overgrown, and it was always possible that there would be infected that were lying prone in the brush. If any of them came onto the road and followed them after they had gone by, the two people closest to the rear of the column, Hampton and Colleen, could dispose of them. The Chief said he didn't want to lead a parade of moaning, infected dead to the front gate of the base.

The first of the infected dead stumbled into the open trail near the middle of their column. Tom stepped toward it and silenced it quickly. As he pulled his blade free, he pushed it backward into the bushes. After the first one was gone, it seemed as if there was a constant flow. No one talked because there was never a need to. They just went about the business of doing what they had done since the beginning, and seven years of practice made them perform like a well-oiled machine.

The column moved forward at a steady pace until they gradually noticed there were no more infected dead coming out of the trees on either side. They were past the open end of the kill zone, and they knew they were probably under the watchful eyes of trained killers. The Chief put his machete through a loop on his belt, and the rest of them took it as a signal to do the same. They kept walking quietly and with confidence that the US military wouldn't just gun them down. They were being assessed and judged on their merits, and the Chief was counting on a high score.

Old Rondy Trail came to an abrupt end at a simple gate with a no-trespassing sign dangling from it.

Kathy said in a low voice, "If there's something taped to the other side of that sign, you'll need to gag me, or my laughing will attract a horde."

The Chief smiled at her because the sign also reminded him of the simple gate and sign that led to the first shelter on Mud Island. He couldn't help himself, and he flipped the sign over to expose the other side. He didn't see anything unusual, but he heard the faint click of metal on metal somewhere in the trees.

Cassandra whispered, "Someone just turned off their safety on a weapon."

The Chief turned to face the column of his friends and said, "This is it. Everyone disarm before they have to order us to. We're about to find out if anyone in our armed forces was able to keep things together from the beginning."

Cassandra and Jim Miller were the first to recognize the sound in the distance. It grew louder with each passing second, and they mouthed a word at each other.

"Humvee."

The Chief told everyone to remain calm and just stay relaxed. To Jim Miller, he said, "Jim…you look like you're standing on a parade ground getting ready for inspection. Don't you even remember how to stand like a civilian?"

Jim had to smile at the sarcastic question, but he shifted his weight so it would rest on one hip instead of straight down the middle. It was hard for a career military man to break old habits.

The Humvee arrived less than one minute later. It drove up to the gate on the other side, and a soldier behind a 50-caliber machine gun casually aimed it along a line a few inches above their heads. Inside the vehicle, soldiers sat without moving and sized up the newcomers as if there was no hurry. Whether they were still in the US Army or not, they behaved as if they were. There was a measure of discipline as well as superiority that they had always deserved.

The back seat door on the passenger side swung open, and a man wearing camouflaged clothing stepped into view. The rank on his shoulders was of a Colonel, but he was younger than most men his rank prior to the apocalypse. He was wearing a sidearm, although it was clear that he didn't think he would need it. He calmly walked to the gate and stood facing the Chief. He had to tilt his head backward, but that seemed to amuse him. He leaned to one side to get a better view of the column behind the Chief, and everyone saw him do a double-take.

"Well, I'll be...hi everyone. My name is Colonel Don Daugherty. Then again, Captain Miller already knew that. That is you, isn't it, Jim?"

Jim Miller did his best to keep a straight face as he said, "Never heard of him," but he couldn't stop the smile that spread from ear to ear. Captain Miller walked to the front of the column and held out his hand across the gate. Colonel Daugherty shook his hand warmly, and then the two men broke out laughing and did their best to hug each other with the rusty metal bars in between.

The Chief turned and found his column had broken ranks and gathered in a loose group behind him. They had their arms crossed and were watching Captain Miller and Colonel Daugherty with great interest. When he looked at Kathy, she shrugged her shoulders at him.

"Let's get you guys over to this side of the gate," said the Colonel.

A soldier unlocked a chain that held it in place and swung it open. They all filed through, and it was closed behind them.

Kathy said to the Chief, "I guess we didn't need a flag. We just needed to put Jim up front."

Colonel Daugherty heard her comment and said, "No, the flag was what got you this far...that's for sure. We've been wondering how a well-armed militia wound up on our doorstep under the Presidential Seal. I can imagine there's quite a story behind that. We also noticed you weren't carrying the flag the first time that you crossed the Old Rondy Trail."

He saw their reaction and continued, "Yes, we've been watching for a bit, but that can wait. I've got a truck behind me that's big enough for all of you. Everyone load up, and let's get going. We can take care of the rest of the introductions back at the base. Jim, how about riding with me?"

It wasn't lost on anyone that the Colonel never even mentioned their weapons. As soon as they were all in the back of the truck, they put their heads together.

The Chief said, "No guard riding with us, and they let us keep our weapons. Either that's coming later, or things are better than we hoped."

"I guess we'll know soon enough," said Kathy. She was watching the Humvee behind them and noticed the 50-caliber machine gun was pointed at the sky.

Shannon didn't like being separated from Jim and said, "Is he going to be okay? Do you think that Colonel knows what he did?"

"That seemed like real friendship to me," answered Kathy. She wanted to reassure Shannon, and that was the best she could do.

The Chief said, "Grown men have a hard time faking hugs. I think it was real."

Despite themselves, they had to laugh at the Chief's attempt to sound macho. They had seen him hug everyone, and he was the last person who had to act macho. Someone his size never got accused of being too sensitive.

The truck bounced over the bumpy trail for over a half-hour, and they wondered what was happening behind them inside the Humvee, but all they could do was go along for the ride.

******

Colonel Daugherty handed Captain Miller a silver flask and suggested a sip might help him take the edge off the unexpected reunion. Miller didn't know exactly what he meant by that, so he went along with it and accepted. He handed it back and waited.

After a pause in which the Colonel also took a sip, Jim began to ask what was happening, but his old friend stopped him.

"I'll answer all your questions, Jim, but let me fill you in on a few things before we get to the base. We don't have much time. Our scouts recognized you immediately, and there are a few people who aren't happy about the way you deserted with a hundred or so people and a bunch of Army property."

"Word gets around," said Jim.

"It does, but as it turned out, you were right. It was a dumb idea to bring the infected back to the ships. They lost containment, and now most of those people are dead."

Jim didn't feel vindicated by being right. There were plenty of people on those ships who were his friends, and he would always feel guilty for leaving them behind.

"Because you were right, there are people who are willing to forget about you deserting. You saved a few people. The problem is that we have a few staff officers who still want to go by the exact letter of the Uniform Code of Military Justice. What they can't get through their heads is that the UCMJ never considered the possibility of a zombie apocalypse."

"So, am I going to be pleading my case, standing trial, or what?"

"Well, that depends on you."

"You mean I have a say in it? I'm not following you."

Colonel Daugherty thought it over and said, "We obviously need good people right now. We've lost our hold in too many places to be cutting off body parts just because we don't like what they did. Just by virtue of your survival, you're an asset. I don't know how many people have survived out there in the world, but survivors are special people now."

"What do you need me to do?"

"Just start by telling me what you've been doing since you deserted. Where are the soldiers who left with you, and what can you tell us? While you're at it, tell me what's with the flag with the Presidential Seal on it. Is he alive? Do we still have a continuity of government? We lost contact with almost everyone years ago. You might be the best source of information to arrive at the Joint Base in years."

Jim Miller didn't know where to start. He thought about his first day on Mud Island when he stood in front of the big vault door. Then his mind flashed ahead to his lost time stranded at the bottom of Fort Sumter.

"Don, I think I'm going to need help from that group of people riding in your truck. They can help me fill in the blanks, and there's a lot to tell you. Oh, and we went to England. Wait until you hear that story."

12

Congressman Roy Burgess

Alaska - 1969

He was only in his first term as a junior Congressman from Alaska, but Roy Burgess was reading the handwriting on the walls. The United States had beaten Russia to the Moon, and they weren't happy about it. They were even making noise about taking Alaska back from the US and were claiming native Alaskans were actually native Russians.

The youngest Congressman ever elected to the House of Representatives wanted to reopen the bases on the Aleutian Islands, and he was talking to anyone who would listen about pulling resources from the Vietnam War and invading Russia from the east. He argued that Russia was too busy watching the Germans and NATO, and they would never expect it. He wasn't making friends with congressmen on either side of the aisle.

The only ears that were receptive to his ideas were people in the Department of Defense and the Pentagon. There were plenty of well-placed officials and officers who felt like the money being wasted in Southeast Asia could be put to better use, and they also believed Russia was helping North Vietnam. An invasion of Russia was justified in their eyes, and Alaska was too valuable to lose.

It was during one of his attempts to sway the opinions of a few key

Pentagon officers that the discussion about shelters was broached. He had already treated them to an expensive dinner in one of Washinton's best restaurants, but the conversation became less inhibited over drinks. One of the officers asked if any of the others had heard about the hippy who was getting big money for a shelter project, and he thought the money could be better spent in Vietnam.

Congressman Burgess countered with the argument that Alaska had been the best state in the Union for the Pentagon budget, so any money spent on shelters or Vietnam could be put to better use in his state. He was, however, very intrigued about the new topic, and he wondered who he had to pressure to find out more about the shelters.

As it turned out, he didn't have to leave the table to learn more. None of the officers wanted to be outdone by the others, and even the rumors about the hippy were treated as facts. Of course, Congressman Burgess promised them he was at least aware of the shelters, and his position on appropriations committees gave him access to the information they were sharing. It wasn't the first or last time that information about the shelter projects would be leaked, but the one piece of gossip that was missing from the discussion was the name of the person pulling the purse strings. If he couldn't find out who was making the decisions about the money, he wasn't going to get in on the deal.

It took several months for Burgess to track down the man everyone called the hippy. He caught up with Titus Rush close to home in Oregon. It was only by chance that he had learned the hippy was talking before the members of some club. He thought anyone who had long hair and talked about the end of the world was probably a bit crazy, but somehow, this guy had gotten the federal government to listen. Congressman Burgess felt like he was persuasive enough to get the hippy to support him.

He was wrong. Titus Rush knew who he was before the Portland meeting even began. He surprised the Congressman by walking straight to him.

"Congressman Burgess, welcome to our meeting. I'm Titus Rush, and I wasn't aware that you had been invited. Is there something I can do for you?"

Burgess was caught off guard for a couple of reasons. He couldn't recall ever having a hippy shake his hand, and the man was obviously telling him that it was a private meeting. He had to regroup the way any politician would, and that was by throwing his perceived influence around.

"Well, Mr. Rush, I'm here as an interested party. As a member of Congress, I'd like to see where the money is going, and I learned that you might be spending some of it."

"I'm glad you're interested, Congressman, but not only are you out of your congressional district, this is a private meeting."

Burgess tried his best to make a demand that he should be afforded the opportunity to know what they were doing because he was a member of Congress, but Titus stopped him by shoving a business card in his hand.

"If you have any questions about the nature of our organization, you can feel free to call the number on this card. I'm sure they'll be more than happy to help you."

The Congressman recognized the card and didn't need to read the number to know what it was. It was embossed with the name of the President's Chief of Staff. He also knew he would get a less-than-polite response if he called the number. He had stepped on the Chief of Staff's toes with his demands to invade Russia.

"Now, if you will excuse us," continued Titus, "we have a full agenda, and I'll have to ask you to leave."

Congressman Burgess got yet another surprise when two large individuals stepped in front of him with the obvious intent of removing him physically if necessary.

He voiced his usual protest that included, "Do you know who I am?"

One of the men said, "Yes, we do. The Congressman from this district told us who you were when you came into the room."

Having to leave the meeting before it got started meant Congressman Burgess would be forced to wait longer at the airport, but he put the time to good use. He called each of the Pentagon officers who had spoken too freely over drinks and used their indiscretions against them. He arranged another dinner in a more private setting and told them when to be there.

Their second meeting was two weeks later, but it was the beginning of a long relationship that he would foster through many consecutive terms in Congress. As the officers became eligible for promotions, he would make sure there were no delays. They made sure he got the money he needed for something he called his 'special project.' With his military connections in Alaska, it was no surprise that he was able to divert money and personnel to work on Attu Island.

He had originally planned to reestablish a military presence on each of the islands and then push for an attack on Russia, but since the Congressman was diverting funds, he had to keep it secret from everyone except the officers who were involved. Army engineers were used to classified projects, and this was just another chance for them to do something special, even if they couldn't talk about it.

The 'special project' took six years to build and another year to completely supply. When it was finally finished, Burgess went on a tour of the facility accompanied by the officers who had helped him with the project, and they were all impressed. He might not get to invade Russia, but he was going to survive if it ever worked out the other way around. The group made a pact that included them and their families. If the end of the world ever arrived, they would have somewhere to go.

There was one last detail to consider, and it was relatively easy to arrange. The present and future base commanders of Elmendorf Air Force Base were all included in the secret. Under their watch, they could upgrade the 'special project' and refresh the supplies.

******

No one inside the small circle of Pentagon officers could have predicted the changes in Russia. Congressman Roy Burgess certainly didn't see it coming. In 1969, he wanted to invade Russia, but in 1985, he was in a position to benefit from their willingness to allow American businesses to invest in their country. When Mikhail Gorbachev became the General Secretary of the Communist Party in the Soviet Union, he instituted the policy of *glasnost* and opened the doors to Russia.

The policy caused sweeping changes around the world, and Alaska was no exception. Russian investors found business opportunities in Alaska, and they learned quickly that they would benefit from a friendship with the Congressman. Of course, he couldn't accept donations directly from wealthy Russians, but he could keep his campaign coffers full with generous donations from their American-owned businesses.

His friendships with Russian businessmen took an unexpected turn when his seat as a Congressman was challenged by a popular candidate, and for the first time in his career, he found himself with only a slight lead in the polls. The margin of error was so small that it made the media call the race a tie. Burgess knew he would win if he could squeeze just a little more money out of his foreign friends, and he invited one of them to sit down for dinner in Dutch Harbor.

The wealthy Russian investor, Vladimir Dorokhov, hadn't become rich by accident, but he wanted more than campaign promises from Congressman Burgess. He wanted something personal, and he had heard rumors in Alaska. There were rumors that the Congressman had forged alliances that allowed him to engage in an underground enterprise in the Aleutian Islands, and the rumors had been enough for him to use some of his influence with the Russian navy to investigate.

When they met for dinner in Dutch Harbor, Dorokhov knew the American would want to talk business even before the meal was served. Over drinks, Congressman Burgess went straight to the point and told Dorokhov how grateful he would be for his support.

"Vladimir, I'm glad you agreed to meet me for supper. As you can see, there are business opportunities on the islands that are ripe for picking. All you need is a well-placed friend to make sure the business licenses are expedited. I can be that friend."

"Da, comrade. We have both done well through our acquaintance."

Dorokhov had a very strong accent, but his English was excellent. Still, Burgess had never really gotten used to being called 'comrade.' After all, it wasn't so long ago that he had wanted to invade Russia.

"But," Dorokhov added, "I would like to enjoy my supper before we engage in business propositions. It is always so much better to discuss joint ventures with the comfort of a full stomach."

Burgess thought Dorokhov was an egotistical pig, but he gave him a big smile across the table. It almost made his face hurt because he wanted to do anything but smile. He wanted to know what it was going to take to get this self-righteous Russian to cough up a few million dollars.

As they finished their drinks, the food arrived, and Burgess thought, "Of course, he ordered enough food for an army. It will take him an hour to get through the appetizers alone."

The Congressman reminded himself why he was there in the first place and decided to enjoy his own supper. Dutch Harbor had the best seafood, so he figured he might as well take advantage of the meal that he was planning to write off as a business expense. It beat watching the Russian eat.

Burgess caught himself checking the time on his watch and wondered if Dorokhov had noticed. He had always been a terrible poker player and avoided the backroom games that would often spring up during sessions of Congress. He figured that Dorokhov was playing him over supper, but all he could do was go along with whatever the game was. It turned out that the meal was being used for higher stakes than he suspected.

Dorokhov leaned back in his chair, finally satisfied with the amount of food he had consumed. Burgess thought the dessert alone had enough sugar in it to induce a coma.

"So, Comrade Burgess, I am ready to discuss business. I thank you for allowing me to indulge in this fine food without the bitter taste of negotiations on my tongue."

"You're welcome, Vladimir, but it doesn't have to be bitter. I'm sure we can come to some arrangement that we both would consider to be a sweet deal. What can I tempt you with? Perhaps you would be interested in some land or maybe shares in a few businesses. I'm sure some of my friends would be happy to accommodate you."

"I have land, and I have businesses. What I am interested in would be insurance."

Burgess didn't think Dorokhov was talking about insurance in the traditional sense, but he couldn't think of anything else that fit the word's definition.

"What kind of insurance? I'm not following you."

Dorokhov seemed to think that was funny because he laughed so hard that he had a coughing fit. Burgess felt like everyone in the restaurant was watching them, and he wished he had chosen a more private setting for this discussion. By the time Dorokhov quit coughing, the waiter had visited the table out of concern. Burgess assured him it wasn't serious, but the waiter wasn't satisfied until he heard it from the Russian himself.

After a few sips from his drink, Dorokhov said, "Comrade Burgess, you know what I am talking about. You have insurance, and I want insurance, too."

Of course, Congressman Burgess had life insurance, car insurance, home insurance, and medical insurance. He had to think for a minute or two about what other insurance Dorokhov was talking about.

The only thing that finally came to his mind was something he referred to as 'My little insurance policy,' but that was only around people who knew exactly what he was talking about, and they were all people who had a stake in the same policy. If they wanted to keep their share of the insurance policy, they had to keep their mouths shut.

He thought to himself, "He can't be talking about Attu Island, or could he?"

"Don't start laughing again, Vladimir, but I really don't know what you're asking for."

Dorokhov saw that Burgess was ready to play dumb all night if he had to, and as tempting as it was to play dumb along with him, he was ready to get down to business.

"Comrade Burgess, how much money do you need to win your reelection campaign?"

"Well, uh, I think it's going to be a close election, and I want the public to think I'm getting all the financial support I need, so I think about fifty million should do it."

"You could buy a lot of insurance with fifty million dollars, comrade."

The Congressman felt like screaming and even slapping the arrogant Russian, but he faked that painful smile again.

"Vladimir, why don't you just tell me what you want?"

Dorokhov leaned across the table and said, "I want a piece of *your little insurance policy.*"

All pretense of anything close to a smile was gone from either face. The piercing gaze Dorokhov was giving Burgess dared him to lie about the shelter on Attu Island. The indignation Burgess felt for the apparent betrayal by one of the officers who had been in on the deal to divert taxpayer dollars to build the shelter was overwhelming. His mind rationalized it as treason even if he was sitting across from the Russian willing to do the same for campaign dollars.

"Who told you about that?"

"What does it matter who told me? It is enough that I know."

The staring contest that followed their mutual implied accusations went on long enough for the waiter to notice. He thought he had neglected them, and he could see they were clearly upset. He rushed to the table with two more cocktails and offered them on the house.

The waiter had no way of knowing that he helped distract them from their impasse. Both men sipped their drinks and relaxed just enough to see the other man's side of the situation.

Dorokhov went first.

"Comrade, I am not asking for my country. I am only asking for myself and my family. Indeed, you have more than just a root cellar with a supply of canned food. I am sure you could accommodate a friend and a few relatives. If we are ever faced with circumstances that require…how you say…extreme measures, I am sure you would not turn my family away."

Burgess wasn't the kind of person to let the betrayal go, but he didn't let it show. He was determined to ferret out the officer who had talked about the shelter. It had to wait because he knew Dorokhov wasn't going to tell him, but he could assuage his hurt feelings with enough money.

"If I had known you were talking about *that* insurance policy, I would have said one hundred million dollars instead of fifty."

Dorokhov burst into laughter again, and the waiter felt like he had accomplished his goal with the free drinks.

"Now, there is my American friend. I will make all the financial arrangements through the proper channels in the morning and send you confirmation. When can we arrange for a tour of *our little insurance policy?"*

The last thing the Congressman wanted was to share his secret shelter with anyone, but especially with the Russians. He didn't doubt Dorokhov would tell friends, and they would tell their friends, and so on.

He thought, "I might as well build them a shelter." He also entertained ideas on how to make Dorokhov think he was getting in on the deal but actually wasn't. It wouldn't be hard. "I'll just change the locks."

"We're not that far from Attu Island. Why don't we spend the night here, and after your investment shows up in the right accounts, we can make a detour."

Dorokhov was ecstatic. He made some calls and then announced to Burgess that the transfer of funds would be completed by the time they finished breakfast.

******

The following day was shrouded in the typical heavy fog, and Congressman Burgess preferred it that way. It wasn't ideal weather for flying, but the helicopter would be able to land them within walking distance of the entrance to the shelter.

There were actually two entrances. One was a tunnel that was hidden among the craggy cliffs on the side of the mountain above the shelter, and the other was a cave that could only be accessed by water. The water entrance had been used to supply the shelter because the boats were able to deliver goods without being seen by airplanes or satellites. The tunnel entrance was convenient for short visits to the shelter, and Burgess decided to omit the existence of the water entrance from his tour.

During breakfast, they received the confirmation of the one hundred million dollar contribution to the Congressman's campaign, and even though he knew the money would be easily construed as allowing foreign influence, it was a large enough sum for him to buy his way out of trouble if someone questioned it.

A helicopter was waiting for them, and a short ride later, they were landing on a level plateau on Attu Island. Burgess led Dorokhov to the tunnel entrance and showed him the first of many security measures. He explained to Dorokhov that he would provide him with all of the necessary codes for the different locks, and he had to ensure the codes were stored safely. He also told him the locks were upgraded as technology evolved, and he would receive updates whenever a new security measure was added.

Dorokhov had no illusions about his American friend. A Congressman who accepted illegal campaign contributions wasn't someone who could be trusted. He had already exploited one officer's financial needs to learn about the shelter. He would exploit him further in order to keep up with the security measures, and he would learn how far Burgess was willing to go to break his word. He already noticed how quickly Burgess entered codes and wondered what lock-out features were being kept from him.

The tunnel ended at a large door that Dorokhov rightfully guessed was initially designed for a bank vault. Its rounded edge sat seamlessly embedded in the rock wall that surrounded it. His low whistle of appreciation gave Burgess a small measure of satisfaction, and he boasted that it could withstand a direct hit from a nuclear weapon. Dorokhov doubted it, but he was impressed.

Burgess dialed in the combination without disclosing the numbers, but Dorokhov knew he would get them by the end of the day. He also planned to return to the shelter frequently to test his ability to get inside. If he were ever denied entry, there would be a leak through the proper channels that would be a nightmare for the American politician.

If Dorokhov was impressed by the shelter door, then no single word could describe what he felt once they were inside. The first room was a lavishly decorated atrium with several hallways branching away from the center. Between the hallways, there were elevators and doors that were labeled as emergency exits. Stairwells could be seen through small windows on the doors, and they appeared to go up and down.

"I have to admit," said Burgess, "I stole some of the ideas for the design, but it's not like anyone will care if we ever have to use this place. Follow me. I'll show you some of the good stuff."

It took four hours to show Dorokhov everything that Burgess thought he might want to see. At first, he marveled at the fine dining areas, the suites with their oversized bathtubs and ornate fixtures, and the entertainment facilities. The gyms, the saunas, and the miniature golf courses were all things one might expect from an all-inclusive vacation resort, but something was missing, and Dorokhov was waiting for Burgess to explain it to him.

Burgess showed Dorokhov one of the lounges that could seat more than a hundred people. It was a place where they could enjoy drinks and Cuban cigars. The Russian decided to broach the uncomfortable subject that was nagging at the corner of his mind, and he used the lounge as the stage for his performance.

Dorokhov chose one of the tables and seated himself. He greedily rubbed his hands together and said, "What shall we have? I'm in the mood for a brandy to warm my stomach."

Burgess took a seat at the table, but he looked around the room as if Dorokhov had lost his mind. He was beginning to wonder if the wealthy Russian was seeing people sitting at the other tables.

"Vladimir, why don't we sit at the bar so I can get us each a brandy?"

Dorokhov acted surprised and said, "We must serve ourselves?"

"Well, yes. Who did you think was going to do it?"

Dorokhov went from surprised to deadly serious as if a dark cloud had passed over his face. He regarded Burgess in a way that made the American feel very uncomfortable. The protracted glare and silence confused Burgess, and he didn't know what was causing it.

"Do you plan everything this way?" asked Dorokov.

"I'm not following you. What are you talking about?"

Dorokhov threw his hands in the air and raised his voice.

"Do you realize how often you have said that to me in the last twenty-four hours? You do not plan well, or you would understand. Explain this to me. Why did you build this shelter?"

"So I would have a safe place to go if there was ever a major catastrophe."

"Pick one," said Dorokhov.

"Pick one what?"

The incredulous glare on Dorokov's face was enough to make Burgess think harder, and he realized what he meant.

"A nuclear war," he blurted out.

"Fine," said Dorokhov. "A nuclear war. Now tell me...how long would it take for you to get here if there was a nuclear war? Would it take maybe two...three hours?"

"Well, I guess about that long," stammered Burgess.

Dorokhov continued, "Let us suppose you live that long, and you do make it to the safety of your shelter. Where are the cooks, the waiters, the cocktail waitresses, the housekeeping staff, the mechanics who fix the elevators, and the security forces to protect the occupants? You built all of this like some resort, but how to staff it never occurred to you. Is your wife going to be in the kitchen preparing your meals? She does not do that for you now."

Congressman Burgess was stunned. He had left the logistics behind the shelter's operation up to the officers included in the deal, and he assumed they would staff the shelter with military personnel. He never assumed they would arrive alone, but it crossed his mind as he was sitting with the angry Russian that it would not be a good idea to tell him the shelter was going to be staffed by the United States Air Force and Army.

Dorokhov proved to be much more savvy than Burgess had given him credit for when he asked his next question.

"How many people will this underground *resort* employ?"

"Excuse me?"

"A hotel this size in New York, Madrid, Moscow, or Beijing would employ over one thousand people. Do you think you could move one thousand people to this shelter in two or three hours? It would take days because every staff member would have wives, husbands, children, and parents they would want to bring along. Even if everyone made it on time, you would have maybe two weeks before the staff would become unhappy about the way you run things. They would revolt and throw you outside."

Burgess saw how wrong he had been. He had assumed that he

would continue to live in the manner he was accustomed to and that there would be people who would be grateful for the roof over their heads.

"What should I do?" he asked.

"Leave it to me, comrade. I will fix this. The good news is that we are not likely to have a nuclear war soon."

Congressman Burgess went from the smug knowledge that he would survive an apocalypse along with a few close Pentagon officers to the humble realization that he needed to bring in an outside business partner to fix his mistakes. The officers weren't going to like it, and he still planned to change the locks as soon as possible.

******

Dorokhov wasted no time giving the shelter a complete makeover. An engineering and design team arrived the next day, and one week later, a transport ship loaded with supplies arrived on the island's northern side. Congressman Burgess had been forced to disclose the entrance that could be accessed by water when Dorokhov had been skeptical about the prospect of using the tunnel entrance for some of the large furnishings inside the shelter. Even the vault-sized door wouldn't fit through the tunnel and had to be installed from the inside.

The transport ship didn't leave for several weeks as the engineers converted the underground hotel resort into a fortified shelter. When it was finished and the ship had left, it was time for Dorokhov to take Burgess on a tour. Before they walked through the door, Dorokhov had had to ask Burgess some of the same questions he had asked when they were seated in the lounge.

"Why did you build this shelter, comrade?"

Burgess remembered how the questions had worked out the last time, so he didn't tell Dorokhov he wasn't following him.

"I built it to have a safe place to go during an apocalyptic or catastrophic event. Do I need to pick one again?"

"Pick three, comrade."

"Okay…I'll pick a nuclear war again. I'll also pick a pandemic and, I guess, an earthquake."

"Ah, I see that you are having a hard time forgetting about nuclear war despite the improved relationship between our countries.

Remember, we will be sharing this safe place, so we will assume the threat is from someone else if it is a nuclear attack. Your other events are interesting choices. I do not think an earthquake will make us run for a shelter."

"Okay, you can change earthquake to a meteor strike," said Burgess.

That amused Dorokhov for some reason, but it made more sense than an earthquake.

"An interesting choice, comrade. Our scientists would most likely tell us when the meteor is coming well in advance, and we would have plenty of time to get to the shelter."

"What's your point," asked Burgess, "or are you just playing games?"

"Do not lose your patience, my friend. I simply want you to understand what you will see when we open that door."

Congressman Burgess was getting a bad feeling. Somehow, he had gone from getting rebuffed by a hippy to making a deal with a Russian. Of the two things, he had been bothered more about the hippy, which didn't say much for his general sense of right and wrong, but he suddenly felt like he had signed away his soul to the Devil.

Vladimir Dorokhov entered the combination on the door and spun the locking wheel. The first thing Burgess saw was a man in uniform holding an AK47. The uniform had a patch on one shoulder with a Russian flag on it.

"What's this?" demanded Burgess.

Dorokhov managed to keep a straight face, but he knew Burgess wouldn't be happy. He was ready for the reaction.

"What did you expect, comrade? We have to be sure that no one invades our safe place while we are not here. Did you not plan to make the same arrangements with your generals?"

If Burgess were honest with Dorokhov, he would admit that was the plan from the beginning. He also planned to change the combinations on the locks and even add a few more features to keep Dorokhov out of the shelter. He had to wonder if Dorokhov suspected that.

"How many men did you bring?"

"No more than necessary. There are fifty service people who will cook and clean and fifty more who will provide protection. I selected people who do not have families. Of course, you should do the same. As you will see when we tour the facility, our soldiers will learn to live together under one roof."

The tour took several hours, and the shelter bore no resemblance to the luxury hotel it used to be. Although their private quarters were still lavish compared with the rest of the facility, it was very utilitarian. Although Burgess didn't really object to the changes, he was preoccupied. There was going to be no easy way to tell his military friends that they would be sharing the shelter with Russian soldiers.

13

Standard Flight 260

The Aleutian Islands - The Beginning of the Infection

"Mayday, mayday…this is Standard Flight 260 carrying the Governor of Alaska on an unknown course and altitude. Our last known location was Amaknak Island. Instruments are malfunctioning, and visibility is zero."

Michael Bailey repeated the message and then listened for any response.

"I hate to say it," said Ramos, "but there's no reason to assume the radio is even working. It's a miracle we're even in the air."

Bailey wasn't someone who gave up easily, but he returned the microphone to its hook. He knew that it didn't do much good to broadcast a distress call because they had been flying without instruments for so long. For all they knew, they were flying in a big circle and were back over the mainland.

Ramos heard the resignation in his copilot's voice when he asked, "How long before we reach Russia?"

Despite the situation, Ramos allowed himself the opportunity to at least smile.

"We're in serious trouble, Mike. I still feel like we're going down, but there's a lot more water down there than land, so we have to face facts. Even if we can stop our descent in time, the odds are that we'll be over water. This thing won't float very long."

"What about our passengers?"

Ramos shook his head, and Bailey took it to mean what he had already been thinking. The Senator was definitely dead, and the Governor was probably dead. What the Senator had become was anybody's guess, but there was no reason to believe the same thing wasn't going to happen to the Governor.

Ramos said, "We can't get medical help for either of them and even if we could get to a hospital, I'm not sure there's anything anyone can do. I've never seen anything like that before. Senator Worth was eating the Governor's hand. I mean literally. She was chewing on a big chunk of it."

Bailey hadn't been able to see everything that had happened, but he heard the screaming, and the coppery smell of blood was unmistakable. Despite believing what Ramos was saying, he felt like he should see it for himself, but there was another part of him that felt like it was something better left to the imagination. He opened his mouth to speak but stopped.

"Do you hear that?" said Bailey.

"Hear what?"

Ramos thought he was talking about hearing something in the passenger compartment, and he checked the door to be sure it was locked.

"The sound of the rotors…it's different. It's like the sound is bouncing back at us from somewhere."

Both men had a lot of stick time in the Sikorsky, and they knew if they were blindfolded, they would still be able to tell the difference between flying, hovering, and landing just by the sound of the rotors. They reflexively checked the altimeter, which wasn't moving, and then they both strained to see through the fog.

The sensation of breaking through the fog and seeing the water under them was like dreaming about falling. They pulled up and braced themselves at the same time. Even at a one-degree angle of descent, the seemingly solid black surface of the water appeared to be rushing up to meet them. The impact was loud, and the rotors bowed toward the surface at full speed. As the tips touched the water, they were like high-speed oars slicing through the low waves, and the torque they placed on the machinery that drove them caused the fuselage of the helicopter to rotate.

It could have been much worse, but they were so level when they impacted the surface of the water that the rotors were making contact on all sides. It was better to rotate than to flip over because the rotors on one side dug deeper than the other.

A rotor broke loose on one side and flew past the cockpit. It clipped the windshield and left Ramos and Bailey facing open wind and spray, but they knew the rotor could just as easily have gone through the cockpit and killed them both. As a matter of fact, the cold wind felt good, and it was a relief not to be flying blind anymore.

The relief didn't last long because the cockpit was slowly filling with water. They undid their seatbelts and grabbed the survival kits under their seats. The cushions were designed to be used as floatation devices, but they had the added benefit of an inflatable raft. Bailey pushed it out through the missing windshield and then climbed out as he pushed it ahead of him. Ramos was right behind him, and he slid from the nose of the helicopter into the water.

"Bailey…wait. Don't inflate the raft yet. My feet brushed against something. Can you touch the bottom?"

Bailey let his body bob downward as he pointed his toes, and he was surprised to feel the slippery sand below the water. He turned in the water and saw that they had landed inside a natural breakwater. The helicopter only sank a couple of feet further before it stopped. The rotors were still above the water.

The unspoken questions were mounting up, but one of them was whether or not they should open the side door and let the Governor out. They clung to the fuselage of the helicopter and stood on it where they could find footholds, but during those first few minutes, they both waited for the other to broach the question of what to do about their passengers. When Bailey opened his mouth to speak while looking in the direction of the passenger compartment, Ramos stopped him.

"Don't think about it. Even if either of them is alive, they won't survive long, and after what I saw in there, we won't survive if we try to help them."

Something in the distance caught Bailey's eye. It was directly behind Ramos and wasn't moving, but unless his eyes were seeing things, someone had momentarily turned a flashlight on and off. As his eyes adjusted to the darkness, he could just barely make out the shape of a boat. He pointed at it so Ramos would turn around. It took Ramos a moment, but he finally saw it, too.

******

It was such a relief to find the breakwater and the calm water behind it. As soon as the anchor was in place, the three Russian survivors were ready to collapse from the strain of traveling so far in the dense fog. Their nerves were shredded, and all they wanted to do was sleep, but the realization kicked in that they had actually done it…they had escaped from Russia, leaving something unexplainable behind.

"I could sleep for a week," said Pavel, "but before I do, I think we should celebrate our freedom."

"We still do not know what is happening in America," said Oleg. "Bodies in the water are not a good sign."

"You are such a sad case, Oleg. We can worry about that tomorrow after the sun comes up. Tonight, we should make something to eat and toast our success. We talked about it for months, then we stocked the boat for a month, and then we did it despite the new problems with this strange disease. Right now, there are more people trying to do exactly what we did, but we made it, and they will not."

The boasting by his brother-in-law was usually after he had been celebrating with a few drinks, but Oleg saw the way Galina was smiling, and he realized Pavel was right. They were still not in America, and they had to worry about the disease, but plenty of people were having to face it head-on back in Yelizovo. At least they had escaped from it.

"I am actually starving," said Oleg, "and I think we would all sleep better with a little food and vodka in us."

Galina went to the galley and put on a big pot of water to boil potatoes and cabbage. She added a large portion of cured meat and decided they could spare some carrots. They didn't know if they needed to ration their food, but the occasion called for a little more than bread and butter. Speaking of which, she sliced several large pieces to go with the meal.

It was the morale booster Pavel had wanted it to be. They ate out on the main deck with a lantern on the table, and the rest of the world seemed so far away. The heavily salted stew was a savory version of comfort food, and Galina had cooked far more than they could eat, but that just meant they didn't have to stop eating until they were really full. They laughed and sang as they added more vodka to their glasses.

Oleg and Pavel both grew serious at that exact moment, and Galina thought she had missed something that had been said. They had stopped laughing, and neither was lifting their full glasses to drink. Then she heard it, too. The unmistakable 'whump whump whump' sound of helicopter blades turning but not at high speed.

None of them could tell where the sound was coming from. It could have been right above them or on any side, and they all three twisted and turned with their eyes aimed at the low ceiling of fog. They also ducked as if they thought the helicopter was going to hit them.

It emerged from the thick fog like a frightening ghost only about fifty yards from the bow of the *Svetlana.* It was graceful but also obviously in the middle of a controlled crash landing.

"There," shouted Oleg, even though the others were also glued to the specter that invaded their privacy. He reached across the table and shut off the lantern, plunging them into darkness.

"Everyone stay quiet," said Pavel. "Sound will carry at night and give us away."

All three of them stayed low and watched as the nose of the helicopter tilted upward. It landed on the water hard enough to send a wave all the way to them, and they had a moment of fright when a rotor whistled through the air in their direction.

"What if they need our help?" asked Galina.

Pavel snapped, "What could we do for them?"

Oleg crawled across the deck toward the door that went down to the cabins.

"I am getting my rifle. There could be more of them."

Even in the dark, Galina and Oleg lifted their heads in the direction of the place where the helicopter had magically appeared. At least, that was where they thought it had come from. The only reason they had been able to see it at all was the running lights reflecting from the fog.

Galina said, "We might be the only people who can help them, and they may be able to help us, too."

"Have you forgotten that we have Russian accents? We might not be as welcome here as we hope to be. Wait until we know more about them," said Pavel.

"What do you expect to learn from here? Can you see better than me?"

Neither of them had a really good view of the downed helicopter. They could see its dark shape, and they could tell there was movement on the front of it, but without light behind it, they didn't even know if the movement was people at first. Then, they heard breathless voices as the men struggled through the windshield of the helicopter.

Oleg returned with his rifle and fumbled with it in the dark. He was cursing at it because the magazine wouldn't engage. He only needed a moment to see better, so he clicked on his flashlight just long enough to push the magazine in place. Even though he turned it off almost immediately, Pavel fumed with so much anger he was sure his eyes were glowing red.

"Do I have to tell you everything to keep us alive? Why not just shoot up a flare for them?"

Oleg didn't appreciate the sarcasm and said back too loudly, "How can I shoot at them without bullets in my gun?"

"Hello? Can you hear me? We saw your light. Is it safe to come to you?"

They didn't know how to respond. There were so many unknowns that they were paralyzed into silence. Oleg, Galina, and Pavel thought of themselves as being ordinary, polite people, and they almost felt compelled to answer during that first moment after hearing the question, but then they were ashamed of their own silence. In the darkness, they could almost feel each other beginning to give in.

Galina said in a low voice, "The first Americans we meet need our help, and this is how we answer?"

Pavel had been calling the shots since they had left Yelizovo because the *Svetlana* was his boat, and Oleg wasn't convinced it was safe to help the Americans, but he heard the shame in his wife's voice. They had a golden opportunity to earn the gratitude of someone in need, and they had been too afraid to take advantage of it.

To Pavel, he said, "We must help." Then, in a louder voice, he called out in the direction of the helicopter, "Do you have the sickness?"

The confusion in the voice of the man who answered was obvious.

"The sickness?"

It was rare for Galina to take the initiative around her assertive husband and more assertive brother, but things were moving too slowly for her. She stood up in full view and walked to the railing. She searched her mind for the way an American would speak under the circumstances.

"How many of you are in the helicopter, and are any of you not acting normal?"

She thought she had chosen the wrong words for a moment because the pause that followed was longer than she expected. She was about to ask the question again when the voice across the water said, "I think that's what I meant when I asked if it was safe to come to you. Are we talking about the same thing?"

"These Americans seem like they are afraid of us," said Galina. She cupped her hands around her mouth and called out in a clear voice.

"There is a sickness. It is making people eat each other. It was on the television. Have you been bitten by another person?"

This time, the answer came back immediately.

"No, it's just the two of us. I'm the pilot, and I'm with my copilot. We haven't been bitten. Can we come to you?"

******

On the other end of the conversation, Ramos and Bailey quietly debated what to say. They had pulled themselves up onto the nose of the helicopter just to be out of the water. For some reason, being in the water on such an ink-black night made them nervous. Their eyes adjusted to the gloom, and the island had taken shape in front of them. Then they saw how close they had come to crashing into it and considered themselves lucky to be alive.

"They're Russian," said Bailey.

"We can't be too choosey about our friends right now," answered Ramos. "I don't think we need to tell them about our passengers yet. We weren't bitten, and if they aren't sick, they at least have a boat. All we have is a raft."

Ramos called across the water to the boat and told them they weren't bitten. A few seconds later, they heard the engine on the boat and the sound of a winch retrieving the anchor.

"That beats swimming to them," said Bailey.

It didn't take long for the *Svetlana* to get within a few feet of the wreckage. Ramos and Bailey tossed their gear up over the railing and then accepted the hands that were offered to help them climb aboard.

"Thank you so much," said Ramos. He introduced himself and Bailey and then thanked them again.

Galina introduced her husband and her brother.

"I am Galina Volkov. We are from Kamchatka, Russia, and we would like political asylum."

Galina said it as if she was surrendering themselves to the authorities. Ramos felt like he was supposed to say something back like, "We accept your surrender," but he simply said, "Glad to meet you," and shook each of their hands. He noticed the AK-47 Galina's husband had in his free hand.

"We aren't armed, in case you were wondering."

Oleg acted like he had forgotten he was holding it and apologetically sat it on the deck table where they had been celebrating.

"We also haven't been bitten," said Ramos, "and you may actually know more about what's going on than we do. All we know is something we saw on the news before we left on an assignment this morning."

Galina had become the spokesman for the group, and she said, "All we know is also from the television." She didn't feel like explaining what had happened when they left Yelizovo and were forced to take injured refugees.

She added, "You did not see the news yesterday? You have been flying a long time?"

Galina knew that her Russian accent was not as severe as her husband's or her brother's, and their way of asking questions could sound accusatory. She asked in a softer, inquisitive voice, and it tended to set people more at ease, especially men.

"To tell you the truth," answered Ramos, "Bailey and I knew we had this assignment coming up, but it was a spur-of-the-moment thing. You know, the people we work for had us on standby. We decided to get as much sleep as we could and tuned out the world. We heard some of the other pilots talking about it and caught one news report before we took off. Can you tell us what's happening?"

While Ramos was speaking, Galina noticed that Bailey was distracted by the smell of the stew that still simmered on a deck stove nearby. There wasn't much of a breeze over the water, so the aroma hung in the air like the fog. Anyone who was hungry would be drawn to the appetizing smell.

"We were having supper when your helicopter crashed. Would you care to join us?"

Oleg and Pavel stared at her as if she had committed a crime, but the two Americans didn't seem to notice. Apparently, Ramos had been aware of the smell of the cabbage and meat as much as Bailey. He just hadn't let on. As soon as Galina offered, they both accepted so quickly that she led them to the table. Oleg and Pavel felt like onlookers but followed behind them. Oleg removed his AK-47 from the table and leaned it against the gunwale.

"I'm sorry," said Mike Bailey, "but I don't think we even had a chance to think about food today. We even skipped breakfast because we thought we would have time to eat when we stopped at Dutch Harbor."

Adam Ramos wondered for a moment how forthcoming they could be with the Russians and thought for a moment Bailey was giving them too much information. His hesitation was short-lived when Oleg asked them where Dutch Harbor was. The three refugees seeking political asylum were as innocent as children, and they could tell them anything without risk.

Ramos answered, "It's on one of the Aleutian Islands between here and the mainland. We were flying there for the company we work for when we ran into trouble."

Ramos and Bailey exchanged looks that were short enough but conveyed the same question. It wasn't a matter of national security anymore. It was a matter of life and death for the five people sitting together on the deck of a fishing boat. They didn't know how the Russians would take the revelation of what was happening inside the passenger compartment of the half-sunken helicopter.

Galina scooped out generous helpings of the stew and passed it around. The two Russian men hadn't been able to finish eating either, and soon, the silence was only broken by the tapping of spoons inside the dishes. She made sure everyone got bread and butter to go with the hot meal, and the magic of 'comfort food' relaxed everyone.

"This is delicious," complimented Ramos and Bailey seconds apart.

Oleg gave into the camaraderie of the shared perils they were all facing and extended their generosity even further. He told them he would be right back. When he returned, he had five bottles of his own homebrew beer. The occasion was festive, and it put them in a mood that allowed them to discuss their situation more openly.

"So, you left from the Kamchatka Peninsula. What was it like there?" asked Ramos. "What can you tell us about the news?"

"Not good," said Pavel. "People were shooting at the boats that were leaving. They were calling it an infection, but I think they were wrong on the news. People who die do not wake up and eat people. I think they were *zhivoy mertvets.*"

Galina reflexively did the Sign of the Cross, a Catholic recognition of the Christian belief in the Holy Trinity. She quickly touched her forehead, the center of her chest, and both shoulders. Oleg wanted to do the same but simply bowed his head. Ramos and Bailey both paused with their beers partway to their faces.

"Zhivoy mertvets?" said Ramos. He didn't speak Russian, but in most languages, the second word sounded like it was referring to dead people.

"Zombi," said Pavel. "Dead people who wake up and eat people."

"You don't think a disease, an infection, can make people do that?" asked Ramos.

"No, it is just evil," said Pavel. "Evil like *vampir*. *Vampir* is not a disease. You can become *vampir* by a bite too."

Bailey said, "Wait, are you saying that's what's happening? When we saw reports yesterday, we just thought it was some kind of cult thing, you know, like Heaven's Gate. People thought if they killed themselves at the right time, they were going to hitch a ride on a comet that was passing the Earth. They said it was really a spaceship that was coming to pick them up."

"I do not know of this Heaven's Gate thing," said Galina, "but this is no cult. We saw news that showed videos of dead people pulling the living to the ground and eating them."

"We picked a bad time to cut ourselves off from the outside world," said Bailey. "That's happening everywhere?"

Bailey couldn't stop himself from sneaking a glance across the water to the helicopter. He understood it had happened inches from them, and the only thing that had saved him and Ramos had been the privacy door between the passenger compartment and the cockpit. Ramos saw the glance and knew what Bailey was thinking, but their three hosts had missed it.

They all sat in silence and sipped their homebrew, and Oleg passed out shot glasses of vodka. The food and the alcohol were making them feel warm, comfortable, and, above all else, safe. Ramos and Bailey were both mentally debating if it was the right time to tell them what was inside the helicopter. Neither of them wanted to spoil the good mood. It was Pavel who asked the right question that made it inescapable for Ramos and Bailey.

"So, you did not see enough of the news to know you should stay home. What trouble did you find in Dutch Harbor?"

The tone of Pavel's question was more of a statement of fact than an accusation. It was obvious that he meant the trouble they had 'run into' in Dutch Harbor was related to the same things they had seen in the Russian port where they had escaped.

Ramos drank the shot of vodka, and Oleg immediately refilled it. The Russians knew he was working up the courage to tell them something because he drank the second glass of the strong liquid before answering the question.

"We didn't know what was happening at Dutch Harbor. We only knew that people were shooting at us. The fog was so heavy that it really wasn't safe for us to land, but we needed fuel, and as Bailey already said, we figured we could get something to eat while our passengers took care of their business."

"Passengers?" said Galina.

It was like the group effect it would have if someone standing in a crowded plaza suddenly stopped and began staring at the sky. The longer it went on, the more likely everyone would be doing the same thing, whether there was anything interesting to see or not. Galina's gaze moved in the direction of the helicopter, and everyone joined her, even Ramos and Bailey. Oleg reached for his rifle.

"You won't need that," said Ramos. "They can't get out."

The skeptical expressions on their faces said what they were thinking, but they waited for more reassurance. They had taken the Americans at their word when they said they hadn't been bitten, and it suddenly occurred to them that it was a question that could no longer be asked in the expectation of getting the truth. No one would ever admit to being bitten if it was a death sentence.

Oleg said, "Show me your arms and hands. Put them near the light."

"Now you think we lied about not getting bitten?" said Ramos.

"Wait," said Bailey, "how do you know one bite is fatal anyway?"

"They said it on the news," said Galina. Her voice was just as soft and even as it was when they had first come aboard, but there was a serious undertone that conveyed the message that she agreed with her husband.

Pavel said, "People who get the bite…they get sick, and then they die. They wake up and bite their families and friends. Then they get sick and die. That is what they said on the news."

"Not everyone, though…right?" asked Ramos.

"Yes, everyone," said Pavel. "Roll up your sleeves and hold your arms near the lantern."

Oleg lifted the Kalashnikov to hold it in both hands and stepped back from the table. He used the barrel of it to gesture toward the lamp.

"Okay," said Bailey. "Listen, we're all going to have to trust each other, but I understand. You don't need the gun for us to respect your wishes. Here…I'll show you."

Bailey rolled up both sleeves and put his arms close to the lantern where everyone could see them. He rotated them several times, and the Russians were satisfied.

"Mr. Ramos?" said Galina. "Now you, please."

Galina felt like time was moving slower than her mind. Her mind was rewinding to the memory of the moment when they had helped the two Americans come aboard the boat. There was something about the way Oleg and Pavel had extended their hands to pull them up.

Time caught up with her thinking when she realized what it was that had seemed odd about such a simple gesture, and she heard Ramos offering his token objections to being treated like this.

"I don't know what you expect to prove by this."

He was unbuttoning his sleeves and rolling them up, but his arms were in his lap, unlike his copilot, who had done it in full view by the lamp. When he finished, Ramos stood and placed his hands in view, but he too quickly claimed himself to be clean and pulled his hands back again.

Galina's mind went into rewind again, and she realized Ramos had done everything with his left hand. "Sure," she thought, "he could be left-handed, but even a left-handed person uses their right hand too."

"Put your right hand by the lantern again and keep it there," said Galina.

"Ramos?" said Bailey. The horror was written in the lines on his face because he remembered seeing the flecks of blood on his friend's hand after he had put the oxygen mask on the Senator. He hadn't thought much about it at the time and even started to ask Ramos about it, but he had been distracted by the other events that followed. Flying the helicopter had become his entire focus.

"It's nothing," insisted Ramos, as he held his right hand in the light where everyone could see it. "I cut myself when we went out through the windshield of the helicopter. It's just a cut."

It wasn't a big bite mark like the chunk the Senator had pulled from the back of the Governor's hand. It was a cut along the inside of the third finger in the crease where the finger meets the hand. Even in the uneven light of the lantern, there was a yellowish tint in the middle.

"That's infected already," said Galina.

Ramos laughed nervously and said, "I'm fine. It's not even that deep."

"Why didn't you say something so we could have bandaged it?" asked Oleg. He had seen plenty of people get wounded on the battlefield and not even notice until later, but this wasn't the battlefield, and he was beginning to suspect that Ramos had known more than he had admitted to.

Ramos snapped back, "Well, that's easy to explain. Look how you're all acting. Even my copilot is looking at me like I'm lying. You're acting like a simple cut means I'm going to die."

"That's what it means if the cut came from the teeth of one of the *zhivoy mertvets,"* said Oleg.

Ramos might have convinced them if not for Bailey. He was right when he described the way his copilot was looking at him. Bailey knew the truth even if he hadn't asked about it when it happened.

Oleg motioned toward the bow with the barrel of the rifle.

"Move over there," he said, and his menacing tone allowed his Russian accent to become stronger. "Sit down facing the bow and place your hands behind your back."

"Wait, Mike, you can't let them shoot me. It's just a cut from the windshield."

Galina made eye contact with Mike, and she saw the truth. His eyes couldn't fill in the details about how or when it happened, but they told her Ramos was lying.

Oleg and Pavel took Ramos to the bow and sat him down when he didn't do it himself. While Oleg held the gun on him, Pavel tied his hands behind his back.

"Leave him tied so we can see the cut," said Galina. "I am also going to clean it. If it turns out that he is telling the truth, we will know if it heals."

Ramos pleaded with her the entire time she was cleaning the wound, but she didn't even speak until she was done.

She returned to the others, where her husband and brother were keeping a close eye on Bailey.

"You knew he was lying, but you did not know he was bitten? Please tell us everything about your passengers and what happened. You should also know that I could smell the wound even after I cleaned it."

14

Yacht

Attu Island - The Beginning of the Infection

On an average day back home, people would open an internet browser, search for their favorite news source, and scan the headlines. If they didn't have a computer or internet service, maybe it was the television or newspaper. Regardless, people could only fill the vacuum in their lives with information, and the squad of soldiers on Attu Island had been living in an information vacuum.

Before things had gotten weird, it was all considered to be part of the deal. They were soldiers, and soldiers didn't always get what they wanted. When someone complained about being bored, not knowing what was happening back home, or who had won the ball game, there was always someone to remind them that no one forced them to sign up. Even though there was no one around who could give a firsthand account of what it was really like in World War II, complaining about anything usually elicited a comment or two about what would have happened if the men in the foxholes at the Battle of the Bulge had whined about not having a current newspaper.

When Private Hupp got the satellite link to work in the main salon of the yacht, and the TV came to life, nothing could have been more captivating. They were glued to it as if it were a window to a different world. The time difference between what they were seeing on their screen was about nineteen hours, so the broadcast they were watching said LIVE, but the date and time were yesterday.

"I've never been able to wrap my mind around time differences like that," said Private Ritter.

It wasn't surprising when Mullins said, "I've never been able to wrap my mind around you, Ritter. Every time I try, I just get a headache."

They all laughed, including Ritter, but they settled down when Hupp turned up the volume. There was a young woman behind a podium at the White House who had just gotten a new question from a crowded room full of reporters.

"No, it's not true that the President has left Washington DC for a secure location."

Someone handed her a note, and she said, "I stand corrected. The President is at Andrews Air Force Base getting ready to depart for an undisclosed, secure location. Next question."

The reporters erupted, yelling over each other until the woman singled someone out in the crowd.

"What is the White House advising the public to do?"

"Stay calm and let local law enforcement do their jobs. If you can help in any way, you should offer your services."

The next question was more direct, and it wasn't something that could be brushed off with the type of placating answers the woman had been giving.

"The police are shooting people in the streets, and there are reports they're even shooting each other. Are you saying that's their job now?"

The young woman leaned toward the microphone, and everyone in the room waited in silence as she appeared to be searching for the best answer to the question. They were shocked when she suddenly stood upright, put her shoulders back, and turned her head in the direction of the man who had handed her the note.

"They left me behind? I'm the President's Press Secretary. I was supposed to go with him in the event of an emergency, not stay behind and cover for him."

With all the dignity she could muster, she walked from behind the podium to the door. There were questions shouted at her, but she didn't act like she heard them. The man who had informed her of the President's departure stepped up to the microphone and raised his hands to get everyone silenced.

All he said before following the Press Secretary out the door was, "Go home."

"That channel wasn't too helpful," said O'Reilly. "Can you get something that tells us what the hell is going on?"

"I'm trying, Sarge, but the satellite connection isn't actually a TV service if you know what I mean. Give me a minute," said Hupp.

"I don't want any 'talking heads'. Get me something that's showing what's happening in the streets."

The only light in the salon was the TV set, and everyone became serious when Hupp succeeded in his attempt to get a major network's broadcast. It was New York City, and the network spokesman, a gray-haired man in an expensive suit, said they had moved their cameras up to higher floors because their lower floors had been compromised.

Mincy asked, "What does he mean by compromised?"

The only answer she got back was a "Shhhh."

The cameraman was aiming downward from the tenth floor, so he was able to pan left and right for blocks.

"My family lives in New York," said Private Talbot.

No one told her to "Shhhh."

The obligatory black and white banner about graphic content being disturbing to viewers ran across the top of the screen while a red and white one traversed the bottom with headlines about death tolls and other apocalyptic messages.

"This is it, isn't it?" said Mincy. "This is the big one."

It was almost as if the cameraman heard her. He had zoomed in on the chaos in the crowded street below and inadvertently found a ridiculous subject to watch. A homeless man wearing a "sandwich sign" was attempting to bite another man who he had pinned to the side of a car, but the bulky sign was getting in the way. The harder he tried, the more the sign came upward between them, but it was the message on the sandwich sign that had caught the attention of the cameraman and probably Private Mincy. It said, "The End is Near." The man pinned against the car finally broke free and ran, but he didn't make it far. He pushed his way into a crowd that succeeded where the homeless man had failed. When he fell to the pavement, the crowd fell on his back like the rats had done on the beach. The writhing mass of bodies was eerily similar.

A large gathering drew the attention of the cameraman, and the gray-haired man in the suit felt as if the scene below needed to be narrated.

"We see police officers in riot gear dispersing tear gas on the crowd, but it doesn't seem to be working on them. The crowd isn't falling back. We can practically smell the tear gas up here."

He must have been telling the truth because he coughed a few times before pulling his head inside the window. His eyes were red-rimmed, and a producer wearing a headset went to his rescue with a wet rag. He carried on as if he were trapped in the same nightmare as the people in the streets. Maybe he would be later, but it wasn't likely to be the sting of tear gas in his eyes that made him scream.

As is often the case, unimaginable events elicited comments from the soldiers watching the chaotic situation, and Ritter couldn't resist. He got the ball rolling by asking, "Where was she with that wet rag when sandwich-guy was trying to make a meal out of that dude?"

"For real," said Talbot. "She must be an intern or something."

Other comments overlapped until O'Reilly shut them all down.

"Stow it, you guys, or we'll put all of you outside to stand guard while we watch."

The banner running across the bottom of the screen said, "Infected dead overwhelm crowds of refugees in Time Square as New Yorkers evacuate."

The police front lines were visible after the tear gas cloud disappeared, and they could see several officers use tasers on people who were pushing against their plastic shields. The blue arcs of electricity appeared to make their bodies twitch, but they continued to push. Instead of falling down in spasms on the ground, they kept reaching for the officers.

Every soldier in the salon wanted someone to tell the police they had to shoot their attackers in the head, but they had to watch helplessly as the officers learned what they already knew. When the frontline went down under the relentless pressure of the crowd, the next row of officers instinctively pulled their friends backward, but the infected dead always fell on their prey as soon as the officers went down. Those officers being pulled backward were already being held in place by as many as six attackers, and the attackers were already biting their victims.

The guns came out as fellow officers were lost, and the cameraman stayed with the action. The soldiers saw that the police had learned where to shoot the infected dead the same way they had. The withering barrage of gunfire melted away the massive crowd of infected dead, and the narrator, who had resumed his commentary from a spot behind the cameraman, said that the police had the situation under control.

"We can see that there were many, perhaps dozens, of injuries among the ranks of law enforcement, but it appears that they have reestablished their frontlines and removed the injured officers to safety where they can treat their wounds."

Mullins got up and walked straight to the TV. He put his face only a few inches from a spot before he said, "Check this guy out. Isn't he the dude that 'sandwich guy' was trying to eat? Now he's trying to eat someone. Is that how the infection spreads?"

Corporal Mullins hadn't been up and down between Sergeant and Corporal because he was dumb. He just lacked self-control. O'Reilly and Gleaton moved up next to him to be sure he had spotted the right man. It was hard to tell because he had been partially eaten, but they felt like he was right.

Lieutenant Gleaton said, "It still could be just close contact that gets you infected."

He was already shoulder to shoulder with Mullins, but when Mullins turned toward Gleaton, his nose was practically in the Lieutenant's ear.

"By close, do you mean this close, Sir? Because I had to grab that one trying to bite Talbot by the neck. Do you think that means I'm infected?"

Lieutenant Gleaton made a vain attempt to back up from Mullins, but O'Reilly was there, and he was several inches taller and much bigger.

O'Reilly leaned forward and said, "I think Mullins is trying to tell you that it spreads by bites, Sir. If close proximity can spread it...well, we're all going to be rat food soon, so let's be optimistic."

The cameraman zoomed in on the wall of plastic shields. The police were definitely eliminating the attackers, and the bodies were creating a natural barrier for them. They were able to shoot from a greater distance, but that wasn't doing anything to help people who hadn't been infected yet. From where the camera was located, they could count dozens and dozens of cars that were drawing the attention of the infected dead. That led them to assume the cars were occupied by living people.

Ritter said, "Let me get this straight. If you get bitten, you die. If you die, you start biting people. That means all of those police officers who were pulled back to safety but got bitten are a risk to the people who saved them."

"You don't always make sense," said Mullins, "but you got it right this time."

Corporal Mullins was a bit rough around the edges, and he picked on Ritter so often that it was expected. There was something different this time, and it worried them all.

"So, that's New York," said O'Reilly. "Hupp, can you try to find another broadcast? Come back to that one if you can't find anything better."

"Sure, Sarge. Now that I have the hang of this system, I can check almost anywhere."

"Anything closer to home?" asked the Lieutenant.

A few moments later, they were watching a broadcast from Los Angeles, and it was ugly. The camera was located on a section of freeway where vehicle traffic was at a total standstill. As for foot traffic, it was flowing between the cars like a river. From time to time, people with guns would stop long enough to shoot between the cars, but it wasn't clear what they were shooting at. The camera never moved, and their guess was that the reporter and cameraman had joined the flow of people who were escaping.

There didn't seem to be an end to the mass of men, women, and children who ran by the camera, but suddenly there were only cars and trucks. The river of running people had dried up. Everything was still.

"What happened?" asked Talbot.

"Wait for it," said O'Reilly. "Wait for it."

Between the cars about a hundred yards from the camera, there was movement. It was still too far away to tell what was happening, but a lone figure took shape. It appeared to be a man who was doing his best to run, but he would only make it a few steps before he fell down. When he got up, he lifted a pistol and fired a few shots back in the direction where he first appeared. Then he tried again to run by leaning against cars.

Behind the man, there was suddenly another river of people, but this river was flowing more slowly. They filled every gap between cars that were within the frame of the camera lens. There was no way to estimate the number of people in that slowly advancing river, but the soldiers didn't need to hear a number to understand what it meant to the city of Los Angeles.

They silently watched as the man stood between the cars and waited as the flood approached, and no one thought less of Shirley Talbot when she couldn't hold back a sob. Most of them wanted to yell at him to keep running, but when the unknown man lifted the gun one last time to put the barrel against his own head, they agreed with his decision. For millions of people in the world, it was a far better fate than what they got.

O'Reilly said, "Find me a talking head, Hupp."

An airport was the next location, and there was an attractive, dark-haired reporter standing in front of one of the massive runway windows where passengers could sit and watch the planes come and go. Hupp turned up the volume, and they all recognized her southern accent.

"From what we're hearing, this frightening scenario is playing out all around the world. Flights are still coming in and leaving, but the status boards are filling up with more and more canceled or delayed flights."

She gestured toward the window, and the cameraman dutifully turned to show a crowded runway where flights waited for clearance to take off.

"We've been told that there are over one hundred flights that have taxied away from their gates and are waiting to take off, so there are around twenty-five *thousand* people on airplanes that are in line. We tried to find out how many planes were waiting to land, but we were unable to get an exact number. When we pressed for more information, we were told, "Too many."

The reporter said, "Hold on," and put one hand on the side of her head. Everyone knew that she was listening to an earpiece and receiving new information.

"We're being told to leave as soon as we can. We don't know why because everything here seems perfectly normal, with the exception of the even larger-than-normal crowds. We'll move closer to the gates to see if we can learn anything to report before we leave."

The reporter led the way toward the gates, and the cameraman did his best to stay focused on her and the TSA checkpoints ahead. She glanced back at the camera and attempted to fill in the gaps with useless information, but the cameraman had stopped advancing. The reporter was obviously confused, but gunshots cleared that up in a hurry. Still, she wanted to cover the story, so she didn't take cover the way everyone did around her.

The cameraman had worked with her before, and he knew her as being determined and talented. She was one of the few he had worked with who appreciated his part of the job. He wanted to help her get the story, but he never wanted to have the camera aimed at her at the exact moment she died. She was facing him when her entire body jerked, and a red spot blossomed on the front of her white and floral printed blouse. Her eyes were opened very wide, and the expression on her face was as if she was waiting for the answer to a question. Then she collapsed to the floor.

It was doubtful that the cameraman tried to record her after the stray bullet hit her, but it was so sudden that he sat the camera down without turning it off. He ran to her and did what he had seen medics do in the field. He checked for vital signs, and then he began giving her CPR.

All seven members of the Attu Island Army squad were standing in front of the television as if their encouragement would help. They had all been trained in CPR, and they counted along with the cameraman as he pumped her chest with his fingers laced on top of each other. Mincy had the palms of her hands on her cheeks, Talbot had hers clasped together in prayer. No one noticed the new bandage on her arm. Most of the men had their hands balled into fists, either at their sides or in front of them. They aimed their ferocity at the TV as if the cameraman needed their energy.

When the dark-haired reporter's body jerked in one long spasm, they couldn't have cheered harder for her or the cameraman for saving her life. They hugged each other and cried openly, and O'Reilly was even ready to approve another round of drinks. Then the unthinkable happened…the reporter's long arms circled around the cameraman's neck and pulled his head down to her waiting mouth. With a feral shake of her head, she pulled back from him and tore away an incredibly large piece of his face. He fell backward onto the floor, and only the lower half of his body stayed in the camera frame.

The previously jubilant squad of soldiers watched in stunned silence as the blood-soaked woman crawled onto the man's legs and further until she was no longer visible. The cameraman's legs bucked out of control, and they didn't have to see what was happening to know how it all ended.

The question they all had on their minds was obvious, and they searched each other's faces to see if anyone had even a spark of understanding they could share. O'Reilly walked away from the group and set up a row of shot glasses on the bar. They all quietly followed him and accepted the drinks. Mullins was the one who broke the silence.

"We all saw it, and we all know what it means. I don't need to see it happen again to understand. If anyone doesn't get the picture, now would be a good time to speak up."

Most of them just studied their empty glasses, but no one asked for more information.

"Hupp, can you get us a different broadcast? I think we've seen all we want to of Atlanta for now."

Private Hupp made some adjustments on a console, and when the new station appeared on the TV, there was a collective groan from the squad. They all recognized Anchorage.

******

Anchorage was a city of just under three hundred thousand people. On bright days, the Chugach Mountains seemed to reflect light down on the city, making it appear to be a painting rather than an actual city. It was beautiful in every sense of the word…but not today.

It was the middle of the night, and the fog that blanketed Attu Island seemed to stretch to the parking lot of the Sullivan Arena. The chilly, foggy weather was cooperating with the catastrophe that had covered the world. As Mullins had said earlier when they walked along the soggy beach, "Great night for just about anything to go wrong."

He hadn't known at the time how right he was. Standing in front of the wide-screen television on the yacht, he felt like he had it pretty good compared to what he was seeing. He wasn't over the shock of watching what had happened to the reporter in Atlanta yet, but he was having to wrap his mind around a familiar place being overrun by dead people. He had parked his car by that arena a hundred times, and it was always because of something fun. It wasn't what he would call a fun place to be right now.

The local news channels had all retreated to the arena, apparently because that was where the municipal authorities had told everyone to go when the hospitals had become too crowded to receive more patients. There were schools and churches that were also designated as shelters and first aid centers, and a banner at the bottom of the screen was listing them. The Sullivan Arena was mixed in with the other names, but it was a popular choice because it was centrally located.

Reporters were lined up on the roof of the arena, and they were doing their best to stay on camera as they moved from side to side, pointing at the chaos below the building. The entire scene was bathed in red, flashing lights as ambulances had found random places to park. The paramedics unloaded their stretchers and rushed them inside to the triage areas. Many of the patients were connected to IV bags that were held high by the people trying to save them.

The banner on the TV said there was an update from the police. It said not to go to any of the shelters and that it would be safer to stay at home. It went on to say that injured patients with bite wounds should be sedated if possible, but that the hospitals could not offer treatment at present. The second part of the update was about a different part of the unfolding apocalypse. It said the police had been given the authority to use deadly force against anyone who disobeyed a lawful order.

"What does that mean?" asked Ritter.

Mullins said, "I was just starting to think there was hope for you. Don't you remember when we got here and we told those people to stop? They didn't stop, so we shot them. That's what they mean. I'll bet there are cops everywhere telling people to stop or they'll shoot."

One of the reporters pointed toward a fire engine below them. It was extending its ladder toward the roof of the arena, and there were already people on it waiting for it to reach the ledge. When it came to rest a few feet from the cameras, several TV stations caught footage of police in tactical gear climbing up the ladder. Even before they all reached the roof, they turned toward the crowded parking lot and poured a barrage of bullets into the sea of people. The screams from the crowd were drowned out by the sounds of the weapons, but when they stopped shooting for a few seconds, there were a few screams and calls for help, but mostly there was silence.

The reporter was doing her best not to cry, but she was failing. She said through big sobs that they didn't know why the police were shooting everyone. She had just finished making the comment when the shooting resumed. One of the officers stopped firing long enough to approach the reporters. The broadcast stayed on the air just long enough for the soldiers on the yacht to hear him tell reporters to turn off their cameras. There were protests, but the screen went blank. The banner reappeared at the bottom of the screen. It said that viewers should lock their doors for safety.

"Should I try to get another station?" asked Hupp.

O'Reilly had a better idea, and he whispered something to the Lieutenant. Gleaton nodded, and the Sergeant told Mullins to take Mincy, Talbot, and Ritter onto the beach and make sure the perimeter was secure.

Mullins gave him a suspicious look and said, "Sending the kids out of the room?"

"I'll fill you in as soon as I can, Lou."

O'Reilly only called him by his first name when it was about something he preferred to keep between them. Mullins caught the familiar gesture, and he trusted O'Reilly. He knew when to argue with him and when to help him.

Mullins raised his voice in the direction of the soldiers and said, "Mincy, Talbot, and Ritter…you're with me. Let's move out and make sure the beach is still secure."

If there was any hesitation, none of them let it show, but they couldn't help thinking about what they had seen, and they knew there was a chance that they would find more dead people outside. They went down the steps to the swimmers' platform and clicked on their flashlights.

"Someone pop a flare when we get to the bow," said Mullins.

In the salon, O'Reilly said, "Hupp, you've done good, but what's the chance you can raise the Joint Base on this gear?"

"I can try from the bridge or from the communications center, Sarge. This boat has a pretty impressive setup. I think we can talk with anyone in the world as long as the power holds out."

"Lead the way, Private."

The communications center was a small room. The officer and NCO had expected it to be bigger by what Hupp had said, but as he explained, it wasn't the size of the room that mattered. It was the quality of the equipment. There was a computer with a large wall-mounted monitor on a compact desk, and Hupp booted it up. A password window opened, and Hupp typed just like he was on his own computer.

"Wait a minute," said O'Reilly. "How did you know the password?"

Hupp sheepishly grinned and said, "People are lazy, Sarge. This boat is so new that I figured the crew hadn't bothered to change the password that was used when someone set up their WiFi. If the boat broker did it for them when they bought the yacht, he would've used the name of the boat, and I saw plenty of monograms around this thing to guess the boat is named *Virginia.*"

O'Reilly shook his head, but he had to admit, these young people they were stuck with on this rock they called an island were a sharp bunch.

A menu came up with a list of connection options. It was an easy choice because one of them was labeled *Satellite Communication.* There was one that said *SOS Distress Signal,* but he told Hupp they didn't need to be rescued...yet. O'Reilly pointed at *Satellite Communication,* and Hupp clicked on the selection. Another menu opened, and Hupp didn't ask which one to select before choosing one because the choices included *Military Bases.* The logos of the bases in Alaska appeared as a grid of boxes, and Hupp clicked on their base. It was like joining a conference call over the computer, and it even emulated the sound of a telephone ringing.

It rang twelve times before a recorded message was activated. The message said they had reached Joint Base Elmendorf-Richardson, and the channel was not secure. Due to the nature of a developing threat, no transmissions could be accepted at this time.

"Hang up and try again," said the Lieutenant.

Hupp went through the selections a second time and got the same results. As soon as the message began, he selected the option to connect again. This time, the face of an angry Specialist appeared on the screen, and she erupted into a string of profanity-laced critical comments about the unknown caller's heritage and life expectancy. She stopped short when Lieutenant Gleaton replaced Private Hupp in the camera frame. She just as quickly launched into an apology.

"Save it," said Gleaton. "Tell me about the developing threat."

"Yes, Sir. Would you like for me to get the Duty Officer?"

O'Reilly touched Gleaton's arm lightly and then pointed at his watch.

"Don't bother, Specialist. Just tell me what's going on. We're stuck out here on Attu Island, and we could use a ride home if something's happening that we should know about."

"Attu Island? Sir, an exfiltration team was dispatched to your location yesterday. They didn't arrive?"

The implications of her answer caused O'Reilly to lean in front of the camera and ask her, "Do you think we would be asking you for a ride if they had arrived?"

This time, the Specialist didn't ask if they wanted to speak with the

Duty Officer. She just disappeared from her station. A moment later, she was replaced by a Lieutenant who introduced himself and went straight into something that sounded like a prepared speech.

"Operational security has been compromised, and all available resources have been redirected toward a defensive posture. Secondary objectives, such as the repatriation of units deployed to foreign territories or remote domestic locations, shall be delayed until further notice. Once all threats are neutralized, attempts will be made to bring all assets together under one command."

Before Gleaton or O'Reilly could say a word, the connection was terminated, and the Joint Base logo reappeared. Gleaton was so furious that he clicked the links to reconnect. The message read by the Lieutenant appeared on the screen below the logo word for word. Gleaton did the connection steps all over again. He was on his fifth attempt when O'Reilly gently stopped him.

"I think we're on our own, Sir, but when we get back to camp, Hupp can try on our secure gear."

15

The Last Detail

Attu Island Shelter - Before the Infection

The shelter that was manned by a joint force of United States and Russian military troops remained a secret for over fifty years. There were the expected disagreements from time to time, but neither side wanted their respective governments to know the truth. Problems were dealt with quietly and on the Russian side, brutally.

The Pentagon officers who had kept the secret would have lost the stars on their shoulders if they had been discovered, so they quietly retired from service without disclosing what they knew. There were rumors, but nothing ever surfaced that caused an investigation.

Vladimir Dorokov and Congressman Roy Burgess died ten years apart. Dorokov had a massive heart attack, and Burgess died in a hospital after a prolonged illness. Despite the turn of events, Burgess had all the time he needed to change the combinations on the doors and install some additional security measures that would prevent intruders. Without a replacement for Dorokov, the shelter was finally controlled by the Americans.

As for the soldiers and support personnel assigned to the Attu Island shelter, they were shipped home so gradually that they hardly noticed there were fewer people living with them inside the massive structure. The existence of the shelter was classified as Top Secret, and if anyone ever talked about it to family or friends, it was something that generated no interest.

Only two people had sufficient knowledge of the shelter even to be curious about it. One of them, Governor Brandon Burgess, the son of the long-time Congressman Roy Burgess, never went to the shelter. When his father died, he discovered a folder that told him enough to know it wasn't something he could share with anyone. It would ruin the family name if anyone found out his famous father had misdirected tax dollars.

The other person who was curious about the shelter was the current Commandant of Joint Base Elmendorf - Fort Richardson. His predecessors didn't leave a complete paper trail, but Lieutenant General Patterson found enough breadcrumbs to make him wonder if there had been a top-secret operation in progress on Attu Island. He decided to send a detail of soldiers to the island with minimal information, and when the time was right, he would have them explore the suspicious location. He told the officer in charge of the squad that the operation was under the direction of SATCOM and that he would be given more information later.

Attu Island Shelter - The Beginning of the Infection

"We still have a job to do out here," said O'Reilly. "Lieutenant Gleaton, Sir? Would you mind telling me what that job is? I mean, now that someone has left us hanging out to dry on this hunk of ugly rock, you might as well tell us."

The young Lieutenant didn't feel like he deserved to be treated the way he was when he contacted the base. His squad also deserved better, so he nodded in agreement.

"Everybody should be together for this, Sarge. I'm sure you wouldn't mind waiting until we get back to camp."

"Actually, Sir, I would mind. I have a feeling that things are a lot more dangerous out here than we thought. I just need to know enough to help me keep my people safe."

O'Reilly had never bucked the system before, and he was known for his even-handed approach to officers and enlisted people, so it wasn't lost on either of them that he was being a bit more on edge with his boss. Gleaton considered it and knew he had to give the NCO something.

"Don't be disappointed in my answer, but I don't think our mission out here and the strange events tonight have anything to do with each other. I think it's just bad timing."

"No disrespect intended, Sir, but I think you have a future in politics. Did you just tell me there's nothing you could say that would help me keep my squad safer?"

"That would be a fair interpretation," said the Lieutenant.

O'Reilly said, "I don't know why that makes me feel like you answered my question because I still don't know what our mission is, but I'll accept it for now."

Gleaton didn't want to lose O'Reilly's support, so he quickly added, "I'll tell everyone at the same time when we get back to camp. I promise."

Hupp had stayed out of the exchange between his two superiors but held up a hand to get their attention.

"Do y'all hear that? I think it's Mullins."

All three of them listened. Hupp was right. He was further from the yacht than they thought, but he was yelling. It didn't sound like he needed help, but he was definitely letting everyone know he wanted them to come to him.

O'Reilly and Gleaton left the salon of the wrecked yacht and navigated the slippery stairs to the swimming platform. Hupp took a few moments to gather a few of the communication components that might be useful but caught up with them on the beach. Ritter, Talbot, and Mincy saw them coming and waited for them, and then they all ran to the sound of Mullins' voice.

The fog hadn't lifted an inch, and Mullins would have popped a flare if he was in trouble, but O'Reilly considered the possibility that Mullins was unable to light up the area.

"Someone give us some light," he yelled. "Make it a red one."

Corporal Mincy had anticipated the order and had a flare ready to go. She aimed it so it would be over the approximate area where Mullins' voice came from. The red burst painted everything a bright shade of red, but they could see him almost immediately. Beyond his position, there was a kind of movement that was already becoming familiar to them. The sideways swaying of a crowd walking in his direction with a slow determination made the squad break into a run.

They formed up on the left and right side of Mullins, and O'Reilly asked the Lieutenant to give the order. He didn't hesitate, and they all fired together. Since they knew it would take headshots, it was over in seconds.

As soon as they were all eliminated, Corporal Mincy asked, "Where did they all come from?"

Mullins pointed toward the base of the mountain.

"Remember that path of disturbed sand when we thought one of them might have walked inland? It was more than one. They probably reached the dead end, then heard our gunfire and came back."

"Which means," said O'Reilly, "we just made enough noise to call for more of them."

Ritter said, "You think there could be more?"

The red light of the flare made it easier for everyone else to see the way the Sergeant and the Lieutenant looked at each other. There was something they both knew. The others all turned toward Private Hupp because they knew he had been inside the communications room while they were outside. He did his best to avoid their questioning gazes.

O'Reilly made a command decision. "Listen up, people. Something's happening on the mainland. Hell, it's happening all over the world. The yacht might not be the last boat to reach our little corner of paradise, and if I'm reading this right, not everyone will show up by boat. We're going to move out and double-time back to camp, where the Lieutenant is going to give us a briefing. Let's go."

The squad moved quickly because none of them had the urge to be exposed on the beach any longer than they had to. On the way toward camp, they were surprised by the number of rats they saw going in the opposite direction.

Mullins phrased it best when he said for the whole squad, "At least there won't be any of the furry little predators around our camp."

Before they turned inland to go toward higher ground, they stopped twice along the beach and shot several more people who seemed to be walking right out of the water. Even as they were taking care of the ones already on shore, three more stood up in the gentle surf.

Private Talbot asked, "Is that what you meant, Sarge? I don't see any boats."

"Yeah, Talbot. That's exactly what I meant. Everyone keep in mind that some may have walked ashore already. Watch for tracks, and when we reach rocky ground, I want flashlights checking every shadow."

Once they were away from the beach, they crossed rugged terrain where nothing could leave footprints. The flashlights turned on, but on higher ground, they were traveling with their heads in the fog.

Ritter said, "This is spooky. All we need is for one of those things to pop up out of nowhere."

O'Reilly usually told them to knock off the chatter, but even he was reassured to hear their voices. Most of all, he wanted to hear each of them so he would know they hadn't lost anyone.

"Those things used to be people, Ritter," said Mincy. She was having a bit of difficulty processing the fact that they were each responsible for several kills in such a short time.

Mullins answered, "They weren't people when we shot them, Mincy."

"If they weren't people, what were they?" she snapped back.

"I think," said Mullins, "we can all agree they used to be people."

Shirley Talbot said, "We can't go around calling them that."

More than one of them said, "What do you want to call them."

O'Reilly was mentally ticking off their names on a list to keep track of who was there. He was just about to ask Hupp and Lieutenant Gleaton what they wanted to call the things that used to be people when Hupp spoke up.

"Zombies…we should call them zombies."

Gleaton said, "Do you believe in zombies, Private Hupp?"

"I do now, Sir."

O'Reilly realized that he had the same word floating around in his mind, but he couldn't quite bring himself to say it until he heard Hupp get it out in the open. It still didn't just roll off his tongue the way he wanted it to.

"If no one has any better ideas," he said, "we're going to name them in the long-standing military tradition until we know what they are. We're going to call them Personnel, Infected Transients, or *PITS* for short. Any objections?"

"Why Transients?" asked Private Hupp.

O'Reilly answered, "Look up the word, Hupp. One of the definitions is something that produces results beyond itself. I think it's fair to say these things exceed expectations. I don't understand how they even manage to walk."

No one objected, but giving them a name to go by only made it easier for them to know what someone else was talking about if they wanted to say they saw one. One reporter had called them 'infected dead,' but it was easier to call them PITS. It didn't make anyone feel better either way.

They reached the plateau where their camp sat well above the beach, and they had a reason to be grateful for the first time since their arrival on Attu Island. Nothing could climb up to the camp on three sides, and the fourth side was a steep climb. A PIT could crawl up the rocky hill, but it would be difficult.

They all went to the mess hall except Private Hupp. Since he had been there for the brief exchange between the Lieutenant and the Joint Base, there was nothing else he needed to hear. He already knew their mission, and he didn't really want to be there when the rest of them found out an exfiltration team had been sent to get them a long time ago.

O'Reilly told everyone about the transmission and what they had learned, which was close to not much at all. What they knew for sure was that they were on their own for the time being. He turned the meeting over to Gleaton with the announcement that the Lieutenant was going to tell them about their mission.

It was only five sets of eyes on him, but Gleaton felt the stare of each one. It wasn't that their mission would be such an unbelievable task. It was going to seem like a dumb thing to be doing when they could be home with families to deal with whatever was happening in the world.

"Okay," he began, "let me start by saying the Commandant of the Joint base specifically created this mission. No one else in the Air Force or the Army knows about it."

"We're not a Black Ops unit," said Ritter. "We aren't even Special Forces, Sir."

"No one would mistake you for a Ranger or Special Forces, Ritter," said Mullins.

They had to wait for the laughing to stop before he could continue.

"I said it was top secret. I didn't say it was an impossible mission. The code name is *armageddon*, and the CO wanted to keep it small. He wanted us to explore the island after he figured out where he wanted us to search."

"Search for what, Sir?" asked O'Reilly.

"Some kind of installation hidden on the island…something like a fallout shelter or doomsday bunker."

"Why all the cloak and dagger stuff?" asked Mullins. "If the government put it here, why not tell us what we were supposed to be looking for? It's not like we would've written home about it."

Gleaton thought it over and realized he had been asking himself the same questions, and given the current state of affairs, he didn't see why he couldn't be honest with them.

"The best answer I can give you is simply that I don't know either. The CO said he would let me know where and when to search, and he never gave the order to start."

"Wait a minute," said O'Reilly. "Are you saying he told you where but not when?"

Gleaton nodded. "He said the search should be on the side of the mountain. There's a path about two hundred yards north of here that may lead to a tunnel."

"Great," said Mincy. "On an island infested with rats, I was really looking forward to going into a tunnel."

There was a moment of silence when everyone had a chance to digest what they had just been told, but it slowly dawned on them all that the two problems weren't related to each other. There was something they were supposed to find, but the plans were interrupted by the arrival of the infected personnel.

"That's what you meant back at the yacht when you said this was just bad timing," said O'Reilly.

Gleaton nodded at him. He didn't have anything more that he could tell them.

"I know you have questions," he said, "but I don't have any answers. I think we should stay where we are for the night and go hunting for this top-secret installation tomorrow. Hopefully, we won't have as much fog, and at least we won't have to go down to the beach and deal with PITS."

"What about back home, Lieutenant? Can we find out what's happening?" asked Mincy.

"We can listen for broadcasts, Corporal, but I don't think we're going to be able to communicate with anyone."

Lieutenant Gleaton hesitated before he gave her his answer, and everyone noticed. He could tell by their expressions that they were waiting for him to tell them what he was holding back. He broke down and told them the truth.

"The last orders I got were never rescinded. They included no direct communications with anyone except SATCOM, and SATCOM isn't talking. We can monitor transmissions, but we can't disclose our location. I can tell you one thing. I have a family on the mainland, too, so I'll do everything I can to get permission for us to communicate with them."

******

It was hard for any of them to sleep that night. They tried to get settled in, but they felt more like keeping busy. Shirley Talbot broke away from the group for a bit to change the bandage on her arm. She said the PIT that grabbed her arm scratched her with a fingernail, and it itched a lot, so she wanted to clean it out better. A couple of them started letters to their families back home, but no one finished. There wasn't much they could say, and there was no promise that they would ever get mailed.

Mullins had been correct in his observation about where the rats would or wouldn't be. They were not scratching at the camp doors, which should have been a relief, but it made them wonder how many PITS there were if they satisfied the appetites of so many rats.

Most of them ended up playing cards and just watching the clock, but Mullins decided they needed something to help them get their day off to a good start. He went to his kitchen and did an inventory of their supplies. If they were really on their own, they were probably going to be rationing their food soon. The best thing he could do was make sure that nothing spoiled, so he put together a large breakfast. He was greeted like a conquering hero when he called them to chow earlier than usual.

As they dug in, he yelled, "Don't any of you dummies go and get sleepy after you eat. This meal is supposed to charge you up."

It was sunrise when they finished breakfast, and despite seeing a few yawns, O'Reilly suspected the squad was more nervous than sleepy after a big meal. They squinted at the morning light because they weren't greeted by rain or fog. For the first time in weeks, it was a clear morning.

They didn't have long to feel elated after they had gotten off to a good start. To their surprise, the remains of a human body were only about twenty yards down the steep slope they walked up only a few hours before. Whether they wanted to call it a PIT or an infected dead, this one had been a crawler, and it had crawled even as the rats had eaten it. If that wasn't disturbing enough, there was a dead rat between the teeth of the PIT.

Ritter, who was never at a loss for words, could only say, "Wow."

O'Reilly knelt down to get a closer look at the rocks on the path that led back to the beach. They were streaked with blood as far as he could see.

"The rats were eating it the whole time it crawled. They must've gotten to the brain here."

"Sarge," said Private Talbot, "If it took that long to reach the brain, there couldn't have been much left of it by then."

"What're you saying, Talbot, or are you just making observations?"

"I'm just making a point about how determined they are. It seems to me that they're just going to keep coming if you don't stop them. Don't let them corner you, is all I'm saying."

"I don't plan to, Private. Besides, that's what we've got each other for, right? You did make a good point, though. None of us can get separated from the rest of the squad."

They strung out in single file and followed the path down to the beach. It didn't take long for them to confirm where all of the rats had spent the night. The beach was littered with bodies and rodents, and the big breakfast Mullins made for them became more of a curse than a blessing. Most of the PITS weren't moving anymore, but if they were, they were also eating rats. One in particular was still on its feet. It had a rat pressed against its face, but it had dozens clinging to its body. It was eating the rat as if it was unaware that it was being eaten.

"Should I end it?" asked Mullins.

"Don't bother," said Sergeant O'Reilly. "It'll be over soon enough, and we might need the bullet."

They kept a wary eye on the beach as they skirted the eastern shore of the island. They were going to be walking further than they had since coming to Attu, so they weren't sure how far it was before pushing inland. According to Lieutenant Gleaton's estimate, they would need to watch for anything that resembled an entrance to a cave. It could be large or small, but he suspected it would be difficult to see from a distance. After talking it over with O'Reilly, he decided to send scouts to higher ground while everyone else followed the shoreline.

Corporal Mullins and Private Ritter were walking along a ridge about a quarter of a mile above them when Mullins shot off a white smoke flare. The rest of the squad moved from the beach to the rocks and searched for the best path to climb higher. Mincy found what they were looking for, and they fell in behind her as they navigated the treacherous terrain. No one had to warn them to be careful. The last thing any of them wanted to do was make someone else have to carry them back to camp because of a careless step and a broken ankle.

They eventually reached a plateau that angled sharply down toward the mountain. At the bottom of the plateau was an opening in the rock face that was about the size of a garage door. It had to be what they were looking for.

"No wonder no one could see it from the beach," said Gleaton. "It's twenty yards below the top edge of the plateau."

"We're going in there?" asked Ritter.

"The PITS won't make it that high, Private, and I don't think the rats are going to come home any time soon," said O'Reilly. "Besides, you and Mincy can stay out here and keep watch while the rest of us go inside."

They clicked on flashlights and stepped carefully into the dark opening. O'Reilly unwrapped a chem stick and dropped it along the side of the tunnel near the floor. That was when he realized the tunnel was man-made. The floor was smooth concrete.

"I think we're in the right place," he said as he pointed at the floor.

Over the years, the tunnel had been explored by rats, but there was very little debris. Inspection of the walls showed that they had been coated to prevent the rodents from burrowing into any of the cracks. No roots from vegetation outside had been able to penetrate the walls, and no spider webs hung from the ceiling.

They knew they had reached the end of the tunnel when they came to a large door. In their wildest imaginations, they couldn't have known their reactions were the same as a Russian businessman and a Congressman decades ago. Nor could they guess that they had also called it a bank vault door.

"We're definitely in the right place," said Lieutenant Gleaton, "but how in the world are we supposed to unlock that?"

O'Reilly turned toward Hupp and asked, "What's that game you're always playing?"

"You mean Sudoku, Sarge?" asked Hupp.

"Yeah, whatever, Hupp. Doesn't it look something like this?"

He pointed at a large square grid next to the door.

Mounted on the wall like a permanent plaque was a metal grid that was perfectly square. The grid was subdivided into nine smaller grids, and each of them contained nine squares. Some of the squares had numbers in them, but most of them were blank.

"Do you think this might be a clue that will give us the

combination?" asked the Sergeant.

Hupp only needed a moment to examine the plaque before he answered.

"This looks like a Sudoku gameboard. There's no doubt about it," he said.

"So you can fill in the rest of the numbers, right?"

Hupp shook his head. "If you're asking me if I can beat this with the given numbers, the answer is definitely, but this isn't like a computer version. It only starts you off with twenty-five numbers. That means you have to get fifty-six numbers right. If you miss a number along the way, you won't know until you can't put in another correct number."

O'Reilly frowned at him.

"I didn't say I want to learn how to play Sudoku, Hupp. I want to know if you can do this one. You went to cryptography school. Can you make sense of this?"

Hupp let out a frustrated sigh and said, "And I'm telling you, this one is likely to take time. Twenty-five numbers aren't much to start with. It's going to take a while, but even if I beat the game in twenty minutes, what does the game have to do with the lock? A combination lock has around sixty-four thousand possible combinations. How will eighty-one numbers on a Sudoku board help you figure out a combination?"

The lock on the massive door was a standard combination lock, and they knew there was no possible way they could try every combination. Hupp was correct that they needed to know only six numbers, and they were also going to need to figure out the relationship between the game and the lock.

Hupp added, "There has to be a key that will tell us which numbers on the Sudoku board are the combination and what order they'll be in."

"Do you have somewhere else you need to be, Private?" asked O'Reilly.

"No, Sergeant."

Hupp knew the question was rhetorical. He sat down his backpack and rummaged through the contents. He dug out a notebook and pencil and sat down across from the plaque. Everyone else got comfortable to wait while he figured out the puzzle. What he didn't tell them was that he already had a fair idea which of the numbers had something to do with the combination.

Of the twenty-five given numbers on the board, three of them were

0's, and twenty-two were the numbers 1 through 9. Twelve of the numbers had circles around them. Anyone who played Sudoku would know there aren't any 0's in the game. The grids should only use the numbers 1 through 9. Hupp knew he would have to replace the 0's with the correct numbers that would, in turn, allow him to do a complicated puzzle.

He thought to himself, "This is going to take a long time. There are only thirteen numbers that don't have a circle around them, but I don't know if that even has anything to do with it." He didn't realize he mumbled and sighed again until the sergeant warned him.

"If I hear one more heavy sigh, the rest of us will go outside and wait while you do the puzzle by yourself."

Two hours later, Private Hupp thought he was going to run out of notebook paper before he finished the puzzle. Doing it on a digital device was much easier because it would tell him when a number was wrong, but on notebook paper, he wouldn't find out if a number was wrong until he hit a dead end. Every time he came to a dead end, he had to backtrack to find out where he had made a mistake. He felt like it would have been easier without the distracting zeroes already filling three of the boxes. It was like doing a crossword puzzle with a pen. It made you commit to your answers even if they were wrong.

"Ah, man…why didn't I think of that sooner?"

Hupp drew the puzzle again, but this time, he left the 0 squares blank so they wouldn't mess with his thinking. The mind has a funny way of dealing with mistakes, and he immediately found the puzzle was easier.

"I'll just circle the numbers that had zeroes in the squares when I'm done," he mumbled. Saying it out loud triggered something in his mind, and he added, "That could mean the number one with the circles around them might be the clues."

O'Reilly glanced at him, but he could see the young soldier was almost excited as he filled in the numbers, so he stayed quiet.

It only took twenty minutes for Hupp to finish. When he was done, he studied the results for a minute and laughed hard enough to grab at his sides.

Everyone moved closer to see what he thought was so funny, but all they could see was a bunch of jumbled notes and wadded-up pieces of paper. Hupp flipped back to his first page of paper and held it up in one hand.

"Does anyone else see what I see?" he asked.

* * *

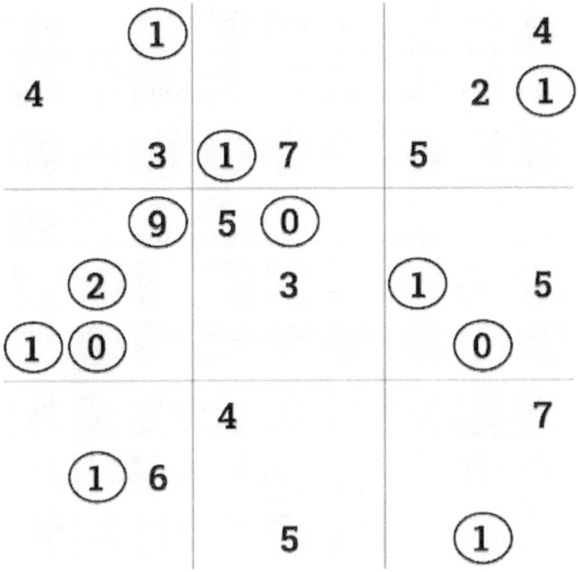

Mullins said, "I think he's lost his mind from trying too hard to solve the puzzle."

"That's just it," said Hupp. "I almost lost my mind trying to solve it, and most people would've given up."

"Get to the point," said O'Reilly. "You figured it out?"

"Yeah, Sarge. I figured it out when I realized what the 0's and circles mean. They're nothing but distractions. The rational mind is always going to take what's given as fact in a puzzle and try to make the pieces fit. The simple truth is that there are no 0's in Sudoku, so I eliminated them. After I had them out of the way, I saw that I was left with circles around some numbers but not all of them, but this time, I did what a rational mind would do and eliminated the numbers that weren't circled. Here's what I had left."

Hupp handed O'Reilly a piece of paper with a row of numbers on it. There were seven ones followed by a two and a nine.

1 1 1 1 1 1 1 2 9

O'Reilly wanted to say something sarcastic, but instead, he decided to let Hupp have his moment of triumph.

"Go on. Somehow, I get the feeling you're going to tell me the combination is in those numbers."

Hupp said, "Most people want to remember a password by leaving a clue. One grid has all the numbers circled, so I figured that's a clue that the 1, 2, and 9 are in the three pairs of numbers in the combination. I decided all those extra 1's had to go somewhere, so I paired three of them with the first three numbers."

Hupp took back the piece of paper and added two more rows of numbers to it.

1 1 1 1 1 1 1 2 9

11 - 12 - 19

1 - 1 - 1

O'Reilly thought he saw where Hupp was going with his explanation, but he wasn't sure yet.

"You're saying 11 - 12 - 19 is the combination? In what order, and what are the extra 1's for? Why not 21 instead of 12?" he asked.

Hupp was beaming and savoring the moment.

"Consistency is important to the pattern. You wouldn't be able to use 91 in the combination, so I put the 1's in front of the key numbers. Once I had the numbers, I assigned them their corresponding letters from the alphabet because they would spell out a word that would tell us the order. Obviously, you could assign a letter to 19, but not 91. I got this when I made them into letters."

11=K 12=L 19=S 1=A 1=A 1=A

K - L - S - A - A - A

A-L-A-S-K-A

"Eleven equals K, twelve equals L, nineteen equals S, one equals A, one equals A, and one equals A. So, that gives us K, L, S, A, and A. Rearrange the letters, and you get ALASKA. Throw out the vowels, and you have your combination," said Hupp.

O'Reilly smiled and said, "LSK...12 - 19 - 11. You're a genius, Hupp."

Lieutenant Gleaton said, "I can go one better than that. You just got a field promotion to Corporal."

16

Reunion

Joint Base Elmendorf-Richardson - April 2023

Their arrival at the base was a novelty to the people stationed there, and large crowds of Army and Air Force personnel turned out to see the civilians they were already calling the 'militia.' The Chief was glad they had chosen not to wear the British Navy coveralls they sometimes wore on missions. The outfits had proven to be durable, but it would've been confusing to their hosts.

When the truck stopped and they climbed down from the back, there were hushed whispers about the Chief's size. He was used to it, and he did the same thing he always did. He flashed a big smile at the onlookers. There were two things that people agreed on when they met the Chief for the first time. He was one of the most unique physical specimens they had ever met, and he had an infectious smile. Despite the fact that he and the people with him bristled with weapons, the crowd felt compelled to smile back.

Colonel Daugherty said, "I can see your friend is already charming the troops."

"That's just the way the Chief is," said Jim Miller. "When you talked about being an asset because I survived, I couldn't help but think about how many times I wouldn't be here if not for him. He's your real asset."

"Well, let's get you guys a place to stay before you meet with the brass, and by the way, that's going to be soon. I'll send someone by to process your people and bring them up to speed about the base."

"Process my people?"

"Sure...I assumed you'd all want to stay. We could use some people who've spent a lot of time in the field. We've got some folks who've earned their stripes fighting the infected dead, but your group has literally lived out there."

Jim Miller had already made up his mind about one thing. He didn't plan to tell their hosts about the shelters. He hoped it was something they could eventually share, but he didn't want to say anything without talking to the Chief. Something was making him feel unsettled. He didn't have a clue what it was, but he was experiencing a nagging feeling a friend of his had labeled as 'free-floating anxiety.' He couldn't put his finger on the source of his anxiety, but until he figured it out, he planned to hold his cards close to his vest.

On the long trip from South Carolina to Alaska, the Mud Island family had spent hours talking about the possible scenarios that would play out once they arrived. Besides keeping the AC-130 and Miller's identity a secret, they had considered the implications of disclosing the network of shelters. If the United States Air Force and the Army were still functional, then the shelters would go a long way toward rebuilding society. On the other hand, what they had to consider was the possibility that a rogue military command would be a threat to the shelters. They had already seen that disaster play out in Wyoming and Huntsville.

Colonel Daugherty led the way, and Jim signaled the Chief and others to follow. It felt strange to be walking around in the open, but the sense of security they all felt within the base meant the combined units of the Air Force and Army had secured the area. As a matter of fact, they noticed that no one else was even armed.

It was a short walk to a standard issue field tent big enough for a large squad to use. It had been specially erected within the last hour when advance word had been received that they had guests.

"We're sleeping in a tent?" asked Kathy. "Is it going to be warm enough?"

Cassandra answered for the Colonel, "It's called TEMPER now, Kathy. It's short for Tent Expandable Modular Personnel, and we've slept in worse places, right?"

Kathy caught the wink that Cassandra discretely gave her. Captain Miller wasn't the only former military member of the group, and apparently, she was sensing something was a bit off, too. They watched the Chief to see if there were any outward signs that he was picking up on any red flags, but if he was seeing any, he was hiding it well. Of course, that's why he couldn't get any of his oldest friends to play poker with him anymore. He was just too hard to read, and right now, he was making everyone like him.

"This will do just fine," said the Chief as he extended a large hand to Colonel Daugherty.

After the Colonel shook his hand and announced he would give them a few minutes to get settled in, they filed into the tent. They exchanged lighthearted chatter, but they spread out and did a thorough search of the tent for bugs. They had been given folding cots and blankets, so there weren't many places to conceal electronic hardware, but they wanted to be sure before they talked.

They gathered together in a circle on folding chairs and cots to compare notes and lay out a plan.

"Without any way to sweep for electronic devices, that's the best we can do," said the Chief. "I don't imagine they're going to give us much time before Jim gets invited to a private interview, so let's get our cover stories straight."

It only took a couple of minutes to agree on one of the stories they had concocted on the way to Alaska, and it excluded any information about the shelters. They could always say they withheld that information until they were sure they weren't disclosing something that was a threat to national security.

"Okay," said Kathy, "the next order of business is personal. None of us are married or even in a relationship. That removes leverage if someone gets interrogated. We also don't let them separate us or take our weapons."

"I've been thinking about that a lot," said the Chief. "Why doesn't anyone have weapons? Why didn't they take ours? Are they going to try to take ours?"

Hampton said, "I'm not the military expert here. For that stuff, I'll defer to you guys who served, but from my personal point of view, they didn't because they can't, or they couldn't yet. So, that leaves the leverage issue. When they take Jim in for a private meeting, they could hold him hostage until we surrender our guns, or they could come at night."

"They could've done that already," said Iris. "They already had Jim separated from us, so they could've taken him to a different place. They also had us bunched up in the back of the truck, and all they had to do was point that fifty-caliber machine gun at us, and we wouldn't have stood a chance. I think they need us for something, and they plan to ask us first. If we refuse, then we might see them change their tactics."

"So, we're still in the intelligence-gathering business for now," said the Chief. "Everyone got their story straight?"

The timing was good because Colonel Daugherty chose that moment to arrive. With him was a woman wearing an Air Force uniform with Staff Sergeant stripes.

"This is Staff Sergeant Harlow. She's going to give you all a basic orientation. You'll need to know things like the location of the latrines, showers, and mess hall. If you don't mind, she's also going to collect some information from each of you for our personnel records. Jim?"

Daugherty held aside the flap at the entrance of the tent. The Chief gave Jim Miller a discreet nod that no one else could see, and Jim left with the Colonel.

"Hello, everyone," began Sergeant Harlow. She was pleasant enough and clearly a bit nervous. She appeared to be in her late thirties, slim to the point of being too thin, hair pulled back into a ponytail that made her look even more gaunt.

Susan noticed a slight tremor in Harlow's hands as she pulled a folding chair around to sit. The rest of the group noticed it, too, but Susan was the one who interrupted the NCO as she began her presentation.

"I'll be your liaison until you know your way around and get assigned to duties. If you have any questions, don't hesitate to ask."

"I have a question, Sergeant. What's your first name?" said Susan.

The question wasn't expected, and even though Harlow opened her mouth, she didn't seem to know how to answer for a moment.

"Uh…Tina," she stuttered, "but I don't know if they would want me to tell you that."

Susan stopped her and said, "Don't worry. When someone else is around, we'll call you Staff Sergeant Harlow."

That seemed to put her at ease, and they saw her visibly relax. The Chief and the rest of the men hung back from them as the women in the group subtly drew closer. If they were reading the situation correctly, Susan wanted to take the lead.

Susan laid one hand on the Sergeant's hand to stop her from writing for a moment.

"Tina, before you get started, when's the last time you ate?"

The question was as unexpected as the request for her first name, and judging by the pause from Tina, she was just as afraid to answer. The women didn't wait for the pause to end. Colleen dug into a backpack, pulled out an MRE, and got it ready to eat. Shannon, Iris, Kathy, Cassandra, and Anne all drew their chairs and cots into a tighter circle with Tina.

The men slowly moved in pairs to different parts of the large tent. Garrett and the Chief took up positions by the entrance. Tom and Hampton went to the back corner where they could listen for outside traffic. There was a flap that could be folded aside and tied open, and they used it to get a view of the main runways where planes still sat in rows. Jon and Sim did the same thing at the opposite corner.

Tina Harlow was caught off guard, but she couldn't resist the gentle concerns of the strangers. The MRE version of pasta couldn't be called fine cuisine, but the smell was almost worth savoring to someone who hadn't eaten lasagna in years. To someone who hadn't eaten meals on a regular basis, it was heavenly. She stared at the food as Colleen heated the package, and they could see tears well up along her eyelids.

Susan opened a bottle and shook out a pill.

"Here, take this before you eat, Tina, and let me check you out. I'm the doctor for this crew."

Tina accepted the pill and took it with a drink offered to her by Kathy. She didn't even ask what it was.

Susan said, "That was a multivitamin."

She took Tina's hand and inspected her fingernails. Just as she suspected, there were signs of anemia, and the nails were brittle. Tina didn't resist as Susan completed a physical because she was too busy eating. Colleen let her feed herself, but she made her give the spoon back after each bite to keep her from eating too quickly.

While Tina ate her food, Susan explained to her what she was finding and told her she wanted to monitor her for a few days. She also asked her what had happened at the start of the infection, how they had survived, and how many other soldiers were in need of basic medical care. She seemed afraid to answer at first, but then she opened up.

Tina's Story - The Beginning

"The base went to an alert status at sunrise when a civilian ambulance arrived. I was already on base because I was on sentry duty at the munitions storage facility. There are a lot of hospitals in Anchorage, so the guards posted at the gate got really worked up about an ambulance that was making a high-speed approach with flashing lights on. They sent out a broadcast over the base alert system so all of us sentries would know something was going on."

Tina paused to collect her thoughts because it had been seven years since that day, and a lot had happened since then.

"Take your time," said Colleen.

"Even though they knew it was likely to be an emergency for an ambulance to be using its siren and lights, they didn't open the gate. They weren't allowed to, as per standing orders. One of them stood in the road with a hand raised like he was supposed to while the other sentry put himself in clear view with his M4 where the driver could see it.."

"Did the ambulance stop?" asked Colleen.

"From what I heard," said Tina, "it was close. The ambulance driver braked hard and stopped just in time. He was yelling something about an injured officer. They said he had three stars on his uniform. They could've gone to the medical center in town, but they figured the military would want him at the base hospital."

Susan said, "If the patient was a Lieutenant General, you can bet they preferred to have him on base."

Tina continued, "The guard still needed to see who was inside the ambulance. You know, he couldn't just take their word for it, and he really didn't want to believe the base commander was who he would find on the stretcher in the back. The driver yelled for someone to open the doors, so they were swinging wide by the time the guard got there."

"Was it him?" asked Susan.

"It was definitely an Air Force uniform, but the guard couldn't be sure. The man had an oxygen mask on and was covered by so much blood that he could have been anyone. The EMT holding the mask in place gave the guard the General's jacket, and there was no mistaking the three stars on each shoulder or the nametag on the breast pocket. The other side of the jacket was almost completely covered by the

General's campaign ribbons. The EMT told him the wallet was in the pocket if he wanted to see his ID."

"Did the EMT know what happened to him? Where was his driver and security detail?" asked Colleen. She knew the General wasn't likely to be driving himself.

"I don't know, but the guard made a judgment call and decided there wasn't time for them to answer a lot of questions. By then, there were Air Force Security Police on standby inside the front gate, and he yelled for them to escort the ambulance to the hospital. After that, he called the hospital and the Duty Officer."

"That probably made everything get crazy," said Susan.

"More security officers were sent to all points of entry to the base," said Tina, "and an order was issued to restrict all movement to essential services. Over thirty thousand people worked on the base, and since it was still so early, most of them hadn't arrived yet. Traffic was backed up for miles from each gate. Guards screened cars one at a time and turned away nonessential personnel. All active duty personnel received an automated message to report to their respective units unless they were on duty somewhere, which I was."

Colleen asked, "Did they ever find out what happened to the General?"

"We didn't know until later, and by then, it didn't really matter, but the General had gone to an early morning breakfast meeting with the Mayor. On the way, his car had been hit by a car that was driving on the wrong side of the road. By the time the ambulance could make it through morning traffic to the wreck, the General's driver was already dead. One of my friends who was stuck in traffic told me a lot about what happened out there."

"What did you mean when you said it didn't really matter?" asked Colleen.

"Well, you probably know from experience what happened when the General died at the hospital."

"All too well," said Susan.

"After the ambulance left for the base with the General, his security detail had to sort out the cause of the accident with the local police, and that was when they learned for themselves that there was something else going wrong."

"By something else, you probably mean the infection was spreading," said Susan.

"Right," said Tina. "The driver of the other car had been trying to reach the hospital when he crossed the centerline of the highway. He was badly injured in the accident, but the EMT with a second ambulance noticed an open wound on the man's leg that had been crudely bandaged by someone else. When she peeled back the gauze that was wrapped around his leg, she saw that a large piece of the muscle was gone, and there were several smaller wounds that matched human bite marks."

Tina went on to describe the events of that morning as if she had watched it on the news instead of living through it. Much of it she heard from people who survived long enough to reach one of the gates.

******

In the early morning hours before sunrise, a pattern of similar injuries was reported across the city. Every ambulance available was dispatched to calls, and by sunrise, drivers were refusing to respond to more. Those EMTs who saw for themselves what would happen if a patient died abandoned their vehicles and went home on foot. Some went back to the hospitals with patients, but as soon as the stretchers were unloaded, they parked their vehicles and left the keys on the dash. Some of them drove home with ambulances so they could use the flashing lights and sirens to navigate the congested roads more quickly.

The guards at the gates were told only to admit military personnel, and if their dependents were with them, they could be allowed on base if they presented their dependent ID cards. Civilians who worked on base were escorted to a place to turn vehicles around.

It was two hours later when the guards at all gates were told to stop anyone who was wearing a bandage. By then, the base hospital was as full as the hospitals in Anchorage, and over a thousand vehicles had entered the base. Less than an hour after that, Base Security Police were responding to reports of assaults, specifically related to human bite wounds, and the order was given to close all gates.

Spiked strips called stingers were spread across the pavement at every gate, and barricades were erected. Armed Security Police were given the order to shoot anyone who attempted to enter the base, and even though they didn't question the order, they were surprised that the specific wording of the order was to aim for the head. Within one hour, there were shots fired at all six gates, and most of the people who were shot were wearing Air Force or Army uniforms.

Word spread rapidly outside the gates, and people who were trying to enter the base began fighting their way through traffic to go in the opposite direction. Uniformed people who didn't believe they would be shot only needed to get close enough to the front of the line to see what had happened to cause others to turn around.

From inside the gates, guards and Base Security Police watched as steady streams of vehicles approached, did U-turns, and drove away, but less than an hour later, the process stopped. Somewhere at the other end of the column of vehicles leaving the base, there was a traffic jam. It didn't move again.

By ten o'clock that morning, people had gotten tired of sitting in their cars. Some were facing the gates, some were parallel to the gates, and some were part of a long row of tail lights that disappeared in the distance. There was a ripple effect as car doors opened in all directions. The doors of the cars farthest from the gates opened first, and it resembled a sporting event where fans would do a 'wave' from one side of the stadium to the other.

At first, the doors opened, and people got out of their cars. After a few seconds, they ran. Most of them ran toward the gates until they were too close. Warning shots were fired, and the general direction of the runners was to go left or right along the perimeter of the base. Then came a lull when there were no runners...just empty cars with their doors open.

Between the cars at a great distance, crowds were gathering, and the crowds moved forward at a slow but steady pace. The gates coordinated with each other, and they all reported they were observing the same phenomenon. The immediate speculation was that the people who had been turned away were coming back together. The order to shoot anyone who attempted to enter the base was confirmed to all gates, but riot control measures should be used first.

At each gate, a squad of soldiers wearing gas masks moved forward and launched tear gas canisters into the advancing crowds. They withdrew and waited for the gas to do its job. The people walking slowly toward the gates were all unaffected, and a second round was launched. It became obvious that the approaching crowds were a threat just as a timely message was received at each gate. The message was that guards and police should not wait until people attempted to enter the base. They should shoot anyone walking in the direction of the gates.

Humvee-mounted fifty-caliber machine guns were rolled into place at the gates, and the process of elimination began. Of the thirty-two thousand people who would have been on the base on a normal day, less than eight thousand were inside the gates. Two thousand of them were at the base hospital with human bite wounds. Unknown to anyone was the fact that two thousand more with bite wounds were either at their duty stations or somewhere in the dependent housing neighborhood.

The paralysis that gripped the base was the result of preparation. The Joint Base was prepared for everything from a nuclear attack to natural disasters…things that sadly made sense. They were also prepared for a biological event. Quarantine units stood ready for patients who needed to be isolated from the general population. Specialized storage units held the latest equipment and life-saving supplies. There were even mobile refrigeration trailers and morgues for contaminated bodies. The problem was that the people who were supposed to implement the responses were already victims of the event, and that was because no one planned for a zombie apocalypse. The quarantine units were empty.

Over on the runways of the Air Force Base, there had always been contingency plans for disasters. Plane crews would have designated rendezvous destinations and be ready to fly with only a moment's notice, but all of the contingency plans relied on the people who would help get the planes in the air. A grand total of three airplanes were able to scramble from the runway, but it wasn't clear where they would go because none of them had a complete crew, and their coordinated plans were to fly as a squadron. The pilots eventually decided to return to the base where they believed they would be most useful. Once on the ground, they learned how wrong they were.

It took only three days for the base to be overrun by the infected dead. Of the four thousand who survived those first three days, only four hundred were left after seven years.

******

When Tina was done telling them about the beginning, they wanted to press her for more details about what had happened over the following seven years, but the Chief announced from the entrance to the tent that the Colonel and Jim Miller were coming back.

Tina Harlow became more agitated than she had been when she first arrived.

"I haven't gotten a single bit of information from you guys. I'm in so much trouble."

Kathy said, "Let me have your notebook."

Tina handed it to her. Kathy hurried over to the far corner of the tent and sat on a bunk. She wrote as fast as she could, listing their names, ages, places of birth, and what they did before the apocalypse. She wouldn't finish before the Colonel arrived, but she could make a good show of being cooperative for Staff Sergeant Harlow.

Jim came in first with the Colonel close behind him. Everyone watched Jim closely for any sign he could give them about the way things had gone for him, but he acted like he was returning from nothing more than a reunion with an old friend. At least he wasn't in leg irons. As a matter of fact, his demeanor was encouraging.

The Colonel asked Staff Sergeant Harlow to show him the information she had collected just as Kathy managed to slip her the book. She had managed to get enough done to make it at least look like she was doing her job. It wasn't that the young sergeant was afraid of the Colonel, but they could all see she was seeking his approval. He appeared to be satisfied, and he announced to them all that Captain Miller would brief them about what they had discussed. In the meantime, he had arranged for food to be brought to their tent. He held the flap of the tent open for Tina to leave first, and then he followed. To the members of the Mud Island family who had military experience, that was a departure from protocol that bothered them.

After Colonel Daugherty and Sergeant Harlow were gone, everyone was eager to hear what Captain Miller had to say, and he was just as anxious to tell them. He pulled up a chair, and everyone gathered around.

"I'll get right to it. Things are bad here," he began. "They may be preparing a meal for us, but we're probably carrying better rations than they have."

Susan said, "That would explain the vitamin deficiencies Sergeant Harlow has. I don't think she's had a decent meal in months."

"Almost no one here has been getting a good diet," Jim continued. "The list of things I'm going to tell you about will blow your minds."

"It's not just food?" asked the Chief.

"No, besides food, they don't have any medicine, not much ammunition, and very little fuel. The base is largely secure because of the steps they took early in the spread of the infection, but they're hanging on by their fingernails. One big horde would overrun the place, so they send out squads to the border fences and call the infected to them. They use pikes to kill the infected."

Kathy asked, "What happened? How'd it get this bad?"

"The usual way," he said. "They expended everything they had at the beginning. They tried to treat their wounded, and once they found out that was a mistake, it was too late to fix it. They lost the hospital and all of their medical supply facilities in the first week. After that, they sent patrols into Anchorage to search for supplies, but none of the patrols ever returned. They didn't really know what they were up against."

Garrett said, "What about the planes and the helicopters? They couldn't fly out in search of supplies? And what about the people in the Army who knew you had deserted?"

Jim shook his head. "The planes and helicopters were useless without pilots, and they lost most of the flight crews on the first day. Colonel Daugherty said they sent a few helicopters to see if they could find any organized military units that had survived. They lost radio contact with them, but one reported back that they had been conscripted by another unit. The others were just like the ground patrols. They disappeared without a trace. From what I gathered, this base is down to about four hundred hungry people."

"You still haven't gotten to the part about your old buddies who were experimenting on the dead," said Hampton. "How do they fit into this picture?"

"They showed up, but they hadn't learned any lessons from their first stupid mistake. They came in and took over just like they owned this place, and in the name of national security, they did it all over again. They had higher-ranking officers with them, so the Joint Base stood down and let them assume command. Daugherty told me they lost a lot more of their people when the infection broke containment, and they were forced to use most of their remaining munitions just to get control again."

"Where are they now?" asked Tom.

"A few are in the stockade, but most of them escaped. Daugherty figures they went somewhere in the Aleutian Islands. The rest have been locked up for a long time, but they're still threatening court martials for anyone who doesn't let them out."

"Any chance they might come back and try to retake the base?"

Captain Miller shook his head.

"I asked Daugherty the same thing, and he said his best guess would be that they found another place to continue their experiments and aren't interested in them anymore. There was one thing, though. He said they seemed particularly glad to leave after they ransacked the base commander's office. He thinks they found something they were looking for."

The Chief said, "We'll have to be careful not to run into them. It sounds like things have been worse here than almost anywhere, but is there any chance that they're holding back?"

"What do you mean? Do you think they're hiding something? No, from what I saw, the only thing that Daugherty wasn't telling the truth about was that there are higher-ranking people he reports to. He was holding that back at the start because he was trying to find out if we were doing the same thing. He thought we might be part of a larger force that was sizing up the opposition."

Iris had been listening closely to the discussion, and the Chief had noticed how quiet she was. It seemed like she had been rescuing people from the infection since the first day, but they had all lost count of the times they had gone looking for help but wound up becoming the saviors.

"I have a question," she said. "How are we going to get four hundred people resupplied? I mean, we could start using the plane to shuttle in food, medicine, and ammunition, but that would be a short-term fix at best."

"Good point," said the Chief. "As usual, my wife sees the bigger problem." He gave her hand an affectionate squeeze before going on. "The first thing we can do is get a runway clear if there isn't already one we can use. We can bring in the plane and give them the rest of our supplies. Then, we can make a trip to Anchorage to see how bad it is. If it's survivable now, we might be able to recover enough supplies for them to figure out a long-term solution. If not, well, we could always start relocating them to the shelters."

"I suggested that," said Captain Miller. "Daugherty told me that some of the Air Force people would like to hook up with other units that survived. I guess we could fly them to Wyoming. Some of the Army people want to do the same thing. After Alaska, I'll bet they'd love the shelters in the South."

The Chief said, "That's settled then. I know everyone's tired, but let's get the plane over here so we can get these people fed."

It took well into the night, but the AC-130 was finally at the base, and hot meals were being distributed. The meal the base had prepared for them didn't hold a candle to the MREs they unloaded from the plane. Four hundred grateful people had been given hope.

17

The Cave

Attu Island - The Beginning of the Infection

Michael Bailey did his best to describe the events that had led to their arrival on Attu Island. He didn't have to lie about anything because the only part that didn't sound feasible was how far off course they had gotten. He even told them about when he had noticed his pilot and his friend, Adam Ramos, had gotten the cut on his hand. He didn't know why Ramos had lied about it, but when the Russians told him what they knew, he understood why they had tied him up.

When he told them about the Governor and the Senator, they became alarmed. They wanted to take the boat to where the helicopter protruded from the water and set fire to it, but he convinced them there was no way the things inside the passenger compartment could get out. He also thought they had most likely been killed in the crash or drowned by now.

"You are not listening to everything we are telling you," said Galina. "They do not die unless you smash the head with something. They do not drown."

"But you can burn them?" asked Bailey.

His question made them stop and think, but Pavel answered, "I think if you set the helicopter on fire, it will blow up, and that will destroy their brains."

Oleg spoke up and settled the issue.

"If they cannot get out of the helicopter, we can leave them there. Maybe fish or crabs will get inside and eat them."

"I can't believe we're even talking about something like that," said Bailey. "A week ago, we would never have thought about what would kill other people if a helicopter crash didn't."

Pavel nodded and said, "It is a different world. A week ago, you would not have thought about being on a Russian fishing boat with your friend tied up."

They all glanced involuntarily toward the bow of the boat. Michael Bailey had guilt written all over his face, and for a moment, he felt ashamed that he hadn't defended his friend.

Galina saw his eyes drop to the floor and said, "You must not let yourself feel that way. If you try to save him, we will all die."

"The fog is lifting," said Pavel. "We should try to move closer to shore while we can see where we are going. Are you going to help us, Mister Bailey, or are you planning to help your friend?"

Bailey didn't need to think about it. He already knew he had done the right thing, even if it made him feel guilty.

"I don't know what's going to happen to us, but I feel like my best chance of staying alive is by doing everything I can to help you guys do the same thing. Besides, it's not like I have many choices. Don't get me wrong. I'm grateful that you happened to be here. If you hadn't been, I would've been stranded with my friend, and I wouldn't have known about what he's going to become."

The fog was lifting higher by the minute, and the cliff face was making a rare appearance across the cove. The steep wall of rock rose straight up from the water, and the fog moved slowly up the face of the mountain like a thin, white curtain. There was a dark blemish along the base that seemed out of place.

"What is that?" asked Galina.

Binoculars only helped a little in the dim morning light, but as the fog lifted higher, Pavel could make out more details.

"I am not sure yet, but I think the cove goes into a grotto or a cave. We may be in luck. The entrance is big enough for me to steer the *Svetlana* inside."

"What if we get stuck in there?" asked Oleg.

Pavel laughed as he answered, "Then we get stuck in there. It would be better than getting stuck out here."

"We need time to figure out what we're going to do," said Bailey, "and that would buy us some time even if we do get stuck."

Working together, they pulled in the anchor and got ready to maneuver the boat into the cave. Ramos pleaded with them again when they got near him, but they had other things to worry about at the moment. They might get only one shot at navigating into the cave, so they needed to be focused. Oleg pulled a cloth sack over the helicopter pilot's head to keep him from distracting Pavel.

There was very little current inside the cove to pull them away from the entrance, so Pavel just gave the engines a slight burst of forward speed. He cut them off almost immediately and let the boat coast. As they drew closer, they could see that the entrance was larger than they had first thought, and they knew it was a golden opportunity for them to hide inside until they could figure out their next move.

Pavel turned on a spotlight that seemed to be a solid beam as it cut through the middle of the entrance. It disappeared into the blackness, and they all strained to see if the beam stopped on anything. It didn't reflect back at them, but they all watched so intently that it felt like they were being pulled into the opening instead of entering under their own power. The gap in the cliff wall grew in size, and what had first appeared to be a small entrance turned out to be room for a much larger boat.

"We won't get stuck in here," yelled Bailey.

As they crossed the threshold of the entrance, the sound of their engines echoed back at them, and the vibrations caused the ceiling to shower a cloud of fine dust on them. It wasn't as thick as the fog had been, but since it was solid, it got into their eyes and mouths. They were forced to pull scarves across their faces to keep from breathing it in.

Pavel reversed the engines and shouted, "Brace for impact!"

The command surprised the others because they still couldn't see anything in front of them. They braced themselves against the nearest solid objects and held on because of the order, but the impact never came. The only light around them came from the spotlight beam and the pilothouse, where Pavel frantically did his best to slow their forward speed until they came to a complete stop.

Silence surrounded them as soon as the engines stopped, and the dust that swirled around them thinned as it settled. Pavel turned the control that rotated the spotlight to the right, and they all recoiled in surprise when the light immediately bounced back from a wall less than six feet away. They were coasting very gently toward the wall at such a slow speed that it was easy for Oleg to quickly loop a rope around a cleat on a manmade dock. He and Bailey dropped bumpers over the side to cushion the boat when it made contact with the pier.

"Where are we?" asked Galina.

No one answered because they were all wondering the same thing. Under the cloth sack by the bow of the boat, Adam Ramos was the only one who said anything, but the rest of them were too stunned by what they were seeing to pay attention.

Pavel rotated the spotlight to the left, and they got their second shock within two minutes. The wall on the left was only about thirty yards away, but the space between the *Svetlana* and the wall was mainly filled by another fishing boat. They had coasted into such a narrow gap between the boat and the pier that was so thin that the outriggers from the two boats were touching each other. Ramos complained again under the cloth sack, but none of them could take their eyes away from the sight only a few yards away.

The phantom boat was drafting deep as if it was totally full, and they could see just enough of the area below the waterline to know it had probably been painted bright red a long time ago, but it had faded with time as rust had consumed the hull. The two fishing boats were similar, but the old derelict had deeper gunwales, which meant it had been used in rough seas. The gunwales, or sides that enclosed the deck, were higher to keep the crew from being swept overboard in bad weather. Pavel was the only one who could see the deck because he was in the pilothouse of the *Svetlana.*

In the stillness that surrounded both boats, it was easy for Pavel to see and hear the movement on the deck. At first, the dim light made the flat surface appear to ripple, but then the shapes became more defined. They stood up and shook off the layer of dust that had blanketed them. Oleg, Galina, and Bailey could hear a rustling sound like old newspapers being blown by the wind, but the movement was below the higher gunwales. They could see the cloud of dust that drifted upward, but they didn't know what it was until they saw the heads appear. Even then, they didn't know what Pavel already knew. They were all wearing Russian army uniforms, and they were all dead.

Pavel's first instinct was to turn off the spotlight so the soldiers wouldn't see them. The blackness was even more blinding because their eyes had adjusted to the beam of light, and the sounds coming from the other boat were even more frightening. He turned the light on again. It was better to be able to see the nightmarish crowd of dead soldiers than it was to hear them so close by.

"They can't get to us," said Bailey.

A thumping sound came from somewhere on the side of the *Svetlana* that faced the other boat. Oleg and Bailey leaned over their own gunwales and aimed flashlights at the water.

"There are more in the water," said Oleg. "What happened here?"

Once it became clear that the dead soldiers weren't a threat, Bailey and his new friends had the luxury of time to figure out what they were going to do next. Pavel rotated the spotlight and probed the darkness. His view of the wall on the port side was partially blocked by the other boat, and there was a cloud of dust still settling over the soldiers that continually shuffled against the gunwales. He kept the light aimed at the darkest spot, and as his eyes adjusted better, he saw the curved shape of a tunnel entrance.

"Over there," he called out to the others.

They saw that he was pointing to something beyond the other boat, but from the deck, they couldn't see what was there. He aimed the spotlight directly at the spot.

"I think I see a tunnel," said Pavel.

"Can we get to it from the dock on this side?" asked Galina.

Pavel repositioned the spotlight on the dock where they had tied their mooring line and then turned it to follow the path around the wall. It disappeared behind the other boat.

"I think we can walk to it," he said.

Bailey climbed onto the dock and carefully walked on surprisingly solid boards that went past their bow. It was a horseshoe-shaped dock that curved to the left and went behind the other boat. He saw that Pavel was right about being able to walk to the tunnel, but he had to get closer to the other boat than he liked. Even worse, there was a ramp that went from the dock to the port side of the other boat, and the gate at the top of the ramp bulged under the weight of the dead soldiers pressing against it. If they detected him, that pressure might increase and force the gate open.

Oleg and Galina approached from behind Bailey, and he held up one hand for them to wait. He pointed at the ramp and then to the gate. They pressed themselves close to the wall and crouched as they walked the last few steps. They were all careful not to shine their flashlights anywhere except by their own feet. Bailey led the way into the tunnel.

Once they were away from the cavern and the boats, the silence in the tunnel seemed to be complete. None of the sounds of the dead in the water or on the boat penetrated the darkness.

Bailey whispered, "Why are there dead Russian soldiers here?"

Oleg snapped back, "How should we know? We did not lead them here. They are all dead, so it does not matter."

"I wasn't accusing you of anything. I was asking for your opinion. There are so many on that boat that I don't think they were here by coincidence. They must've known this cave was here."

Galina said, "What is this?"

Her flashlight illuminated a room at the end of the tunnel, and inside the room was a large door. Bailey let out a low whistle when he saw it.

"How did that thing fit through the tunnel?" he asked.

"Even more important," said Galina, "we either have to open that door or go back out the way we came in."

Attu Island Shelter - The Beginning of the Infection

Lieutenant Gleaton and Sergeant O'Reilly both deferred to the newly promoted Corporal Hupp. He figured out the combination, so he should have the honor of turning the dial. He rubbed his fingertips together dramatically and leaned his head against the door as if he needed to hear the tumblers inside the lock. When the last number was selected, he turned the huge silver wheel in the middle of the door clockwise. It spun easily, and this time, they all heard something. Massive steel pins were retracted into the door, and it opened a few inches toward the soldiers.

O'Reilly pulled the door open the rest of the way. As he did, the lights turned on inside. They pulled their sidearms out of reflex even though there was no apparent danger. All they could see was a hallway with something facing them that resembled a guard shack.

"Anyone see anything?" asked O'Reilly.

They advanced as a column into the hallway and inspected the guard shack, but they didn't find anything interesting. Hupp checked the locking mechanism on the door and reported that it could be locked or unlocked from the inside so they could pull the door shut behind them if they wanted to. O'Reilly suggested to Lieutenant

Gleaton that they send Talbot back through the tunnel to get Mincy and Ritter. He thought it would make more sense for them to have one person stay in the guard shack inside a locked door than to leave two people outside.

Fifteen minutes later, Ritter was complaining about getting to sit inside the guard shack while the rest of them went deeper into the underground facility.

The hallway made a right turn after going straight for almost twenty yards. Only a few feet past the turn was a door that could have been in any jail. Steel bars ran from the floor to the ceiling, and the lock was surrounded by a metal case. The door stood open, but stepping through it gave everyone the sense that they would be captives if the door shut behind them. O'Reilly told Corporal Mincy to secure the door in the open position with the strongest zip-ties she had.

"What is this place?" asked Talbot.

O'Reilly said, "I'll be sure to let you know when we figure that out."

The impression that it was some kind of prison was reinforced a few yards later when they came to rows of cells on both sides of the hall, and the last thing they expected was what was inside them…not to say they expected anything at that point. They hadn't expected to find the vault door or the bleak gray walls of the corridors.

"This place is about as depressing as it can get," said Gleaton. The words had just gotten out of his mouth when an arm reached through the bars of the cell on his right.

"Be careful," said O'Reilly as Gleaton and the rest of the squad recoiled away from it. "There are PITS in the other cells, too."

There were eight cells, with four on each side of the hall, and there wasn't much room to walk between them. As the six soldiers eased forward through the narrow gap between the outstretched arms, the chorus of moans became so loud that they could barely hear each other.

Corporal Mullins shook off the grip of a hand that had caught enough material on his jacket to hold on. The hand immediately grasped at him again.

"Any reason to keep these things alive, Sarge?" he asked.

Mincy added, "I was thinking the same thing, but we can't shoot them. We'd be deaf after the first round."

The creatures had their faces pressed against the bars, and there were at least thirty pairs of arms waving around. O'Reilly did a mental count.

"I see about fifteen to twenty on each side. Everyone stay well back, but get out your bayonets. Aim for their foreheads without going too deep, but if your blade gets stuck, just let it go. We can retrieve it when we do clean up."

They didn't need to be told to work both sides at the same time, and they split up into two groups. They were constantly dodging the hands of the caged dead people, but stabbing their foreheads was easy since they didn't try to move their heads out of the way.

"Lost my blade," said Talbot.

Mullins immediately pushed another into her hand, and she went back to work.

She said with a smile, "I should've guessed you would be carrying a spare."

The distraction of reaching for the second blade and talking to Mullins made her get too close to a grasping hand, and she screamed in pain as the squirming fingers got under the edge of the bandage on her arm. The gauze wrap pulled loose, and the adhesive holding the sterile pad in place ripped free. When Talbot screamed, the others all turned to help her, and none of them missed seeing the long flap of skin that came off with the bandage. They also saw the long streaks of infection that stretched from her wound to her elbow and wrist.

Mullins swung his bayonet like he was chopping wood and severed the hand that was holding the gauze. A second swing removed the other hand that had gripped her clothing when she had stepped closer. One final swing went through the bars and split the creature's forehead in half.

He pulled Talbot away from the group to the section of the hall away from the cells and sat her down against a wall. A quick look at her arm was all he needed to know what had happened, but he still wanted to treat it quickly. He dug into his backpack and tore open the disinfectant pouch. With one hand, he poured it on liberally, and with the other hand, he found the tube of antibiotic gel.

By the time the rest of the squad had finished the clean-up of the cells, Mullins had Talbot's arm completely bandaged. She was afraid to make eye contact with them when they gathered around her. She knew from the reports they had seen what was going to happen to her, and she felt guilty for not telling them.

Mullins stood up as they gathered around her, but he couldn't face any of them, either. He turned away from them, and O'Reilly saw the toughest man in his squad make a quick swipe across the corner of his eye with a big hand.

O'Reilly and Gleaton both knelt down by Talbot as Hupp and Mincy stayed back a bit. Unsure what to do, they made themselves busy cleaning off their bayonets and checked the action and magazines of their handguns.

Shirley Talbot finally lifted her head far enough to make eye contact with the sergeant and then the lieutenant.

"I'm sorry I didn't tell you," she said in a voice barely above a whisper.

"Nothing to apologize for," said O'Reilly. "You must've been too scared to say anything. This happened at the boat?"

She nodded and said, "I don't wanna die, Sarge, but I know I'm gonna. That's why I didn't tell you, but I also don't wanna become like them. Don't let me become like that, Sarge. You gotta promise me."

Talbot's cheeks were wet from the tears that streamed down them, and O'Reilly put a big hand on top of hers.

"You didn't think we would put a bullet in your head as soon as you told us, did you? We might've been able to do something about this."

She shook her head. "You saw the reports. There's no cure. Besides, I didn't even know it was a bite myself. Remember how dark it was out there on the beach? I thought I just got scratched. By the time I knew what it was, it was already bad, but I should've told you."

"I know, Talbot, but even now, I'm not ready to give up. We don't know for sure that bites are fatal. We're going to keep changing those bandages and get you better."

Lieutenant Gleaton knew the sergeant had a special relationship with his squad. Even a newcomer would be taken under his wing on the first day. He was respected by his people because they knew he had their backs. Gleaton wished he could have that kind of bond, but he knew an officer's role was different. Command decisions were his to make, but the heart of the squad would always be Sergeant O'Reilly.

He tugged at the sergeant's sleeve and got him to step away from the group. Mincy, Hupp, and Mullins took it as their chance to console Talbot, so they closed in on her and offered words of encouragement.

"Check out that bandage job," said Mincy. "Mullins isn't just the best cook in the Army. He's a glorified medic."

Gleaton kept his voice low and asked O'Reilly, "What do you think we should do? It seems like those news reports were clear, but man...I don't think we can just start killing our own people."

"I agree, and we have a few other options right now. If we can find the keys to one of these cells, we can make her comfortable while we wait this thing out. She's tough. She might just get sick as a dog and then pull through."

"You said we have a few other options. What else can we do?"

O'Reilly said, "We could take her with us, but keep an eye on her. We could have her take over for Ritter at the big door. If it were me, I'd want to be useful to the rest of the squad. Laying in a cell waiting for the end isn't how I think she would want to go out."

The lieutenant frowned and was having a problem with the choices.

"She doesn't look like she feels too well, but I haven't noticed her having a hard time swinging her bayonet. We're already down one man by leaving Ritter at the door, and if we take her with us, someone's going to have to keep an eye on her. Even if she does a good enough job, that's still like being down two people."

O'Reilly nodded to show he understood and said, "Hey, Talbot. Can you make it to the guard shack on your own and relieve Ritter?"

Lieutenant Gleaton was right. Private Talbot didn't look like she felt too good. There was perspiration beading on her forehead, and she kept wiping at her nose like she had a cold. She also winced when she moved her bandaged arm.

"I ain't ready to quit, Sarge, but I could use the rest. I can make it back to relieve Ritter, but maybe someone could go along with me so they can show him the way back to here."

It was obviously a good idea, but O'Reilly suspected it was more likely that Talbot needed support than Ritter needed a guide because they hadn't gone far from the entrance yet.

"I'll go," said Mullins.

As rough as he appeared at times, everyone could see he was a bit more worried about Talbot than he wanted to admit. He helped Talbot to stand, and she leaned on him as they walked away together. Talbot turned back toward the squad to smile at her friends. No one said goodbye even though they felt like that was what was happening.

Mullins and Ritter came back together only a few minutes later. Ritter had read the situation correctly when he saw Mullins practically carrying Talbot to the guard shack. He had helped her get comfortable on a stool and gave her his water. The way she was pouring sweat, he figured she needed it more than him. He had also taken off his foul weather coat and draped it around her shoulders.

The rest of the squad could read the grim expressions on their faces, especially Mullins', and his somber face sent the message that he didn't want to share comments or feelings about Talbot. His jaws were clenched so hard that his mouth was just a straight line. He wasn't responsible for what had happened on the beach, but that would never stop him from feeling like he was.

The squad moved off again without saying a word. Corporal Mullins went right by the rest of them and took the lead. Everyone else fell in, and when he pulled his bayonet out in place of his semiautomatic handgun, everyone did the same except Ritter. He wound up at the rear of the column, and going past the cells with their dead occupants in them gave him enough reason to pull out his pistol. He could see that they had all been killed with bayonets, but he didn't want to let anything get that close to him.

The narrow corridor ended at another guard post, but this one seemed more like a main entrance. The room was larger and had a counter facing outward from the corridor where they had been. A solid steel door appeared to be the only way out of the room.

O'Reilly said, "This room is like the central booking area of a jail, and we just came from the holding cells. I guess we have to see what's on the other side of that door."

They fanned out on both sides and waited for O'Reilly's signal. When he motioned to go, Mullins pulled open the door but waited to go through. The next hall was larger than the one by the jail cells, but the lights were off. They knew there were lights on somewhere because the other side of the doorway wasn't pitch black.

"I wonder how this place can have power," said Lieutenant Gleaton.

O'Reilly answered, "I was asking myself the same thing. I don't hear any generators. Whatever provides the power, I have plenty of other questions I want answered first."

"Like what?"

"Like, are there any living people here or just more of those things in cages back there? Worse yet, are there any that aren't in cages?"

The squad used their urban combat training to make steady progress through dark corridors until they reached the source of the light. When they turned the corner from the last of the unlit hallways, they were speechless.

They entered an immense, square courtyard that had a ceiling at least one hundred feet above them. The middle of the courtyard was furnished sparsely with wooden benches that surrounded a podium. It had the appearance of a town square where announcements were made. All four sides around the square were identical, and each side resembled apartment entrances. There were ten levels on each side with landings that ran from one corner to the next, and a quick count revealed twenty-five closed apartment-style doors per floor. The main level in the courtyard only had doors at each corner, and they had just entered through one of them.

"I count one thousand doors," said Private Hupp.

"This is going to keep us busy," said O'Reilly. "We have to clear every one of them, and until we know for sure, we can't assume there are just rooms behind those doors. It may look like a hotel, but there could be more places just like this. It's a big mountain."

Mullins said, "We need to split up, Sarge."

O'Reilly nodded.

"I agree. Mincy, you're with me to keep sweeping this main level. If you don't mind, Lieutenant, I think Hupp should go with you in case you come across useful intel about this place. I suggest you go up one set of stairs and start on the first level. Mullins, you've got Ritter. Check out the second level. That's a hundred doors per level, so let's rendezvous back here in one hour."

"What should we do if we find someone?" asked Mullins.

O'Reilly gave it some thought and said, "If they're alive, attempt peaceful contact. If they're PITS, don't engage unless you have to. We have to assess the threat first."

They set their watches and split up. Sergeant O'Reilly led Corporal Mincy straight along the left side of the courtyard toward the next door. Unlike the doors on the upper levels, this one stood open, and the darkness inside beckoned them like a trap. Mincy was glad to have O'Reilly leading the way. She didn't need to be told to turn on her flashlight as they went inside.

Just like the hallway they had entered from, the door gave them more options than they needed to find. Corridors stretched out in front of them and to the left and right. Closed doors were placed at regular intervals.

"This is going to take forever," mumbled O'Reilly.

He motioned toward the first door, and Corporal Mincy nodded. She positioned herself to one side of the frame and gently turned the doorknob. It was unlocked, and her nerves were tingling as she pulled it open.

There was an immediate flurry of activity inside the room as dark shapes moved toward them. O'Reilly lashed out with a large boot and kicked the door shut. Christine Mincy pinned her back against the wall and waited for something to open the door, but despite the thumping that came from the other side and echoed down the corridor, the door remained shut.

"PITS," said O'Reilly, "and they obviously don't know how to turn doorknobs."

"What're we going to do about them, Sarge?"

"One thing's for sure," he answered as he dug around through the contents of his backpack. He produced a large stick of red chalk and scrawled *PITS* in big letters. "We can't go through every room shooting at anything that moves in the dark."

18

Dead End

Attu Island Cave- The Beginning of the Infection

"How much food and water do we have left?" asked Micheal Bailey.

Pavel glanced in the direction of the bow where Adam Ramos was still tied with his hands behind his back and a cloth sack over his head.

"Maybe two weeks if we do not feed your friend," he growled, "and much longer if we do not feed you."

Bailey knew that Galina wasn't going to let him starve, but he didn't push his luck with her brother. The boat belonged to him, and Pavel took any opportunity he could to remind him.

They were back together on the *Svetlana,* and they hadn't been able to devise a plan beyond staying where they were or sailing back out of the cave. Neither plan would solve their immediate problems. If they stayed put, they would eventually starve or die of thirst. If they sailed out of the cave, they still had nowhere to go. If things were as bad as they appeared to be, they wouldn't have to worry about food or water for very long in the outside world.

Oleg had wanted to go back to the big vault door to see if he could open the combination lock on the door. Pavel had sarcastically suggested that Oleg had seen too many American movies because he thought he could press an ear against the door and listen to the tumblers inside the lock. The two had exchanged insults until Galina stepped in and reminded them they were both going to die squabbling over something stupid.

"We could at least try," said Oleg angrily. "Is it better to sit here and do nothing?"

Pavel retorted that they could find a way to make a bomb and blow the door open, to which Oleg replied that Pavel should have watched more American movies so he would have known what happened to Butch Cassidy and the Sundance Kid.

Galina got tired of the bickering and left the wheelhouse. Michael followed her even though it was at the risk of upsetting either of the men. The last thing he wanted was to have her husband get jealous or her brother to get protective, but he also couldn't stay in the wheelhouse with them and referee as they fought.

Galina was already crossing the main deck, and he saw that she was walking straight toward Adam Ramos near the bow. From the door of the wheelhouse, he could see that Ramos was squirming more than before and appeared to be tugging at the ropes on his wrists.

Michael had a bad feeling about the way the sack on Ramos' head was moving. Then he saw why. Ramos was literally chewing a hole in the cloth over his mouth.

"Galina, wait," he yelled.

Galina reached for the top of the sack, thinking that the helpless man was becoming desperate or maybe having difficulty breathing. Adam Ramos rolled over onto his back with his legs flailing. She tried to stop herself, but she had leaned forward too far. She fell when her legs became tangled with his. Her eyes became wide with horror when she saw the wet hole in the front of the sack, with teeth and lips biting hungrily at the air.

A hand gripped her hair and pulled, and Galina was sure it was Ramos trying to end her life, but as she was lifted away from the snapping mouth, a foot shot past her and connected with the cloth sack. Michael pulled her away with one hand and stomped on the covered head of his former friend. Even though Michael clearly heard neck bones break, Ramos still bit his teeth together furiously.

Oleg and Pavel arrived as Michael delivered a second kick. Oleg grabbed Galina, and Pavel delivered a right hook to Michael's face. Michael fell where Galina had been only a moment before, and he found himself dodging the faceless bites of the thing that Adam Ramos had become.

"What are you doing?" screamed Galina.

She broke free from her husband and grabbed a pole that was mounted on the inside of the gunwale. It bore a resemblance to the pole used by firemen because it had a spike and a hook on the end. Pavel used it to hook nets and lines that were in the water, but Galina used it as a weapon. She drove the spiked end through the middle of the cloth sack.

Galina wanted to pull it free and use it on her brother, but she had lunged with it so hard that it was stuck into the wooden deck under the body. When she couldn't pull it free, she spun around and punched Pavel in the nose hard enough to break it. He would have gone over the gunwale if not for the pier behind him.

Michael was in the process of separating himself from the body of his friend when Galina got her arm under his and helped him to his feet.

"You idiots," she shouted. "He was saving my life already by the time you got here."

Oleg helplessly held out both hands, palms up. Galina glared at him, but she was more angry at Pavel. She shook a finger at him where he lay on the deck holding his bloodied nose.

"You have been waiting to do that since we brought the American on board your boat, but it is time for you to realize it is no longer *your* boat. It belongs to all of us now."

Pavel waited until he felt like it was safe to approach his sister again. He stalled a bit by removing the body of Adam Ramos from the boat. When he squeezed into the galley with the others, he offered Michael an olive branch in the form of a generous cup of vodka.

"It will not last, so we might as well drink it," he said.

Michael didn't reach for it immediately, but Pavel kept his arm outstretched.

"I am sorry, Mikhail."

Referring to him by the Russian version of his name made Michael soften a bit. He understood Pavel's resentment a bit. Here they were, three Russian immigrants who only wanted to be free, and the first American they encountered needed their help. He took the cup and nodded his thanks.

All four of them sat together and drank vodka as they commiserated about their dead end. They couldn't go forward or backward, and their supplies wouldn't last forever. If they hadn't been drinking, maybe they wouldn't have hatched a plan to board the other boat.

It was Pavel's idea. He speculated that the number of infected dead on the boat meant they had a large supply of food. All they had to do was get to it. Pavel said it would be easy because the dead would fall for any distraction. The others would simply stand at the bow of the boat and yell while he would climb over the stern. He could get inside the boat without the dead soldiers ever noticing.

If they had waited until they were sober, they would have reconsidered, but the vodka only made them feel like they were ready for anything. They noisily stumbled out of the galley and climbed onto the pier, then circled around to the other fishing boat. By the time they reached its bow, the infected dead were crowded against the forward gunwales making more noise than them.

Michael, Oleg, and Galina used their hooked poles to beat loudly on the bow of the boat. The infected dead reached hungrily for them just as they thought they would. Their taunts gave Pavel the distraction he needed. He crawled on his hands and knees along the port side of the boat until he reached the stern, the he climbed easily onto the boat and was almost laughing as he descended through the door below the wheelhouse.

Once he was inside the boat, Pavel didn't see the humor in the plan anymore. It was too dark, and the boat smelled like death. He knew that smell, and he was suddenly aware that they had assumed all of the infected dead on the boat were outside on the main deck. He clicked on his flashlight and was surprised that he was alone. He let out a ragged breath. He didn't notice he had been holding it out of nervousness.

Letting out his breath had one major consequence. It meant he would be forced to inhale again, and when he did, the stench overwhelmed him. His coughing fit induced by the smell of decay was enough to wake the dead…literally. Shadows moved just out of reach of his flashlight beam as the infected inside the boat gathered at the bottom of the stairs. By the time they were where he could see them clearly, he knew he couldn't go down.

Pavel backed up the stairs and kicked his foot out at the first one to climb close enough. It fell backward, taking at least six more with it. He could hear his sister and the others still yelling and taunting the infected dead on the main deck, so he decided it was time to leave. When he pushed open the door he had entered only moments before, it slammed into several infected dead that had come to investigate the new sounds coming from the bottom of the stairs. He pulled it shut in time to keep it from being forced open again, but his freedom was limited to two stairs.

He made a second, well-aimed kick that cleared the stairs again, and for a moment, he wondered if he should try to go down. One quick peek out the door was enough for him to know he would never make it out the way he had come in. He wondered if the others would ever realize what had gone wrong.

Pavel made his decision. He would wait until the stairs were full before making his next kick. Then, he would jump over the infected dead while they were on the deck, and he would make his way forward. If he was right, there would be a hatch he could climb through onto the main deck.

He counted twelve infected dead below him, and the steps would only hold about six, so he had to hope the others would go down like bowling pins. Pavel backed up as close to the door as he could, lifted his right foot, and aimed at the head of the closest one.

The entire boat moved under his left foot, which was still firmly planted on the step. Pavel swayed to his right, and his foot missed the infected dead by so much that it landed on the creature's shoulder. He braced himself with both arms in the narrow gangway and fought to stay upright on one foot while the infected dead hung onto his right leg.

Everything after that happened so fast that he wasn't sure what was up and what was down. The boat seemed to sway again, and the door at his back opened wide. He was pressed hard against it because the infected dead in front of him still had his leg on its shoulder and was pushing it even higher. All he knew was that he was falling, and the dead were falling with him.

Pavel landed so hard that it knocked the wind out of him, and he pressed his eyes shut so he wouldn't see what was about to bite him. The bites didn't come, and he opened one eye to see why. A pole passed over him, and he lifted his head in time to see the pointed end pass through the forehead of the infected dead. The hands holding the pole lunged forward, and he felt his leg finally set free.

Strong hands under his armpits lifted him to his feet, and he came face to face with Oleg. His brother-in-law had a big smile on his face.

"Pavel, you idiot. The American had a better plan."

Oleg took Pavel by the shoulders and turned him around to face the dock. He saw that the boat was about six feet from the pier, and the gunwale on the port side was open. A plank was extended over the water and through the opening. There was no sign of the infected dead on the deck.

While Galina and Michael used their boat hooks to force the infected dead back down the stairs, Oleg guided Pavel to the opening. Heads bobbed in the water between the boat and the pier, and hands reached helplessly toward them.

"Michael said we should open the gangplank door and then push the boat away. The dead walked right through it and fell into the water. All we had to do was call them to us. Now we will help to kill your friends inside the boat."

Pavel was still in a daze and just a little bit drunk, but even he had to laugh along with Oleg.

"I like the American's idea better than my own."

The two men went back to the door and found Galina and Michael squeezed inside the narrow opening. One by one, they lured the infected dead onto the steps and then used their long poles to spike them through their heads. There were still a couple of them trying to come up the stairs, but the job was mostly done.

When there were no more infected dead to dispose of, they carefully descended into the galley and worked their way through the bodies toward the hold. They stopped from time to time to use their spikes on a few that were pinned under the weight of the bodies, but when they reached their goal, they weren't disappointed. It might only mean they had more time before they would get hungry, but the hold was full of canned food. Being a Russian fishing boat, they weren't surprised to find there was also a generous supply of vodka. The bonus was that there was also a large cache of weapons and ammunition.

Pavel put his arm around Michael's shoulders and pulled him into a bear hug.

"Mikhail, you are now my brother as well. Together we will survive this thing."

Despite everything they had going against them, Michael couldn't help feeling like Pavel was right.

******

An hour after the teams began their search of the mysterious underground facility, they returned to the courtyard to make their reports. They rested on the benches in a circle and pulled out notebooks with the details about each room. They knew they would have to know how to locate them again, so most of their notes were maps.

O'Reilly and Mincy broke the bad news that they had encountered PITS in so many rooms that they couldn't begin to give an estimate of their numbers. They had labeled the doors and made notes of their locations. They weren't surprised to learn that the other groups had also been forced to label the doors of rooms they couldn't enter.

O'Reilly said, "We ran into a group of six PITS that were just wandering around outside the rooms. I don't know how long they can function, but I got the impression they haven't been here long. They were all dressed in Russian officer uniforms. We had to dispose of them the way we did in the jail cells, but we noted where we left the bodies. As for the good news, we found a fully stocked storeroom and kitchen. The food is mostly canned or boxed, but there are some big freezers stuffed full of beef and poultry."

"We can fill in some blanks for everyone," said Lieutenant Gleaton. "We found an administrative office that wasn't overrun with PITS, so we were able to search for records. Everything we found was written in Russian, but our new Corporal knows a lot more than we ever suspected. He speaks a fair amount of Russian and two other languages. It seems that this place was some kind of doomsday shelter built by the Americans and Russians together."

"I can't wait to find out how that happened," said Mullins. "How do you suppose they got the idea to put it on this miserable island?"

Gleaton went on, "Me too, but there wasn't enough time to go through everything. The most interesting stuff was a record of everything that's happened in the last two weeks."

More than one of them said with surprise, "Two weeks?"

They suddenly felt exposed being out in the open in the middle of the courtyard, and they all nervously scanned the levels that towered above them. If there had been a sniper taking aim at them, they would have been sitting ducks.

"Take it easy, everyone," said Gleaton. "We know what happened, and that group of officers you ran into were all that was left of a Russian company that defied orders and got out of Russia while they could. They must have known where this place was and how to get inside. Their orders were to provide ground support for a Russian Navy base somewhere on the Kamchatka Peninsula. They arrived around the same time that we got that report of an incursion SATCOM wanted us to investigate."

"How did they get here, Sir?" asked Corporal Mincy.

"Good question," he answered. "Hupp found a reference to several boats and something about boats going back to Russia to bring more troops, but things went sideways fast. Did anyone else notice how clean this place is? I mean, there aren't any signs of a fight. There aren't any blood trails, no bullet holes in the walls, and other than the Russian officers O'Reilly and Mincy found, they're all confined."

"I was wondering about that," said O'Reilly.

Corporal Hupp held up a journal and said, "The last entry in this thing describes the measures the Russians took to contain the infection. They apparently brought it with them because soldiers who were infected by bites didn't tell anyone. It says here that they isolated the seriously infected in cells, but they ran out of cells and put them inside the hospital facilities. They tried to treat the wounded, but the bites were always fatal."

"We're gonna need those facilities," said Mullins.

They all understood what he meant. If this infection was as bad as they thought, they needed to contain it better than the Russians had. It had wiped them out in only two weeks.

"Talbot," said Ritter. "If the bites are always fatal, what about Talbot?"

No one wanted to put it into words, but it had been a mistake to leave her at the guardpost. She wasn't going to survive, and while she was unconfined, she was a threat to all of them.

"I'll go," said Mullins before O'Reilly could choose who to send.

O'Reilly said, "Take Mincy with you. Put Talbot in a cell and make her as comfortable as possible. Don't worry about guarding the back door. I don't think we're going to have any visitors who can figure out that combination lock. Just check it while you're there."

After they left, O'Reilly asked Hupp if he had finished. Hupp said there was one more thing he thought might be important. The journal said something about the main entrance being accessed by boat, and the secondary access was by land.

Hupp added, "We came in the back door, so we need to find the main entrance to see if it's secure."

"That would explain why we didn't see anyone coming or going to the island," said Lieutenant Gleaton. "They've been moving right under our noses the whole time. Good thinking, Hupp. We need to make finding the main door a priority."

"Do you think the Russians knew about us and our base camp?" asked O'Reilly.

Hupp shook his head. "There's no mention of us in here, Sarge."

Private Ritter said, "Mullins and I went up a level. You guys won't believe this place. Most of the rooms are just bunks and tables, but a few of them are really nice. They must've been reserved for officers...no offense Lieutenant."

"None taken, Private. Did anyone find anything else we should know about now?"

"The journal also says there's an armory around here somewhere," said Hupp. "It says they planned to transfer weapons and ammo to the armory from the last ship. It was also bringing the last contingent of soldiers. There's nothing about the ship arriving, though?"

Mullins and Mincy came back a lot sooner than anyone expected. It was easy to tell they had been running because they were winded.

"She's gone," said Mullins. "Talbot's not at the guardpost anymore."

Mincy said, "There was a trail on the floor down the hall, but we couldn't find it after those jail cells."

"A trail of what?" asked O'Reilly. "She wasn't bleeding the last time I saw her."

Mullins said, "Let's just call it body fluids, Sarge."

O'Reilly nodded and said to Lieutenant Gleaton, "If it's okay with you, Sir, I think we should lock ourselves into the mess hall for the rest of the day. We can get some hot food and spend some time figuring out how we're going to clear the rooms with PITS in them. I also don't want anyone stumbling over Talbot, so we should do everything as a group."

A few minutes later, they were secure in the mess hall. The double doors at the entrance of the large room were fastened together with long zip-ties, and for added protection, they stacked tables in front of them. There was a small window in each of the doors that had wire mesh reinforced glass in them. Hopefully, they wouldn't see any faces peering in at them through the glass.

By the next morning, they had figured out from the journal where they would find the main entrance. They had also done an inventory of the food in the storeroom and reached the conclusion that the Russians had planned to feed a hundred people for several years. Whatever their plans had been, a squad of six people wouldn't starve in a decade. The supply of protein bars alone would keep them alive twice as long.

That was definitely good news, but the icing on the cake was the armory. Apparently, the last ship hadn't arrived, but some of the contents of the armory had been delivered. There were several sublevels, but they were so expansive that there was a general agreement that they would keep finding hidden stairwells as long as they kept looking for them.

Ritter complained constantly as they carried a case of ammunition from the armory to an upper level where O'Reilly told them he wanted someone to act as overwatch. They didn't know why the Russians had a supply of standard-sized NATO ammunition, but they weren't too worried about it. The fact was there was so much of it that the Army squad would be more likely to run out of food before running out of ammunition.

"Why does everyone put ammunition in basements?" asked Ritter. "Then, when they need a case of it, they want it hauled upstairs even higher. Why not store it upstairs and then carry it downstairs."

Christine Mincy was lifting her end of the case by a rope handle and answered Ritter, "You do realize you said the exact same thing before we were told to carry this upstairs, right? My answer was the same then as it is now. If they stored it upstairs, you would be the grunt assigned to carry it up there."

"That doesn't make sense," he answered. "I wasn't here when this ammo was stored in the basement."

Mincy was always one step ahead of Ritter because she had him figured out on the first day. It wasn't that he was a bad soldier, and he wasn't really lazy, but every unit had a whiner. She had him pegged as the whiner as soon as they were introduced to each other.

"Let me explain karma one more time, Ritter. If this ammo had been originally stored upstairs, karma says one of three things would have happened. One, you would've been told to carry it higher. Two, you would have been the original person to carry it upstairs. Three, you would have been the original person to store it upstairs, but then you would have been told to carry it higher."

"If I'm the original person who put the ammo here, why was it stored in the basement?"

"Because karma would have made you carry it from the basement to a higher level just like you're doing now, right?"

Ritter was quiet the rest of the way to the floor where O'Reilly said to put the ammo. He was busy figuring out how karma had him doing exactly what he was supposed to be doing. When he sat his end of the case down, he thought he understood.

"So, you're saying I'm doomed to carry the ammo no matter what?"

"Yes, and I was put here to explain it to you."

"That means I have bad karma?" he asked.

"No, Ritter. That would be me," said Mincy.

There was a loud whistle from below, and they went to the balcony. Sergeant O'Reilly signaled with a hand for them to join him in the courtyard. By the time they got there, Mullins had arrived too.

O'Reilly said, "Lieutenant Gleaton and Hupp have already left for the main entrance. We're going to join them, but Mullins came across more fresh tracks left by Talbot, and it's possible she's in this area, so keep your head on a swivel. Mullins, you bring up the rear."

It didn't take long for them to reach the main entrance using the map Hupp had copied from the journal. Gleaton and Hupp were only waiting for the rest of the squad to arrive before opening the big door that rivaled the door at the back entrance in size. As soon as they had assumed a defensive position around the door, Hupp spun the huge locking wheel in the center. It spun as if it had been lubricated recently until it came to a stop.

******

The locking wheel may have spun quietly, but when the door opened, it opened on hinges that had been exposed to the salt air that carried the mist from the cave full of seawater. The sound from the protesting metal hinges was amplified as it carried down the tunnel to the fishing boats that were stranded inside the cave. Michael, Pavel, Oleg, and Galina all heard it as the wail of a banshee hidden inside the depths of the mountain. They also felt the air move as if it was sucked away from them toward the tunnel.

Inside the entrance of the shelter, the sound of the hinges wasn't as pronounced as it was in the cave, but the six remaining members of the Army squad felt the rush of air and smelled the familiar scent of the ocean. They immediately moved forward into the dark tunnel toward the echo of the sound that could only be coming from the place the journal had described as the ocean supply area. It was too dark for them to be moving without their flashlights on, and they felt like sitting ducks, but without them, they would be moving blindly toward the water. They felt like they had no other choice.

They didn't know what they expected to find, but they were surprised to find the dock with a fishing boat tied to it. They were even more surprised to find that the first fishing boat was blocking the view of a second, smaller boat, and the water around the two boats was choked with the bodies of Russian soldiers.

They fanned out to the left and right of the first boat keeping a close watch for anyone moving. Mullins led the way onto the gangway that was still in place, and he immediately went to the door that led below decks. There were bodies of PITS on the afterdeck near the door. O'Reilly followed, and on his signal, he went up as Mullins went down. Both reported no movement within seconds, but Mullins added that the PITS at the bottom of the stairs appeared to have been recently eliminated. He also said the boat was carrying munitions.

They rejoined the rest of the squad under the cover of the bow ahead of the gangplank, and O'Reilly leaned closer to Gleaton to report.

"Something's really strange out here. The PITS have all been dead for a few days, but it's our opinion that they were just put down permanently in the last few hours."

"Why's that, Sergeant?"

"The ones in the water aren't bloated yet, and if you look close enough, some are still moving. Give them another day to soak up enough water, and they'll sink. Then when they decompose, the gases that build up inside them will make them get bloated and pop to the surface like fishing bobbers."

Mullins added, "There are bloody footprints on the boat and the gangplank. Whoever wiped out the PITS walked off the boat and went that way."

"How do you know the PITS didn't make the footprints?" asked Gleaton.

"With all due respect, Lieutenant, we all have the same amount of experience with these things, so you probably noticed they don't exactly walk in a straight line. I can't picture any of them even walking the length of that gangplank by accident. Any that tried landed in the water. Those bloody footprints are from more than one person, and they go that way."

Behind the gunwale at the bow of the *Svetlana,* Michael Bailey couldn't believe his eyes. The flashlight beams moved with dizzying quickness at times, but in random moments, he recognized the uniforms of the newcomers. He knew he could be shot in the dim light, but there was no other choice. He stood up and raised his arms as high over his head as he could. His three Russian friends were slower to believe it was the right thing to do, but one by one, they stood up beside him.

A beam of light crossed over them, stopped, and then jerked back to shine directly at them.

They heard a woman's voice yell, "Sarge."

When Corporal Mincy saw the four people on the bow of the other boat, her first thought was the same as the rest of the squad. They were ragged enough to be PITS, but PITS didn't raise their hands.

"Well, not that high," she finished the thought. "They reach, but they don't raise."

Another voice, a man's voice, called out with authority, "Put your hands behind your head and don't move."

19

Rat Island Shelter

Attu Island - The Survival Years

Changes needed to happen quickly at first, but then things only changed gradually as they adapted to their new life. The squad of US Army soldiers had been sent to Attu Island to investigate the possibility that the shelter existed, but once they knew for sure that it was real, it didn't matter to anyone except them and the four strays they had taken in at the beginning. The days inside weren't boring, and there was enough to keep everyone busy as the days went by. Days became weeks, and weeks became months.

The first few days had been long hours of debriefing and piecing together their information combined with the folder given to them by Michael Bailey. As it turned out, his thin file was the key piece of information that explained everything. The Russian soldiers had been quick to make their escape from their country once the infection began, and they apparently already had enough information about the shelter to open the door inside the cave.

The discoveries about the origins of the shelter paled in comparison to the discoveries within. When the Russians had originally redecorated the shelter, they had removed most of the amenities that had been installed by the Congressman. His version of a shelter was more like a hotel. Their version had turned it into a fortress.

Corporal Hupp discovered an entry in a journal that said the Russians had also changed the name of the island to Ostrova Krys'i. It didn't matter to the Russians that there were already islands named Rat Island because it seemed to them they would never be able to eliminate them from the shelter once they got inside. They did, however, manage to completely seal the shelter, and when it had been abandoned by both the Russians and the Americans, the rats eventually died off due to starvation. Once Hupp told everyone else about the name change, they were all more than happy to accept it.

Exploration of the Rat Island Shelter was expected to take months because they kept finding new sections. Just when they thought they were done, they would find a door that hadn't been opened, and there wasn't a room behind the door. There were more doors, and those doors led to new and surprising discoveries.

The explorations eventually uncovered the communications center they had expected to find, but the equipment was antiquated. Some of it was useful, but the best option was the yacht they had found on the beach at the beginning of the infection.

Lieutenant Gleaton sent O'Reilly, Mullins, and Hupp back to the yacht to cannibalize it for parts, and they returned with good and bad news. The island was overrun with PITS in such large numbers that they were eliminating the rats, but the good news was that more yachts had run aground. It was risky, but they liberated enough parts from nine yachts, and Hupp was able to construct an array of receivers that enabled them to keep tabs on the outside world.

The strays, as the squad called them, had an interesting story to tell, but the part that had the most impact was that they had actually been in a city when it all started. The soldiers had been on Attu Island and were only vaguely aware that something bad was happening. Everyone asked them more than once what it had been like, each one of them in search of any piece of information they may have forgotten to mention. In particular, they wanted to know if they had heard anything about their hometowns.

Michael was important to the survivors because he had given them answers to the existence of the shelter when he presented the folder from the Governor of Alaska. The three Russian immigrants were valuable additions to the team when it came to earning their keep. It was as if they felt the need to express their gratitude for being given a safe place to be. They translated documents when Hupp got stuck, and

Galina took great delight in cooking. She and Mullins bumped heads in the kitchen at first, but after a month, they would have missed each other if they had to cook alone.

Michael had an entirely different set of skills. There wasn't a need for a helicopter pilot inside the shelter, but it wasn't really a surprise to find out he was an ace mechanic. He said he considered it a necessary part of flying helicopters because they couldn't carry a mechanic with them every time they took off.

The population of the shelter was officially at ten people, but there was a nervousness they all carried because of the size of the place. Everyone, even O'Reilly, felt like they had to sleep with one eye open. Mullins commented that the place was so drab with its gunmetal gray walls that it didn't seem like the lights were ever bright enough. They stared at shadows for so long that they started to move.

The three strays said it was typical Russian decor and that there was a standing joke about interior decorators in their country. Ritter took the bait and asked them what it was.

Oleg said, "What do you call a Russian hitman? An interior decorator."

"I don't get it," said Ritter.

"It means," said Mullins, "that the only way you're going to get any color added to a room in Russia is if a hitman whacks someone in the room."

"I still don't get it," said Ritter. "Why not just paint the room?"

"Let me try," said Galina. "Private Ritter, our country is not known for being colorful."

"So, you're saying that this place was decorated by Russians?"

"That's a shocker," said Mullins. "He actually got it."

The dull colors and dim lights made more than the shadows move. It made them feel like something would walk out of the shadows at any moment, and they would be faced with the terrors that had consumed the outside world.

They decided that everyone would live on the second floor in the hotel-like section of the shelter. There were enough rooms in a row, and one person could stand watch over the balcony that ran the length of the row. Since there was a set of stairs on each end, they blocked one end off with a net made of ropes, and that gave them the luxury of only needing to post one guard above the other set of stairs. From the vantage point of the second floor above the stairs, nothing could come out of the shadows and climb the stairs without being seen.

Routines became the only saving grace for the ten people inside the shelter. Galina would wake up before the rest of them and begin preparing breakfast. The squad kept to their military schedule even though they couldn't tell if it was day or night outside, so they all took advantage of her exceptionally good food.

After breakfast, O'Reilly led the others, with the exceptions of Lieutenant Gleaton and Corporal Hupp, on searches of the unexplored corners of the shelter. Gleaton and Hupp secured a room and turned it into a communications center so they could keep tabs on the situation outside.

By midday, the search teams would return for lunch and then go to their other assigned tasks. Preventative maintenance included cleaning weapons and inspecting the systems that kept them alive. The power that gave them lights and recirculating air had to be coming from somewhere, and the water coming out of the taps was purified. That meant it was a priority to locate the power source.

Using the records uncovered by Hupp, they found the third entrance to the shelter, and it was not like the others. Located at the top of a ladder that scaled the wall thirty feet above the highest level in the shelter, there was a simple platform big enough for four people and a steel door. Just climbing the ladder made each of them feel like they needed a safety harness, and looking down wasn't recommended.

Mullins made the first climb by himself, and he shouted down that the door wasn't locked. When he pushed it open, he discovered why. It opened onto a vertical cliff face that ended on the rocks at the base of the steepest mountain on Attu Island. Another ladder made of rungs that were implanted directly into the rock of the cliff rose to dizzying heights, but the worst part was that there was no platform. Mullins leaned out, gripped the first rung, and faced upward. There were three old wind turbines above that were so far away they appeared to be tiny. They were a rusty red color and didn't look exactly like the white blades on turbines in modern wind farms. They were bulky rather than sleek.

When he climbed back down to the rest of the squad, the first thing Mullins said was that he knew why the door was unlocked. It would be a scary climb for anyone who was afraid of heights. The second thing he said was that they would need to use safety lines if they were expected to do maintenance on the wind turbines. Everyone was relieved when Pavel and Oleg volunteered for the job. Pavel made the first climb up to the turbines and came back exhausted, but he reported that the turbines were a Russian design. They were definitely old, but they appeared to be functioning well.

Talbot didn't show up for three months. On that morning, Galina woke up and went to the kitchen as she always did. The corridors were as dark as ever, and she was probably the only member of the team who didn't bother anyone to escort her.

Galina preferred to let Oleg sleep because he was always so tired when he came to bed. He was always trying to show the Americans he was useful, and the climbs to and from the wind turbines had taken a toll on him. He had privately told her that the worst part of the climb was after he entered the base of the turbines. When he volunteered for the job, he didn't know they were two hundred feet high. By the time he reached that ladder, he was beyond exhausted.

Oleg was so sound asleep when she left for the kitchen that she didn't even bother to be quiet. She passed Corporal Mincy at the top of the stairs. She had been on guard duty and was ready for Galina's breakfast.

"What's on the menu today, Chef?"

Galina laughed at the joke, but she liked the nickname. Just like her husband, she wanted to be part of the team.

"What would you like for breakfast, Christine?"

"Is it too much to ask for blueberry pancakes, bacon, and eggs?"

"As you Americans like to say, no problem," she said with a big smile.

Mincy returned the smile and asked, "Are you sure you don't need an escort to the kitchen?"

"I'll be fine. It is not far from here, and I will yell if I need you."

Galina went down the stairs and across the courtyard. Mincy watched her every step of the way until she disappeared down the dark corridor. Several seconds passed, and she knew Galina must've made it to the kitchen without a problem.

In the dark hallway outside the kitchen, Galina didn't see the movement in the shadows. She unlocked the double doors that entered the dining room and went inside. She wasn't sure what was different than any other day, but when the door swung shut behind her, something made her reach up and lock the door from the inside. As soon as she flipped the light switch up, the dining room was bathed in bright light, and whatever small sense of dread she had felt was washed away instantly. She didn't look back toward the door, but even if she had, she wouldn't have seen Shirley Talbot's face on the other side of the glass because it was so bright in the dining room that everything inside reflected from the glass.

Galina immediately disappeared through the door of the kitchen and went to work laying out the supplies for breakfast. Talbot lost interest in the empty dining room and moved on.

Just under an hour later, Mincy arrived at the dining room just as Galina unlocked the door from the inside. Mincy was already starting to say something about the smell of bacon in the air when she felt something wet on the handle of the door. She held her hand up in the light from the dining hall and saw that her fingers and palm were covered in something brown and greasy. She sniffed at it and recoiled.

Quick thinking saved her. The smell of rot on her hand made her remember the yacht and their first encounter with the PITS. Mincy backed Galina into the dining room with her other hand and grabbed the latch on the door, all in one motion. With her own reflection in the glass of the small window, she saw the eroded face of Private Talbot.

Even with the door between them, the sight of Shirley Talbot unnerved Mincy. They hadn't known each other long, but they were part of the same squad, and they had been the only women assigned to the detail. From the first day, she had taken Talbot under her wing, and in some ways, she felt responsible for what had happened to her. Now, Talbot was working her mouth against the glass as if she could bite her way through it.

Mincy reached to her hip and wrapped her hand around her Baretta M9, but then she stopped. She could easily shoot Talbot through the glass, but something told her she didn't want to spend a few years looking at the hole where she had shot her friend. It was hard enough to kill Talbot, or they would have done it before she became a PIT.

"Galina, get me a long kitchen knife while I keep an eye on her."

"What are you going to do?"

"I have to go out there and do it. Don't ask why. I don't really want to explain it."

Galina ran to the kitchen for the knife, and Mincy was left with nothing to do but watch Talbot's grotesque face. She was horrified but curiously detached at the same time, and she found herself drawn to the tragedy of what her friend had become. Mincy stepped closer to the window until her own face was almost touching the glass, and she was aware that her breath fogged the window, but Talbot's breath didn't. For some reason, that little detail made her more sure of what she had to do.

Galina returned with a large kitchen knife that would do the job.

"Stand over there. I'm going to use the door to knock her down, then I'll hurry out and take care of her."

Mincy gripped the blade in her right hand with the blade pointed outward. She unlocked the door and threw her weight against it with her left shoulder as hard as she could. The impact knocked Talbot backward and down just as Mincy hoped, but since her face had been against the glass, she was thrown further than Mincy had wanted.

It had also been too bright in the dining room. In the dim light of the hallway, Mincy had to locate Talbot before she could eliminate her. White dots floated across her vision as she tried to adjust her eyes, and Talbot had the time to get back to her feet. At the exact moment when Christine Mincy could finally see her target clearly, a hand gripped her shoulder and pulled her backward.

Mincy didn't have the chance to form expectations about who was pulling her away from Talbot. The grip was so strong that it could have been O'Reilly or Mullins, but as she was spun around, she only knew that she didn't recognize the face. Time seemed to slow down, but only because she suddenly felt like she wasn't going to have enough time to survive. Alone with a knife in her hand, she knew she couldn't take on two of the infected creatures they called PITS.

Something clicked in the mind of Corporal Christine Mincy. There was a time in hand-to-hand combat training when she was fighting face-to-face with another trainee. The training officer had grabbed her from behind to test her reactions. She had surprised him by letting her body drop to the mat instead of resisting him, and when he came at her on the ground, she had dropped him with a strategically placed kick.

This time was different, though. Her training officer wasn't trying to bite her, and the other trainee hadn't continued to fight her. Christine dropped the knife, and this time, when it went to the grip of her Glock, she drew the gun and fired two shots into the face of the PIT that had pulled her backward, readjusted her position, and fired two more shots into Shirley Talbot. It was over in seconds.

The door to the dining room had swung shut after Corporal Mincy had rammed into it. Galina didn't see what happened, but the deafening blasts of the Glock made her legs become weak. She dropped to the floor and waited for what seemed like an eternity. When the door opened again, it was Oleg, and behind him was Corporal Mincy, being pulled inside by Sergeant O'Reilly. They were followed by the rest of the living population of the Rat Island shelter, and they were frantically checking her for wounds.

"Corporal Mincy," yelled O'Reilly, "are we good? Were you bitten?"

Her ears were ringing after firing four rounds in the confines of the hallway, so O'Reilly's voice seemed like it came from miles away. She kept shaking her head from side to side, trying to let him know that she couldn't hear him but also saying that she was okay. He finally understood, and he also couldn't find any wounds. O'Reilly sat heavily on a table and let out a tremendous sigh of relief.

"Where did that PIT come from?" he yelled at no one in particular. Everyone had expected Talbot to show up sooner or later, but the other guy was new.

Mullins spoke up for everyone and said, "Your guess is as good as ours, Sarge. All we can do now is make sure this doesn't happen again."

"You bet it won't," bellowed O'Reilly. "Right after chow, I want everyone on patrol again. If this place isn't completely clean, then we need to make sure there aren't any holes where PITS can get inside."

None of the survivors inside the shelter took O'Reilly's anger personally. They knew that he took responsibility for their lives and even blamed himself for what had happened. That made them even more determined to make it up to him. Above all, they felt like they had failed Christine Mincy. She was okay, but they could see her hands shaking as they took turns giving her a hug.

Everyone had expected to run into Shirley Talbot sooner or later. They knew she was out there, and even though the corridors and rooms were dark, there were the occasional smudges on the floors or walls that meant she had passed by. Now, they weren't so sure, and they had to wonder if there were more of them out there.

Over breakfast, there was very little conversation, and none of it was small talk. There was none of the usual banter that kept everyone lighthearted. The low voices of O'Reilly and Gleaton didn't give away what they were thinking, but they were in agreement that something had to change. No one could say they had become complacent, but they should never have allowed Galina to go to the kitchen alone, and Mincy should not have followed by herself.

O'Reilly stood up to speak, and everyone took it to mean he and the Lieutenant had reached some decisions.

"Listen up, people. I think it goes without saying that we're glad to still have Corporal Mincy with us, but we also know how it could've turned out. I won't say she got lucky because I think her training saved her life. I would want her with me in close-quarters combat after what I saw today. That having been said, it shouldn't have come to that, so we're making some changes."

Ritter raised his hand and then asked, "You think there's more PITS out there, Sarge?"

"You just hit on two of the changes at the same time, Private. Both of them are how we think of these things. Lieutenant Gleaton and I don't think everyone is taking these infected people seriously because we haven't had as much contact with them as the rest of the world. We need to remember they're infected, and they're dead. If we called them zombies, it would feel like a joke every time we talked about them. By calling them PITS, we've minimized the danger they represent."

"What else can we call them?" asked Ritter.

"We all saw the broadcasts on the yacht, and Hupp has been able to tune in a lot of radio signals. It seems like the whole world is calling them the infected dead. I want all of us to call them the same thing. Maybe it'll make us remember they aren't living people anymore, and they carry an infection that can't be cured. If you get it, you're gonna die."

"What's the other change?" asked Mincy.

"You already know, Corporal. From now on, if I see one of you somewhere, I had better see two of you. We're going to keep searching this facility to figure out where the other one came from and to see if there are more. There will hopefully come a time when we decide the problem has been dealt with, but until then, we're under the two-man rule. I don't care how you do it, but if you go anywhere away from the second level, find someone to go with you."

After they all finished eating, all ten of them went into the kitchen and took over the dishwashing and cleaning so they could secure the door and leave as a group. Their first stop was the second level, where they all put on as much protective clothing as they could. O'Reilly said they were going deeper into the shelter than before, and they would do it every day until it was done. Any room that still contained the infected dead would be cleared before they moved on. It would be hard work, so everyone was included. Oleg, Pavel, Galina, and Michael were all glad to do their part.

Over the next four hours, the squad moved from room to room as if they were in a foreign country fighting a war. Rooms they had previously marked as being occupied were entered one at a time, and the infected inside were systematically eliminated. If the rooms were lightly populated, they used bayonets. If they were crowded, the doors were propped open, and the squad fell back to a defensive posture and shot the infected as they came out. The headcount at the end of four hours was eighty-three, and they were still on the first level.

The hardest part of the job wasn't clearing the rooms...it was disposing of the bodies. The shortest distance to travel with them was the entrance where the boats were docked, so they decided their only choice would be to haul them out and dump them into the water. There was a slight current that pulled at the water inside the cave when the tide went out, so the bodies eventually drifted through the entrance into the lagoon.

After a break to eat field rations, the squad went back to work. They were relieved to find the first room was unoccupied, but O'Reilly said he still wanted the room to be closely inspected. It turned out to be a good idea because the contents of the room gave them all the emotional uplift they needed.

Hupp had already uncovered information that showed how the Russians had renovated the shelter after it had been built. The Americans had intended the shelter to be a comfortable refuge in the event of a catastrophic event, such as a nuclear war. The Russians didn't understand the need for luxuries and had virtually stripped it of the decadence installed by the Americans. They had purged the rooms of unnecessary comforts, and they undoubtedly planned to dispose of the items, but some of it was just stored in unused rooms.

One discovery, however, was a recent delivery that must have been brought to the shelter by Russians who had a taste for American movies. The squad felt like they had found a long-lost treasure. There were thousands of Blu-Ray videos stacked on shelves that went from the floor to the ceiling. Blu-ray players were still in sealed boxes next to more boxes of TV sets. Even Sergeant O'Reilly was momentarily held captive by the discovery. They hadn't enjoyed any entertainment that didn't involve board games or a deck of cards since arriving on Attu Island. Things were about to change for the better.

All ten of them felt like kids in a candy store, and they indulged themselves for a few minutes checking the titles. There was everything they could possibly want, but the unanimous first choice everyone wanted to watch was the movie about a pandemic in New York that turned people into crazed, fast-moving zombies that could only come out at night. An Army doctor was stranded in the city and worked on a cure by himself. They had all seen the movie, even their Russian friends, but they identified with it and wanted to see it again.

O'Reilly said, "All right, people. Time to move out. Someone mark this room on the map, and we'll come back later to check out a few movies."

As they moved deeper into the shelter, they saw more signs that the infected had been in the area. They weren't confined to closed rooms, so the squad was forced to move quietly as they followed fresh trails. They came to a door that was propped open with a rubber wedge at the bottom. The trail of body fluids led straight to it, and it was dark inside.

Mullins was in the lead, and he gave hand signals to the others that he couldn't see anything inside. O'Reilly tossed him a chem stick, and motioned for Mullins to throw it in across the floor. Mullins activated the chemical light and then threw it around the corner of the door. It bounced and rolled, but then it disappeared.

"Flashlights," said O'Reilly.

They didn't need every light to see they had found one of the nerve centers of the shelter. The beams from their flashlights barely reached the opposite wall, and the room hummed with the vibrations from equipment that was stacked along the walls. The chem stick Mullins had thrown into the room had disappeared because the floor was at least ten feet below the door. A short platform extended outward only a few feet from the door, and a ladder was attached to the end.

When they turned on their flashlights, it was like someone had kicked over an anthill except louder. The floor below them was full of the infected. They filled every space between the equipment, and every one of them began incessantly groaning louder than the sound of the equipment.

O'Reilly cautiously approached the ladder and shone his light down on the infected. They reached for him with outstretched arms. He watched in disbelief as the ones at the bottom of the ladder were crushed by the weight of the others.

"I'm glad they can't climb ladders," said Mullins.

"Me too," said O'Reilly, "but we can't wait for something to break down in here before we clear this room, and it won't be easy."

"We can reach them with spiked poles," said Mullins.

"That wasn't what I meant. How are we going to get them out of there after we spike them? There must be a couple hundred of them in here. If we kill the ones closest to us, the rest are just going to climb their piled-up bodies until they're able to climb onto the platform with us. You handled supplies for us, Mullins. How do you think we should do this?"

Corporal Mullins thought O'Reilly was joking with him at first and laughed. When O'Reilly didn't crack a grin, he realized the comment wasn't rhetorical.

"Supplies never tried to bite me, Sarge. What makes you think I have an idea?"

"I was just talking about volume, Corporal. How can we move this many bodies fast enough? If we have to carry them all one at a time, it's going to take days or even weeks."

"Oh, I see what you mean, Sarge. We have to kill them up here. If we kill them down there, we won't even be able to get their bodies out. How can we get them up here before we kill them?"

"Now you're just messing with me, Mullins. I'm asking you how you would get them up here before you kill them. Any ideas?"

"You know we have a couple of forklifts, right? Why don't we rope them and then use the forklift to pull them out? We could use the other forklift to carry a load of them to the dock and dump them in the water."

"That's at least an idea," said O'Reilly. "Do the forklifts still work?"

"If they don't, we've got some pretty good mechanics in the squad, Sarge."

It seemed like a good idea at the time, but it needed some fine-tuning. The forklifts were old, but a little bit of light maintenance got them both running. The problem was successfully roping the infected. Mullins managed to get a rope over the head of one, but the rope became tight before he could get it past the neck. The infected resisted his attempt to free the rope again, so he used a spiked pole to kill it. When he used the forklift to pull the infected onto the platform, all he got was the head.

Mincy suggested they might have more luck if they dropped the rope and made it miss the infected. Then when one stepped into the lasso, pull it tight and haul them up by their legs. That worked better than getting the rope around their heads, and they had a steady flow of catches and kills for a while, but sometimes they only hauled up a leg, and they had to try for the rest.

Half of the squad went back with the other forklift and removed the bodies from the other rooms while the other five lassoed the infected in the large electrical facility. After six hours, they knew they would have to spend several days to clear the room.

"Let's just hope we don't find more rooms like this one," said O'Reilly.

******

It took a month for them to clear the infected dead from the Rat Island shelter, but when they were through, they felt like they had inspected every possible hiding place. They also located the storage areas where the Russians had put some of the amenities they had removed from the original shelter. To improve morale, Lieutenant Gleaton allowed Mullins to run raffles and competitions for some of those amenities.

The Russians had provided an ample supply of vodka when they occupied the shelter, but they hadn't disposed of the scotch, bourbon, rum, gin, and tequila that the Americans had stockpiled. Those items weren't raffled or put up as prizes. They were closely inventoried and then put on a rationing schedule. There was enough to last a few years, even though everyone would have been perfectly fine to consume them all in one night.

Everyone got used to the idea that they would probably be inside the shelter until long after the liquor was gone, but the news from the outside never changed. There was only less of it. After the main broadcasts ended and there were only Civil Defense broadcasts, they heard the same reports every day. Gradually, even those ended.

20

Rogue

Joint Base Elmendorf-Richardson - April 2023

"Let me get this straight," said the Chief. "You think there are ex-military units that went rogue and are nearby?"

The Chief decided he needed to confront Colonel Daugherty about Captain Miller's former commanders on the off chance they would have a run-in with them.

"No, I didn't say they're nearby," said Colonel Daugherty. "I said they were here not long ago. They left in a hurry after they found something in the safe that belonged to the base commander at the start of the infection."

"Do you know what they found?"

"Not a clue, but it seemed like they couldn't care less about us anymore. That's how some of them wound up in the stockade."

"What do you mean?" asked the Chief.

"Well, the way we saw it, they were high-ranking officers from all branches, and our base was at their disposal, but they tried to conscript people stationed here to go with them. They also took large amounts of our supplies, what little we had left. I had the support of my junior officers and the units originally stationed here, and we stood up to them. It turned into a fight that cost people on both sides. Some of them escaped."

Hampton had been listening in on the conversation, and he asked the Chief if he would mind a suggestion. The Chief trusted him and said he was all ears.

"We need to know exactly where these people are and what they're doing," said Hampton. "If not, we're going to stumble across them one day and lose some of our own people, especially if we hang around Alaska."

The Chief understood quite well that some units had done better than others. Back at the beginning of the infection, he had met Captain Miller by coming to the rescue of Miller's unit. He had dumped precious fuel from his plane on the infected dead who were on the verge of overrunning the Army near Columbia, South Carolina. They might not have survived without the Chief's help, but they were trying their level best to put up a good fight against the infected.

Since that night, they had many more encounters with military units that had given in to the temptations posed by the new world. In Huntsville, Alabama, the military officers had allowed a sheriff to dictate policy in return for a few creature comforts. The NCOs had kept their fidelity to the service and just needed help from the Chief and his friends to get back on the right path.

The Air Force units in Wyoming had splintered because some people just knew how to influence weaker minds. If they had stayed together, maybe the silos would have eventually become functional societies on their own. The Chief and the rest of the Mud Island family were there every time to help those units get on their feet again.

The one time they saw it happen the other way around was when Captain Miller showed up on their doorstep. He brought one hundred people and lots of equipment with him, but he was also doing something that went against his own nature...he was deserting. It wasn't something that came easily to him, but it was either leave or become a part of a unit that didn't prioritize the safety of its members.

The command that Captain Miller belonged with was comprised of members from all branches of the US Armed Forces. When the infection began, those individuals and units that survived reorganized into a large fighting force in the Atlantic Ocean. It was just a fraction of the former superpower that protected the United States, but it was still the only hope the country had of fighting back against the infection. They had an entire fleet of Navy ships, squadrons of planes and helicopters belonging to all of the branches of the service, and thousands of servicemen, but the senior ranking officers were making a mistake that would cost them everything.

The Chief realized he had been reflecting on the past and what that combined force could have meant to the survival of the whole world. He hadn't noticed that he had tuned out Colonel Daugherty and Hampton.

"Where'd you go, Chief?" asked Hampton.

"I was thinking about what you said. We've been focused on helping here, but if they're still out there, they could still be doing their thing."

"Which is?" asked Daugherty.

"The same thing they've always been doing. Experimenting on the infected dead and getting their own people killed in the process. Imagine what we could have done to fight back against the infected if they had focused on that instead of exposing everyone to the infection by bringing it back to the ships."

Daugherty said, "We wanted to help them at first, but you're right. They would've gotten the rest of us here killed if we had allowed them to bring the infected on the base. I can't believe they brought them back to their own ships."

"As you know, that didn't go so well," said Hampton.

"If you were them, where would you have gone?" asked the Chief.

Colonel Daugherty gave it some thought and said, "I have two ideas. You know those guys in the stockade? They talk too much when you get them separated from each other."

"I'm listening," said the Chief.

"I think some of them know more than they're saying, but they don't know you're former military. They also don't know you well enough to know that your personal code of conduct would stop you short of torturing them for a little intelligence."

Hampton snorted.

"The Chief may have relaxed his code of conduct a little since the start of the infection."

"In that case, maybe we can have you talk with them privately to see what they know."

The Chief spent another hour with Colonel Daugherty getting as much information as he could from him about the officers in the stockade. Some of them were hardcore, but most of them would be glad to sell their souls to get out of jail. That meant he had leverage going in, and if they wanted out badly enough, he wondered how fast they would cough up some details if they were requested by the right person. He decided to send in the heavy-hitters.

Kathy, Iris, and Colleen were sitting in a comfortable meeting room on a sofa, waiting for the arrival of the young Ensign. Morris Boone had been assigned to his first ship for only one week when the infection began. Practically overnight, he had gone from being a wet-behind-the-ears junior officer to being a survivor of the biggest test to ever face mankind. He had watched his senior officers make one mistake after the next until they had reduced a task force to a few dozen people with very few resources. Morris was very nervous.

They had selected Ensign Boone from the officers they had in captivity because they didn't think they would need to use unacceptable tactics to get him to talk. They also thought they could take advantage of his ego by leaving other men out of the room. He might let his guard down a bit if he didn't feel threatened, and if the Chief had interrogated him, the man would have felt so threatened that he was likely to have a heart attack.

"Ensign Morris Boone?" said Iris.

"Yes, Ma'am," he said as he cautiously sat down in a recliner across from the sofa.

He was clearly surprised to find himself facing three attractive women, and the one who had spoken to him had incredibly striking silver hair. That's why he had responded as if he was speaking with someone who was more of a mother figure.

"My name is Iris. The lady on my right is Kathy, and this is Colleen. We have a few questions for you."

Iris hoped she was reminding Ensign Boone of the days before the infection. If he respected his mother or had sisters and a girlfriend, then they could appeal to his softer side.

Kathy asked, "Did you lose close family to the infection, Ensign?"

"Everyone has, Ma'am."

He stumbled a bit on the last word because he could guess they were about the same age, but she had an air of superiority about her… not in a bad way. It was more like she was a leader.

"Are you three in charge now?" he asked.

"Heavens, no, we aren't in charge," said Iris, "but we figured you would rather talk with us than the guy who is. You see, we all have things in common, and there's no need for us to be on opposite sides. Wouldn't you like to be let out of your cell and be useful again? We can't do anything about the people we lost, but we can fight back against the thing that killed them."

"That's what we've been trying to do," he said, "and now that we're close to having a safe place to do the job, all we wanted was a few people to help us."

Boone leaned forward in his recliner and delivered an explanation that sounded more like a rehearsed speech. He was clearly sold on the ideas of his superiors which told the three women he was easily manipulated. He explained to them that the experiments were necessary for them to find a cure for the infection and that they could only find a cure if they had a large number of test subjects. He added that they could only have a large number of test subjects if they could have ready access to them. That was why they had to bring them back to the ships with them in the first place.

All three women recognized Boone was not only giving a well-rehearsed speech, but he was also delivering an indoctrination philosophy. It sounded like something that had been said to him repeatedly, and even worse, he was saying it to them with conviction. He had really bought into the ideas that had failed so badly.

Iris wondered if he had ever been faced with any tough questions about the need for a large test population when they could learn practically everything they needed to know with one of the infected dead.

She asked herself, "What could they learn that was different from one or two of the infected? Why would they need more?"

Then she realized the answer to her own question, and it made her feel cold all over. She didn't notice that she herself had leaned forward when Ensign Boone did. Maybe it was her subconscious mind picking up on something about him, but when the answer came to her, Kathy and Colleen were watching her reactions as much as they were Ensign Boone's.

"Iris?" said Kathy. "What is it?"

Colleen saw that Iris' lower jaw had dropped, and her mouth was open. It was an expression of shock or possibly horror as if she was sitting in the presence of a monster.

"Ensign Boone," Iris began in a shaky voice, "were you and your friends experimenting on uninfected people?"

Boone's expression didn't change. He had no more of a reaction than a serial killer would have when asked if he would kill again. Kathy and Colleen didn't keep the same composure. They both felt the revulsion that Iris had a moment earlier, and it was a moment of clarity.

"Is that how the infection broke out of containment on the ships?" asked Kathy.

Boone's composure broke enough for anger to break through, and his teeth clenched together as he said, "People didn't follow orders. If they had just listened, we would have finished our work, and we weren't just a bunch of friends. We were in charge. It was our job to save the world, and anyone who died because of our experiments died for a good cause."

"What's he saying?" asked Colleen. She probably understood what was happening but couldn't believe her ears.

Iris said, "He's saying they needed to test the cures on healthy subjects, and the healthy subjects became infected."

"Who were the healthy subjects?" asked Kathy hesitantly.

"I'm not saying another word," said Boone.

"Who was first?" asked Iris. "Did you start with healthy refugees, or did you use your own people…military personnel? Wait, let me guess. When all ships were ordered to put to sea as quickly as possible, you had to do it without full compliments."

Iris turned to Kathy and Colleen.

"Remember the HMS Ambush had to take people from other boats, and they even accepted civilians they rescued and made them members of their crew."

She faced Boone again and said, "You put to sea with civilians on board. Your ship met up with the fleet at a rally point, and someone assumed command. Your command assessed the total complement of survivors and the command assets. Am I right so far?"

Ensign Boone returned her gaze with a contemptuous glare.

"I'll take that as a yes. Once the assets were assessed, it was determined that your command couldn't maintain its fighting capabilities if it was going to be forced to expend material assets to support nonessential personnel. In other words, what were they going to do with all the people?"

"We didn't have a choice," blurted the Ensign.

He had seen the expression on their faces change from kind to disdain. It was the same change he had seen years ago when they had begun separating families. First, they had taken the men. If they could perform a useful function, they were put in uniforms. If they couldn't, they were taken to the labs. No one could object, or they would receive the same treatment.

Iris was calculating the steps as if Boone had said the first one aloud.

"What did you do when you didn't have enough men? You went through the men without families first, but there weren't enough of them. You made the decision to take all of them, but you eventually went back for their families. I mean, who would know?"

Kathy and Colleen said almost simultaneously, "You used children as test subjects?"

Under their accusing eyes and questions, Ensign Boone couldn't keep himself from answering if they were wrong.

"No, we didn't do that. We weren't monsters. We reevaluated our capability to rescue more survivors."

"What the hell does that mean?" asked Colleen.

"I can answer that," said Kathy. "Instead of rescuing survivors, they started capturing them. Let me guess. You sent raiding parties to the mainland from the ships. When they saw families, they ignored their pleas for help. If they saw men alone, they picked them up. The men thought they were being rescued."

The women had easily gotten under the overzealous Ensign's skin, and he didn't see where it mattered anymore how much they knew, so he angrily explained it to them. In his misogynistic mind, he felt like they needed help to understand.

"It wasn't the way it looks."

"Why don't you tell us how it was so we can understand better?" asked Colleen. She used a tone of voice that was almost helpless like she couldn't possibly understand if she didn't have him to guide her.

"There were too many survivors, and we couldn't help them all," he began, and to the women, he showed the first, faintest hint of sincerity. There was a glimmer of regret as he remembered those days seven years earlier.

"Every time rescue crews came back, they said the same thing. For every ten they picked up, one hundred more were on the ground. There was no way to screen them to be sure they weren't infected. You don't know how many times they came back with someone who had a bite wound. Sometimes, everyone in the same rescue was infected. Can you imagine what it was like? You expend resources, you send out a crew in a helicopter to rescue people, and they come back with ten who are already infected. What were we supposed to do with them, throw them overboard? They couldn't be cured, and they were only good for one thing."

"You locked them up and watched them die so you could study the progression of the infection," said Iris.

"They were treated humanely and kept comfortable."

"I'll bet they were," said Kathy.

Iris said, "What happened next? Wait, let me guess again. You were also losing crews who went out on rescue missions, so you stopped sending them. That's when you turned to the test subjects you already had in large supply."

"I told you already. We didn't have a choice."

Colleen asked, "What happened when you took healthy family members away from their loved ones? Is that when the rebellions started?"

"Rebellions? You mean the traitors who tried to stop the tests and the cowards who deserted."

Kathy said, "I wouldn't call them cowards. The ones we've met were some of the bravest military personnel in the world."

"Yeah, I heard you have one of them with you. Let me have five minutes alone with him, and I'll show you how much of a coward he is."

All three women had to laugh at that empty threat.

"Sonny," said Iris, "Captain Miller would play with you like a big cat and tiny mouse."

Kathy had picked up on something she knew Captain Miller would be glad to know.

"You said traitors and deserters. How many people left?"

He hung his head with his eyes to the floor and said, "I don't know. Ships broke away from the fleet with full crews and disappeared. Some of them became like pirates and raided civilian vessels for supplies."

"How was that different than what you did?" asked Iris. "You took people, and they took supplies, but both of you were handing out death sentences."

"We were trying to help."

Boone said each word slowly and emphasized the last word.

"Forgive me if I don't agree to the difference," said Iris. "So, you're saying the whole thing fell apart."

"There weren't enough crews left to maintain confinement, and the infection spread on every ship. We had to evacuate."

Colleen couldn't resist twisting the screws a bit and said, "Funny how it was desertion when other people did it, but it was evacuation when you did it."

"I'm no deserter. I had orders to leave, and they didn't."

"And you always follow orders," added Iris. "You said you were finally close to having a safe place to do your work. What were your orders once you got there?"

"You're not tricking me, lady. I'm not telling you anything about our plans."

"You already did," said Iris.

Iris knew that right-handed people always looked to the left when they tried to remember something that was said or when they tried to do math in their head. She didn't think he was trying to do math, so she knew he was trying to remember what he might have said that would give them a clue where his command had gone. They had kept him talking long enough, and they had gotten him angry enough that he wondered if he had said too much.

"I didn't tell you a thing."

"You told us enough," said Kathy as she stood up.

Iris and Colleen joined her, and as they stood, she said, "Are you familiar with the advice to be careful what you ask for because you might just get what you want?"

Before Ensign Boone could answer, the door opened, and the largest man he had ever seen walked into the room.

"Who's this? Is he supposed to scare me?"

Boone was obviously scared because he stood up too. It did nothing to make him feel better, though, because he got to see exactly how small he was compared with the stone-faced man who was staring at him as if he were his next meal.

Iris said, "You told us that your diminished command found a safe place to continue their unsanctioned, inhumane tests. They found the place through some piece of information they located here on the base."

Boone's eyes moved to the left again, and she knew he was trying to remember when he had said that. He couldn't remember, and he had no way of knowing they had gotten that part from Colonel Daugherty.

"You told us that you would have gone with them if you hadn't been captured, so that means you know where they went. You also said you wanted five minutes alone with one of the deserters. This man is here to grant your request. Let us know if you decide you need more than five minutes."

The Chief thought Iris gave a masterful performance. She delivered her unrehearsed speech as if she had taken weeks to prepare. There was the perfect mixture of fact and sarcasm in her tone and her choice of words for the Ensign to have no doubt that he wasn't going to last five minutes alone with the big man. The women paraded past him out the door in single file, and the Chief had to resist the urge to make eye contact with her. Instead, he kept his eyes on the Ensign to make him as uncomfortable as possible.

Kathy stopped behind the Chief and said to Boone, "He knows everything you did on the ships, and he's had seven years to want payback for what you did to his family. So, he's only going to ask you one question, and he's only going to ask you one time. What is the exact location of the rest of your command? If you answer him, he's under orders to walk away from you. If you don't answer him, he has no obligation to do anything but get his payback."

When the door closed, leaving the Chief and Ensign Boone alone, Boone was busy trying to remember the big man and if he had been dumb enough to do something to his family. A moment of eye contact told him it didn't matter what he remembered as long as the man remembered, and his mouth was opening to ask the question he would only ask once.

Iris, Kathy, and Colleen stepped into the next room and moved a few feet from the door.

"Do you think he'll talk?" asked Colleen.

Iris said, "If he knows anything, he will."

"You were really great in there," said Kathy. "It was everything I could do to stay in my seat after the part about testing on healthy people."

"I know, I was disgusted too," said Colleen.

The door opened again, and the Chief pulled it shut behind him as he joined the women. All three had their eyebrows raised in expressions that asked the obvious question.

"You softened him up pretty good," said the Chief with a huge grin. "He started talking before I had a chance to say anything. It looks like we're going out to the Aleutian Islands."

******

One of the things that made the Mud Island family stand out from other survivors was the way they filled crucial jobs without being concerned about whether or not they should be doing something else. They all had skills, and they naturally assumed duties without anyone holding their hands.

Garrett Carson couldn't get enough of tinkering with the AC-130, and Sim had joked with the Chief about losing the plane to him. The Chief had other plans for Garrett's skills, but he let him have his fun for now. The plane would be well-tuned during its stay in Alaska if he left Garret alone with it long enough.

Ensign Boone had plenty of information to share with the Chief, but it presented him with a lot of problems. The powerful weapons on the AC-130 would be useful if there was a fight out in the open, but if all of the new intelligence was correct, they would need transportation that had been either neglected or cannibalized for parts. Fortunately for them, they had four pilots. Hampton could fly fixed-wing planes, but the Chief felt like they could teach him how to handle a Black Hawk fast enough. Now all they needed was something to fly.

The Chief, Garrett, and Jon King all met in a hangar that housed several helicopters in various states of repair…none of them good. The only good news was that they were all Sikorsky UH-60 Black Hawks, and they would get them where they wanted to go if they could be repaired.

"How long would it take to get three of these in the air?" asked the Chief.

"I guess that would depend on how long it took Lockheed Martin to get us all the parts," said Garrett.

Jon added, "We would need the contract approved in the budget first."

The Chief decided to play their game and said, "I have a friend in the Pentagon. He fast-tracked the contract, and the parts were delivered here already. All we have to do is remove them from where they are currently located and place them on machines where they are most likely to result in operational aircraft."

They had a good laugh remembering the days when there was red tape in the way of any project, but they knew what the Chief was getting at. If they had any hope of gaining ground on the rogue military and stopping their misguided projects, they needed the Black Hawks.

"How many birds do we have that can be cannibalized?" asked Garrett.

"Luckily," said the Chief, "we have over a hundred, plus we have at least a few parts that were left on the shelves in supply. There's another thing that we have in our favor that no one thought of already."

Garrett and Jon waited while the Chief savored the moment. His grin told them that he was about to reveal one of his epiphanies that made him unique among the survivors.

"When the infection began, a general order was sent out that recalled all of the helicopters, but according to Colonel Daugherty, at least six tried to land at the Sullivan Arena in Anchorage to pick up military personnel who were stranded. None of them are accounted for," said the Chief.

Jon said, "Not to rain on your parade, but what makes you think they're any better off than all of these specimens we have at our disposal?"

"I agree," said Garrett. "If they could have made it back, they would have. They're most likely rusted hulks of crash sites by now."

The Chief nodded. He knew it was a long shot, but there was always the possibility that the crews had become incapacitated or they had run out of fuel. The aircraft could be just sitting there waiting for new tires, fuel, and a little tender loving care. They wouldn't know until they checked.

"If we get one of these aircraft capable of flying, we can go to Anchorage and find out about the others. With any luck, two of the six will be serviceable. How about it? Can you two miracle workers get one in the air?"

"I only have one question," said Garrett. "Where in the world did you get the idea we were miracle workers?"

It took a week before they were ready to test the engines on a newly assembled Black Hawk, and they only added enough fuel for one attempt. They figured if the engines worked, they could take it for a test flight, but if it blew up, they didn't want it to be a total loss. The test failed, and they wound up spending another week learning from their mistakes. When they fired up the engines the second time, the UH-60 warmed up on the runway long enough for them to fly it across the base. When they landed in front of the hangar, Colonel Daugherty was waiting with the rest of their group to celebrate the success.

"So, you're really going after them."

It was more of a statement than a question.

"I don't suppose you'd like to tell me what Ensign Boone said that gave you any idea where to go."

"If I told you, then you would want to go along," said the Chief.

"They took some of my people," said the Colonel.

"And you feel responsible," answered the Chief. "Would it make you feel better if I told you that I learned enough to know that people will die on this mission if we don't take along people who are ready for this? I've already decided some of my own people aren't going."

Colonel Daugherty seemed caught off guard.

"How many of your people are you taking?"

"Actually, I planned on briefing you as soon as we got three Black Hawks operational. We need about a dozen of your best people, and I would prefer people with experience dropping from a helicopter by rope."

Daugherty's expression changed when he understood what the Chief wanted.

"You're going where a helicopter can't even land. One of the islands?"

The Chief placed a big hand on the Colonel's shoulder, which was something only he could do.

"Baby steps, Colonel. Once we have three operational Black Hawks, I'll tell you everything. If we don't get that far, then we have to figure out a plan B."

******

They lifted off for Anchorage the next morning. The Chief could only take along a modest crew, but the Black Hawk could carry twelve people. If they got lucky, they would need three pilots, but they had four who could fly if they needed to. That meant the other nine people were for protection, but if they weren't busy, they had to be able to handle a wrench. He also had to guess what spare parts were likely to be needed the most, so a pallet was assembled from his list. They would airlift it to the Sullivan Arena and fly back for more if they had to.

On the pallet were four new front tires and eight smaller rear tires. It was a foregone conclusion that they would need to be replaced. They only brought enough fuel and oil to get the helicopters back to the base if the engines started. The assortment of spare parts was just the best guess of the avionics maintenance crews who worked for Colonel

Daugherty.

The Chief, Garrett, and Jon were accompanied by Captain Miller, Hampton, Kathy, Tom, Cassandra, and four soldiers who Daugherty swore were his best mechanics, but they were also combat veterans. The soldiers also knew the area well and would save them valuable time and fuel locating the Sullivan Arena.

21

Fresh Air

Attu Island - January 2023

Six or seven years on Attu Island was more than anyone could have wanted, but there were no other choices left to the occupants of the shelter. There were times when people became stir-crazy and talked about leaving, and there were times when they all felt like living inside a mountain shelter just to stay alive was like living on the Moon. There was a whole world out there before they arrived on Attu Island, and they all wanted that world to be the way it was the last time they saw it.

When the isolation became too much for anyone to bear, O'Reilly would assign that person to assist Corporal Hupp for a day. All it took was a few minutes in the communications room with Hupp to convince any of them that there was nowhere else to go. He began recording everything he heard because news was becoming scarce, and there were fewer messages to record with each passing day.

Regular news broadcasts had stopped years ago. Distress calls had become the new connection with the outside world, but he was under strict orders to ensure the calls were one-sided. There were a few that came from boats that must have been close to the island, and he could have easily directed them to safety, but he had too many recorded messages that warned against taking in strangers.

To maintain perspective, Gleaton and O'Reilly had regular meetings with the Rat Island survivors to remind them of why they had survived. They played a selection of Hupp's recordings that included what went wrong when people let the infection get inside their shelters. It was amazing to hear one common theme played over and over. Someone survived, they tried to save someone else, and they also became infected.

There were only ten occupants of the shelter, but debates over what they should do about other survivors raged among them. Some of them felt guilty about surviving. Some of them just couldn't stand being inside anymore. Some of them wanted revenge against the infected. Emotionally, the years took their toll, and by the time the newcomers arrived, some of them didn't care about surviving anymore. Morale was at its lowest point, and something knocking at the door was a welcome distraction…even if it meant running the risk of letting the infection come inside.

Hupp was in the communications room when he saw an indicator light turn red. The last time it had illuminated was when a large group of the infected dead had stumbled into the tunnel that led to the big vault door. There was a sensor that said something was there, but there were no external cameras to tell them what was on the other side of the door. It had been the only time Lieutenant Gleaton pulled rank on Sergeant O'Reilly and ordered the door to be opened, and he had promised not to do it again when they were done dealing with the infected that had swarmed the door.

Now, the light was red again, and all Hupp could think of was the possibility that this was the time when it was someone who really needed their help. He found O'Reilly walking from the dining room to his quarters.

"Sarge, we have a red light indicator on the tunnel."

"Keep your voice down, Hupp. You know what happened the last time."

Hupp shifted his weight from one foot to the other, clearly nervous about bringing up the tension they had all been feeling.

"It's been a long time, Sarge. I heard Mincy and Galina talking about asking if we could at least go outside, and the Lieutenant told them he would talk it over with you. You know, do a patrol or something…let people breathe some outside air."

O'Reilly stood about six inches taller than Hupp, and sometimes he used his height to put a stop to conversations just by stepping closer to the other person. He took a half step toward Hupp but stopped short. He was well aware that opening the door was dangerous, but he was also aware that everyone had their tipping point, and there were a few people who were about to reach theirs. Opening the door to see what was in the tunnel might serve as a reminder to some of them, and if it turned out to be nothing, maybe it was time to patrol the island. Maybe it was time to breathe some outside air.

"Use the PA system, but try not to sound too excited. Tell everyone to gear up and assemble in the common area. I'll catch Lieutenant Gleaton and let him know what's going on."

Fifteen minutes later, everyone was in combat gear and ready to go outside. If something was in the tunnel, they would deal with it, but O'Reilly said he also wanted to know what was happening on the rest of the island too. He felt like it wasn't unusual that the infected dead had stumbled into the tunnel once before, but he didn't see how it could happen twice unless the island was really crawling with them.

Michael, Oleg, Pavel, and Galina had all begged to be included. They had petitioned Gleaton and O'Reilly several times over the years about becoming soldiers just like the rest of the squad, and they had been given enlisted ranks but only symbolically. Still, O'Reilly didn't see how he could let everyone else go outside without them.

Before they opened the door, O'Reilly thought about any last words he should say to them. He studied their eager faces and remembered how young they had all seemed when they first made camp on the plateau. They had complained about the rats, and they had complained about the perpetually damp island, but they had been new soldiers, and complaining was what new soldiers always did. Only Mullins hadn't complained. He had seen too many good reasons to complain in the Middle East.

"All right, people. When I open that door, I expect there will be infected dead out there. Don't waste ammo lighting up the place. Mullins and I are on point, and we'll deal with hostiles. If we need help, we'll say so. After we clear the tunnel, we're going topside for some fresh air. Everyone ready?"

There was a chorus of answers. No two were the same, but they all meant the same thing. They were ready to see the sun again. O'Reilly signaled Mullins to open the door, and everyone held their breath.

Mullins spun the locking ring and then pushed hard on the big door. It swung silently open, and as it did, Mullins and O'Reilly took aim at the tunnel outside. Nothing moved. There was no growling, no stench of rotten flesh, and no surge of bodies toward the opening. O'Reilly panned his flashlight around the space outside, probing every corner, but there was nothing to see.

"Hupp?"

"Yes, Sarge."

"Any chance that red light was caused by a faulty sensor?"

"Don't know, Sarge. Could also have been rats."

The answer caused O'Reilly and Mullins to both aim their flashlights at the floor of the tunnel. Sure enough, rats ran in the opposite direction.

O'Reilly stepped through the opening and gave the order to move out.

Hupp said, "Lock the door, Sarge?"

"Only if you remember the combination, Corporal."

There was a nervous chuckle from almost everyone as they followed O'Reilly and Mullins into the tunnel, but they went silent as the door closed behind them. Whether Hupp remembered the combination or not, there was a small amount of worry that the door might not open the next time he turned the dial. They were leaving home, and they didn't know it until that moment.

The tunnel seemed longer than they remembered it, but eventually, the faint light at the entrance grew until they were shielding their eyes. They had never experienced a nice day on the island before the infection, so they didn't expect to see the bright sun shining from a clear blue sky. One by one, they emerged onto the outcrop of rock that sloped upward at the tunnel entrance.

O'Reilly remembered when they had discovered the tunnel. The reason it remained so well hidden was because the entrance was lower than the lip of the small plateau outside. He signaled for everyone to stay down while Mullins advanced toward the ledge on his stomach. Mullins extended his head to be able to see the beach below, then motioned for O'Reilly to join him. O'Reilly didn't know what to expect, but he wasn't prepared for what he saw.

If there had been blankets and beach umbrellas, and if the people had been wearing bathing suits, it would have seemed like a normal day on a beach in Southern California. There was nothing normal about the crowd of people wearing water-soaked clothes, and there was nothing normal about the extent of injuries they could see. Some were missing limbs, and some were tripping over their own intestines as they were being dragged through the sand. Rats fed on the eviscerated organs even as they rode on them.

"What do you see?" whispered Lieutenant Gleaton.

"It's not good," said O'Reilly. "It looks like Venice Beach on a busy day, complete with the weirdos and the homeless people."

Gleaton had to see for himself, but he stayed as low as he could.

"That's a surprisingly accurate description, Sergeant. The only thing missing is the vendors. Any suggestions about getting away from the beach without being seen?"

"We can try popping smoke down the beach to the left, but personally, I think there are too many for us to bother. I estimate six dozen just on this stretch of beach, but there's no reason to suspect it's any better elsewhere."

Mullins said, "We can go up the rock face above the tunnel to the next plateau and then angle downward toward our old base camp. If the infected spot us, they will follow away from the tunnel entrance."

"Agreed," said O'Reilly.

He pointed toward the steep path that cut across the side of the mountain to the left of the entrance. Corporal Mincy took that as an order to go, so she led everyone away from the plateau. After everyone made it far enough away without being detected, the Lieutenant followed them. O'Reilly and Mullins waited to be sure they made the ascent without being detected before rejoining the column.

Once they were away from the beach and no longer in danger of being spotted by the infected, they relaxed a bit and enjoyed the fresh air. There were shared smiles as they took in the view of the mountain that rose above them on the right.

Mincy said in a low voice, "Who would ever believe that there's a huge shelter under that mountain?"

Mullins aimed a set of binoculars toward the summit of the mountain.

"You see that crevasse that looks like someone split the mountain open with an axe? There's a pass that goes right through there, and on the other end of it must be the wind turbines."

"No wonder no one would suspect what they were for," said O'Reilly. "They're impossible to see from out here."

They made good time once they were going downhill. Other than a few rats, they didn't see anything moving, but whenever the trail gave them a view of the beach, they knew why they were safer inside. The few dozen they had seen below the tunnel entrance were just a fraction of the total that wandered along the beaches of Attu Island.

Eventually, they came to the last part of the trail, where they had a good view of their old camp. The curved huts were still there, and the small radio tower still stood straight up in the middle of the camp, but the weather had erased the paths they had made to keep from falling over the cliff in the fog. The paths wouldn't be needed on such a clear day, but it wasn't the lack of the white stones that concerned any of their group. It was the presence of people in US military uniforms who were obviously not the infected dead.

A sentry assigned to keep watch in their direction sounded the alarm, and the Rat Island survivors found themselves facing a superior force with weapons aimed in their direction. To make matters worse, a squad of soldiers came up from somewhere behind them. If it had been a typical day on Attu Island, the fog would have been useful, but they were completely exposed.

"Stand down."

The shouted command came from somewhere in the middle of their old camp, and a Navy Commander stepped into the open area between the huts. All around him, the odd mixture of Army, Navy, Air Force, and Marine uniformed personnel lowered their weapons. The Commander actually lifted his hand in a friendly wave and then gestured for them to come down to the camp. The squad behind them had lowered their weapons too, but they waited where they were for further orders.

O'Reilly asked the Lieutenant in a low voice if he had any orders.

"I don't see that we have a choice but to comply, but remember when we talked about what the US military would do, we agreed they would combine forces. This could be our best chance to be rescued."

Gleaton moved to the front of the column and took the lead. They were followed by the squad behind them, but everyone had shouldered their weapons. The Navy Commander walked toward them at a brisk pace and extended his hand to Gleaton before he was even in reach. Gleaton felt like he was supposed to salute the senior officer, but the man had such a broad, friendly smile across his face that Gleaton accepted the handshake. O'Reilly managed to salute before the Commander gave him the same welcome.

"Where did you guys come from? Don't tell me you're the squad that was sent out here by the joint base commander seven years ago because it doesn't look like anyone's been living in this camp for at least that long. Oh, where are my manners? I'm Commander Evans, and this is what's left of the United States Joint Military Command. We're the last line of defense against the infected dead."

Commander Evans gave the appearance of the kind of commanding officer who was by the book. His camouflaged uniform appeared to have been laundered and pressed recently, and his grooming was immaculate. If they had asked him about his pristine appearance, they knew he would say it was important to set an example for his troops, as if it would help their morale. His gray hair and square jaw gave them the impression that he was more about how he saw himself in a mirror than how he influenced morale. His blue eyes added to the illusion that he would have fit right into a World War II uniform, but he would have been on the other side.

It was a lot for Gleaton's squad to absorb. From where they were standing, there were a few dozen armed personnel on the plateau, but as they moved lower toward the camp, they gained a view of the beach down below. There were several amphibious landing ships pointed toward the beach with their ramps extended, and they were in the process of unloading supplies. Guards were shooting the infected dead as they gathered on the beach near the boats.

"How's that working out, Sir?" asked O'Reilly.

"What's that, Sergeant?"

O'Reilly noticed a pause before Commander Evans said his rank and recognized it for what it was. It was a reminder that he was an NCO, and Evans was an officer.

"Just askin', Sir. The only comms we've had in years would lead us to believe there hasn't been much of a defense against the infected. We haven't heard any communications referring to a joint command."

Evans paused again, and O'Reilly distinctly interpreted the pause as a warning. The Commander was sizing him up as an adversary or, at the very least, as a malcontent.

Gunfire erupted on the beach, and everyone turned toward it. It was obvious that the people on the beach were outnumbered by the infected dead and were going to need backup.

"With your permission, Lieutenant. Would you mind sending your squad to assist?" asked Commander Evans.

Red flags were going up in O'Reilly's mind, and he knew Gleaton well enough to know he was seeing them too. If this was, as Commander Evans put it, the last line of defense against the infected dead, it was a thin line if they needed the help of ten survivors.

They weren't in a position to refuse, so O'Reilly gave the order for the squad to move double-time to the beach and engage the infected. Lieutenant Gleaton stayed behind with Evans, and O'Reilly didn't blame him. He hoped Gleaton would be able to learn how this pompous naval officer knew they had been detailed to Attu Island seven years ago.

O'Reilly sized up the squad that had followed them on the trail and noticed their leader was a corporal.

"Mullins, drop back to those guys behind us. Pull rank if you have to, but make sure they stay with us down to the beach. See what kind of intel you can get about these people."

Mullins was the right man for the job because he knew what buttons to push with enlisted men. He could see in the eyes of the Corporal that he was inexperienced, and he could use that.

"What's your name, Corporal?"

It was a question, but to the young corporal, it didn't sound like a request.

"Corey Haskell, Sir."

Mullins made eye contact with Haskell as soon as the last word slipped out. It was treated as an insult when someone like Mullins was called 'Sir.'

"Corporal Mullins to you, Haskell. Call me 'Sir' again, and I'll make lunchmeat out of you."

Mullins waited a few beats as they got closer to the beach. They were moving in behind a sizeable horde, and O'Reilly gave the signal for everyone to use bayonets first. Mullins told Haskell to order his men to do the same.

"What's the story, Haskell? Give it to me quick because we're about to get busy."

It was even amazing to Mullins how easily he got intel from Haskell. Some people were just an easier mark than others. In the span of three minutes, Mullins learned that the newcomers had been part of a much larger force that had collapsed from within after a series of mistakes. They had managed to make it to Alaska from the East Coast, where a fleet had been making a stand. They had regrouped at Joint Base Elemendorf-Richardson but had overstayed their welcome. Now they were looking for some kind of shelter that was supposed to be on Attu Island. Mullins made a mental note that the last part about the big base in Alaska meant these people couldn't be trusted.

The infected dead were focused on the people who were unloading supplies, and they didn't have a clue that they were being attacked from behind. O'Reilly's squad engaged them first, but Mullins and Haskell moved into the fight quickly. Dozens of the infected went down in the first minute. After the pace became slower, the squads became more spread out as they worked their way along the beach. The only infected dead left standing were those that were too far away to reach with bayonets.

O'Reilly gave the order to conserve ammunition even though they had plenty back in the shelter. He was curious, though. It seemed to him that Commander Evans and his larger force needed help more than they did. He set up a perimeter to protect the people unloading supplies, then he took Mullins aside to find out what he had learned. He agreed that it sounded like the base in Alaska didn't like something about this unified rescue operation, but he didn't see how they could back away and pretend they weren't interested either.

"Good job, Corporal. Keep an eye on things down here while I go find out more about this so-called 'last best chance for survival' thing the Commander has going here."

By the time O'Reilly reached the plateau, he saw Lieutenant Gleaton coming to meet him. His guess was that Gleaton wanted to fill him in without the Commander hanging around to hear him.

"Why do I get the feeling I'm not going to like what you have to tell me, Lieutenant?"

"Because you won't like it. You could tell just as well as I could that there's something hinky about this operation."

"No kidding, Sir. Are they low on ammo or something? If they're the rescue force, we're in trouble."

"I don't know what they are yet, Sarge, but they know about the shelter."

"Mullins got that out of their squad leader," said O'Reilly. "What do they want to do with the shelter, use it as a home base or something? It's kind of far from the mainland to be a good place to make a stand against the infected dead. It's more like a place to hide."

Gleaton nodded. "I thought the same thing, but there's something else. Our old chow hall is packed full of the infected."

"You mean they're putting the bodies in the chow hall?"

"No, not the bodies. They aren't killing them first. They've been catching them and putting them in there. Don't ask me why. I haven't found out yet."

"That can't be good," said O'Reilly. "The Russians were doing the same thing when we found the shelter. Remember what we talked about then? Some of the rooms were laboratories. You don't think these people are working on a cure, do you?"

"Not successfully," said Gleaton. "Like I said, I didn't get enough out of Evans to know what they're doing yet."

"Did you have to give up the shelter?"

"Unless you can tell me a way not to, Sergeant, I had to. They're getting organized to go there now. If we could leave and pretend they aren't here, I would order it, but they have us outnumbered."

Commander Evans came out of the former SATCOM hut and walked toward them.

"There you are. I'm glad you're both together so I can introduce you to my senior NCO."

Behind Commander Evans was a very large man. He was dressed in combat gear with a SEAL pin over his breast pocket. He didn't have any stripes on his uniform, so neither O'Reilly nor Gleaton knew what rank he was. All they could tell for sure was that the man looked dangerous, and if he was really a Navy SEAL, then they were right to be careful around him.

Evans said, "This is Chief Clemenza. Report to him from now on."

Lieutenant Gleaton visibly stiffened.

"Excuse me, Commander, but I won't be reporting to an NCO. I'm an Academy graduate, and this squad is my detail."

"Of course it is, Lieutenant. My apologies. I meant your squad will be reporting to him from now on. You will be reporting to me since I'm your new CO."

Evans walked away without waiting for a response, leaving them with the big NCO. Clemenza had a feral grin that sent the message that he enjoyed the exchange. O'Reilly felt a moment of respect when his Lieutenant addressed Clemenza.

"What are you grinning about? Do you think something's funny? Wipe the grin off your face and bring yourself to attention in my presence."

The grin faded, but there was something in the big man's eyes that said he wouldn't forget the verbal reprimand from Gleaton. O'Reilly didn't know what the man's story was, but he had known plenty of people like him in the military. He wasn't a team player, and it was better not to let yourself get into a position where he was behind you. He looked out for himself and didn't care much for officers.

Chief Clemenza said, "Commander Evans has ordered me to take an advance party to our shelter."

"Whose shelter?" said Gleaton and O'Reilly at the same time.

Clemenza didn't answer, but his intimidating eyes were locked onto O'Reilly's now. O'Reilly was too experienced with the bullies in uniform to take the bait.

"I'm busy following the last orders given to me by my commanding officer," snapped O'Reilly. "You'll have to clear it with him first."

The big man seemed like he was off balance for the first time, and it wasn't something he was accustomed to. His grin was gone, and along with it, the overconfidence he had displayed.

The tense standoff may have swayed in favor of the two soldiers, but they both knew the inevitable outcome. They would be forced to turn over command of the shelter to the Navy.

Lieutenant Gleaton asserted his authority one last time and ordered Chief Clemenza to remain where he was while he conferred with 'his' senior NCO. He motioned for O'Reilly to step aside with him.

"We don't have a choice, Sergeant. Round up the squad and prepare to move out. We always knew this could happen. As a matter of fact, it's what we should have wanted. We couldn't ask our people to stay underground for the rest of their lives, and we don't have to like these people. If we were in their shoes, we would be finding smaller commands to absorb. Just wait until this bunch meets up with a General."

Gleaton smiled when he said the last part, and it had the desired effect on O'Reilly. Commander Evans would be forced to hand command over to someone with more rank eventually.

Sergeant O'Reilly did as ordered and gathered his squad from the beach. They had a hundred questions, but he only had the time to give them the basics.

"Treat it like any other change of command, but keep an eye out for anything unusual and report back to me or Mullins. Oh, and watch out for that big guy. He seems like he's a wildcard."

The hike back to the shelter was subdued compared to when they stepped out into the fresh air that morning. As much as they wished they had kept their heads down and avoided contact with the newcomers, they knew if they had it all to do over again, they would have welcomed them. The shelter wasn't their prison, but it wasn't where they wanted to spend the rest of their lives.

Corporal Mullins worked his way down the line until he brought up the rear of their column. It put him directly in front of Clemenza. He didn't like having his back to him, but it didn't scare him either. He just wanted to be sure he was first in line if the big man tried to start something with his friends. Clemenza was followed by six Marines.

"Hey, Mullins. You're career Army, aren't you," said Clemenza.

It was more of a statement than a question.

"That's right, and my guess is that you're just here because you don't have anything else to do."

Clemenza surprised Mullins with his answer.

"You've got me all wrong, man. Just so you know, I haven't picked a side yet."

"What's that supposed to mean?" he asked over his shoulder.

"Your Sergeant will know."

They didn't talk the rest of the way to the tunnel entrance, and Mullins had a lot of time to think about the odd comment. He wouldn't be able to talk it over with O'Reilly until they were inside the shelter, and he wished there was a way to stall them from opening the door because he had a bad feeling that the guy he had been warned to watch out for had just warned him about the Navy officer.

Once they reached the tunnel, it seemed like they got to the big door to the shelter faster than before. Corporal Hupp dialed the combination and opened the door wide.

Inside the shelter, O'Reilly noticed there was something different about Clemenza. As he took a tour of the facility, he didn't make any derogatory comments. As a matter of fact, he appeared to appreciate what they had accomplished inside. He asked logical questions about the history of the shelter and what it had been like to live inside it for so long.

When they reached the power plant, Clemenza was busy long enough inspecting the generators connected to the outside power source for Mullins to have a brief exchange with O'Reilly. O'Reilly was just as baffled by the message. Either Clemenza was trying to set them up, or he really was a wildcard. He asked Mullins what he thought since he had always accepted Mullins as somewhat of a wildcard himself.

"Something about it felt familiar, Sarge. Remember that TV show where they would dump a bunch of people off on an island or some remote location in the jungle and let them pretend to be surviving against the elements? They were contestants in a big game, but they acted like it was real and even made alliances with each other. I felt like Clemenza was letting me know he's not sold on being part of their team."

"The question is why," said O'Reilly. "You think he's not sold on their mission? I know I'm not. Why would a group that size need us to clear the beach for them? Another ten minutes and those supply people would've been overrun."

Mullins asked, "What is their mission?"

"You didn't know? They're going to beat the infected dead."

Mullins rubbed the stubble on his chin and said, "I don't think they're making much progress with that. You think that's what Clemenza was trying to tell me?"

"I hope so. If we can sway him to our side, we'll be able to keep tabs on the Navy officer. If I read him right, you might be the one to tip him in our direction with a little help from our private reserve."

O'Reilly slipped Mullins the keys to the room where they had stored the best liquor for special occasions.

"Try not to drink it all, and don't let him know where we keep it."

Trusting Mullins with the keys to the liquor room wasn't something O'Reilly would have done before now, but things had been different before. He knew that Mullins was a bit hard-nosed, but he knew which team he was on.

"Thanks, Sarge. I'll let you know what I find out."

22

Joint Base Evans

Attu Island - January 2023

The shelter had functioned well with only ten occupants, but for most of them, it was like a return to civilization by having so many new arrivals join them. They were a blend of men and women from all branches of the military, and there were lots of stories to share. O'Reilly's squad remembered how excited they had been when they picked their own bedrooms, and they hadn't seen half of the hardships experienced by the new occupants.

Galina needed help in the kitchen, and there was plenty of it. When people learned there was real food to cook, there were more volunteers than she needed. Oleg, Pavel, and Galina were all surprised at how the Americans treated them as equals. It didn't matter to anyone where they had escaped from. They were all escaping from somewhere.

The tables in the dining room buzzed with conversations about the rest of the world. Hupp, Ritter, and Mincy were like celebrities and sat at different tables where they were told the details about their hometowns. There were stories about how the hordes gathered together and walked along interstate highways as if they had places they needed to be. In some states along the coasts, the infected walked right into the water until they were washed away. There was proof of that on Attu Island because so many of them washed up on the beaches.

There wasn't really any good news, but there were some interesting rumors. It didn't take long for the discussions to turn in the direction of what the military was doing to fight back. Christine Mincy learned at her table that the joint force had suffered extensive losses. She was told about how they ran out of supplies, in particular ammunition, and were forced to be on the defensive most of the time. They had begun their mission on ships but were forced to abandon them and travel on land. They had air support at first, but without bases where the planes could land, refuel, or be repaired, the planes gradually disappeared.

"Tell me about those rumors you mentioned," she said to the group.

"We've heard someone is fighting back," said one of the Marines. He was probably close to her age, but the last seven years had taken its toll on him. She had noticed when he ate his supper, he chewed slowly as if he was savoring each bite, and she had felt sorry for him.

He said, "Most of the rumors seem to be in the South in places away from big cities. We've picked up some radio traffic from a few people who say they were helped by a group of survivors who've put a dent in the number of infected dead."

Another man who gave the appearance of someone who had given up a long time ago said, "They can dent all they want, but it's simple math. As long as there are living people, there will be the infected dead. We're their replacements."

"That sounds a bit cynical to me," said Mincy.

"Try living out there a while and watch them eat your friends, and see if you don't become cynical," the man answered.

Wanting to change the subject, Mincy turned back to the rumors.

"I was raised in the South. I would expect it to be tougher there because the weather is warmer. I've heard the cold weather slows the infected down during the winter months."

"It does," said one of the Marines. "At least until things thaw out. Some of the people who joined us said they hunted for frozen ones when it was cold."

"I was stationed at a base in Corpus Christi when it all started," said one of the Navy guys. "We were cornered by them because so many came from Houston. We had to fly out over them, and you don't want to see a horde like that. They were walking into the Gulf of Mexico like they thought they could walk on water."

The same discussions were taking place around the room, but

anyone could see there were a few solitary individuals who had nothing to say and kept to themselves. There were also some who seemed to be watching everyone else. They were the ones O'Reilly had told them to spot. If things went sideways, O'Reilly said they would be the ones who would be dangerous.

With so many rooms available, it wasn't difficult to accommodate everyone, but O'Reilly wasn't happy when Commander Evans told Lieutenant Gleaton that he was reassigning rooms in order to integrate the squads better. He said it would help them to establish an identity as one unit. O'Reilly saw it as a way to spread his people out so they couldn't communicate with each other.

Mullins had some interesting information that he had gotten from Chief Clemenza. Thanks to the large supply of good bourbon, they had become buddies, and Clemenza had shared what he knew about the Commander and his people. He even told Mullins he wasn't worried if he passed the information to O'Reilly, and he actually expected him to.

Clemenza told Mullins he had run into the Commander and his people around Kansas City, and he didn't have anything better to do, so he went along with their big scheme to take back the country from the infected. He said he had already seen some plans from another government agency go wrong, and he was just curious about how this one was going to play out.

In the late hours of the night, O'Reilly, Gleaton, and Mullins got together in one of the empty rooms and went over what Mullins had learned.

"So, Clemenza isn't really fond of Evans?" asked O'Reilly.

"Naw, he thinks the guy is pompous. Apparently, Evans doesn't learn from his mistakes."

Gleaton said, "What's that mean?"

"Clemenza said that Evans was part of the big government response to the infected dead. There was this big plan for all of the branches of the military to unite under one command. It was something that was cooked up by the Pentagon as a contingency for this type of thing."

"There was an emergency plan for a zombie apocalypse?" said O'Reilly. "Why am I not surprised that it didn't work?"

They were far enough away from everyone else, but when they started to laugh, they quickly reminded each other to keep it down.

"Actually," said Mullins, "it started as kind of a game to help the planners think about how they would respond to any kind of apocalypse. They were focused on nuclear wars, but what they did was make a plan for a zombie apocalypse and then substitute nuclear war in the plan. The thing is, they accepted both plans just for the hell of it."

O'Reilly said, "So when the infection broke out, someone said to activate the plan?"

"Yep. They got the President out of Washington and scrambled the military. They had a fleet park off the coast of Virginia, and they started doing something really dumb."

"Which was what?" asked Gleaton.

"The plan was to cure the zombies, or more likely, find a cure for people who got infected," said Mullins.

They waited for him to go on because both of them were thinking the same thing, and that was how they would find a cure without test subjects. Gleaton was a West Point graduate, so he had taken his fair share of elective courses in college. He was familiar with the experimental paradigm and knew any experiment had to be done with at least two groups. There was the experimental group and the control group. One got the cure, and the other didn't.

O'Reilly might not have gone to college, but he was a voracious reader before the infection, and he knew the same thing about experiments.

"You're talking about experimenting on humans. They had a plan that allowed for that?"

"Yes, Sarge. According to Clemenza, they didn't have a shortage of infected dead, but to make the plan work, they needed people who were infected but not dead yet."

"Where did they get those people from?" asked O'Reilly. He dreaded the answer, but he had to ask.

Mullins took a big swallow of his drink and then refilled the glass.

"Clemenza said they sent patrols into populated areas and rescued people. They sorted out the ones who had been bitten and let the uninfected ones go."

"Wait a minute."

Lieutenant Gleaton stood up from his chair, and O'Reilly had to convince him not to go confront Evans.

Gleaton said, "But they rescued people and then threw them back. That's insane."

"I'm not saying it isn't, Sir. We just have to be careful how we go about setting things right. If what Clemenza said is true, we have to remove Commander Evans from command and figure out how to try him for his crimes, but he has a core of people mixed in with the innocent ones. Our people have identified them, and they outnumber us."

O'Reilly got Gleaton to simmer down so Mullins could tell them the rest of what he had learned.

"It got worse than that," said Mullins. "The people who were infected died later because they couldn't find a cure. They wound up with lots of infected dead on the ships, and at first, they just tossed them overboard. The problem was that they needed to keep some of them for tests. Remember some of those broadcasts we used to get? A lot of them warned not to keep the infected alive. You know, not alive in the sense that they could still function. They said the infection would always break out of containment."

"Is that what happened?" asked O'Reilly.

"I wish it was," answered Mullins. "They realized they needed subjects that hadn't been bitten yet."

This time Gleaton and O'Reilly both reacted, and Mullins wasn't sure what to do. They were ready to go after Evans. It took some convincing, but he got them to understand that they needed to hear the rest and then make a plan.

"You both outrank me, but I've seen some things in my career that I can't unsee. I know that you gotta plan this out, or you won't make it past his door without getting a bullet in you. We can get him alone if you want, but you can't get to him in the middle of the night."

"What happened on the ships?" asked O'Reilly.

"They told the rescue parties to bring back people who were bitten but not dead, and they gave them orders to bring in healthy people too. Families were glad to come in together, thinking their loved ones were going to get medical treatment. They put them in cells together."

Mullins didn't have to tell them what happened next, but before he went on, he had to get them to calm down again.

"Clemenza said he was told that there were mutinies on the ships. People deserted. Patrols went out for more subjects but didn't come back. As crews became smaller, the infection did what all infections do. It broke out of containment, and more people died. Evans abandoned ship, taking with him his strongest supporters."

Gleaton said, "You mean most of these people weren't with him at the start. Where'd they come from?"

"He picked up strays along the way. There were a lot of military people across the country who were cut off from their commands.

They were glad to join up, but they didn't know what Commander Evans and his people had done before. There's one last thing, a few of the enlisted men were stationed with us at Elmendorf and Fort Richardson."

Since they were all in the Army, they saw themselves as being stationed at Fort Richardson. One of their private jokes was that the Air Force was 'over there' at Elmendorf, and they were at the Fort where soldiers were supposed to be.

When Mullins was done telling them what he had learned, he added, "Don't get mad at me, but I helped Clemenza do something."

They waited for him to go on because they couldn't imagine what it was he could have done for Clemenza.

"He said he never wanted to be part of anything the Commander did, and it wasn't his business to do anything about it. He just wanted to leave, so I helped him. I told Hupp not to tell anyone. You know how he is. He would've told you tomorrow, Lieutenant, but he was too afraid of me to stop me."

"Does he know what this island is like?" asked O'Reilly.

"I tried to tell him, Sarge."

"Did you tell him about the rats?"

"That didn't seem to bother him. Are you mad at me?"

Both Lieutenant Gleaton and Sergeant O'Reilly seemed unfazed by the admission and shook their heads.

O'Reilly said, "It would've been nice to have him on our side against Evans and his people, but I'm glad he told you everything. At least we know what we have to do."

They never got the chance to make a plan.

******

Commander Evans was waiting for them in their quarters when they arrived. There was no ceremony, no speeches, and no offer to join their side. The only thing Evans had to say was that he had trusted Clemenza and been wrong. He apologized for what was about to happen, but it was for the good of all mankind. O'Reilly, Gleaton, and Mullins were handcuffed and escorted away to the holding cells where they had eliminated the infected dead upon their arrival in the shelter.

It was quiet as they crossed the main common area of the shelter, and they noticed the guards on the different levels of the shelter were all watching them as if they expected to get the opportunity to open fire with their M4 rifles. As soon as the door was opened that led into the darker corridors near the holding cells, there was a loud chorus of shouting. They recognized the voices of the rest of their squad and found out quickly why they were upset.

The other holding cells were full except for the one reserved for them, and a soldier stood with the door open, waiting for them to go inside. Theirs was the first cell in the narrow corridor, and they had to walk between the other seven cells to reach it. They saw all of the familiar faces of their squad and even some they didn't recognize. They all had hoped to be rescued by O'Reilly and Mullins, but they were becoming resigned to their fate now that they saw their best hopes in handcuffs. Once the door was closed, they were told to put their hands through the bars so the cuffs could be removed.

Lieutenant Gleaton yelled louder than the rest of them, "Evans, you took an oath when you became an officer. You're a disgrace to the uniform."

Evans paused long enough to shoot a piercing stare in the direction of the cell where Gleaton was pressed against the bars. The man had all of the same features as the first moment they had seen him, but in the dim light of the corridor, the deep lines of his face and broad smile had become a menacing leer. They hadn't instantly liked him when they met at their old base camp, but if they had seen the way his eyes stabbed at Gleaton now, they would have recognized the monster in him.

Commander Evans walked closer to Gleaton's cell and said in an eerily soft voice, "Just think, Lieutenant, years from now, when people teach the history of the infected dead, they will talk about the brave men and women of Joint Base Evans on Attu Island. They will honor those of you who sacrificed their lives so that a cure could be found, but they will praise those of us who were daring enough to risk our place in history by making the decisions about who would live or die. I'll make sure that the records clearly indicate that you volunteered your life so you will be honored."

Gleaton gripped the bars tightly, and he would have spit in Evans' face if his mouth hadn't become so dry. At that moment, he had little doubt that the madman would carry out his threat.

As much as O'Reilly wanted to offer words of encouragement to any of them, especially Gleaton, he didn't know how they could possibly get out of the cells. Corporal Hupp was in the cell directly across from his. Once Evans and his men were gone, O'Reilly motioned for him to get closer.

"Anything in the old records about these cells?" he asked Hupp.

The shake of Hupp's head said it all. He couldn't recall seeing Hupp appear more defeated. The young man had always been up for any challenge that gave him the chance to display his talents. At the very least, O'Reilly hoped Corporal Hupp would be able to pick the locks on the doors or find a way to pop the hinges, but now Hupp was looking at the bars like he wanted to use his eyes to super-heat them until they melted.

"You aren't Superman, Corporal. Just keep thinking about it. There might be something you missed or just haven't thought of yet."

Hupp wasn't the only one who was trying to dial up superpowers to break out of the cells. Everyone was moving around as they inspected the bars, the ceilings, and the walls. Besides the ten original occupants of the Rat Island shelter, now known as Joint Base Evans, O'Reilly estimated there were at least twenty more prisoners. They were undoubtedly people who had fallen out of favor with Evans by becoming too friendly with O'Reilly's squad. He could hear some of the muted conversations in the other cells, and it was a mixture of anger and resignation.

"What's he going to do to us, Sarge?" asked Ritter.

Someone in his own cell answered before O'Reilly could.

"He's going to kill us and say we were all volunteers. He's done it before."

O'Reilly recognized the voice. It was one of the women who had opened up to Mincy in the dining room.

"Why are you in here with us?" asked Mincy from her cell. She was three cells down from O'Reilly's on the same side as him.

"You know why. Just look around you. We were the ones who were stupid enough to fall for his orders to get friendly with you people. If we had been smarter, we would have warned you guys. You could've turned the tables on him and locked him up first."

Mullins said, "We were working on that. We were just a little too slow. We didn't think he would move on us so soon."

"Where's Michael?" asked O'Reilly.

Ritter said, "They took him somewhere else, Sarge. They said he was going to be first."

"Do you know where they have their lab?"

Ritter shook his head. "They kept us all out of the loop."

Michael hadn't been part of the original detail, but just like the Russians, he considered them to be one of his people. The years together in the shelter had made all of them feel like family.

O'Reilly could hear their Russian friends whispering in their cell next to his, and he had been around them enough over the years to pick up some of their language. He couldn't tell what Pavel was saying exactly, but he heard enough to know he had a plan. He tapped on the bars lightly to get their attention without drawing the interest of everyone else. He had a nagging feeling that one reason Evans had been a few steps ahead of them was because he had planted spies. He wouldn't be surprised if one of the people in the holding cells was there to keep an eye on them.

Pavel moved closer to the bars that separated them, and O'Reilly scanned the other cells to see if anyone appeared to take notice. There were a few occupants of the cells who were keeping to themselves, but they could have been simply scared. What Evans had in mind for them was enough to make the average person sick to their stomach.

"You have a plan?" whispered O'Reilly.

"When they come for us," said Pavel, "I will be the loudest. I will demand that I be allowed to die for my new country. When they open my cell, Oleg will stab them with a knife Galina carried with her from the kitchen. They underestimated her because she is just our cook."

O'Reilly thought about it for a moment, and he saw a way that it might work. The corridor between the rows of cells was narrow, and if the guards got too close to either side, the people in the cells could reach them. All he had to do was get everyone in the plan without a spy tipping off the guards to their plan. The problem was that he had no idea how to do it before running out of time. He realized he had no choice.

"Listen up, people," he said in his best command voice. Everyone became quiet, knowing that Sergeant O'Reilly was the one most likely to have a plan.

"When they come for the first test subjects, they will most likely come for Lieutenant Gleaton."

Gleaton glanced at O'Reilly and gave him a nod that said he agreed.

"They will expect us to resist, but no matter what they do, we have to create enough chaos to keep them off balance. When they come through that door, the first thing they're going to do is demand that everyone has to go to the back wall of the cells. Do the opposite. Rush the bars, reach for them, and create confusion. Mincy, Pavel has something for you. He's going to pass it through the other cells to you. You'll know what to do."

Pavel wasn't willing to give up the knife yet, but when he made eye contact with O'Reilly, he saw the slight wink of his left eye and knew it was deliberate. He didn't know what O'Reilly was planning, but he had learned to trust the big soldier. He crossed his cell and handed the sharp kitchen knife to Private Ritter. From there, it was passed to the first cell to Corporal Mincy.

While the knife was being passed, O'Reilly whispered to Gleaton and Mullins, "Watch the other cells for any reactions that aren't normal."

"Define normal," said Mullins.

"Anything acting not like everyone else when I drop a bomb on them."

O'Reilly surprised all of the prisoners with the next announcement.

"Okay, now for the best part. I have nine friends in here. The rest of you are all in the same boat as us. We're all going to die if we can't pull this off. The problem is that one of you is a spy for Evans."

The cells erupted into a riot of movement. O'Reilly was watching for anyone who was surprised but trying to hide it at first. He figured he would have no more than three seconds to spot the spy before he or she realized they needed to react like everyone else.

If O'Reilly had said there was someone in each cell who was already infected, it would have caused the same reaction. People tried their best to create space between themselves and their cellmates, and at the same time, they recoiled as they bumped into people behind them who had done the same thing. In the cell with Corporal Mincy, he saw one of the soldiers he didn't know, and he was processing what he had just heard for almost three seconds.

The man was sitting on one of the wall benches behind Mincy, and up to the moment of the big announcement, he appeared to be despondent. He had his right elbow resting on his right knee and his chin resting on his upturned palm. He watched the knife passed to Mincy into his cell with detachment, and O'Reilly had thought he saw an eyebrow go up. When O'Reilly said there was a spy in the cells, his chin remained on his palm while everyone else spread out. Three seconds later, he looked around the cell as if he had been exposed.

Mullins yelled, "Mincy, behind you."

The man moved faster than Mincy could turn around, but O'Reilly and Mullins weren't the only ones who had zeroed in on the man. That was what O'Reilly had gambled on. Everyone who wasn't a spy would notice the one person who didn't act paranoid. It was Ritter who intercepted the man as he sprung at Mincy's back. Ritter caught the spy by the back of his collar and swung him face-first into the bars between the cells. Someone in the next cell delivered a well-aimed punch to the man's face.

Using belts and bootstrings, the man was bound and gagged. It didn't take long to get him securely tucked under a bench where he wouldn't be seen by the guards when they came back.

"Good job, people. That's one problem out of the way. Now, I want everyone to get up against the bars at the front of your cells. When the guards come in, they're going to expect something, but Mincy is the wildcard. She knows what to do."

From a distance, O'Reilly caught her eye, and he saw that she understood.

They didn't have long to wait. Evans was apparently eager to get on with his experiments and earn his place in the history books. The occupants of the cells began making noise as soon as they heard the door open from the main part of the shelter, and they kept up a constant chatter to be sure the guards didn't get suspicious.

Four armed men came in together and shouted for everyone to move to the back walls of the cells, just as O'Reilly suspected. Their first mistake was that they came into the narrow hallway in a group instead of in a line. Their second mistake was that they thought they could intimidate their prisoners with rifles instead of handguns, and there wasn't enough room to maneuver. As soon as they pointed the barrels at the prisoners, they were within reach of grasping hands on both sides. They were pushed and pulled from both sides, and maybe they would have broken free in time if not for Corporal Mincy.

While the men grappled with the extended arms that came through the bars, one arm reached for them near the floor. The long blade of the kitchen knife pierced the calf of one man and then swung sideways to sever the Achilles tendon of another. Their screams caused the other two soldiers to panic and lose the fight with the hands that pulled them against the bars, and Corporal Mincy showed them no mercy. After using her knife to kill each of them, she reached through the bars to pull the keys to the cells off one of the bodies.

Mincy opened all of the cells, and they gathered up the weapons carried by the soldiers. O'Reilly made sure that the four rifles and four handguns were distributed to his own people, but he made it clear to the others that they would all be protected.

"What should we do with these guys, Sarge?" Mullins gestured at the two dead soldiers and the two wounded ones. Both of them were lying on the floor, holding their hands against blood-soaked legs and crying.

"We're not like Evans. They have med kits on their belts. Put them in separate cells, but don't tie up their hands so they can bandage themselves. Put the dead ones in a cell together. When they turn, the others can get a close look at what they wanted to do to us. The spy can figure out how to untie himself."

O'Reilly saw that the man was glaring at him from under the bench, and for a moment, he was mad enough to consider putting him in the cell with the two who were going to turn, but he refused to let Evans make him become someone no different than him.

"All right, everyone. Let's move out," said O'Reilly.

Mullins said, "Where are we heading, Sarge?"

"The power plant. That place is a maze down there. Plus, you might remember Ritter complaining about it when I had him hauling stuff down there."

They all remembered Ritter whining about moving weapons and food from the main storage areas, but now Ritter could only smile when he understood why. At the time, he had commented that it was just like the Army to have a Private move a sandpile from one place to another for no reason.

"Hey, Sarge," said Ritter, "just let me know when you need something moved again. I'll be glad to help."

It didn't take long to reach the power plant using some of the back corridors and service tunnels. In some places, they almost had to turn sideways to fit between the pipes, but O'Reilly doubted Evans had ever learned about the deepest levels of the shelter.

When they finally reached their hidden cache of weapons and food, he told everyone to gear up. If their escape hadn't been discovered yet, it would be soon, and Evans would have his people combing the shelter for them. He singled out one of the Marines who had come over to their side and asked her if she thought any of the others still with Evans would help them.

"Not a chance, Sarge. They were the ones who fought for him the hardest back at the base in Alaska. They'll do the same thing here."

Mullins was busy packing magazines for his weapons in his belt, but he leaned closer to O'Reilly. The power plant wasn't as brightly lit as other sections of the shelter, but there was enough light for O'Reilly to see that his face was covered with sweat. As a matter of fact, when he ran his hand over his own head, it came back wet.

Mullins said, "I don't remember it getting this hot down here before, even when we were clearing out the infected dead. Is something overheating?"

It wasn't just the two of them who were sweating. It was everyone, and Hupp confirmed it when he broke open cases of water. He caught O'Reilly's attention and nodded to the unasked question.

"It's not the power plant itself, Sarge. I thought it was the HVAC system, but nothing was overheating. I checked it already."

"Why's it so hot then?"

Hupp said, "I smell something like sulfur. I don't know where it's coming from exactly, but my first guess is that it's external."

"You mean it's coming in from the outside? That can't be good," said O'Reilly.

23

Sullivan Arena

Anchorage, Alaska - April 2023

Garrett piloted the Black Hawk from the Joint Base to Anchorage because the Chief was one of the people most likely to be needed on the ground if they couldn't land. That meant he would be the first one to drop to the ground at the end of a rope. He had done it before, and he had been in helicopters plenty of times since the beginning of the infection. This time, he wanted to be on the ground if they were forced to crashland the helicopter.

The memory of his crash landing in Charleston, South Carolina, was still fresh in his mind even years later, and he wondered if the scene would be that much different than it had been before. People had tried to escape from the infected dead by taking shelter behind the gates and walls of a minor-league baseball stadium, and the parking lots surrounding it were too full for a ground landing. Not to mention the fact that a ground landing would have been a harder crash than what he had chosen to do. He didn't want to try it again, but he had lined up with a charter bus and used it to cushion the blow. The roof of the bus had collapsed, but their forward momentum had been enough for them to survive.

Over the comm system headset, the Chief told Garrett that he wanted to make a few passes over the city after they located the arena and lowered the pallet of spare parts and supplies. He said he wanted to see if the city was deserted or infected or if survivors would come outside when they heard the helicopter.

All of the soldiers knew the area well and directed them to the Sullivan Arena. There was light snow the night before that had covered the desolate scene below them, but it made the fresh tracks easier to see. They circled twice before they determined the tracks led away from the arena. There was no way to tell if the tracks were made by survivors or by the infected dead, but their arrival would act as a summons to either of the two choices. They would just have to wait to see who would show up.

Garrett hovered the Black Hawk over an open area and sat the pallet of supplies down as gently as possible. They could see several of the Black Hawks they hoped to salvage, and he managed to get the pallet close to one. The soldiers dropped separate lines and slid easily down to the side of their cargo. While the Chief and his people took a few minutes to explore the city, the soldiers would set up a perimeter and be ready to either get to work or be picked up when their ride returned.

They steered a new course that followed the tracks until they disappeared at the closed door of a business, and the Chief told him that was a good sign. If the tracks had ended at an open door, it would have been likely to be an infected dead, but survivors would have closed doors behind themselves.

"Mark this spot on a map so we can check it again later," said the Chief.

Garrett dropped their forward speed as far as he could, and they navigated across the city, following the main streets. The rotor wash caused the loosely packed snow to swirl below them, but the city was eerily quiet. Rain, followed by freezing temperatures and then followed by snow, had caused the city to shine, but the deserted streets were nothing more than a reminder of what had been lost.

Some of the streets were still choked by the traffic that had ground to a stop on the first day. Other streets had been cleared, and the derelict vehicles had been used to create barricades. The Mud Island family had seen it before.

Hampton said over his headset, "Reminds me of the beginning when everyone was trying to close off the town I lived in, except it was bridges instead of streets. These people most likely put up their barricades to keep the infected dead out of their blocks, but someone inside was already infected. Before long, the barricades were keeping people in who were trying to get out."

Kathy added, "Smaller groups ran out of food and had to forage. If they found anything worth bringing back, they eventually brought the infection back with them too. Anyone who survived without the help of a shelter or lots of weapons and supplies deserves to survive now."

What Kathy had said was still fresh on their minds when they returned to the block where they had seen the tracks end at the door. It was open now, and a small horde of infected dead were crouched around a large red stain in the white snow. All they could think was that someone had survived seven years and then run out of luck. They had heard the helicopter fly by and then exposed themselves to the infected.

The Chief tapped on Garrett's arm and pointed in the direction of the arena. Garrett nodded. There wasn't any sense in exploring too much of the city. They might find more survivors, but if they drew them out into the open like that last person, all they were doing was giving them the opportunity to make a mistake.

Hampton said, "We'll be at the arena too long to get away before the infected or survivors show up. Do we have a triage plan?"

"That's what Cassandra and the soldiers are for," answered the Chief. "They're going to keep the area clear while we see if we can get another bird in the air. Survivors will be taken to the roof of the arena for infection screening."

They hadn't been gone long, but there had been enough time for the soldiers to mark a safe landing zone for Garrett to use. Flares were at the corners, and an X was spray painted in red at the center. Everyone was out of the Black Hawk and running to do their jobs as if it were a competition. They expected to have no more than fifteen minutes to identify helicopters that could fly, but they hoped for an hour.

The Chief was pleased to see how efficiently the four soldiers from Fort Richardson had secured the landing zone. They had unpacked a rope ladder and managed to navigate barriers inside the arena to get it to the roof. If survivors arrived while they worked, they would be told to climb the ladder, where they would be met by Cassandra.

If survivors couldn't climb the ladder, the odds were that they were already infected. Tom would be pulled from helicopter duty to inspect them to see if they had other injuries or illnesses that prevented them from climbing. When he asked what they would do if they found someone was already infected, the Chief told him what he already knew. They could leave on their own, or they could ask for help to do what they couldn't do themselves. It would be considered a merciful act.

The helicopters all needed batteries, and even though they had an external unit to jumpstart them, they wanted to make battery replacement a priority. If the starter systems had been the newest versions and were in good condition at the beginning of the infection, it was possible that they would start easily. According to the mechanics at the base, it was a good possibility that the UH-60 Black Hawks had the 2015 starter generators installed, so they were less than a year old when they landed the last time.

There were four helicopters in the parking lot, which meant there were two missing. All they needed were two, but if they had time, they wanted to at least find out if they would all fly. There was also the question of whether or not the fuel had degraded. Working in pairs, the Chief was with Garrett, and they had the battery installed just as Jon and Hampton began the start sequence on theirs. Everyone stopped for just a moment as the rotors that had sat still for years turned loudly in protest.

The starter sounded much smoother than they expected, and the turning rotors increased gradually to warm up speed. They were just as lucky when Garrett started the second one. The Chief gave him a thumbs up and hurried with his tools toward the third helicopter. He heard a single shot from a sniper rifle above the roar of the Black Hawk rotors and saw Cassandra waving an arm at him from the roof of the arena. When she saw she had his attention, she pointed to the west of the parking lot toward downtown. She held up her right arm with her fingers spread wide. That was the signal for five or more survivors. Next, she held up her left arm and closed her fingers into a fist. The left arm was the signal for sightings of infected dead. The closed fist meant she had eliminated it.

The Chief wasn't surprised that there were more survivors than infected dead because of the freezing cold. The group they had seen when making a pass over the city could have been inside the building with the closed door until the door had been opened by a survivor foraging for supplies.

Even though they had hand-held radios, they were using hand signals to avoid detection. They were making a lot of noise, but they had to be careful not to give away too much information if there was someone listening for radio broadcasts. The Chief repeated the signal back to Cassandra, and she understood he wanted her to lead the survivors to them. She shot a flare straight up and watched as the people in range of her sniper scope pointed at it. They increased their pace and headed directly toward the arena.

A third Black Hawk roared to life, and the Chief hurried to where Kathy and Captain Miller were excitedly loading their gear into the passenger compartment. He ducked under the spinning rotors to give them new orders.

"We're way ahead of schedule, and I don't trust this much good luck. Let's pass on the fourth bird for now. As soon as these three are hot enough to fly, we'll gather everyone up and go back to the base."

The Chief trusted his gut. After all of their years of survival, they had been through good and bad times. He felt like he was in a casino playing with house money, and his best bet would be to cash in his winnings and go home. He checked on the progress of the survivors that Cassandra had signaled and saw that there were twelve people, and they were all lined up and scaling the rope ladder. Tom was at the bottom with them, helping them to get started.

When the first of the survivors reached the roof, Cassandra had just begun screening them when one of the soldiers fired his sniper rifle at a target somewhere on one of the side streets of the city. His left arm shot into the air, and he waved it frantically. That meant he couldn't bother to count the incoming infected, but then he used both hands to make the old time-out signal used in sports. The Chief counted to five before the soldier took his hands down. They had five minutes to be clear of the area.

Garrett had seen the same signal, and after letting his Black Hawk run for another minute, he lifted it into the air. He wanted to warm up longer, but five minutes was just about right for him to land on the roof of the arena and retrieve most of the survivors. They would need two helicopters to get all of them and their snipers, so he had to get in and out fast.

On the roof of the arena, Cassandra was doing a triage of the excited people. After seven years of foraging for food and medicine, dodging the infected dead, and enduring the freezing temperatures, they were finally being rescued. They all wanted to shake her hand or even hug her, but she had to remember any of them could be infected, and they didn't have much time.

The first of the survivors to reach the top was a woman, and

Cassandra pulled her to one side, believing that the survivors would have sent their injured people first. One sniper stayed at the corner of the rooftop nearest to the street where he could see a small horde trudging through the snow. At that distance, he was one hundred percent accurate, so he was buying them valuable time. Cassandra saw that the woman had bright eyes from the excitement and wasn't favoring either of her arms. She had too little time to be totally sure, but the woman didn't appear to be infected.

"What's your name?" said Cassandra.

"Katrina."

The woman was about to say something else, but Cassandra stopped her. Even as she spoke, Cassandra could see the Black Hawk flown by Garrett as it turned to line up with the rooftop. They had cleared debris left behind by the news crews in the first chaotic days of the infection.

"We have minutes before we have to go. I need to be sure no one in your group is infected, but I don't have time to make everyone strip and be inspected for bites."

"None of us are infected," protested Katrina.

"Forgive me for saying that I don't know you, so I can't just take you at your word. We have a plan for this that I don't have time to explain, and you can accept the plan or choose to stay here on the rooftop."

"What do you want me to do?"

"Gather your people together as they arrive and tell them what I just told you. If any of them disagree, tell them to go immediately to the far corner of the rooftop, but tell them they have two seconds to decide if they're staying or going with us."

They were arriving over the edge at a steady pace, and Katrina did as she was told. Cassandra didn't spot any bandages, and despite the fact that they were as banged up as any group of survivors they had ever found, they seemed to have managed the hardships well enough. Once they were all there, Tom came up last. He left the rope ladder hanging over the edge because it might be the way someone else survived in the future.

Katrina approached Cassandra and said, "Everyone agrees to anything you say to do."

"Good," answered Cassandra. "Have everyone drop their gear and weapons in a pile."

Garrett landed as if on cue, and Tom directed ten of the people to the open cargo door. He climbed into the copilot's seat and told everyone to strap in. He also told them he was under orders to eject anyone who showed signs of infection for the short trip. He smiled and added that he could tell the difference between the infection and air sickness. He was glad to see a few of them had a sense of humor and laughed.

The first Black Hawk lifted from the roof of the arena, and the second one, piloted by the Chief, landed where the first had been. Cassandra and one of the soldiers loaded the gear into the cargo area while Katrina and a young boy climbed inside. She had stayed behind to let the others all go first. Cassandra climbed into the copilot's seat to ride shotgun for the Chief.

The last two helicopters completed the operation by retrieving everyone else, and they got a good view of the horde that entered the parking lots. They still had another minute or two, but they understood why it was a good idea to trust the Chief's instincts.

It was a short trip back to the base, and in no time, the Black Hawks were landing near a crowd of cheering people. It wasn't just a welcome party, though. Colonel Daugherty had anticipated their success and had every flight mechanic available ready to inspect the helicopters. It was one thing to trust them to be in the air for a few miles. It was going to be altogether different on the next trip.

The new group of survivors was surprised to find so many people were still inside the base, but those last few miles between Anchorage and the military installation had been a virtual killing field to anyone who tried to cross it, and from what they could see, the personnel may have had a secure place to be, but they were running out of food. They were worried that they might have been better off staying in the city, but once they learned more about the plans of the Mud Island family, they understood why there was a new reason to hope.

******

"They have a four-month head start on us," said the Chief. "Who knows what damage they've done with that much time?"

The Chief felt like they were getting things done fast, but he had a sense of urgency that was making him feel jumpy. He didn't know how much resistance to expect, but he knew their adversaries were ruthless and driven by a god complex that made them feel like anything they did was justified. Over supper with Colonel Daugherty, he was venting nonstop.

Colonel Daugherty said, "You promised me something, Chief. Remember? You said you'd tell me where you were going once you had three working helicopters. You have four."

"You know anything about the local politics?" asked the Chief.

"A little."

"It appears that Alaska had a Congressman who got involved with the Russians. They had a real estate deal on one of the Aleutian Islands. It was a crazy idea that they would be able to survive an apocalypse if they worked together. The plan was passed down to the Congressman's descendants. The Joint Base commander was investigating it when the infection broke out."

"You have to be joking," said the Colonel.

"I wish I was. That Ensign knew far more about it than I had expected, but other than the name of the island, he didn't know the exact location. You wouldn't happen to know anything about Attu Island, would you?"

The Colonel almost spit out a swallow of coffee when the Chief said the name of the island.

"I can think of safer places to develop where someone could ride out an apocalypse."

"Why?" asked the Chief.

"To start with, you're trading one apocalypse for another. What were they planning for, a nuclear war?"

"Probably. I don't think they considered a pandemic that turns people into crazy predators after they die," said the Chief.

The Colonel shook his head and asked, "What do you think is the single greatest threat to that island?"

"At the moment, it would be the rogue group that wants to do illegal human tests, but my guess is that you have something else in mind."

"Mother nature," said Colonel Daugherty. "Attu isn't volcanically active, but it's part of the Ring of Fire. Last time I checked, there were about fourteen active volcanoes on the coast of Alaska, and there are about eighty hot spots. The Kamchatka Peninsula isn't too far away, and there are at least as many volcanoes and hot spots there. You're more likely to get blown up by a volcanic eruption on the Aleutian Islands than a nuclear war."

"But Attu isn't volcanic?"

"It doesn't have an active volcano on the island, but if I remember my college geology classes correctly, lava can break through to the surface between volcanoes. I think that's called volcanic initiation. It's more likely to happen along the edges of tectonic plates where they overlap."

The Chief said, "You paid attention in that class, it seems. So, what are the chances of a new volcano popping up there?"

Colonel Daugherty laughed, "I didn't major in the subject, Chief. If I had to guess, I would say it would be more likely to see a new volcano pop up on one of the Aleutian Islands than someplace like Columbus, Ohio."

"I guess they're lucky it never happened," said the Chief. "Do you know anything about Attu Island?"

"I know the Japanese invaded it during World War II, and there was a nasty battle there to take it back, but it hasn't had an indigenous population since then. The US had a LORAN station out there until satellites replaced them. I think all that's left there is a small monument now."

"Apparently," said the Chief, "there's been something out there for about forty years or so that was a well-kept secret."

"How soon are you leaving?"

"We're having a briefing in the morning. I'd like for you to be there. We don't know much about the location of the installation, so I want to go over how we're going to find it. I think our best bet will be to search the island from the air."

"If the weather is clear," said the Colonel. He had a slight amount of skepticism in his voice.

"You don't think we'll be able to see it from the air?"

"Sometimes the sky is so clear out there that you wouldn't believe it," said Daugherty, "but most of the time it's so foggy that you can barely see your hand in front of your face."

"I'm feeling lucky," said the Chief.

The next morning, everyone gathered in a briefing room to discuss the plan. The room was full, mostly with people the Chief didn't know. They were there because they had heard through the grapevine that the new people were planning something that would free them from the isolation they had endured in Alaska. Most of them were from other states, and even though they had nothing to go back to, they would be glad to be somewhere else.

The Chief stood on a raised platform, and his people were all along the front row. He could see by the crowd of eager faces that they wanted to know what could be done to help them lead normal lives.

"Good morning, everyone," he began. "I assume you're here to find out what we're planning. I won't be able to tell you everything because we have limited information. What I can say is that we have four Black Hawks that can make the trip to where we're going. That means we'll be taking along about thirty-six people, including myself and my combat-ready friends."

"Where are we going?" called out someone in the sea of faces.

"Our first objective is Dutch Harbor. There's a small airport there where we hope to find fuel. We can top off our tanks, so we should have plenty to reach Attu Island and then use it again as a refueling point on the way back. If all goes as planned, we will clear the runway there so we can also fly our AC-130 that far, then use it as a resupply point."

Hands went up around the room, and most of them were people who wanted to volunteer for the mission. The Chief thanked them all and told them that his crew would be screening volunteers after the briefing. He said they would be selecting people with combat experience.

"Wheels go up in two hours. If you're selected to go, try to be ready in no more than one hour."

"You haven't told us the rest of the plan," said the person who had called out earlier.

"When I said where we were heading, I said we had limited information, so this is a plan for the worse and hope for the best scenario. At this point, the plan is to get there."

Not to be deterred, the guy asked again but in a different way.

"So, you mean we should hope for slow zombies but plan for fast ones?"

The expression on the Chief's face was priceless, and the laughter from the people who knew him the best spread contagiously across the room.

******

The Black Hawks lifted off on schedule. Against the Chief's wishes, all of his close-knit family was included in the mission. He had argued that they didn't need to take everyone because they had plenty of combat veterans, but if they were going to make the trip on schedule, he could only argue for so long.

They were spread out among the helicopters as pilots and copilots, and the Chief realized the first part of the plan had taken care of itself. They would need to leave some people in Dutch Harbor to clear the runway at the airport, and that might be a good assignment for people he trusted.

The Chief had felt lucky about the weather, and he had been right to feel that way. It was a cool and clear evening when the helicopters circled the airport on Amaknak Island. The island was located north of Dutch Harbor and was actually surrounded by Unalaska Bay and part of Unalaska Island. It was a good thing they hadn't wasted fuel in the AC-130 because the runway was littered with the wreckage of small planes and vehicles. The chaos that happened around the world also found this remote place in the Aleutian Islands.

There were no signs of living people or the infected dead, and the Chief gave the order to land. The UH-60s sat down in front of the main terminal between parked vehicles, and the first order of business was to ensure the area had no hidden surprises. The second order of business was finding more fuel.

The crucial question of fuel had been an aspect of the plan that the Chief had only shared with a few people. The pilots all knew everything because they would be watching their fuel gauges the whole trip. There was always the possibility that they would find the fuel trucks and tanks at the airports empty or contaminated. If they were, they would have to 'island hop' until they found some.

The Chief had a list of five locations ready for them to try if the worst-case scenario happened. If they flew straight to Attu Island without stopping, they would be at the outside edge of their range without enough fuel to even make it back to the closest island that might have fuel. It was better to know for sure where they could find fuel than to be running on fumes when they got to Attu Island.

Within minutes of landing, the area was secured, and the fuel trucks parked within their landing zone were checked. The Chief's feelings of good luck went further than having clear weather, and they were able to top off their tanks in less than an hour. The Chief passed the order for guards to be posted in shifts, and they would be spending the night at the terminal after they cleared the runway of debris.

Kathy and Cassandra organized a team to explore the Dutch Harbor terminal, which was roughly the same size as the terminal in Minnesota, where they had been reunited with the crew of Executive One. The two airports weren't very similar in design, but they could have changed places with each other, and no one would have minded. They met the basic needs of passengers, and that was all.

With darkness settling over the island, they knew they had to make a fast survey of the surroundings without missing anything. The terminal doors stood open, and the good news was that no infected dead were trapped inside. When they reported to the Chief, he said there were no signs of people or infected dead from any of the crews, and that concerned him more than if they had found a few of either.

Kathy asked, "Do you remember the first time we went to the Guntersville lakes and we discovered the infected had walked into the water by the seaplane docks?"

"Yeah, and we were caught off guard because they were able to walk out of the boathouse by the water. Why?"

"Did anyone check the water?" she asked.

The Chief turned in the direction of the bay that surrounded Amaknak Island. The runway had been built along the edge of the bay, and he understood what Kathy was insinuating.

"Let's get everyone to walk the length of the banks and check the water before the sun completely sets. Tell them to pay close attention to any spot that could be used as a boat ramp. Check for slopes that the infected could use to walk out of the water."

Kathy's concerns about the water saved their lives. They had seen hordes on land more times than they could count, and some of the hordes were so large that the infected dead numbered in the thousands. They had seen the infected dead in the water, and they had seen blue crabs feeding on them. They had never seen anything like what they found in the bay next to the runway.

Because the sun was going down, the crews from the helicopters used flashlights. They spread out quickly and aimed their beams toward the water, moving left and right and causing a disturbance along the bottom of the water near the shoreline. At first, they didn't understand what they were seeing, and that nearly cost them their lives.

One of the crewmen at the furthest end of the runway yelled a warning to everyone along the line of light beams and began running as fast as he could back toward the area they had secured. When the

Chief saw the way the others along the line were gathered with him as he ran by them, he made a split-second decision. Only one thing could make military men and women run away that fast. Something was coming out of the water after them.

"Let's get the Black Hawks in the air," yelled the Chief.

He dove inside the UH-60 nearest to him and hit the starter. He hoped Garrett, Jon, and Hampton were doing the same thing. As the darkness settled over the landing zone, the beams of flashlights from the dozens of crewmen waved wildly and were extinguished one by one as people boarded the helicopters. The Chief heard Iris call out from behind him that there were twelve people in their chopper, including him, and he didn't hesitate.

The Chief lifted off a few feet and then elevated as he moved forward. He would have preferred to warm up longer, but he knew he should just be glad they had refueled when they arrived and not waited until later. His Black Hawk passed over the terminal roof by only a few feet, and he put the craft into a tight turn to the left that would bring him back over the runway. He wanted to see that the other three helicopters had all made it away from the landing zone, and he wanted to know what had caused the evacuation. He couldn't believe his eyes.

When the first crewman, Staff Sergeant Bateman, understood what he was seeing, his first thought had been how the Chief had reacted when he had jokingly said to hope for slow zombies but plan for fast ones. The Chief hadn't laughed even though almost everyone else did. Bateman realized that it might not have been funny to the Chief, just like what he had seen wasn't funny to him.

His beam of light from his flashlight made him feel like he had disturbed a school of fish because the water swirled. Then he saw it wasn't the water moving. It was something below the surface, but he wasn't sure what it was. There was a mass on the slope that resembled a garbage dump. Clothing and other debris appeared and disappeared beneath spider-like creatures that were roaming over the refuse, and it didn't completely register in Bateman's mind what the creatures were…or what the debris was until the creatures moved in his direction.

Snow crabs and Tanner crabs that were bigger than any crabs he had ever seen stopped feeding on the destroyed bodies of the infected dead and walked out of the water. He didn't know if they were attracted to the light or to him, but he was more concerned about whether or not he was faster than them. It occurred to him that he had never seen a live crab before. He had only seen Alaskan crabs on a seafood buffet table. He didn't think they normally got as big as buffet tables.

As Bateman ran past the next person in line who was also holding a flashlight, he yelled, "Run."

Being a bit of a clown in the Chief's briefing, Bateman had enjoyed the fact that his joke had gotten some laughs, and he had remembered a second joke about a zombie apocalypse.

'I don't have to be able to outrun zombies. I only have to outrun the guy standing next to me.'

It had also seemed funny at the time, but when he glanced over his shoulder and saw what had come out of the water, he really wanted everyone else to run as fast as him. He yelled over and over at everyone to run.

With everyone accounted for on the helicopters, they hovered for a minute over the unbelievable sight. The entire landing zone was covered with immense crustaceans. There was no point in waiting, and the Chief decided they would fly through the night. They turned to the west and flew toward Attu Island.

24

Escape

Attu Island - January 2023

The power plant was too hot for the escaped prisoners to hide in for long. It was like a sauna, and they could hear the HVAC system for the entire shelter working overtime to keep the temperature down. After only an hour, there were complaints of headaches and dehydration. The squad was drinking the reserve water supply faster than they should, and O'Reilly knew he and Lieutenant Gleaton needed to come up with another plan fast.

"He's gone insane," said Gleaton.

"Who?" asked O'Reilly. "Commander Evans? That much is clear, Sir. The question is how far he'll go. Remember that hut full of infected dead at our old base camp? When they transported them here, I saw some of them were in military uniforms."

"You don't think we could have talked some sense into him?"

"He wasn't hesitating to lock us up, and I don't think it was for our own safety. He was ready to kill his own people, and he already took Michael Bailey. Sir, we have to get out of the power plant. At least we can all load up with rations, and we have weapons now. It was a good idea to hide them here, but they aren't going to do us much good if we die of thirst."

Mullins approached where they were talking. He was drenched in sweat and kept wiping a rag across his forehead.

O'Reilly said to him, "Don't worry, Lou. We're not staying here. This heat would kill us."

"That's good, Sarge, but where can we go? Have you felt the pipes?"

"What about 'em?"

"They're as hot as everything else. Whatever is making it so hot in here is heating up the water in the pipes. I don't think there's anywhere we can go that isn't hot."

"I have an idea," said O'Reilly. "Can we get to the door near the boats from here? If we can get into that cave, maybe we can use one of the boats to escape."

"I think so," said Mullins. "Evans probably has a guard there, but there are plenty of blind corners near that door. We should be able to jump a guard who's not expecting us. Everyone going along?"

"We can't leave anyone here. It's too hot."

O'Reilly called everyone together and told everyone the plan. He gave Mullins the honor of taking out the guard and cautioned everyone to walk as quietly as they could. Over two dozen people walking down the same hallway might cause the sound to carry to the guard.

They strung out in a long column, and Mullins took the lead. The shelter had main corridors that they had always preferred because they were more brightly lit, but there would be more opportunities to be seen by the people loyal to Commander Evans. The smaller, darker hallways were used primarily as maintenance tunnels, and they were barely wide enough for two people to walk shoulder to shoulder. Their advantage was that no one used them unless they liked dark, scary places. Their disadvantage was that any emergency would be harder to handle.

Mullins could have taken them down several different tunnels that went to the back door of the shelter. It was only bad luck that he picked the same one that had rear entrances to the rooms where Commander Evans' people had set up their labs. The doors had small, wire-reinforced windows, and light from the rooms spilled out into the narrow hallways. At each one they passed, everyone had to get down on their knees and crawl past the door, and it was only a matter of time before someone made a mistake.

Ritter raised his head as he crawled past a door. He wanted to see what they were doing inside, and when he saw Michael Bailey chained to a bed, he stopped crawling. No one behind him expected the column to stop, and they piled up on his legs. It was just loud enough to draw the attention of the lab technicians inside the room, and one walked straight to the door and opened it.

Private Ritter was still pinned to the floor by the soldier behind him, so he couldn't even defend himself. The only advantage he had was that the room was brightly lit, and the man's eyes didn't have enough time to adjust to the darkness. He didn't see Corporal Mincy soon enough to block the long kitchen knife she had kept from their earlier escape. She put one hand over his mouth and used her other hand to push the knife upward just below his breastbone. It reached his heart, and he fell helplessly to the floor.

The chaos that erupted inside the room was only partly because of the unexpected arrival of the knife-wielding woman. The distraction had caused another lab technician to back into Michael Bailey's bed. He lost his balance and put out his hand to catch himself next to Bailey's pillow. Bailey's own hands were tied to the rails of his bed, but his head could still turn far enough to reach the arm in front of him. He sank his teeth into the warm muscle and pulled free a large mouthful of flesh.

The scream that erupted from the man reached a higher note than anything he would have thought possible, but the pain of having his flesh pulled away by teeth didn't seem possible either. He cradled his injured arm and turned toward the other lab technicians as if they could help him, but they were all fighting with each other at the main entrance to the room.

Mincy stepped over the body of the man she had killed at the door, and her rage boiled over when she saw what had been done to Bailey. She silenced the screaming of the lab technician, who was holding his injured arm out toward her as if she would help him. In just one smooth motion, she used one hand to pull her 9mm handgun from its holster and the other hand to silence the man.

Behind Mincy, there was panic in the dark hallway. The commotion had drawn the attention of the guard near the back door of the shelter, and he stepped into full view to see what was happening. Mullins was close to the floor and only had to fire one shot at point-blank range, but the guard had a split-second to do the same thing. Unfortunately for the people strung out in single file down the hallway, the guard was holding a Russian AK47 set on automatic. One pull of the trigger as he died was all he needed to send ten rounds into the darkness.

Not everyone who was hit by the burst of bullets was killed. The panic and the fear that more shots would be fired caused everyone to seek shelter by going through the nearest doors, and the column of people was scattered, leaving the dead and wounded on the floor of the hallway.

At the front of the column, O'Reilly's instinct was to make sure his squad was safe, but all he saw in the chaos behind him was the movement of people as they dove for safety. He couldn't tell who his squad was, with the exception of Lieutenant Gleaton, and that was only because his CO was dead. One of the ten rounds had hit him in the chest. After years of living in the shelter together, their difference in rank had melted away, and they had become more like brothers. O'Reilly felt numb.

Mullins stayed on the floor, but he reached into the hallway and grabbed the dead guard's AK47. He aimed it down the main corridor and waited. When the reinforcements he expected arrived, they rushed blindly into the corridor, and he caught them by surprise. They couldn't get to cover in time. He saw at least six of them go down before he ducked back into the darkness.

There wouldn't be enough time for O'Reilly to pull his squad out of the tight hallway and get the door of the shelter open. They would be sitting ducks for the next round of reinforcements. His only choice was to find whoever he could that was alive and pull them into one of the rooms they had crawled past. He tapped Mullins on the shoulder to get him to follow. They made their way back along the line, stepping over the people who had died when they were shot by the guard.

Besides Lieutenant Gleaton, there were three people who had been with Evans before. None of them were moving. Blood trails that led into brightly lit rooms were from the wounded who had pulled themselves free of the tangled bodies in the hallway.

Corporal Mincy had snapped when she had seen Bailey strapped to the table chewing on the lab technician's arm. She advanced on the crowd at the door, moving from one target to the next. She didn't stop shooting until they were all dead. She pulled them by their feet out of the doorway and took up a defensive position near the floor, just as Mullins had done.

Private Ritter had been pinned under people from the start, and the line of people who had fallen on him were lucky because they were still caught up in the arms and legs of people who had fallen over Ritter. The back of the column made the mistake of standing up at the moment the guard had fired his rifle. Ritter couldn't go backward. So he followed Corporal Mincy and joined her by the door.

One room over from them, O'Reilly and Mullins found Corporal Hupp sitting behind an overturned table. A bullet had grazed his arm, and he had a rag tied around it. Mullins untied the rag to inspect the injury. He told O'Reilly that Hupp would be fine, then he took a big piece of gauze from a first-aid kit and covered the wound. Once the rag was tied back in place, they moved toward the front entrance of the room.

Behind another overturned table, they found Galina and Oleg. Pavel was stretched out on the floor between them with his head cradled in Galina's lap. She was gently stroking his hair, pulling it away from a gunshot wound. The sudden realization that made O'Reilly feel like his own blood had drained from his head to his feet was that Pavel had died from a gunshot wound to the head, and Lieutenant Gleaton had been shot in the chest.

O'Reilly rushed back into the dark hallway and aimed his flashlight toward the place where he had left the Lieutenant's body. The beam of light landed on four people, and at first glance, it appeared they were huddling together. They let out a collective groan and bumped against each other as they all reached for the source of the light. O'Reilly backed into the lab and shut the door. Lieutenant Gleaton's face appeared at the small window, and Sergeant O'Reilly felt like he had let his friend down.

Mullins said, "We need to find everyone else, Sarge."

O'Reilly felt Mullins pull at his arm and hesitated, unable to take his eyes away from the Lieutenant's face. Mullins pulled again, and he remembered where they were and what they had to do, but it was too late. The chill that ran up his spine wasn't fear. It was the hatred he felt at the sound of the voice behind him. O'Reilly and Mullins turned to see Commander Evans and several of his soldiers overwhelming Private Hupp, Galina, and Oleg.

"It's no use resisting, Sergeant. You can die here if you want to. We have two of your friends pinned down in the room next door, and the others are being rounded up as we speak."

Evans smiled at his prisoners with an abnormally exaggerated smile that made him appear as if he was suppressing the urge to giggle. He gestured with his own 9mm handgun toward the door where Lieutenant Gleaton was attempting to bite the window.

"Thank you for contributing to my supply of fresh test subjects."

When the smile faded, they could see the menace in his eyes. They also saw the madness. He had them handcuffed while he held his gun on them. When they were pushed into the corridor, they were joined by Corporal Mincy and Private Ritter. They had surrendered when given the choice of giving up or staying inside the lab with almost a dozen people who had died from gunshot wounds and were just beginning to become the infected dead.

Six more escapees were rounded up when they fled from the hallway, and several more who had been shot by the first guard were summarily executed.

Commander Evans addressed his captives as a group and said, "As you can see, when you try to escape, there is only one outcome. You will die."

He appeared to be introspective for a moment, then added, "You're going to die anyway, but you'll at least get to live longer if you don't try to escape. So, you can choose when you want to die. Go ahead and try to escape."

Evans must have thought he was being really amusing because he laughed long enough and hard enough to have a coughing fit. He gestured toward the guards to take them back to their cells.

******

No one who was taken from the cells ever came back. Commander Evans was understanding of O'Reilly's fierce loyalty to his squad, and he played on those feelings. He would send his guards into the cellblock pretending to need another test subject just to keep their emotions on edge.

It was a morning in the first week of February when the guards marched into the narrow space between the cells and focused their attention on Galina. As soon as their squad leader inserted his key into the lock, Oleg put himself between the men and his wife. They backed everyone else away with gun barrels pointed at them, but Oleg refused to move. O'Reilly and his squad shouted from their cells, but they couldn't do anything to help. Oleg was tackled and pinned face down on the floor by four men while two others dragged Galina away.

After they were gone, Oleg threw himself at the bars in a frenzy. He cursed in Russian, and even though the Americans had been in the shelter for over six years with Oleg, Galina, and Pavel, they could only understand a fraction of what he said. They all did their best to console him, but in the end, he went to a corner of his cell and wept uncontrollably.

Later that same day, when the guards brought them lunch, Oleg renewed his attacks at the bars with such fury that he was knocked unconscious before they opened the cell door to pass out food. He was crumpled in a heap on the floor when everyone realized the food actually smelled good. The savory smell was also familiar. Galina hadn't been taken as a test subject. She had been taken because of her culinary skills.

Evans made a rare appearance in the cell block at supper when the food was distributed. He made a short speech to Oleg about what would keep his wife safe and what would guarantee that she became a test subject. Oleg understood his meaning, and it also meant they would eat well before they died.

Oleg Volkov smiled and spoke in a pleasant voice as he made his own speech entirely in Russian. Evans thought Oleg was graciously accepting the terms and promising to behave, but O'Reilly understood enough Russian to know it was a different kind of promise. If Oleg got to keep his promise, the man would be fed to the infected dead in small pieces, and he would be kept alive to watch.

The botched escape attempt provided Evans and his deranged researchers with a ready supply of infected dead to use as test subjects, but he still needed uninfected people. Being angry made it easier for him to sacrifice healthy people. His anger was partly fueled by the fact that he didn't receive the same respect and loyalty from his troops as O'Reilly, but what he failed to understand was that O'Reilly would die for his people. That was why they were willing to do the same for him.

Commander Evans felt like he was betrayed by the soldiers he had put into the cells with O'Reilly's squad. When they escaped with him, he thought they had missed a golden opportunity to be redeemed. It was beyond his comprehension, and he felt like they should get the worst punishment.

Two weeks after Galina was taken, they came for a live test subject. The guards opened a cell and pointed at a young woman who they all knew was a Navy E-4 named Tracey Knight. She was only a Third Class Petty Officer and planned to leave the service at the end of her enlistment, but the infected dead showed up a month before she was due to get out of the Navy. She was on temporary duty in Norfolk,

Virginia, when the Navy ordered all ships to go to sea, and in an unprecedented move, all personnel on shore duty were ordered to go with them.

Petty Officer Knight stiffened her shoulders as she stood up straight. She expected to be one of the people Commander Evans would select because she had called him a coward when he had ordered her to be detained with Sergeant O'Reilly's squad. He not only heard her say it, he had reacted as if she had slapped him. She followed up the first insult with a string of rhetorical questions.

"What? You can't take it? Are you gonna cry now?" she shouted.

When the guards stepped into the cell to take her, three of the men who shared the cell with her blocked their path. The squad used Tasers on all three of them, but instead of moving to take her from the cell, they grabbed one of the three men and dragged him through the door.

The squad leader taunted Petty Officer Knight and said, "The Commander told us to bring the first person who stands up for you because that would make you suffer more. This guy is going to die for you."

By the end of March, six of the military personnel who had been branded as traitors were taken as test subjects. There were only two of them left, including Tracey Knight. Each time they had come for another living subject, the others had stepped in front of her.

"Live," they said as they gave themselves up for her. Then they would face O'Reilly and say, "Keep her alive."

He didn't know how he was going to do it, but he always said back, "I will."

The first week of April went by, and as the second week arrived, the last shipmate of Tracey Knight's was showing signs of mental fatigue. He knew he was next, and he planned to be as brave as everyone who was taken before him, but the stress of not knowing when it would happen made him physically ill. None of the remaining prisoners were sure that the guards would take him as a test subject if he was already sick.

The food that was delivered to the cellblock took such a noticeable drop in quality that everyone suspected something had happened to Galina. Instead of a hot meal, cold canned beans and saltine crackers arrived from the kitchen. The only thing that had been holding Oleg together was Galina's cooking. He ate each bite as if they were back in their old apartment, and in his mind, he had watched her cook it. It was his connection to her, and it was severed with no warning.

"What have you done to my wife? Where is Galina?" he asked when the food was passed out.

His voice rose as they ignored him, and he was convinced they had used her as a test subject. O'Reilly watched the guards for any clue about what might have happened to Galina, and if he had to make a guess, the guards appeared to be uncomfortable. They weren't just ignoring Oleg, they weren't making eye contact with any of the people in the cells. He nudged Mullins and hooked a thumb toward the guards. Mullins watched them closely, the lines across his forehead getting deeper.

"They're afraid of something," whispered Mullins.

"Yeah, that's what I was thinking. Something happened, but I don't think they used Galina as a test subject. I think something has them spooked."

******

The experiments weren't going well, and Commander Anthony Evans lost his patience with the doctors. In one display of his boiling temper, he told the doctors to give him significant results within twenty-four hours or pick someone from among themselves as the next living test subject. They worked feverishly to find one shred of information about the virus that wasn't already known, but well before the deadline, they knew they wouldn't be able to tell him what he wanted to hear.

Out of fear for their own lives, they whispered among themselves about who was the least important person who could be sacrificed. Madeline Logan had been with them from the beginning, but she was still the least qualified researcher in the group. The backstabbing and plotting whispers were responsible for the mistakes that caused the over-stressed lab technician to become infected.

It wasn't a large wound or a bite. It was a needle puncture that went unnoticed by everyone else in the lab. The woman barely felt it herself when the tip of the needle went through the latex glove on her left hand.

She had placed the syringe on a table without replacing the protective plastic cover over the needle and then reached for another syringe next to it. There was a slight burning sensation that itched like a mosquito bite, and she even thought an insect might have gotten under the edge of her glove near her wrist. She peeled back the glove and saw the red streak where the needle had lightly scraped across her arm before it finally pierced the skin. A tiny red dot of blood had smeared when the glove moved over it.

It might as well have been a severed artery to her. She had worked with the doctors long enough to know it would be fatal, but she didn't want to die yet. She also knew if she told anyone about it, they would act quickly. She had seen it happen before. Her pleas and her excuses would fall on deaf ears.

Madeline knew the whispers were about her because they stopped whenever she moved to another table, and they started again when she left. They were also doctors who were more valuable than her. She stripped off her gloves and threw them into a wastebasket as casually as she could and kept her back to the others as she dabbed an alcohol prep pad over the scratch. It burned in confirmation that she had committed the fatal error.

She knew that the act of placing a bandage on her arm would draw suspicion, so Madeline pulled on a fresh pair of gloves and slid a clean piece of gauze under the hem of the glove. She gathered herself together and pretended that she was working as hard as everyone else, and for the rest of the day, she kept telling herself that it was just a scratch.

Later in the day, the three doctors who were considered the most important members of the medical team stood before the desk where the Commander made a show of reading the research notes they presented to him at the end of their deadline.

When they had been working on Navy ships, they had regular meetings around conference tables. They discussed their research as peers and had optimism that they would succeed. The conference tables were replaced after months of failed experiments, and the doctors were eventually seated across from Commander Evans at a desk. Now, at Joint Base Evans, they were no longer allowed to sit.

******

Over the years since the first experiments began on Navy ships in the North Atlantic, Commander Anthony Evans had seen his resources dwindle. When he was given orders to spearhead the program to find a cure for the infection, he was given access to everything the military could offer. Medical bays were transformed into research facilities. Teams of doctors with extensive experience in virology were assigned to him. Civilians who had been rescued were interviewed to see if any had worked for the Centers for Disease Control. He had everything he needed.

Commander Evans was selected for the job because he had been stationed at Fort Detrick, Maryland, as the US Navy's liaison officer. He personally didn't have a research background, and his main function was to provide support for the facility if the Army needed assistance. It was a comfortable job that was basically just a stepping stone for climbing in rank. His wife was happy, and his kids were in private schools.

The facility where he worked was known by the name USAMRIID, United States Army Medical Research Institute of Infectious Diseases. When the evacuation order was given, it was obvious to anyone that there was an infectious disease spreading faster than anything ever known to mankind, and the symptoms meant the research community wasn't going to be able to conduct conventional tests, publish papers, have peer reviews, and schedule endless meetings to discuss their progress.

The decisions that were made in the first few weeks of the infection were mostly made in good faith. The singular goal was to save the human race, and the people in command of the fleet were torn apart by their inability to do more to help. They were essentially thrust into a situation where they had to triage mankind. The question was, who could they save, and who could they sacrifice? If they were going to save mankind, they had to do away with the rules that would have been followed if there was more time, and they gradually realized they had to turn a blind eye to which rules were broken.

The captains turned toward routine shipboard operations and gave Commander Evans a long leash to do his own job. Assault teams that had previously trained for combat were adapted to the role of quick-strike forces. They went ashore under his command and attempted to take control of research facilities where the doctors could conduct their tests, but they could only secure buildings for brief periods of time. The losses they suffered were an unacceptable trade for the lack of progress they made toward finding a cure. He used those losses to justify his answer to the problem.

There were a few officers who argued against Commander Evans when he suggested that they should bring the infected back to the ships where they could be studied around the clock. He saw them as short-sighted and considered them to be his enemies. It never occurred to him that he was a member of the very small minority who had been able to bring family members along during the evacuation and that he was already seen as an outsider. He had no traditional naval duties, and he wasn't burdened by grief like the rest of the officers.

That grief was the one thing that made Evans different from his fellow officers, and it was the reason for his mistakes. If he had lost his family to the infection in the beginning, he might have understood the risks he was taking. He ordered the labs to work around the clock on the ships, and just as it always did, the infection found a way to break out of containment. When his family was caught up in the outbreak, he lost what remained of his objectivity and his humanity.

******

Almost seven years later, with depleted resources and a smaller team of researchers, Anthony Evans was a US Navy Commander in name only. If his command had existed in the free world without the infected dead, it would have been a pariah state, much the same as North Korea. With the doctors standing ramrod-straight before him and in fear of losing their own lives, he was the picture of control as he turned the pages of the daily report. In reality, his eyes were unfocused, and his mind was raging.

Part of him knew he had issued an empty threat. Another part of him wanted to lash out and punish the pitiful men standing across from him. He detested their impotence, but it never occurred to him that he was partially the cause of their failures. It also never crossed his mind that maybe there would never be a cure for the infection. All he knew how to do was to continue being the way he had become.

"Isn't this the same report you gave me yesterday? As a matter of fact, this appears to be the same report I've been reading every day for seven years."

If it was the same report as it had been every day for seven years, it was also the same rhetorical question he had asked them since the beginning. They even knew what he was going to ask them next.

"Is this the same report you're going to give me tomorrow? Why not save us all some time and just give me two copies of it today?"

None of them answered because they also knew he would take out his anger on the first one to open his mouth. They were also silently hoping he would forget about his ultimatum so they wouldn't have to give him Madeline Logan's name.

His temper was on full display for thirty minutes before he threw them out of his office. He didn't ask them for a name, and they were relieved that he had either forgotten about the threat or changed his mind. One thing that stood out in their report also went unnoticed... they had been able to determine that the infection manifested symptoms in left-handed victims more rapidly while it moved slowly in right-handed subjects. They didn't know what it meant, but Madeline Logan wished she had not seen the report. She was left-handed.

25

Inevitable

Attu Island - April 2023

David Clemenza had never been a team player, and he was questioning how he had allowed himself to get so involved with Commander Evans and his band of 'eggheads,' as he liked to call them. Even worse, he knew he should have deserted before letting himself get transported to a barren island that had nothing to offer other than rat stew. There wasn't even any vegetation he could eat.

He had decided it was time to get out of the shelter when Evans started talking about using his own troops as subjects. He wondered how long it would be before one of the eggheads suggested that body size needed to be studied to see if bigger, more muscular people could fight off the infection. All he had to do was find that ladder Corporal Mullins had told him about.

Clemenza could walk right up to either door and overpower the guard if he wanted to, but he preferred to just disappear if that was possible. If he could leave without anyone knowing it, they would waste precious time searching the shelter for him, and by the time they figured out he was really gone, he would have a good head start. When he thought about the way the shelter was built, he put two and two together and came to the conclusion that the ladder that went to the exterior power source was his only option.

The ladder that went up to a small platform wasn't guarded. Either Evans knew about it and didn't think anyone would be crazy enough to leave that way, or he had never been told about it. When Clemenza opened the hatch at the top of the ladder and saw the steel rungs in the face of the cliff, he decided it was the former. The rungs stuck out from the rock face like big staples. If there was another way out of the shelter that didn't involve free climbing, he would be glad to take it. It wasn't that he couldn't climb that far. He just wasn't thrilled with heights.

He made sure his rifle and backpack were secure and reached for the first rung. The metal was cold, wet, and rusty.

"This should be fun," he said aloud.

It wasn't until he had climbed at least twenty rungs before he saw where the ladder went. The wind turbines were shrouded in clouds that swirled as the huge blades turned through them. They were also dark in color, which he guessed was caused by corrosion, and even though he didn't know much about wind power, he was sure they were old because they were noisy. The closer he got to them, the louder the noise got. It was a high shrieking sound like metal rubbing against metal.

Clemenza hoped he wouldn't need to climb all the way to the three wind turbines, and he got his wish when he came to a cleft between a low peak and the mountain. A worn path in the cleft sloped downward, and someone had painted an arrow to show it was a way to go down. He didn't know where it went, but it beat climbing higher.

Half an hour later, he emerged from the path onto the plateau above the outpost that had been built by Sergeant O'Reilly's squad. He felt an odd twinge of gratitude toward O'Reilly and his men for giving him a place where he could hole up until he figured out how to get off of the island. Corporal Mullins had told him while they were drinking that he had buried a footlocker filled with food under one of the huts so the rats wouldn't get into it. He didn't know how long it would last, but he was sure it would last long enough for him to figure out a way to get off Attu Island.

He was wrong, but by the time he was done exploring Attu Island, there was no one in history who knew the forsaken lump of rock better than him. He had found the yacht that was explored years ago by O'Reilly's squad and tried to find a way to make it float again, but he knew that getting it to float was only part of the problem. Without propulsion, he would risk drifting out into the Pacific, where he would most likely die of thirst.

Speaking of thirst, the freshwater tanks at the camp were nearly empty because it hadn't rained in weeks. The food would be gone first, but if it didn't rain soon, he was facing the possibility of going back to the shelter. He had thought about stretching his rations a little by eating rats and had gone so far as to stalk a large one, but when he saw the way they fed on the infected dead, he had to wonder if it was safe to eat them even if he charred the meat.

The same was probably true for seafood, but fish might be safe to eat. He decided it was a risk he had to take. In the supplies left behind at the camp was a spool of wire. He decided to use it as a fishing line, and he sacrificed a can of processed meat to use as bait. Making a hook was easy because there was a suturing needle in the first aid kit. It was something he knew he might need later, so he figured he would be careful not to pull too hard when he set the hook.

The canned meat proved to be attractive to fish, but it was even more attractive to crabs that lurked close to shore. When Clemenza threw the line out as far as he could, the water where the bait landed was calm at first, and he watched the fin of a small shark cruise toward it. He didn't need to pull at all to set the hook, and he ran sideways along the beach to guide the fish closer, winding the wire around his hand as he ran. The line was suddenly pulled painfully tight, and the water churned wildly. The shark disappeared under several armored bodies with long legs.

When the thrashing in the water stopped, the line went slack. He wound it around his hand again and felt small tugs that pulled back at him. The end of the line appeared, and a crab surfaced with it. His first thought was that he could eat that crab for a week, but he had already seen them hanging onto the infected dead the same way the rats did. Not to mention the fact that this crab was big enough to give him a good fight.

Clemenza watched the crab walk up the beach in the same detached way someone would watch a car wreck. It was inevitable, and everything was moving in slow motion. He suddenly realized the crab was walking toward him. He had thought he was reeling in the crab as he wound the line around his hand, but the crab was coming faster than his hook. Clemenza got a mental image of himself trying to pull one pincer out of his skin while avoiding another one.

At first, he just backed away from the water, but the crab matched his pace. When he backed away faster, the crab ran toward him faster than he thought possible. He abandoned the fishing line and ran for higher ground. When he stopped to see if the crab had given up the chase, he was shocked to see it was still running. Even worse, there were three more following behind it. Clemenza wondered if the crabs were going to stalk him like prey.

Just like the inevitable car wreck, Clemenza eventually accepted that his only option was to return to the shelter. As far as he could tell, he had been outside for over two months, and he wouldn't have made it that long if not for Corporal Mullins and his private stash. He had explored every possible way of leaving the island and had come to the conclusion that he could only leave one of two ways. He would either be rescued, or he would leave in the stomachs of the crabs. The bad news was that he had better chances of swimming to the mainland than he did of being rescued.

"Where did I put that lottery ticket?" he said aloud after locking the door behind himself. "I think I have better odds of winning that."

Ten minutes after he shut the door, he heard something scratching at the metal frame. He was sure if he opened the door, it would be the crab. He settled back on a bunk and weighed his options. Going back wouldn't be difficult, at least not until Commander Evans knew he was there. That left him only one choice…he had to arrange a change of command.

When Clemenza opened the door in the morning, he had his 9mm Sig Sauer pointed at the ground. If the crab was still there, it was going to die. He took a couple of steps outside and checked the ground all around him. Only about six feet from the door, there was a pile of bones mixed with broken crab legs. From what he could tell, the crab had been the ultimate loser, but it had taken out at least one or two rats. Of course, nothing went to waste. After the rats finished eating the crab, they cleaned up the remains of their fallen comrades.

Out of curiosity, Clemenza lifted his foot and held it over the shell of the crab. He was a big man, and he wore a size fourteen boot. The crab's main body was at least six inches longer than his boot. He didn't want to think about what would have happened if he had run into one of those things at night.

He stuffed a few things in his backpack and slung it over his shoulder with his M4. He didn't need to take much with him because he knew exactly what he was going to do when he got back. His plan was simple. He would find O'Reilly or Mullins and pitch the idea of a mutiny. If they didn't know by now that Evans was crazy, he would tell them things that Evans had done in the name of his precious experiments.

The temperature had dropped a bit, so he made sure he had his gloves ready for the climb down to the hatch. It should be easier going down, but he also felt like he was more likely to make a mistake and slip if it was too easy. If he had some climbing gear, he would be happy to hook a safety line to one of the rungs and rest at the halfway point.

An hour later, when he stood in the cleft between the peaks and looked down at the steel rungs that were hammered into the cliff face, he realized that he hadn't looked back on the day when he had climbed up. The rungs seemed to fade away in the distance and disappear. He couldn't mentally guess how many hundreds of feet he would fall if he slipped, but he knew it was far enough that it wasn't worth knowing if it was four, five, or six hundred feet.

"Jeez…I climbed that far?"

The first step was the hardest because he had to feel for the rung with his feet. He kept a tight hold with his hands and didn't relax his grip with one hand until he had a firm hold on the next rung with the other hand. He also didn't move a foot downward until he had both boots next to each other on the same rung.

Clemenza thought he might be at about the halfway point when he felt the rung under his boots move. He wasn't completely sure that it had moved, but he didn't want to find out the hard way by staying on it for too long. He climbed downward a little faster until his hands reached the rung he had been standing on, and he reached further with his hand for the next rung below it. He felt like he had to know if the ladder was safe because he still had a long way to go.

When he reached for the rung, he mentally pictured it being as solid as all the others, and he imagined it moved. He let out a nervous laugh, wrapped his fingers around it, and tugged. It came completely out of the wall of rock. He held it up like a really large horseshoe and stared at it. His eyes moved to his other hand, and it occurred to him what would have happened if he hadn't felt it move under his foot. In his mind's eye, he saw himself falling backward, unable to even see what he was going to hit when he landed.

"What are the odds that's the only loose one?" he thought.

There was no sense in waiting around and worrying about what could have happened. Throwing caution to the wind, Clemenza climbed down the ladder much faster than before. When he reached the hatch, he didn't hesitate to pull it open and climb inside. He shut the door and sat on the small landing for a half hour.

******

Clemenza had always wondered where Evans had found so many misfits to drag along on his crusade. They were so easy to get past in the dark corridors of the shelter that he thought Evans deliberately recruited nearsighted people. When one guard walked past him, he could have reached out and tapped the man on the shoulder. The guard was so used to the safety of the shelter that he didn't even check the shadows anymore.

There were plenty of hiding spots in the shelter. Clemenza thought more than once that the place wasn't designed by a real architect. There was too much wasted space that could have been used for storage of supplies, and he used those dark, unimportant places to move from one level to the next until he was near the kitchen. Food was a priority to him, and he found a hiding spot under some stairs to wait for the dining room to clear out. He could have used a back entrance into the kitchen, but he figured it would be safer if everyone was gone.

Clemenza watched a pair of soldiers leave, and before the door swung shut, he saw that the room was empty. As soon as they were far enough away, he slipped across the hall and through the door. Unlike the guards, he didn't take anything for granted. He kept his back against a wall just inside the door and listened. The door was open to the kitchen, and he could hear someone in there.

Since the kitchen wasn't visible from the dining room, he couldn't tell how many people were in there. He listened for distinctive sounds that would tell him if someone was cooking or cleaning, and he heard water running at the sinks. It was the right time of day for dishwashing, so he hoped the sound was coming from one person cleaning up after the morning meal. If that was the case, the person would have their back to the door. As added insurance, he turned off the dining room lights. If anyone came in after he went into the kitchen, he would see the lights turn back on.

When Clemenza peered around the corner, he saw Galina scrubbing a large pot. There was a container of food sitting only a few feet away from him on a stainless steel counter, and it was still warm. He could smell it, and his stomach growled. He leaned toward it and saw it was chipped beef in a cream sauce.

"Are you hungry?" asked Galina. "Can I make you a plate?"

She didn't sound at all like she was afraid to find the big man standing behind her, and the offer to feed him was genuine.

Galina didn't wait for Clemenza to answer. She wiped her hands on her apron and got a plate from a stack. She dropped two large slices of freshly baked bread on it and then used a soup ladle to scoop out the chipped beef and spread it over the bread. She didn't seem to mind when he took the plate and dug in as if he hadn't eaten in a long time.

"You are so hungry," she said, and he could hear real concern in her voice. "Where have you been? I have not seen you in a long time."

"I left," he said around a mouthful of food. "Did you make this?"

She laughed, "Of course." She added sadly, "They put my husband in a cell with the others, and they made me their cook."

Clemenza stopped eating for a moment and said, "So, Evans made his move, huh? Is everyone still alive?"

"I lost track of time. I do not know when you left, but the last time I saw you was before Commander Evans came for us. He had us locked in the prison cells, but we got out. We almost got away, but they caught us. My brother, Pavel, was killed, and so was the Lieutenant. They will not let me visit with my husband, but as long as I can send him food, I feel like I am still near him."

Clemenza had never gotten close with people, even before the infected dead arrived. If he helped someone else, it was usually because it was of some benefit to him. A few years earlier, when he saved the lives of some people in Charleston, he wasn't sure why he had helped them, but he supposed it was because the people he worked for were pompous jerks. As a matter of fact, they were just like Commander Evans. He also felt like there was something about the big guy who was the leader of that group of survivors. He felt like he might have saved them as a sign of respect and that the guy would have done the same thing for him.

There was something about the Russian woman that he liked besides her cooking, and he felt sorry for her. No one had asked for the infected dead to wreck the world, but from what he had been told before he left, the Russian refugees had more than their share of hardships escaping from Russia. Their timing had been good, but that didn't mean it was easy.

Clemenza wiped his sleeve across his mouth, and Galina had to smile at how eagerly he had eaten the food. He was also very tempted when she offered to give him a second plate, but he was feeling uneasy about what she told him. Part of him wanted to find out for her if Oleg was still alive, and that made him remember that Evans would most likely have him locked up with the other prisoners if he got caught. He decided that his plan to arrange a change of command couldn't wait.

"Are you allowed to go back and forth between here and your quarters without an escort?"

She shook her head.

"I must wait for a guard who comes for me, and they keep someone near the stairs outside my room. I am not allowed to go anywhere else."

"How long before someone shows up again today?"

"I think about two hours."

"That's not much time," he said. "I'm trying to figure out if you should disappear now or after they tuck you in for the night."

"Disappear? You want me to leave? I have to cook for my husband."

Clemenza realized that Galina didn't have a clue about what was about to happen. She probably wasn't aware that Commander Evans would lock him in a cell with the others if he found out he was back, and he wasn't going to let that happen. He was about to stir things up inside the shelter, and he had to make sure she was safe while he did it.

"I have an idea," he said. "Pack enough canned food for two days and grab a gallon of water. You're not leaving…you're just taking a couple of days off. If everything works out the way I hope it does, you'll be serving food to Oleg in the dining room soon."

Clemenza made himself another plate of food while Galina gathered together the supplies, and he ate the second plate faster than the first. He also grabbed a second gallon jug of water because he had noticed the power plant was warmer than the rest of the shelter. He didn't know why Evans didn't send his troops down to the power plant more often, but it was probably because he didn't consider it to be a great place to hide. The area also had so many escape routes that it was difficult for them to guard them all. They reached the power plant without seeing anyone.

"This is where we went when we tried to escape," said Galina. "Do you think it is safe?"

"It's safe for a short time. If things work out, we won't have to hide for long. By the way, was there anything wrong with the boat you three used to escape from Russia?"

"The *Svetlana*? No, she is a good boat."

"I guess all we would need is fuel, but that shouldn't be a problem from what I heard. Back when that entrance was used a lot, they put in tanks to hold fuel for the trips back and forth to Russia."

"You will take us with you?" asked Galina.

"If that's what you want. I mean, it's safer here on this island, but I was going crazy here before. That's why I left. If there's a way off this rock, I would rather take my chances with those infected things on the mainland."

"If Oleg wants to leave, we will go with you," she said.

"That's fine by me. I could probably use the help on the boat, and you're a great cook."

That comment earned him a smile, and for the first time in a long time, even a time before the infected dead, Clemenza felt good about himself.

"You might get bored down here, but stay here as long as you can. Hopefully, I won't need more than a day to make some changes around here."

******

Madeline Logan didn't feel well, but she managed to make it back to her quarters without anyone noticing the way perspiration beaded on her forehead or the way she walked ramrod straight because every joint in her body hurt. She gasped when the sharp pains lanced through her as she climbed the stairs to her level.

The guard at the top of the stairs lifted his eyes from the paperback he was reading and asked her if she was okay.

"Long day," she mumbled.

She was about to say more, but she saw that he had already gone back to reading, and he didn't look up again while she walked to her room. After she went inside, Madeline got a washcloth and soaked it in cold water. After she placed it against her head, she felt it quickly become warm. She was burning up. She took a couple of aspirin, wet the washcloth again, and laid down on her bed.

When she woke up a few hours later, her head hurt so bad that she could hardly see. She had left a small lamp on, and it felt like a needle had been stuck through her eyes when she opened the lids. She rolled over away from the light, and even though she didn't know where she was going, she walked out of her room.

The guard was only about thirty steps from her door, and she wasn't sure if it was the same man or not, but whoever he was, he was sound asleep. She couldn't have cared less. The stairs made her body hurt just as much going down as they had when she was coming up, but she didn't care about that either.

When she reached the main floor, Madeline discovered it was easier to walk if she leaned a shoulder against the wall. Not only did it keep her from falling down, but it also kept her in the shadows, where she was almost invisible. If anyone happened to look toward the common area where the corridors connected, they wouldn't see her as she circled around it.

Sweat was running down into her eyes when she made a turn that would take her to the cellblock entrance. She didn't know where she was or where she was going. There were no walls for her to lean against as she made the last turn because there were cells on both sides. She slipped into the narrow gap between the bars and caused a general panic inside the cell. It just happened to be the cell that held Petty Officer Tracey Knight and her last remaining shipmate, Carl Bolden. Neither of them was expecting the intrusion, and they scrambled away to the back wall of the cell.

Tracey recognized Madeline because she had seen her in her white lab coat with the doctors. The doctors and technicians kept to themselves because no one wanted to talk about the experiments. She knew what Madeline did, and seeing her so close made her want to pull the monster through the bars by her hair. She might have tried if not for the way she had arrived. Making her and Carl jump away out of fright gave her time to recognize that Madeline wasn't coming for them. On the contrary, Madeline didn't act like she was even aware of them.

Madeline pulled her shoulder out from between the bars and made a failed attempt to stand up straight without holding onto anything. Her grip slipped on the first try, and she had to pull her shoulder out of the gap for a second time. She used two hands on the next try and was at least able to proceed on her trip to 'who knows where.' She worked her way along the cells one bar at a time and didn't seem to notice the occupants inside. They knew she wasn't dead yet, but they knew she was sick. Everyone was fairly sure she would be dead soon.

After Madeline went through the door and made a turn, Corporal Mincy said, "What was that?"

"That," said Tracey with shock in her voice, "was an infected lab technician."

"That's what I thought," said Mincy, "but I don't know if that's good or bad news."

If they could have seen Madeline Logan beyond the cellblock, they would have known that she died before she reached the entrance to the tunnel where Corporal Hupp had cracked the combination years ago. She leaned against the wall and slid down to the floor. Maybe there was something to the theory about left-handed people turning faster because her eyes opened less than thirty minutes later.

When the dead version of Madeline Logan pushed herself into a standing position, it took as much effort as it had before she died, but she didn't need the wall to stay upright anymore. She walked in the direction she was facing when she died and only minutes later found her first victim.

Like most of the guardposts throughout the shelter, there was nothing to keep the guards awake. No one ever checked on them, and more often than not, they slept until they were awakened by the guards who relieved them. When Madeline gripped the sleeping man's arm, his first waking thought was that his relief was shaking his arm to wake him up. When she leaned closer and nestled her face against his neck, his second waking thought was that he was dreaming.

She bit deeply and pulled away his carotid artery. He was in shock in seconds and dead a few seconds later. She fed on him until he began to move again, and a few minutes after that, both of them bumped around in the room by the vault door. They eventually walked into the doorway, and the guard followed Madeline into one of the many tunnels that snaked through the shelter.

******

Over the next two days, Commander Evans had the shelter searched, but as Sergeant O'Reilly had observed when they first discovered the shelter, it could take weeks to explore the entire thing. A day after the first cold meal was served to the prisoners, a detail arrived and shoved a guard into the cell with Tracey and Carl. He looked familiar, and he put himself in the corner as far from them as he could get.

O'Reilly said, "Hey, aren't you the guy Evans has in charge of the watch schedule? What did you do wrong?"

The man turned away from him and acted like he didn't hear the question.

"Petty Officer Knight, you and Bolden bring that man to me. If he can't hear me from there, maybe he needs to be closer."

The man put his hands up in their direction and whined, "Wait. I'll tell you. The cook went missing, and the Commander said I should have had someone stay with her all the time instead of just escorting her. I only did what I was told to do. I was just following orders."

"Were you just following orders when you dragged people out of here to be used as test subjects?" asked O'Reilly. "Speaking of tests, are you missing anyone besides the cook?"

The man didn't answer, but the look on his face told him what he needed to know. When the relief for the guard at the vault door arrived for his shift, all he found was a big pool of sticky blood and a trail that went down into the depths of the shelter. There were footprints that became less evident the further they were from the start. The man didn't know if O'Reilly was talking about the guard at the vault door or the missing lab technician and wondered how he knew about them. No one bothered to tell him about their sick visitor.

26

Arrival

Attu Island - April 2023

"I feel like we've painted ourselves into a corner," said the Chief.

He was watching the fuel gauges and calculating whether or not they could make it back from Attu Island to their refueling point in Dutch Harbor.

There was a light fog over Attu Island, but they saw the sun reflecting off the beaches before they were too close. The Chief had radioed the other two helicopters and told them they would land quickly and cut off their engines quickly to save fuel. He wanted everyone out of the Black Hawks in a defensive perimeter as soon as they touched the ground. If it was clear, they would leave guards posted while everyone else prepared to begin the search for the shelter.

They passed over several small boats and a large yacht that was marooned on the beach, and even though they were much further from the mainland than Dutch Harbor, there were still a few of the infected dead lying in the surf. Everyone saw the massive crabs dragging an infected dead from the beach toward the water. Rats scurried from side to side around the body as they avoided the pincers. It was a competition for a piece of what used to be a living human being.

From her perch in the open door of the second Black Hawk, Kathy commented over the radio, "It seems we've slid down the food chain a few notches out here. I hope we can find high ground where it's flat enough to land. I don't think I need to warn anyone about the threats, but the rats are likely to be coming from higher places like those rocky slopes."

She heard a chorus of acknowledgments from all three helicopters.

Hampton was watching how the rats moved and added, "Everyone try to keep a close eye on the person next to you. The rats are adapting to a threat they've never had to worry about before. It looks like they're hunting in packs. Some keep the crab's attention while others get behind it. They'll try that with people too."

The Chief spotted the camp on the plateau above the beach and angled toward it. He landed quickly and cut the engines off as soon as he was sure there was no immediate threat. Behind him, the other two helicopters were only a couple of seconds slower to land, and people spread out in a circle with weapons drawn.

As the cloud of dust from their rotor wash cleared, the Chief sized up the camp and could imagine what it had been like for the soldiers stationed on Attu Island. The wind from their landing had blown away the dirt that had settled on the stones that had marked the paths between the huts, and he guessed the paths weren't decorated with white rocks to make the place more aesthetically pleasing to the eye.

Cassandra greeted him as he got out of the helicopter and said, "Can you imagine what it was like for the people stationed here when the infection started? They had no way to get home, they had infected dead washing up on their beaches, and they had crabs and rats trying to eat them. I hope they found the shelter."

"And after they found the shelter," answered the Chief, "I hope they got inside and then didn't open the door when guests arrived."

Iris joined them in time to hear what he said and asked, "Why wouldn't they? They would feel like they were being rescued. Isn't that what they were hoping for?"

The Chief had to agree. There were plenty of ways things may have gone at the camp. The soldiers might have become infected. They might have been killed by rats or crabs, or maybe they found the shelter and figured out how to get inside. He doubted they had found a way to leave the island, so it was more logical to assume they were already dead. If they somehow managed to survive, they would have welcomed the arrival of a larger military force with open arms.

"We don't want to waste daylight, so let's check the camp from top to bottom," said the Chief. "Someone find a clue to where the shelter is. The soldiers had plenty of ways to disappear, but hopefully, someone left a trail."

With everyone searching except the perimeter guards, it didn't take long to search the camp, and it didn't take long for them to find the breadcrumb trail they were hoping someone had left.

Shannon went with Hampton to one of the huts, and she spotted the small details that told the story of someone's survival.

"Did you notice the windows are sealed shut, and the doors have a metal rim around them, so there's no gap anywhere?" she asked.

Hampton nodded, "Rats can flatten their bodies and go through incredibly small places. The soldiers probably never got used to the sound of them scratching at the door as they searched for any chink in the armor. See those steel poles and sharpened mop handles in the corner? They probably had to constantly stab at the ground."

"Was this hut used as the chow hall?" asked Shannon. "It seems bigger than the others, and there are folding tables and chairs over here."

"Most likely," said Hampton. "There's a stove back there. Not a bad setup for such a remote place. Someone cared that they got decent meals out here."

"For how long, though?"

Shannon had been fed and cared for by an unknown benefactor for years in her shelter. Despite the fact that she was in some ways marooned the same way as the soldiers on Attu Island, she at least had a seemingly endless supply of food and water. They had to run out of supplies sooner or later in the camp.

Hampton said, "I don't know, but there's something about this place I can't quite put my finger on. It feels like someone was here not long ago."

"What's this?" said Shannon. "Looks like someone left us a note." She held up a piece of paper with writing on it.

"At least we know rats didn't get inside. They would eat paper if there wasn't anything else around. Let me see that."

Shannon handed him the note, and his eyes grew wide as he read it.

"Well, I'll be…," he trailed off. "I can't wait to see the Chief's face when he sees this."

They found the Chief at the communications hut, and he could see by the expression on Hampton's face that they had something good to show him. He held out his hand, but Hampton didn't give him the piece of paper.

"Not so fast," said Hampton. "We need the whole Mud Island family together for this."

The Chief couldn't miss the way Hampton suppressed a smile and wondered for a moment if this was how everyone else felt when he was about to put his sense of humor on display.

When word spread and everyone was present and accounted for, Hampton handed the piece of paper to the Chief with much fanfare. Then he got to enjoy seeing the Chief react to the note.

To whom it may concern, (I always wanted to say that.)

If you're reading this note, I hope you're one of the good guys because I'm going to go after the bad guys, and I'm going to tell you where I went. There's no more food out here and not much water. If you haven't noticed, you can't even fish around here without drawing the attention of things that will eat you if you let them get close enough. On the other side of this note, there's a map that should help you find a big shelter. There are three ways to get inside that I know of, but two are locked and guarded. The third way isn't locked, and I don't think the bad guys even know about it. The only catch is I hope you aren't afraid of heights.

David Clemenza

The Chief did his best not to react because he felt like it was a setup. His expression remained neutral until he reached the signature, and even he didn't possess the self-control needed to hold back a reaction.

"It can't be," he said.

"What is it?" asked Kathy.

She reached for the note, and even though he wanted to follow the map and get their business on Attu Island done, there was time to enjoy her reaction as much as Hampton had enjoyed his. Kathy read the note aloud for everyone to hear, and they were all stunned.

Everyone was talking at once, but there was some laughter at the Chief's expense. Someone said it was a small world, but he was fixated on what had made Clemenza become their hero, not once but twice. He had never been able to figure out why Clemenza had saved them from a terrible death in Charleston, and now he was making life easier for them on Attu Island.

"Hey, Chief," said Kathy, "Clemenza knows you knocked him out once, right? It feels like he knew it would be us reading this note."

"I know," said the Chief. "Frankly, I've always thought we would run into him again. I just didn't know if we would be on the same side or not. I don't know how he got here or what led to this moment, but I won't question fate. Let's get everyone geared up so we can follow this map."

Garrett asked, "Can someone tell my crew why you guys know the man who wrote the note?"

"You're gonna love this story," said Colleen. "We have time while we hike inland. You won't believe it."

The Chief studied the map, and he saw why Clemenza made the comment about not being afraid of heights. He told everyone to pass the word that they should only bring basic supplies and weapons because they would be doing some climbing.

He also wanted four of the fast-ropes they carried in the helicopters. There were at least two ropes in each helicopter, and they were used for troops to descend to the ground when the helicopters couldn't land. Each one was about fifty feet long and made of a strong, lightweight nylon material. He briefly explained to everyone that he, Tom, and Captain Miller would carry the ropes because they were around thirty-two pounds each.

The Chief said he hoped they wouldn't need them, but from what he could tell, they had to make a long climb down a steep cliff. He would tie one end of his rope to something solid at the top and drop the rest over the edge. Then he would climb down with the second rope and tie it to the ladder on the map. If they needed a third rope, Tom would carry it down to where the second one ended and fasten it to the ladder.

The last rope would be cut into short sections, and anyone who was afraid to climb down the cliff could use them as safety lines tied around their waists and then attached loosely to the main ropes by a slip knot. If someone fell, they would have a better chance of only getting bruised when they reached the end of a rope.

The Chief figured the Black Hawks would be safe without a guard unless someone from the shelter came outside and found them. Since he had no way to know what was happening inside the shelter, he decided that six people should stay behind. Two could sleep inside each helicopter more comfortably than inside the huts, and since they had windows, they could see what was going on outside. The helicopters were lined up in a way that allowed them all to see each other, so they could also stay in close contact.

There were volunteers who wanted to stay with the Black Hawks. Not surprisingly, two were people who didn't like the idea of climbing down a sheer drop from the side of a mountain. Shannon had spent too many years in isolation without testing her physical strength, and Anne said climbing a wall wasn't the same thing as flying in an airplane. The Chief wanted the twelve soldiers from Fort Richardson with him because they all had combat experience, so he selected four more to stay behind.

Garrett was still physically fit for a man approaching sixty, but he understood when the Chief pointed out there wasn't any need to protect the Black Hawks if he risked the lives of all of the pilots. Iris and Sim accepted without question when the Chief chose them to stay behind. Both of them knew that the Chief and Cassandra would be more focused on the mission if they didn't have them to worry about. Jon gave in and agreed to stay for the same reason as Garrett.

When they were ready, the column strung out in a line behind Cassandra and walked up the path marked on the map. They waved back at their friends just before they disappeared into the shadows of the peaks that rose on both sides. There were twenty of them in the group, and although no one would admit it, none of them was happy with the idea of climbing down that ladder on the steep rock face.

The Chief pointed upward at the rusty wind turbines way above them and said, "Check out the antiques. At least we don't have to climb up there."

Tom leaned slightly forward and looked at the waves crashing against the rocks at the bottom of the cliff.

"Yeah, Chief…that makes me feel better."

******

David Clemenza could move fast and quietly for a big man, but he had a long way to go before getting to Commander Evans. There were more guards in the area as he got closer, and his luck ran out when one spotted him. Now, he was using his speed to outrun them. Evans had enough respect for Clemenza to give a standing order to shoot him on sight, and he wasn't surprised that they tried.

His advantage was that he had spent more time exploring the darkest corners of the shelter. He memorized the layout and was amused by the way it had been designed without a pattern. It was like a jigsaw puzzle with the pieces forced to fit together, and that gave him the advantage when he found himself running past two infected dead that were wandering around. They didn't see him, but they heard the sound of the men who were chasing him.

Clemenza ducked around a corner and stayed in the shadows to be sure it went as he hoped it would. If it didn't, he had his pistol ready to take care of them. He could hear the boots of three guards as they charged blindly through the dimly lit corridor, and he could see the backs of the two infected dead as they were drawn closer to the place where the merger was about to happen.

The guards were yelling, "He went that way."

He thought the collision was epic. All five bodies went down in a pile on the floor, and the screaming started before anyone was bitten. He could tell the exact moment when the biting started by the pitch of the screams. Shots were fired wildly in the tangle of bodies. One man stopped screaming a split second after he was shot in the face by one of the other guards, and it would have been a mercy killing if it had been a few inches higher. The other two guards were still screaming when Clemenza left his hiding spot to renew his attempt to reach Commander Evans.

He was intercepted a second time by the dining room, and this time he was forced to make a detour back toward the power plant in the lower level. He didn't want to go that way because he was leading people straight to Galina. His only choice was to cross through the main floor of the power plant and let his pursuers be close enough behind him to see him leave the level through one of the many exits.

Clemenza chose a stairwell that he knew went up and down. If he entered it and heard someone coming from above, he planned to escape to the lower level that didn't even have as much light as the dimly lit upper levels. When he opened the door, the air that rushed out at him was hot enough to take his breath away. He stood in the doorway and covered part of his face with the collar of his shirt.

Shouts behind him let him know they saw him, so he went through the door, but the heat was coming from the lower level, and it was far too hot for him to go that way. He went up the stairs three steps at a time, stretching his leg as far as he could. He reached the next level and went through the door. If they were waiting for him, he knew it was all over, but he would go down fighting.

There was only one guard outside the door, and he was surprised when the big man burst through and ran right into him. He didn't even have his weapon in his hands, but even if he had, the impact would have kept him from getting off a shot. The man was unconscious before he reached the floor because he bounced off the wall opposite the door. Clemenza just kept going.

Inside the power plant, Galina saw Clemenza go by and knew that someone must be chasing him, or he would have gone to the dark corner where she was hiding. She pushed herself lower behind the machinery and waited. Seconds later, a group of armed guards ran in the same direction she had seen him go. She heard them yelling as they went through the stairwell door, but she stayed hidden.

It was the right decision because a second group came in after the first group was gone. She saw four men turning in circles as they tried to decide where the men had gone, but the door to the stairwell had shut before they arrived. She watched them go to another door and pull it open.

The power plant was a big room, and the lights were very low, but she could see well enough to tell that someone had come into the room when they opened the door. At first, she thought more guards had come in, but then she saw how they were grabbing each other. Someone screamed as teeth bit through hands that had been reflexively raised in self-defense. Galina covered her ears when one of the guards managed to fire shots at point-blank range.

The fighting at the door went strangely quiet after a few minutes, and Galina knew that it wasn't good news for her. Judging by the feeding sounds on the floor, she was going to be trapped inside the power plant with the infected dead if she didn't move fast enough. She glanced around the corner to see how many there were, and she couldn't tell for sure, but there were as many as five infected dead feeding on four bodies.

The only exit she could reach without drawing their attention was the one the guards had come in through. She stayed close to the shadows of the machinery and went through the door, making sure to pull the door shut behind her. Unsure of which way to go, she chose a corridor on the right and hoped there were no more infected dead waiting for her.

Clemenza heard the men chasing him, but he was far enough ahead of them to know they didn't know where he had gone. They wasted valuable time thinking the semi-conscious man he had run over would be able to point out the direction he had taken, and their voices faded as they went the wrong way.

He tried to circle back to get to the power plant, but when he reached one of the halls that would have taken him there, he saw the fresh blood trail that led straight to where he wanted to go. He knew that any infected dead that went through that door had to be inside, and if his calculations were correct, it could be a lot of them. He hoped he was guessing correctly when he decided that Galina was too smart to let herself get cornered like that, and if she left the power plant, it would not have been through that door.

Clemenza shut his eyes and visualized her reaction to him running by. She would have waited for his pursuers to go by, then she could have left.

"But why?" he said aloud. "Someone opened the door for the infected dead from inside the power plant?"

For a moment, he felt a sinking feeling at the thought that Galina had opened the door to escape from the power plant. If she had, there was nothing he could do for her, but when he gave it more thought, he didn't see why she would have done it. He shut his eyes again and saw a second possibility. More guards had entered the power plant, and they opened the door.

He began following his mental map of the shelter to find the hall that would lead him to the right entrance, and thirty minutes later, he caught a glimpse of her cowering under a set of stairs. When she saw him, she burst into tears and threw her arms around him.

"Come on. We can't stay here," he said.

He was relieved to find her and touched by the emotion that had spilled out of her. He wasn't sure what had made him change so much. Before the infected dead came along, he had not appreciated people. Now that there were fewer people alive, he considered the possibility that it made individuals stand out from each other. He didn't like what he saw that made Evans the monster he became, and he didn't like that the monster thought they were on the same side. Clemenza wanted to be more like Galina and her friends.

The thought of Galina's friends made him realize that he was going about his plan wrong. Maybe he needed more help to get to Evans, and he could get some help if he could reach the cellblock.

******

Commander Evans heard the shouts and the gunshots that echoed throughout the shelter. His first impulse was to surround himself with as many men as he could and join the pursuit. He didn't know for sure that it was Clemenza until a pair of guards reported in to say they had chased him through the power plant. He had gotten away, but they at least had a general idea of which side of the shelter he was on. He had his soldiers spread out at as many key points as possible to cut the shelter in half. They were spread thin, but his plan was to slowly collapse inward on his prey. If he was lucky, maybe he would find out where Galina was hiding too.

Evans became frustrated as the search stretched into a second hour without a single sighting.

"How can a man that big be hard to find?" he shouted at the helpless guards he had singled out. He had a dozen of them standing at attention in the common area while he vented his anger.

None of them wanted to be the first one to speak, so no one answered the rhetorical question. They all knew the Commander well enough to know what the fastest route to the cellblock was. Evans ranted until he was practically spitting on the men.

When he was done, he yelled, "Don't just stand there."

Evans found himself alone after mere seconds went by and realized it hadn't been the smartest move. He pulled his own gun out of its holster and checked the chamber. The common area seemed to be nothing but shadows that moved, and he hurried as quickly as he could to his office. Once inside, he locked the door, went to the farthest corner of the room, and sat heavily in a chair.

******

The massive shelter under Attu Island had become divided into rival camps. There were the prisoners in the cellblock and the infected dead in the power plant. They both were confined by doors they couldn't open. The same could be said of the doctors and lab technicians who had been doing the experiments for Commander Evans. They were confined in their labs by their own fear. They knew from a guard who had taken refuge with them that there was something happening outside their doors. They turned off their lights and sat in corners, unaware they were doing the same things as their leader.

The other two camps were constantly moving, but only one of them was as combat-skilled as Clemenza, and he had put his 'game face' on. The guards were the remaining camp. They moved recklessly through the shelter, ready to stumble on their own mistakes.

One mistake was their lack of coordination. Two groups of guards surprised each other, and they opened fire. Eight men were severely wounded. Another group ran from the sound of the gunshots. Six men ran through the door into the power plant. Four made it out the other side, but all of them were bitten. One of the other two fell in the doorway, and his body held the door open for the others to go through…after they were done with him.

Only one camp was still prisoners, and they were all backed up against the walls of their cells as the infected dead filled the narrow hallway of the cellblock. The infected reached in through the bars at them and waved their arms in the air. They pressed their faces into the gaps between the bars so hard that one got its head stuck.

Mullins put it into words perfectly.

"Does anybody else think it's ironic that we were out there and they were in here when we discovered this place?"

O'Reilly said, "You know what, Mullins? That will be very funny someday in the future if we live to tell about it."

Corporal Hupp said, "They aren't leaving as long as we're in here."

"Are you kidding me? I thought you were the smart one, Hupp," yelled Christine Mincy. "Does anyone else want to be Mr. Obvious next?"

Despite himself, Private Ritter had to laugh at Mincy's question, and it was contagious for a moment. When it died down, they knew they had laughed because the sobering reality was that they were going to die inside the cells if someone didn't come to break them out. That would have to start with eliminating a growing crowd of infected dead, so their hope was growing equally dim.

Mullins surprised everyone. His right arm snapped outward like a whip, and he wrapped his hand around the wrist of one of the infected dead. Pulling backward as hard as he could, he threw his left hand out to get a better grip. His feet slid along the floor of the cell until he braced his boots against the bottom of the door.

The infected dead were slow to realize they could grab his legs, but even as he felt their hands scrape against his pants, he saw that they couldn't bite him. The others saw it too, and O'Reilly grabbed Mullins from behind. He pulled along with Mullins.

There was a loud pop when the infected dead's shoulder separated. It was followed by a tearing sound. Tearing sinew was different than any of them expected, and everyone watched in morbid fascination as O'Reilly and Mullins fell to the back wall of the cell. Mullins had the separated arm across his lap, and it was twitching.

Mullins smiled at O'Reilly and said, "That's one."

Everyone joined in to try to do the same thing to the other outstretched arms, but they learned fast that it wasn't as easy as it looked. Mincy and the rest of them could catch an arm, but they didn't weigh enough to pull a shoulder out of the socket. They decided it was easy enough just to taunt the infected dead over to Mullins and O'Reilly and let them take it from there.

They made slow but steady progress removing five arms when gunshots and shouts disrupted their plan. The crowd of infected dead left the cellblock to pursue prey that was at least on their side of the bars.

"Not that I'm complaining," said O'Reilly, "but even if we had finished 'disarming' them, we would've still been stuck in here with them out there."

Everyone groaned at the weak joke.

******

The infected dead gradually overwhelmed the soldiers who were still loyal to Commander Evans. The living were too spread out in the shelter to know what was happening, and by the time they figured it out, all they could do was try to make every shot count. They were backed into rooms where they could shut the doors, but they couldn't fight off the hordes that waited for them in the halls.

The doctors and lab technicians watched through the small windows of their doors and saw no living people. There was nowhere for them to go, so they waited in the darkness.

Commander Evans ventured from his corner and listened at his own door. When he finally opened it a fraction of an inch, an infected dead slammed against it as it tried to reach the prey that was on the other side. Evans locked it again and went back to his corner.

The only living people left inside who were moving from room to room were Clemenza and Galina. It occurred to him that there were no safe places inside the shelter, and although he had never actually gone to the boats, maybe they could go out the door to the dock inside the cave and use a boat to escape.

When he told her his idea, she shook her head vigorously.

"We have to free my husband," she said. "Oleg and the others need to be set free."

"The cellblock is on the other side of the shelter, close to the other door. I don't think we can get through all of the infected."

"We have to try. I'm not leaving my husband."

He saw by the set of her jaw that she meant what she said, but he didn't think he could protect her while he fought his way to the other side of the shelter. He needed to make her safe first.

"Okay, I'll get them out, but I need to do it alone. The door to that grotto is right down that hallway. I'm taking you there first."

Galina tried to tell him they should stick together, but he was as stubborn as she was. He finally convinced her that he couldn't help her husband if he had to protect her at the same time.

The door was as close by as he thought it was, and he spun the big locking ring to open it. It swung silently open on its hinges and revealed a room with a tunnel in one wall. He flipped a switch next to the mouth of the tunnel and said a silent 'thank you' when the lights came on. He could see all the way to the end of the tunnel to the dock, but there was something moving at the other end. The dark shape was close to the floor, and he saw it raise an armored leg into the air.

"Crabs…I forgot about the crabs."

Galina could see it too, but she hadn't experienced the crabs the way Clemenza had. She hadn't seen how big they had gotten since their arrival at the shelter.

She said, "I think there's something wrong with it. It's not moving right."

He saw what she meant. He was also wondering why the crab hadn't charged down the tunnel at them.

"Stay behind me."

He drew his gun and walked slowly toward it. The crab was lifting a leg in the air, and it was trying to lift a pincer, but it moved like the menacing weapon was too heavy. Clemenza noticed that the crab's shell was almost pink like it had been partially cooked. It was also much hotter at the end of the tunnel than it was by the door. He took a few steps past the crab and out onto the dock. The lamps strung around the grotto revealed the two boats still tied up at the dock, but the big surprise was the water.

Galina stood beside him, and they stared in shock at the sight. The entire surface of the water was hidden by the bodies of crabs. Steam rose from around them, and the smell was unmistakable. It was the aroma of boiled crab.

"Why is the water hot?" asked Galina.

"Believe me," said Clemenza. "I don't have a clue."

27

Closure

Attu Island - April 2023

The rest of the group waited for the Chief to give the signal to climb down. If someone had asked, they would have said it was almost as bad to wait and watch him climb down the ladder as it was to climb it themselves. Some of them couldn't get close to the edge without getting dizzy, so they definitely couldn't watch as the others backed over the edge in search of the rungs with their feet. The rope was helpful as a guide, and the added security of safety lines made them feel like they had a chance if they fell.

The Chief made it look easy, but he was worried about the rest of them. The rocks were so far below him that he couldn't hear the surf hitting them. He tugged on each steel rung as he climbed and was disturbed when he found two holes where one had been. He stuck the tip of a finger into one of the holes. When he pulled it out, he saw there was rust surrounding his finger. That meant the rung had probably come out recently because the rain would eventually wash the holes clean.

He reached into his back pocket and pulled out a white rag. He tied it on the last rung before the gap so it would attract the attention of everyone else as they climbed down to join him. Since there were no other spots like it, he hoped they would all see the rag as a warning.

The end of the first rope dangled just below him, so he looped it around the same rung as the rag. After tying the second rope to the first rung after the gap, he easily climbed the rest of the way down to the hatch. When he lifted the metal door open and peered inside, he saw there was a small platform above another ladder. It went down an inside wall, and the floor below it was clear of any danger. The Chief swung one leg inside and signaled for everyone else to make the descent.

It was nerve-wracking for the Chief to watch his friends make the climb. He could do a lot to protect them, but there was nothing he could do about it if they fell hard enough to pull their safety lines off. As they reached him, he guided them through the door onto the platform. Kathy came down first, and he told her to hold her position halfway down the inside ladder until Cassandra arrived. Then, the two of them could go the rest of the way and be sure the place was clear.

They came down the ladder in a steady stream, but the Chief felt like it took forever. He also felt like he held his breath the entire time. Captain Miller was the last one to arrive, and the Chief couldn't resist giving him a hug out of relief.

"Are you ready to see an old friend, Jim?"

"Yeah, I've thought a lot about this. I don't think Evans will be happy to see me. I have a few things to talk with him about."

Once they climbed down from the platform, they found they were on a level of the shelter that was virtually empty. It didn't appear that it had been used in a long time. They strung out in a long column to begin their assault on whatever waited for them on the lower floors.

******

It wasn't easy for Galina to stay on the boat. The smell of boiled crab meat was overwhelming. If they had been at a restaurant, it might have been appetizing, but it was like a sauna inside the grotto, and Galina felt like she might get sick. She was also worried about what she would need to do if Clemenza didn't come back. He felt like it would be safer if he locked the vault door behind him, and she couldn't stop thinking about how it would all end for her if she was stranded in the grotto. She was forced to wait inside the boat to escape some of the smell, but it was difficult to breathe the warm air.

Clemenza didn't waste any time getting back inside the shelter, and he navigated the maze of hallways and stairs to get to the other side where the cellblock was. He wondered the whole time how he would eliminate an entire horde of infected dead while fighting any soldiers that might still be alive. He didn't know that they were all dead, but it would have only been a small comfort because it meant there would be a bigger army of infected dead to fight through.

Blood trails on the floor told him that things had gotten worse throughout the entire shelter. Twice, he came up behind hordes as they were walking in the same direction as him. They moved slowly, but as long as nothing was behind him, he could follow them. Each time, they made a turn into corridors where some distant noise caught their attention. Once they were far enough along their new courses, he dashed into the hallway he needed to use.

His luck didn't hold after he passed the second horde. He knew he didn't make any noise, but the infected dead at the back of the group turned his way just as he went by. The groan that it made was enough to cause the rest of them to pivot in the middle of the hallway and focus on him. With them following him, Clemenza was worried that he would get caught between two hordes, so he watched for an exit that would take him up one level. He knew the shelter well enough to know there was a stairwell around the next corner on his right. It was there, and a horde was only a few feet past it.

When Clemenza grabbed the knob on the door and swung it open, an infected dead stuck its hand into the gap between the door and the jamb. Clemenza pulled the door shut and heard the crunch of bones, but unless the infected pulled its hand out of the door, there was no way it was going to close. He yanked several times to try to smash the fingers inside the doorjamb, but he had to give up when a second one grabbed at his arm. He ran up the stairs to the next floor and continued across the shelter.

Another problem occurred to Clemenza as he hurried from one dark hallway to the next. He still had to find a way to open the cells. As big as he was, he wasn't strong enough to bend steel bars. His only alternative was to rummage through the pockets of the infected until he found one with the keys to the cells.

The next stairwell that went down to the main floor exited into the narrow hallway behind the labs. He decided that he could take a shortcut through the labs and then cross the common area after he found an infected dead with a key. There were bound to be some near there. He could watch through the window for one to pass by and then ambush it.

The labs were dark, so he cautiously slipped inside the first one he came to and eased the door shut behind him. He stopped just inside the door and listened, and his old training paid off. He could hear people breathing. He couldn't tell how many there were at first, but the infected dead didn't breathe like that. Someone was trying their best to hold their breath, which meant they had heard him come into the room.

Clemenza listened closely for changes in the rhythm, and he guessed there were possibly six or seven people in the room. One of them was trying not to cry. He put his back along one wall to prepare to defend himself.

"I'm only going to say this once," he announced to the dark room. "Anyone who moves before I say they can will die. Is that clear?"

There was a pause before a woman's voice said, "Please don't kill us."

Clemenza cleared his throat and said, "How many people are in here, and does anyone have a flashlight that still works?"

The hesitant woman said, "Seven people, I think, and we have flashlights, but we're afraid to turn them on."

"Who are you?" asked Clemenza.

"Medical staff," she said, then added, "and one guard."

"Is that what you call yourselves? I would call you something worse, but then you would say you've just been following orders. You've been experimenting on people, and you deserve to be out there with the infected because you're no different from them. Where's the guard?"

A flashlight clicked on, but it was held low to the floor and shaded so the infected dead outside wouldn't see the light through the window on the door. Clemenza saw that the man holding the light had a gun in his hand. He knew the man couldn't see him, so he slipped his own gun out of its holster.

"There are two things you need to do for me if you want to live," said Clemenza. "First, put the gun on the floor and push it toward me with your foot. Second, tell me you're lucky enough to have a key to the cells where the prisoners are."

The guard didn't say anything. Clemenza saw in the dim light that he lowered the gun to the floor and then pushed it away with his foot.

Then he waited.

"Well? Do you have a key?"

The guard said, "Oh, I'm sorry, sir."

He redirected his flashlight for a moment. He had been holding a keyring out toward Clemenza with his hand.

"Keep the flashlight on your hand and don't move. Everyone else stay still too."

Clemenza crossed over to the man in long strides and snatched the keyring. Then he backed away from them again.

"Turn off the light," said Clemenza.

The room went totally dark, and he let his eyes adjust again.

"Okay, everyone. Here's how it's going to go. I'm going to the cells to let the prisoners out. I don't care one way or the other if you live or die. You deserve to die here in the dark. Just don't get in my way, and I won't be the one who kills you."

The woman choked back a sob and said, "Please take us with you."

"Lady, there's a long list of people in history who've said they were just following orders when they did something bad to their victims. I almost went down that road myself, but if I can straighten out, so can you. The thing is, I'm not the only jury here. When I let those people out of the cells, they'll kill you if they get the chance. You're better off trying to get out of here on your own."

Clemenza followed the wall to the door and peered through the small glass window. As far as he could see, the common area was clear, so he made his move. The people inside the room heard the faint sound of the door opening and closing, but they couldn't see that he was still shaking his head in disbelief at the arrogance the woman showed by asking him for help.

******

As the Chief led the column deeper into the shelter, they saw more and more signs that the warning Captain Miller had given his superiors years ago was still not being heeded. He had told them not to bring the infected dead back to the ships because the infection couldn't be contained. It was a warning that Hampton had given to the people in his hometown, and it was still true. If you brought the infection inside with you, you would pay the ultimate price for it.

Captain Miller had deserted along with helicopters and a sizeable army of soldiers who trusted him, and his superiors had failed to contain the infection. Now he was seeing it happen one more time on Attu Island.

The Chief motioned for Cassandra to take the lead and dropped back next to Captain Miller.

"They've been here about four months. How long do you think the infection has been loose?"

Captain Miller shook his head.

"I haven't seen any signs of living people yet. They're either all dead or in hiding."

"Well, it stops here," said the Chief. "If any of your old friends are still alive, we're putting an end to their experiments. If they're already dead, we just need to be sure that no innocent survivors are left behind."

Cassandra held up a fist to bring the column to a stop. Then she flashed her fingers to indicate there were infected dead in the corridor. She pointed at her eyes and signaled that she could see between ten and fifteen of them. She put the strap of her M4 over her back and slid a machete from her belt. She was trained in urban combat, and if she felt like the machetes were a better choice at the moment, it was her decision. Everyone behind her switched to their machetes, too.

They had engaged in fights like this one too many times to count. Sometimes, they were forced to fight in total darkness or in places where they were so cramped that they couldn't swing their arms. This time, they had nothing to stand in their way. The lights weren't bright, but the infected were all in the open, where they could be easily eliminated.

"That's round one for the good guys," said Kathy. "Let's find the next batch."

After an hour, they had encountered ten separate hordes in the shelter without finding any survivors. They were also lost. They backtracked to places where they had eliminated the infected dead, but they had no reference points that meant anything to them.

"How long are we going to keep this up?" asked Hampton.

The Chief brought them together into a group and said, "Let's split up into four groups of five people. We haven't come across a horde large enough to beat five of us. If you do, backtrack until you run into another squad that can help you."

"What if we run into another horde?" asked one of the soldiers who had come along with them.

Cassandra answered, "It would be the horde's bad luck. Just stick with us. We've got this."

The four squads went in different directions after they agreed they would all meet back at the same spot in one hour. The Chief reminded them that five people should be able to remember how many turns they had taken, but if they got lost, it would be better to keep moving than to sit still.

******

Clemenza was able to make it to the other side of the wide-open common area after dodging the infected dead twice. If he had tried to eliminate them, the noise might have drawn more of them to the cellblock, so he just hid in the shadows while they went by. When he finally reached the room outside the narrow hallway that ran between the cells, he listened but didn't hear anyone talking. He wondered if he was too late, and he wondered how he could get into the hallway without causing a disturbance.

The problem was solved for him when a lone infected dead wandered into the cellblock from the other side. He heard it groan, and then it became agitated when it saw living people inside the cells. Clemenza leaned forward to see around the corner and almost laughed when he saw what happened.

The infected dead was leaning against a cell door and reaching through the bars. Someone inside the cell was holding onto it by the wrist, and someone else swung a club downward onto its head so hard that the creature went limp. The people inside pushed it away from the bars and threw the club out onto the body.

One of the men said, "What did you do that for? We might need it again."

The other man answered, "We have plenty more."

When Clemenza saw that the club was an arm, he had to throw in his own joke.

"Would you guys like a *hand*?"

He pulled out the keys and went to the cell that held O'Reilly and Mullins. Everyone started talking at once, and Clemenza had to tell them to keep it down.

"Where did you come from?" asked O'Reilly.

"The only living people I've seen in the last few hours were a group of doctors and lab technicians hiding in a room. I got these keys off of the guard who was hiding with them."

"Did you kill them?" asked Petty Officer Knight. Her voice was flat, and he could read by her tone that she hoped he would say yes.

"No, but trust me…they will wish I had soon enough. They're stranded in the dark in a shelter full of infected dead. They won't make it one whole day."

Oleg reached for Clemenza and begged, "Please tell me Galina is alive."

"She's safe for the time being. I took her to your boat in the grotto. It smells like hell out there, and something is making the water hot, but she should be okay until we get there. I didn't think it was a good idea to bring her along while I got you guys out of here."

"You came back just for us?" asked Mincy.

"Everyone has a right to be noble once in a while," said Clemenza. "It was my turn because I've been a jerk for too long."

Ritter said, "I take back everything I said about you, Clemenza."

"I wouldn't be too quick to congratulate him just yet," said a voice they all recognized.

Clemenza turned to see Commander Evans standing behind him with a gun. He had some seriously bad scratches along one side of his face, and he was favoring his left leg, but he was undeniably able to shoot Clemenza if he made a move toward him.

Evans motioned with the gun and said, "Now that you have that door open, Clemenza, you can join your friends inside the cell. Drop your gun on the floor first, and leave the key in the lock."

Clemenza didn't see where he had any other choice. Evans could easily shoot him before he could close the distance between them, and he couldn't miss.

"Sorry, everyone," he said as he dropped his gun and stepped inside.

Evans came closer, and Clemenza thought for one moment he would have an opening and be able to hit Evans with the door as he retrieved the keys from the lock. Evans saw the mistake too, and he aimed the gun through the bars at Christine Mincy.

"She'll be dead before I hit the ground, Clemenza. Move to the back of the cell."

Clemenza reluctantly walked to the back and stood next to O'Reilly and Mullins. Evans turned the key in the lock and pulled it out, then he picked up the gun from the floor.

"You chose the wrong side, Clemenza. After I gather up what's left of my people, we're going to have plenty of infected dead to study, and you're going to make an excellent subject. I'll be back for you later."

For the second time in a few short minutes, the tables turned again. A loud groan came from the end of the cellblock, and an infected dead stepped into the narrow hallway. Evans raised his gun to shoot it but held his fire when two more came in right behind it. He backed away toward the other end of the cellblock thinking he could just retreat, but a chorus of groans from that direction meant he was surrounded.

The horde that came from that direction was even bigger, and Evans had to move fast. He shot the infected dead that was closest to him as he shoved the key into the nearest lock and opened the door. He jumped inside and pulled it shut behind him as he locked it.

Before he could turn around, Mincy took the heavy human arm that Mullins passed to her through the bars. She gripped it by the wrist and swung it like a baseball bat the way her father had taught her. It weighed about eight pounds, and when it hit Evans in the head, it knocked him out cold. He bounced against the bars and dropped the gun. Mincy relieved him of the gun in his holster and handed it to O'Reilly.

Clemenza said, "Does anyone have a plan?"

Mullins said, "Well, we can go back to pulling off their arms, and then we can use his keys to get out of the cells."

"Works for me," said O'Reilly. He shook Clemenza's hand and added, "I'll bet you can pull a few arms off."

"My pleasure," said Clemenza.

******

The single gunshot was the first one they had heard since climbing down into the shelter, and it was nearby. The Chief's squad was the closest, and they moved toward the sound. When they entered the room outside the cellblock, they saw a horde attempting to squeeze into a hallway.

On the other side of the cellblock, the squad led by Cassandra had made rapid progress clearing the maze of hallways on the same level. They didn't know how close they were to the Chief's squad, but the timing was good. They also heard the shot that Evans fired and moved into position behind the other horde.

Tom was behind her and asked, "Guns or machetes?"

"Guns," said Cassandra. "There's no room to swing machetes in here."

There was plenty of room for them to fire their M4 rifles over each other's shoulders, and all five of them took aim.

The Chief's squad had more room than the squad on the other side, but when they heard the gunfire from the other side, they didn't know if it was one of their squads or local guards. It wouldn't be a good idea for them to be swinging machetes if guards came at them once the infected dead were gone.

"Open fire," yelled the Chief.

They were close enough to use their handguns, and the sound was deafening. Their ears were ringing, but the dead fell away fast.

Inside the cellblock, everyone dove for cover and put their hands over their ears. The combination of M4 rifles and 9mm handguns firing on both sides was enough to leave them with hearing problems, but it didn't last long. It was like the finale of a fireworks display. It went on long enough to be satisfied with the results. When the shooting stopped, the infected dead were in a pile that stretched from one entrance of the cellblock to the other.

The occupants of the cells cautiously stood up and approached the doors. On one end, Cassandra peered around the corner to assess the possible threat in the hallway. On the other end of the cellblock, they saw a man as big as Clemenza fill the door from side to side.

Clemenza saw the Chief at the same moment that the Chief saw him.

The Chief said, "I got your note."

Clemenza said, "What took you so long?"

"I didn't know we were supposed to hurry."

O'Reilly sized up the Chief from his cell and asked, "Is he a friend of yours?"

"We've met," said Clemenza.

Both squads pulled the bodies out of the narrow cellblock so they could open the doors. Captain Miller was surprised when he saw who was in the cell with Corporal Mincy. Evans was still unconscious on the floor.

"Is that Commander Evans?"

"You mean my cellmate?" she answered. "Yeah, that's Evans. He's not a friend of yours, is he?"

"I don't think he would say so," said Captain Miller. "What happened to him?"

"He got in the wrong cell and tried to take my bunk."

The grin on her face told Captain Miller everything he needed to know.

******

Galina heard Oleg yelling for her and ran out onto the deck of the *Svetlana.* She couldn't believe that he was finally coming to her. When Clemenza told the Chief about the Russians, he felt like she was the priority. The reunion was worth waiting for, but despite everything the Chief had seen over the years, he was dumbstruck by the boiled crabs that floated on the surface of the water. The smell was overwhelming, and there were so many crabs that they were overflowing onto the dock.

"What's cooking the crabs?" asked Kathy.

Hampton wanted to check the Russian boat that was tied up closer to them, but the smell was too much for him.

As he passed the Chief on the way back to the tunnel, he said, "It's hot down in the power plant, and it smells like sulfur, too. What was that Colonel Daugherty said about this place being in a volcanic zone?"

"Might be something to that," he answered. "Let's go. We have a few things to discuss, so we need everyone to be together for this discussion."

An hour later, everyone was in the dining room. There was no shortage of excitement from most of them, but Commander Evans was nervously watching from a corner where he was tied to a chair. It was a celebration for everyone else, and they were dipping into the food that Galina was happily making in the kitchen.

The Chief stood up and raised a hand to get everyone to give him their attention.

"Okay, folks. I have some decisions to announce. The first one is that we can't take everyone off the island."

The enormity of the statement silenced the few people who were still talking.

"Don't worry," he continued. "We can carry everyone who deserves to leave. The people who are staying behind deserve to be in prison for what they've done. Needless to say, that means you, Evans. You and your so-called medical staff can stay here and experiment on each other if you want to, but we've already got people dumping your test equipment in the grotto. Whatever you decide to do, you won't be able to do it to more innocent people. Attu Island is now your prison."

Captain Miller joined the Chief up front.

"I have something to say, and it may be purely symbolic, but you might have noticed that the Chief didn't use your rank when he said your name. That was on purpose because you stopped being a Commander when you violated your oath to protect citizens of the United States from harm. You are Anthony Evans, and I hereby dishonorably discharge you from military service."

Evans would have protested if not for the gag in his mouth.

The Chief got everyone's attention again and said, "We're leaving immediately. We still have to get back to Alaska. We've begun transferring fuel to the Black Hawks from the shelter, and we have enough to make it to Dutch Harbor."

More than one person raised their hand to ask about the crab problem at Dutch Harbor.

"I didn't mention it before, but when we had to evacuate from Dutch Harbor, I was able to contact Colonel Daugherty and told him what it would be like if we had to refuel there again. Corporal Hupp spoke with him less than an hour ago, and he confirmed that Colonel Daugherty had landed the AC-130 at Dutch Harbor, and the crabs were no match for the weapons on the plane. He's waiting for us there. The Black Hawks have traveled a long way after years of sitting still, so we can't trust that they can make the trip home. We'll all fly comfortably in the AC-130 and get home much faster."

It was a longer walk from the main door of the shelter to where Iris and the others waited with the Black Hawks, but they preferred the walk over climbing the cliff again. They were also able to carry a few supplies from the shelter. When they saw the column of people approaching, Iris and Shannon ran to meet them. After hugs and kisses, the Chief told them they were heading home, and it would be crowded until Dutch Harbor.

It was crowded, but time seemed to go by faster now that the job was done. Captain Miller appeared almost younger after the experience and told Shannon that he felt like a heavy burden was gone now that Evans was stopped.

They made their rendezvous with Daugherty at Dutch Harbor, and the Chief noticed there were fewer crabs even up on the runway, where they had been shredded by the machine gun on the plane.

Corporal Hupp took a water sample from the bay and checked it.

"The water is a few degrees higher than normal. The crabs must've gone to deeper water where it's cooler."

"Well, I think it would be best if we didn't hang around to find out why," said the Chief. "Besides, Oleg and Galina have waited a long time to reach Alaska."

******

Mount Tambora in Indonesia exploded in a volcanic eruption in 1815. As many as one hundred thousand people died as a result of the devastating blast and the following changes to the climate. Over ten thousand died in the immediate vicinity of the volcano.

The eruption on Attu Island wasn't nearly as devastating compared to Mount Tambora. It built up pressure slowly and took its time, almost as if it was punishing the remaining occupants of the shelter.

It began even while the Mud Island family was still on Attu Island, and the Chief knew from a long life of experience that they were giving Anthony Evans and his misguided medical staff a death sentence. He didn't know that the water around the Ring of Fire got warmer on April 11, 2023, because the Shiveluch volcano erupted on the nearby Kamchatka Peninsula in Russia. It set off a chain reaction that caused a new volcano to rise up under Attu Island.

The cooling systems in the shelter were overwhelmed by the heat in the power plant, and it became too hot to breathe inside. The water in the grotto boiled hard enough to sink the two boats that were still tied to the dock. Steam poured from the grotto entrance as the water evaporated, and an immense cloud rose above the island.

Evans and his team were only a few minutes ahead of the lava flow that filled the common area of the shelter, but they made it through the vault door and the tunnel in time to see the eruption. They watched in terror as the mountain above them appeared to shrink inward as if it was drawing in its final breath. One minute later, the shockwave from the eruption came toward them like a giant fist. The debris it carried erased any clues that showed they were ever there.

28

Epilogue

Sixty Miles South of Anchorage, Alaska - July 2023

It had already rained for the first week of the month, and the Chief decided to take advantage of the first sunrise on a clear day. It was a breezy forty-five degrees at the top of the scaffold where he was perched, but the blue sky gave him a breathtaking view of the distant Chugach Mountains. He leaned back and put his feet up on the railing. A sip of coffee took the chill out of him. He was forty feet in the air and could see the morning crew arriving at the refinery.

So much had happened in the short time since they had returned to Joint Base Elmendorf-Richardson. There was a lot to get done and still plenty to do, but for the first time in years, he felt like he had one of the answers he had been searching for.

They had yet to find a large-scale last line of defense against the infected dead, and there probably wasn't a major force out there, but there were still plenty of small pockets of resistance. When he thought about it, he realized that the most successful resistance was his own Mud Island family.

When the infection started, they were spread out across the South, but circumstances and a lot of luck had brought them together. None of them had made a plan to survive an apocalypse, but somehow they had. It wasn't over yet, but he didn't feel like giving up. They had too many reasons to keep fighting against the infected dead.

The Chief had just put his index finger in the air to count the number of places they had been since it all started when Iris climbed onto the scaffold behind him. She rested her left hand on his shoulder and reached around the other side for his coffee.

"I'm getting a sense of deja vu," she said.

"I was just checking out my fingernails."

"Uh, huh. What were you counting this time?"

Iris noticed that the morning sun only made her husband look younger, and she wondered if it did the same for her. His short hair and beard had gone from red to a strawberry color with gray mixed in, and the deep lines of his face made him appear to be wiser but not older. She didn't realize that she had run one hand through her own hair as she studied his face, nor did she know that the sun reflecting from her silver hair and tanned skin made him hold his breath.

"I'm counting the number of things I love about you, of course," he said. His wide smile made her feel younger.

"That worked at the prom, old man. How about coming up with some new material? What's making you so content this morning?"

"Well, since you asked…I was trying to think of the places we've been and which trips were successes."

"Successes?"

"You know, which ones ended with a favorable outcome."

Iris shook her head and said, "You've probably noticed there were a few that weren't so favorable. What about this mission? It turned out pretty good."

The Chief held up his index finger again.

"That was the first one if I count backwards. We found out what happened to the failed combined military force that Captain started out with, and thankfully, they can't do any more harm. It's ironic, but their best bet was to splinter the way they did, and maybe we'll find more of their remnants out there."

Iris added, "This mission has been one of our most successful as far as I'm concerned."

"I'm glad you think so. Can we count it as a vacation? We went to the islands."

"I don't remember saying I wanted to go to the *Aleutian* Islands. If I need to be more specific, I wouldn't mind going to a tropical island someday, but let's get back to my point. This place is a big step for us.

Getting the refinery to produce fuel will help us get to some of the places we want to go, and the supply that's still usable will hold everyone over for a long time."

The Chief knew she was right. After they returned from Attu Island, they couldn't just leave the personnel at the Joint Base to figure things out for themselves. If they hadn't taken the last three months to help them become functional again, they would have made bad decisions that would have led to their end. People were talking about leaving… striking out on their own, and trying to reach homes that didn't exist anymore.

Colonel Daugherty had almost four hundred people on his base who needed a new reason to survive. The Chief knew that they had to show those people what waited for them if they didn't stay together. It was dangerous work, but he organized groups to go on patrols to Anchorage. The idea was to give them practical experience fighting the infected dead and to show them it wasn't something they could do alone. They needed each other.

When the Army and Air Force personnel got a firsthand look at how the world had changed, they understood that going home to Chicago, New York, or Miami were all things they needed to forget. Plus, they found so many survivors in Anchorage who needed them.

Not everyone who came back with them to the base was interested in becoming part of the military, but the influx of civilians meant some adjustments had to be made. The base became a colony that resembled Alaska as it was when it first became a state, but even better because it had a past to build upon.

Iris studied her husband's face again and could tell he was thinking about all of the changes. His smile was a bit wider, and he had gone beyond content to cheerful.

"Are you okay about the people who are staying behind?" she asked.

"Okay? I wouldn't say I'm happy about it, but I'm okay with it if that's what they want. It makes sense, but I'm going to miss them," he said.

******

The others had come to the Chief as a group during breakfast at the mess hall to tell him themselves. They thought it would be easier if he heard it from them personally. The former crew of Executive One was still convinced that the fight against the infected dead had to begin in a colder, less hospitable climate, and they felt like the Joint Base was the support system they needed. The civilians had already started talking about electing Garrett Carson as their first official spokesman, and he had accepted.

The Chief wasn't surprised that Anne, Susan, and Jon still wanted to stay with Garrett. After all, they would have stayed with him on Last Island if it had worked out better. Now that they had a safe place to live, it made perfect sense. What surprised him was when Cassandra and Sim said they wanted to stay in Alaska. Besides being reunited with his old friends, they thought it would be a good time to start a family. He told them if they ever changed their minds, he would arrange transportation. They each took turns to give him a hug and left him alone with plenty to think about.

The news had left the Chief feeling a bit unsettled, and he couldn't quite put his finger on what it was that bothered him. He felt like they were all doing what was best for them, and each of them could make huge contributions to the military base, but he had to wonder who else might decide to stay. When he saw Kathy and Tom working their way toward his table, he knew what had him off balance.

"Mind if we join you?" asked Tom.

Chief Barnes gestured to the chairs that had been vacated by Garrett and his group, but he was afraid if he spoke, it would give away his already fragile emotions. He was big, and he was a good leader, but sometimes, his sensitive side made him turn into a softie, and he fought to hide it.

"So," said Tom, "did you hear the good news?"

"Depends," he answered. "There's been a lot of good news lately."

Before Tom could answer, Kathy blurted out, "Hampton and Colleen made it back to Alabama in the AC-130, and our friends in Huntsville have a plane load of scientists flying out to help us get the refinery running again. When it was at full capacity, it only needed about two hundred people to run it."

"That's the good news?" asked the Chief.

"Sure," said Tom. "What did you expect?"

The Chief took a bite from his breakfast and did his best to act excited about the refinery, but the couple didn't buy it.

"Spit it out," said Kathy, "and I'm not talking about the food."

He almost choked on the last bite, and he had a hard time making eye contact, but he managed to croak out a few words.

"Sim and Cassandra are staying behind with Garrett's group. They want to start a family."

"That's great news," said Kathy. She practically cheered, but then she remembered a similar conversation, and she saw the way the Chief avoided eye contact with Tom.

"Wait, you're afraid that we might want to stay behind with them. You know, settle down and have some kids we can raise together," she said.

"Something like that," mumbled the Chief.

Tom held out a fist toward the Chief, and he obviously expected a knuckle bump. The Chief reluctantly returned the gesture, but he didn't know if it was because Tom was acknowledging his assumptions or if he had been mistaken.

"We already talked about it, Chief. Kathy and I want to start a family someday, but we would worry too much about you going out on your missions without us to protect you. For the time being, you're stuck with us, but I mean what I said back on Mud Island. We're a package deal from now on."

"Are we interrupting anything?"

The cheerful question came from Corporal Mincy, and the rest of the squad came up behind her carrying their breakfast trays. They didn't wait for an answer, and they all pulled out chairs to sit down.

Private Ritter said, "The food around here really improved when Galina and Oleg took over the cooking. Oleg's the mess hall manager, but I think Galina really runs the place."

Sergeant O'Reilly took the seat next to the Chief and gave him a hard slap on the back as he sat down. Not many people could rock the Chief like that. O'Reilly wasn't as big as the Chief, but he was muscular. If he had slapped Ritter like that, the Private might have gone over the table. The Chief took it as a token of friendship.

Mincy took the seat next to O'Reilly, and Kathy noticed she moved the chair a little closer to the Sergeant. She also caught the body language and quick eye contact. They were trying to be discreet, but there were some things that couldn't be kept secret for long. She gave Mincy a wink of approval and saw her blush.

The last person to arrive was still a bit of a wildcard to the Chief, but he had gratefully accepted David Clemenza as a member of the new base. From what he could tell, the man had always felt like a square peg surrounded by round holes, so he struggled to fit in. Clemenza had identified with the Russians because they were also outsiders, but it was Lou Mullins who gave him a sense of balance. Mullins had regained his sergeant's stripes, and for some reason, the two men had been keeping each other out of trouble. The Chief had seen people become brothers in combat, and he felt like they would always have each other's backs.

When the Chief excused himself and left the breakfast table, he ran into Captain Miller and Shannon as they came in the door, and he held his breath one more time.

"Chief, you're just the man we were looking for. Colonel Daughtry offered me a job as his executive officer, but I wanted to let you know before you heard any rumors. I turned down the job, but I recommended Sergeant O'Reilly for a field promotion. I can't wait to get back home. Are we going to Guntersville or Charleston?"

"Actually, I think we're going back to Mud Island. As I recall, it's a great vacation spot during the summer months."

The Chief stepped outside into the early morning air and decided to catch a helicopter ride down to the refinery. He knew of a spot where he could enjoy a cup of coffee and think about the future.

ABOUT THE AUTHOR

Bob Howard (1951-) was born in New Jersey to an Army Sergeant from Ohio and a mother from Romania. He was moved from one Army base to the next, and before he began high school in Huntsville, Alabama, he had lived most of his early life overseas in Germany and Okinawa, with brief stays in Maryland, North Carolina, and Alabama. He credits his imagination to his exposure to different cultures and environments at an early age. He began reading science fiction and fell in love with post-apocalyptic novels. He still has an original copy of the first one he read in 1966, The Furies by Keith Edwards. He joined the Navy after high school and continued to move from one base to another, including a submarine base at Holy Loch, Scotland. He eventually stayed in one place when he got stationed in Charleston, South Carolina. He graduated with a BS in Psychology from the College of Charleston and married his wife of 39 years. His son still lives in Charleston, but his daughter has married and made a home in

Ohio, where the Howard family has its earliest known roots. Through the years, he had one passion he wanted to fulfill, and through The Infected Dead series, he is getting to achieve that passion. Creating a book is something many people want to do but never have the opportunity, and after writing these books he believes the sky is the limit. He plans to write for the rest of his life because it is enjoyable beyond his wildest dreams. As for the zombie genre, he saw Night of the Living Dead when it originally hit the theaters, and he believes until recently, it didn't receive the attention it deserves.

www.ingramcontent.com/pod-product-compliance
Lightning Source LLC
Chambersburg PA
CBHW022205030726
47494CB00019B/397
* 9 7 8 1 9 4 5 7 5 4 4 9 4 *